NOTHING

As thrilling as this good fortune was, Carter knew the Secret Service agents could not be far away. Most likely in suite number six. There was still the need to be deathly quiet. And no time to dally. Silently Carter moved around the foot of the bed and found a position on the man's side. Carter then tucked the Beretta beneath the flap of the overcoat and eased the safety to the off position. Not a sound could be heard. Carter brought the pistol to arm's length and placed the silencer within a half inch of the back of the man's head. Carter smiled. It was not expected to be this easy.

There was a strong temptation to wake them both up. Give the Vice President one last look at life before he tasted death. Carter smiled once more. Lord, this was fun. Carter hated to bring the anticipation to an end. It should last longer. It should be prolonged. It should be more like a glorious sexual encounter. But there wasn't time. Carter could wait. The sexual encounter would have to come later. Carter squeezed gently on the trigger.

The Beretta sent one round into the man's skull. The bullet exited through his right eye and forced its way into the mattress . . . or had it?

SIGNET ONYX

THRILLING SUSPENSE!

- ☐ **RUNNING DEAD by Robert Coram.** Tony the Dreamer was a master terrorist and sexual psychopath . . . a serial killer who combined his bloody business with perverted pleasures. Homicide Detective Jeremiah Buie was a legend of lethal efficiency. He would—and did—do anything to get his man. The killer and the cop—they were worthy of each other. The only question was: which of them was better at the hard-ball game they played for keeps? (175565—$4.99)
- ☐ **STRANGLEHOLD by Edward Hess.** The all-too-real horror keeps mounting, as a cunning killer, with the reflexes of a cougar and an agenda of evil beyond basic blood lust, is countering FBI special agents Martin Walsh and Dalton Leverick's every move, as he keeps sending his prey, not to the mat, but to the grave. (179846—$4.99)
- ☐ **PURSUIT by Zach Adams.** Martin Walsh is the deep-cover FBI agent who usually takes his fight to the enemy. But this time they bring the war to him when they snatch his son in a revenge-driven payback. Walsh, with the help of his partner, strips back layer after layer of a vicious international child-trafficking ring. Nothing short of a sea of blood will stop them. (180607—$5.50)
- ☐ **A TIME FOR TREASON by Everett Douglas.** The premier assassin . . . the premier target—in a supercharged conspiracy thriller. Scorpion's mission is to kill the President of the United States on behalf of some of the most commanding men in America—and a woman who is even more powerful than they are. But, FBI Special Agent Joel Matheson is hot on his trail. (179218—$4.99)
- ☐ **PRAYING FOR SLEEP by Jeffery Deaver.** Michael Hrubek, a dangerously paranoid schizophrenic, has just escaped from a mental hospital for the criminally insane, and he is on a mission to find Lis Atcheson, the woman who identified him as a vicious murderer. (181468—$5.99)

*Prices slightly higher in Canada

Buy them at your local bookstore or use this convenient coupon for ordering.

PENGUIN USA
P.O. Box 999 — Dept. #17109
Bergenfield, New Jersey 07621

Please send me the books I have checked above.
I am enclosing $_______________ (please add $2.00 to cover postage and handling). Send check or money order (no cash or C.O.D.'s) or charge by Mastercard or VISA (with a $15.00 minimum). Prices and numbers are subject to change without notice.

Card #_______________________ Exp. Date _______________
Signature_______________________________________
Name____
Address_______________________________________
City _______________ State ___________ Zip Code ___________

For faster service when ordering by credit card call **1-800-253-6476**

Allow a minimum of 4-6 weeks for delivery. This offer is subject to change without notice.

THE SECOND MAN

Steve Zettler

AN ONYX BOOK

ONYX
Published by the Penguin Group
Penguin Books USA Inc., 375 Hudson Street,
New York, New York 10014, U.S.A.
Penguin Books Ltd, 27 Wrights Lane,
London W8 5TZ, England
Penguin Books Australia Ltd, Ringwood,
Victoria, Australia
Penguin Books Canada Ltd, 10 Alcorn Avenue,
Toronto, Ontario, Canada M4V 3B2
Penguin Books (N.Z.) Ltd, 182–190 Wairau Road,
Auckland 10, New Zealand

Penguin Books Ltd, Registered Offices:
Harmondsworth, Middlesex, England

First published by Onyx, an imprint of Dutton Signet,
a division of Penguin Books USA Inc.

First Printing, October, 1996
10 9 8 7 6 5 4 3 2 1

Printed in the United States of America

PUBLISHER'S NOTE
This is a work of fiction. Names, characters, places, and incidents either are the product of the author's imagination or are used fictitiously, and any resemblance to actual persons, living or dead, events, or locales is entirely coincidental.

Upon such sacrifices, my Cordelia,
The gods themselves throw incense.

Prologue

Twenty-nine years. That's how long it'd been. On the thirteenth of every month—be it a Friday or not—for twenty-nine years, three of Creation's wealthiest men had gathered in this impeccably maintained cedar-shingled hunting cabin sixteen miles northwest of Long Rapids, Michigan. A lifetime of riches had afforded these grizzled fools the best of everything, and the interior of the cabin reflected their capacity to spare no expense. And as with all hunting cabins, stuffed heads, racks of antlers, stuffed fish, stuffed ducks, rabbits, coons, rifles, shotguns, bows, arrows, all of that crap played an important part in the scintillating decor. It was their way. It was their corner of America. They would treat it as they damn well pleased.

Phil was now sixty-four years old—and still as loud and bombastic as ever.

Grant, a year younger—but strength personified.

Art—a baby at sixty-one.

They were businessmen. Their businesses, after twenty-nine years, had evolved mostly into the business of increasing their wealth—on a daily basis. However, on this particular thirteenth, not a Friday but a Thursday, their business was about to branch out into seductive, albeit untrodden, territory—the business of political assassination.

"How many does that leave us?" Grant said as he lifted his pocketknife from the ivory inlaid poker table and began to methodically pick at a fingernail. The table had been covered in a thick green felt and handcrafted out of ebony in 1879 by Trinity of San Francisco. The chips and cards had been placed in the side drawer. Steam drifted up from insulated Eddie Bauer coffee mugs. A bottle of scotch, Black Label, sat perfectly centered on the table. Three garishly etched tumblers were grouped off to one side. And an ancient yellow Labrador retriever named Buck had curled up as close to the roaring fireplace as he could get without melting his frigging dog tags. Buck was not at all pleased with having been dragged away from his overstuffed couch in Long Rapids proper to "go for a little ride with Dad," in December, no less.

"Five," Phil answered. "Let's run through the list one more time. Maybe we can narrow it down a little further—or beef it up—if you lads think it's necessary." He restrained a sadistic grin.

"I'm exhausted, Phil. Let's pick it up tomorrow." Art stood as he said this and attempted a move toward the door.

"Tomorrow's not the thirteenth, Arty boy. You walk out that door, don't ever walk the fuck back in."

Art sat back down without a word. Laid his hands in his lap. A spark exploded from the fireplace. Buck raised an eyebrow, then tucked his tail closer into his body. Phil continued with his list.

"Okay, first we have Oscar Sanchez." He smiled and shook his head as though he might be talking about a long-lost and deeply admired older brother. "*The one and only Oscar* . . . Yes, sir-ee, likes to take out the big targets. More a terrorist than an assassin. Deals in explosives mostly. Has a record as long as the fucking turnpike. Not one conviction. You have to love this bastard. I see a real touch of class there . . . along with that flawless reputation. Plus, if this operation comes off as a terrorist attack, the Feds'll start chasing the goddamn towel heads. The last place they'll look is Michigan."

Phil took a second to let his enthusiasm with the great Oscar Sanchez spread to Grant and Art. Then set his coffee aside and filled one of the glasses with scotch. Held it under his nose and inhaled. Continued, "Next. John Napier. *The Invisible Man.* Nearly all of his strikes have been behind the former Iron Curtain. Always good at long distance. A modern-day Lee Harvey, God bless his soul." Phil performed a mock genuflection. "If things can be handled there, in the old Soviet bloc, we get more than we ever hoped for. We come away very, very clean, and the Russians are left to pick up the pieces. . . ."

He checked his two compadres to be certain he still had their full attention. He did. Though Art seemed to be slipping.

"Okay, after Napier we have Nora Lincoln. Changes her name and face quicker than a lizard trapped on a fucking roulette wheel. But . . . somewhat difficult to get in touch with . . . that right?" Phil looked at Grant for an answer.

"We'll see . . . I'm not a hundred percent sold on using a woman. Besides being bad luck, I see this as a man's job all the way. She's also a little too elusive for my liking . . . but I guess that comes with the territory. We'll just have to see. . . . Move on."

"Okay, number four, Salvatore DiParma. This guy *I* don't like. If we have to lose someone from this list, I say it's him, not the broad. I have no use for these wops. They kill their own. I wouldn't be surprised if they ate them as well. Plus, they don't know shit about following orders. Next thing you know—"

"Can it, Phil," Grant interrupted in a level but at the same time forceful tone. A tone that more than clarified where the strength and power rested at the table. "We know how you feel about Italians. You've got good reason—maybe—but drop it. My sources put DiParma at the top of that list, not the bottom. And that's where he stays. We'll work with the woman, too. . . . We move forward."

Phil sucked in, then slowly released a chestful of the cabin's stale dry air. "You're right," he eventually acquiesced. "We're all tired. This is no time to get hung up on who's who. They're all pros." He took a good-size sample of scotch and smiled. "That leaves us with Carter Perkins. Personally, with what I've read on the printouts, I like this guy the best. He travels in the open. Goes where and when the fuck he wants. He seems about as polished as a ladybug in May . . . a travel writer." Phil grinned as he pondered this assassin's brilliance. "It's so fucking sweet."

Grant looked at Art, who now appeared oddly overstressed, and then back again to Phil. "Anyone you feel like adding?"

"I think we might be pushing it with five," Phil said as he scanned a larger list of names. "In reality we have nearly a year to pull this thing off. Let's start with these and see if one of them can get in close, get the job done—clean. If we start nearing the election, I say then, and only then, do we exercise some of our other options. But there's no point in letting too many folks in on this little plan. Especially if we don't need to."

Art added, "We also don't know if these guys're willing to handle targets this big. Let's see what kind of a response we get." He coughed nervously. "There's no point in rushing things . . . don't you think . . . ?"

This time Grant poured a scotch. After tasting it he pulled a slip of paper from his pocket and said, "I've got a contact for all five of them. I'll pass on the account numbers in Switzerland just in case they want to smell the money. No passwords until it's done, though. They'll get our code numbers if and when they respond and deliver. And we keep our fingers crossed. I assume we're still agreed on the price? Ten million for our friend the President—seven for the Vice President . . . ?"

The other two let their broad smiles serve as affirmation.

Grant raised his glass and added, "And of course, we sign it . . . DOC."

MONDAY

One

Venice, Italy. The day before Christmas and Joe Bradlee was dying of thirst. Thirst. It made him jumpy. Jumpy Joe. Jesus God, he hated that word. Jumpy. A moronic word. And it had an annoying way of tagging after him. Joe never considered himself jumpy. Not really jumpy. His father'd dropped this endearment on him. The old man had loved to call him Jumpy Joe. And when the bastard got a hook in like that, he never let it out.

The goddamn old man. The goddamn thirst. "Christ," Joe thought.

"Water, water, everywhere ... This could end up being a real fucking mess."

Joe Bradlee was too damn old and too damn smart to ignore this dry throat. It was just one more part of what he'd refer to as his left wing. His bubble. What was going on in front of him. What was going on to his left. Right. What was going on behind him. Above him. And more important, what was going on inside. His guts. The thirst was an early warning device. The devil was at hand; you could bet money on it. Something was up.

Joe had just left God's gift to the rich, the magnificent Hotel Malvasi. He'd heavily greased all appropriate personnel. A necessary preparation for the arrival of Number Two. Or Goliath. West Virginia's own. The Panhandler. Whatever they wanted to call him, the Man was coming to Venice. Coming to Italy for a little Christmas R&R.

The Hotel Malvasi employees had thanked Joe profusely for the greasing—these over-extravagant gratuities. There'd been an absolute chorus of *"Molto grazie, signore,"* and *"Lei e molto gentile, signore."* The anticipation of Goliath's arrival had given all the Malvasi guardians a colossal adrenaline shot. But with Goliath, and the excitement, came the men with guns. Men like Joe Bradlee and his breed. And as the Italians knew all too well, men with guns were destined to attract other men with guns.

The last Malvasi employee Joe had spoken with was Nelo. Nelo—a Saint Francis among desk clerks. A man loved by hotel employees and guests alike. Nelo was intimate with every twist and turn of the great Hotel Malvasi. He could spot trouble or an unwanted intruder a mile off. He was guardian of the guardians.

Nelo had graced Joe with one of the sacred keys to the Malvasi Rear Gate. He'd done this as though he'd been handing over the only key to the Vatican. The Rear Gate, a gate used strictly for garbage removal—and Secret Service advance parties.

Joe had dropped this key into his right inside suit pocket, and the tiny piece of bronze now sat comfortably a quarter of an inch from a 9mm semi-automatic pistol. On his way through the kitchen Joe had grabbed a couple of biscotti. One of those oranges with the blood red centers. A large bottle of Pellegrino water.

After Nelo, Joe had spoken to no one.

He was now on his way back to the Piazza di San Marco on one of the Hotel Malvasi's private motor launches with some orange rinds and a half-finished bottle of Pellegrino. He was still, without any logical explanation, feeling very thirsty. Jumpy . . . "Fuck." Something was up. No questions about it.

The Malvasi launches were boats of unparalleled beauty. Gleaming white. Every ounce of brass, chrome, mahogany—polished to within an inch of their lives. And this was launch number one, the flagship. Joe ran his hand over the red leather seat cushion. The leather was soft. Thin-skinned.

The boat cut through the swells.

There was the scent of roses. A half dozen of them, vaguely resembling bleeding apricots, had been arranged in crystal vases near every window. Their odor crowded the air. Collided with the salt coming from outside, pouring in from two open windows. Joe's left wing clicked off the potential venom that could slither through these windows, from grenades to buckshot.

He slid the windows closed and took another hit off the Pellegrino. He put the bottle down on a silver tray, then shook his head. He smiled. Checked his reflection in the glass. Shoved the windows back open and thought, "Come and get me, you motherfuckers."

Nine minutes. Nine minutes from the Hotel Malvasi to the Piazza di San Marco. A nine-minute boat ride. Nine minutes to simulated freedom.

Sunlight shot off the dome of San Giorgio Maggiore and down into the water. It turned the sea to a molten green. The church itself was lit up like a damn MGM set. Joe played with the idea of throwing the helmsman overboard. Taking the launch. Disappearing into the evening's sunset. He found himself wondering if Number Two would have any idea how to grease the palm of the maître d' in the Malvasi dining room if Joe Bradlee were to vanish. The thought of an Italian waiter dragging the Vice President and his family off to a table just south of the espresso machine made Joe want to dump the helmsman all the more.

He finished off the bottle of Pellegrino. Stood out of reflex. He'd become too goddamn comfortable. Besides, "Ya gotta put your face into the wind and get those sea legs in shape," to quote the older Mr. Bradlee. The old salt. The sailor turned cop turned bad. The old man. The man with all the answers. Joe often wondered how someone who'd never asked any goddamn questions could possibly have all the answers. He also found himself pondering whether he had merely stood up or ir if he had *jumped* up. Again he thought, "Fuck." And wondered why his old dead *padre* had come to haunt him on this particular day.

Joe picked up his reflection in the port-side window as he moved to the cabin door. His dark hair and Ray-Bans popped out with an extraordinary contrast to the rest of his lean face. He found himself hoping he wasn't as transparent as the reflection that flew to keep up with him.

He stepped out of the cabin and moved up beside the helmsman. The wind slapped him. Felt good. The dryness in his throat was finally leaving. But Joe understood the thirst had been a message. Understood that fact too damn clearly. In his twenty-one years in the Grid, the protection business, the United States Secret Service, he'd learned to pay attention to every unexplained annoyance. Ninety percent of the time he was right. Something was up. Someone was in town. And it was Joe's responsibility to find out what or who before Number Two deplaned in Italy.

Venice . . . Italy.

Jesus. What a goddamn place to set up a shield.

"Water, water, everywhere . . ."

Even so, one or two things were working in Joe Bradlee's favor. At Christmas there'd be very few people in Venice who didn't belong. Number Two, Goliath, the VP, whatever, would have a short stay. One state meeting on his schedule. Meals would be private—"La Famiglia solamente."

Standard operating procedures had been solidified. The few automobiles needed to bring Number Two and his entourage in from the airport had been checked out. The drivers had been checked out. Like the automobiles, all the Malvasi launches had been checked out. Bulletproof glass had been installed in these babies before the Vice President got out of diapers.

And the local *carabinieri* were more than efficient. In fact, the Italian police in general were very good about handling undesirables—not much bullshit here. You had to love the bastards.

Still, this vice-presidential expedition, as with all

vice-presidential expeditions, had been greeted with a fair amount of grumbling from both the Italians and the Americans. The souls who had been forced to go along with it. Every Christmas or Easter the President would arrange one superfluous meeting in order to drag Number Two off to some far corner of the globe. Anything. Just to get him the hell out of D.C.

Joe had often speculated on Number One's motives for not wanting Number Two around. And there were more than enough. But it always boiled down to one thing: photo ops. Goliath was far more photogenic than Atlas. The Vice President simply looked better with the kiddies on the White House lawn. He looked better sitting around the tree with his lovely wife and daughter at Christmas.

But the effect of these expeditions was always the same. A good thirty people would be shuttled away from their homes and families at Christmas. Or some other goddamn holiday. Joe didn't have a family. And he was actually happy to be in Italy. The country and its people were his. Venice was his. But the reason for Joe's presence in Venice was a crock of shit. Plain and simple.

Bang. His nine minutes of simulated freedom were gone. Over. Finished.

The Malvasi launch nudged into a private berth at the edge of Piazza di San Marco. To the left sat an endless row of jet black gondolas.

Back on terra firma. Back to business. Joe wondered if Louis also suspected that something was up.

Two

Louis Zezzo had been in Joe Bradlee's shadow for three years. He was fifteen years younger than Joe, and like Joe, an ex-marine. A fact not easily forgotten. Louis had a very bad habit of ending nearly every conversation they had with "Semper fi."

Louis was good-looking—in a Louis kind of way. Women seemed to find something tremendously appealing about him. How he carried himself. He had dark, close-cropped hair. Stood six two. And was fighting a slight weight problem. Louis considered a worthwhile meal almost as good as good sex. And he was a Pennsylvania boy.

"No coal miner here," Louis would say. "Just a South Philadelphia wop and proud of it."

Joe often wondered how the son of a Milanese-born tortellini manufacturer could speak only thirty-seven Italian words. And every one with an outrageous Philadelphia accent. But Joe found Louis a breath of fresh air. Especially compared to ninety-five percent of his coworkers. The other stiffs in the Grid. Having Louis on your detail was a little bit like having a devoted dog.

Piazza San Marco or not, Joe hated offices. He trudged up the ancient stone steps and pried his way into the space he'd set up two days earlier for the advance men. The Roadrunners. When he opened the door, he found Louis gazing out the window. Louis turned and pointed.

"That's a heck of a church, Saint Mark's. We should try to take it in before we split."

Joe simply said, "Let's go. I'll give you a tour."

And he was out the door instantaneously. Offices were offices. They reminded Joe of cages. Holding pens. Louis was forced to break into a trot to catch up.

"Yo, slow down. We can't do the church now," he said when he caught up to Joe. "I told the Italians we'd meet them at eleven. Inspector Solfanelli called. Something's up. He wouldn't say what. Not over the phone, anyway. He wanted to make it sooner. I had to stall him a little. What took you so long?" Louis was already a bit out of breath. "Jeez, I gotta lose some weight. Look at this belt. I'm running out of notches."

"Low tide. The boats can't move as quick."

"Right. Tide. I didn't think of that. They have tides here. Sometimes you think these things are rivers . . . the water, that is."

It never failed to amaze Joe how Louis believed absolutely everything he would tell him. Just like a dog.

Together they headed across the piazza until they reached a spot Joe was particularly fond of. He then turned to Louis.

"Did you lock the door?"

Louis thought for a second.

"Wait for me here. I'll be right back."

"Don't forget to grab your overcoat," Joe called after him. "It'll get colder before it gets warmer."

After Louis disappeared, Joe Bradlee stood in the center of the Piazza di San Marco and turned in a three-hundred-and-sixty-degree circle. Like a first-time tourist. In the past twenty years or so he'd come to this precise location and made the same move. Maybe two hundred times. The beauty of it was, nothing ever changed. It never would.

It could be hazardous to stand in a public place and daydream, but Joe couldn't help himself. He was a sucker for Venice. How could anyone be jumpy standing in the sunlight of San Marco? Every time he drifted into Venice it was the same—became harder to move on. But Joe was a Roadrunner. It was his profession to move on. He wallowed in the idea of just once staying behind. He wondered how well he'd mix with the locals . . . Some new clothes. Let the hair grow out a little. Dump the Ray-Bans for the wraparound jobs he'd picked up on the Lido. That was three years ago. The damn things were still in his bag. Always there—never worn. Dusty by now.

Joe spoke Italian like a native. But the Venetians always seemed to mistake him for a Corsican. "Americans make no attempt to fit in," was the most common explanation the Italians gave for making this slight nationality error. Joe had worked hard on his Italian. He liked to think of himself as a blend-in kind of guy. Nothing could be further from the truth. Joe Bradlee was no blend-in guy.

As if to punctuate whatever this quality was, the moment Joe put his hands into his pockets it happened. It seemed as though a freight train had come from behind. Cut him down at the back of the knees. A little spot in the rear of his brain flashed up a twisted image. The image was that of a round man in a black and white shirt. The man turned on a remote microphone, eyeballed a television camera, and barked: "Clipping, Denver, fifteen yards." The image lasted a millisecond and was gone. Joe was on his way down, face first, hands in pockets, watching the cobblestones of San Marco soaring up to meet his nose.

He had every limb and muscle moving in a different direction. Simultaneously. His right leg pulled out from under the weight of the attack and snuck under his left knee, turning his torso to face this new foe. The heel of his left foot dug in for support. His hands exploded from his pockets—spraying a dozen five-hundred-lira coins halfway to the Palazzo Ducale The fingers on his right hand spread wide in preparation for landing. His left hand slid smoothly into the space between his jacket and shirt. He found the handle of his 9mm, not-government-issue pistol. He removed the weapon from its not-government-issue holster. Found the trigger. Cocked the hammer. Removed the safety.

When all came to rest, Joe Bradlee was down on his ass. Knees bent. Elbows between his legs. Pistol pointed squarely between the eyes of the bastard who had taken him out. Joe vaguely resembled a hawk. Hit by a fucking truck.

The view, over the hammer, down the blue steel of the barrel, past the sight bead, was not at all what Joe had expected to see. He slowly returned the pistol to a safe position. Reholstered it. He wondered how it was possible for a boy of four, five at the most, to pack that kind of a wallop. There was no way this kid could have weighed more than forty pounds, but Joe felt as if he'd been creamed by a good-size water buffalo.

Glancing to his right, he spotted the object of the boy's desire. A white rubber ball. Maybe the size of a grapefruit. A big grapefruit. Texas grapefruit. With the words "Venezia" and "Italia" written in green and red more times than one would think humanly possible. If there had been a blank space on the ball anywhere, a star or a half moon had been squeezed in to add a little glitz and sparkle. Joe also spotted, at about twenty yards, directly behind the boy, and approaching like a silver bullet, what could only be the Boy's Mother.

She was young. Young enough. Thirty-two maybe. She had flowing dark brown hair. Sunglasses. Her coat was open. A long gauze-like skirt floated beneath her. Italian shoes. And she was coming on like a rocket ship. It was not going to be a pretty scene. Joe'd been through a few frightening experiences in his life, but only once before had he seen a look like the one in this woman's eyes when she hauled off her dark glasses.

It had been on an August night way back when. On a sand dune just south of the Vietnamese demilitarized zone. "The Look" that night had belonged to a marine lance corporal. They had started out as a platoon of thirteen. Before the night was over they were a platoon of two. The lance corporal and Joe had taken out the better part of a company of North Vietnamese regulars. Ninety-three to ten was the government tally. The body count. And the generals and politicians were always happy with those kinds of numbers. The lance corporal had been awarded the Congressional Medal of Honor. Then a year later, killed, trying to hold up a 7-Eleven in Oakland, California. Joe got a Navy Cross. When they gave it to him, he cried. The senator from Nevada assumed it was because he was only nineteen years old. What a dumb fuck.

The Boy's Mother was on Joe in a millisecond. Killer look. Beating his head with a paper bag. The bag eventually exploded and sent a collection of neckties off into as many directions as there were ties. The beating was accompanied by a small monologue:

"You idiot. Why don't you watch what you're doing? He's only a child. You could have hurt him, you cretin. . . . And don't look at me with that stupid expression."

She continued slapping him with her one remaining tie.

"And don't make believe you can't understand what I'm saying. You can speak English just as well as the next person. I should call the police. *La polizia.* You understand that, don't you? You friggin' idiot."

"Mi dispiace, signora. Scusi, signora. Mi dispiace."

The apology just came out of Joe's mouth that way. She was the first person to have ever mistaken him for an Italian. He liked it. He was also strongly tempted to tell her how attractive she looked in her present frame of mind. It was her goddamn eyes. They were more alive than any he'd ever seen. Brown. Very dark. Almost too deep.

Joe began explaining the situation. In Italian. She appeared to have no command of the language. Shoes or no. She wasn't grasping a word he said. He considered switching to English but decided against it. He was enjoying himself. He was enjoying her. In reality, the woman would have been attractive in any frame of mind. In any language. He found himself praying she hadn't seen his gun.

"Mom, did you see his gun? It's really cool. Hey, mister, show my mom your gun. It's under his jacket, Mom."

"A gun? You've got a gun? A mobster? A goon? I'm definitely calling the damn police. Who the hell do you think you are? Showing a gun to a child? How do I get a policeman around here? Do you speak any English at all? God, you're an idiot."

"Mom, it's really cool."

"I do not want to see his gun, Eubie . . . Are you all right? Oh, angel, look at you, you're filthy. Look at how dirty you got him, you jerk. I don't give a damn if you do have a gun. So there. Fungulo. You don't frighten me in the least, mobster or no mobster. You're a friggin' bum. You probably don't even know how to read."

As if on cue, Joe spotted Louis on his way back from locking the office door—still no overcoat. The idea of Louis blowing his cover with Eubie's mom didn't appeal to Joe. Not in the least. It became critical to move quickly. Again the Italian rolled off his tongue.

"*Mi dispiace, signora. Sono ritardo.*" He glanced at his watch for effect. "*Scusi. Arrivederla.*" If he'd had a hat, he would have tipped it. He then stood and took off across the Piazza di San Marco like a bird.

"*Ritardo?* That's a friggin' understatement," she said.

Louis played it perfectly. He saw Joe streaking toward the Piazetta dei Leoni and assumed they were finally going to see a little action. He had just about reached top speed when he passed Eubie and his mom. Jacket open and flapping. Smith & Wesson .357 model 19 on display for tourists and locals alike. Already out of breath. He didn't particularly notice Eubie and his mother as he went by, but he heard the woman say, "Thank you, Officer. He turned left just after the statue of the lion. Don't go easy on him. He's a jerk."

Joe Bradlee had, in fact, ducked past the statue of the lion and turned left on the narrow Calle dei Specchier, but when Louis made the same turn, Joe was nowhere in sight.

They'd had a rule for these situations: first left, next left, next right. Left, left, right. Louis decided there was no point in running. Joe would be there at the end of this Venetian maze or he wouldn't.

But it was the *wouldn't* that concerned Louis. In the past three years Joe had dragged him off to a hundred different places. Outrageously remote pieces of nowhere. When they'd get there, Joe would stare in silence for twenty-five minutes. Then impart something idiotic like, "This beats hell out of D.C." or "Makes it kind of hard to go back, don't you think?" or "I could live here." Louis knew, sooner or later, Joe wasn't going to come back. He just hoped he wasn't around when it happened.

"He's like one of those birds," Louis once said. "I hate those birds. What are they called . . . ? People don't know when they'll fly away and never come back so they tie their feet down? I mean, I like Joe and all, but you can't figure him out sometimes. I'll take a hound any day."

"Left, left, right." Louis ran it through his head as he walked, and eventually he found himself standing on the steps of San Giuliano, scanning the square that spread in front of him. No Joe.

Joe was actually behind him. In the church. Checking out the paintings.

Louis waited on the steps like a good dog, and Joe exited five minutes later. As he walked by Louis, he simply said, "We're late."

And Louis fell in alongside.

"Why were you running back there?" he said. "I thought you were after someone. . . . I was looking forward to a little rock and roll. What time is it?"

Louis looked at his watch.

"Actually, we're not late," Louis continued. "I told

the Italians eleven-thirty. Not eleven. Earlier seemed better than later. I mean, getting there earlier, not an earlier meeting, or an earlier time for the meeting. Actually, they set the time. They wanted to make it earlier. It's getting cooler. Notice that?"

This banter was something Louis had perfected over his years with Joe. He knew sooner or later he would touch on something that would interest Joe, and Joe would say, "What?" And Louis could get back to his original question. It worked every time. Louis pushed on:

"The problem was, I had no idea how long it would take to get there. If we walked, that is. I figured you'd want to walk. I didn't see a decent *vaporetto* route—"

"What?" Joe said.

"What were you running for?"

"I thought I saw something."

"What?"

"Turned out to be nothing."

Louis shrugged and said, "Semper fi."

And after walking two more blocks they found themselves standing at the door of the area police station. Louis opened it.

Three

The Golden Boy. Secret Service agent Jerry Olsen. He'd been assigned to cover the Vice President from the very first day of Number Two's last campaign. The election had been a little over three years ago. Jerry had been with Goliath ever since. They were perfectly suited for each other. Not an ounce of brains between them, if you were to listen to Louis Zezzo.

Olsen was the classic case of the right place at the right time. Goliath had taken a shine to him from day one and that was that. Dumb fucking luck. Olsen was in. He'd had only two years in service when he'd met Goliath, but now he held one of the senior positions in the Grid. Jerry Olsen was big wood. The man in charge of the Vice President's Secret Service detail. And there was no love lost between Olsen and the advance men—the Roadrunners.

Louis Zezzo had always felt that Olsen's job should have gone to none other than Louis Zezzo, and he wasn't adverse to telling people so. Even though Louis hadn't been with the service when the job was handed out, he moaned about it constantly. But Louis Zezzo didn't get Jerry Olsen's job. Louis would never get Jerry Olsen's job. One simple reason: Louis had been a light-heavyweight boxer for Temple University—Olsen, the golden boy quarterback of Brigham Young. When politicians mixed with cameras, they brought out the Norse gods to shield them. Louis considered this absolute crap.

Joe, on the other hand, had gotten used to being passed over for the glory work. He had many a good friend in the Central Office. Top people in the Grid. People who respected him. Respected the way he got things done and done right. But the Central Office knew better than to let Joe get too close to a politician. Joe understood that. He accepted it. What the fuck.

Jerry Olsen was well aware of how the advance men felt bout him. And basically, he could care less. They had their work. He had his. The less he came in contact with the Roadrunners, the better it was for everyone.

When Jerry, and his precious cargo, had landed at Venice's Marco Polo airport, he'd been pleased. Things had gone smoothly. Goliath, The Wife, and Little Audrey, their daughter, had been ferried out of *Air Force Two,* code name Cardinal, and through an emptied section of the airport terminal. From there they'd been hustled outside and into a waiting Mercedes limousine. No flags on the fenders. No American cars. Not a Lincoln in sight.

But when Olsen jumped into the front seat of the Mercedes, the driver surprised him. He glared at the man and said, "I don't know you. What's going on?"

The driver watched his rearview mirror as the other agents piled into the sedans behind him. He considered saying, "Yeah, well, I don't know you either, dickhead," but he didn't. He simply said, "Harvey." Then handed Olsen an envelope. In the envelope were Harvey's clearance and a short explanation as to why the sedans were being driven by Italian policemen.

"You might as well know it, Harvey, I don't like surprises. Why the changes?"

Harvey thought of pointing out to the Golden Boy that it'd been rather foolish of him to have loaded the Vice-President of the United States, his wife and daughter, and his entire entourage into a bunch of fucking foreign cars that had no familiar drivers, but instead he'd stuck to the facts:

"Lightfoot came down with something last night. We put it to the junk he ate. Probably the *fegato*. Nobody else went near the stuff. Venice is famous for it. You know Lightfoot, right? You would've recognized him, right? Anyway, he feels like shit."

"What the hell is *fegato*?"

"*Fegato*. Liver. Venice is famous for it," Harvey said as he pulled the big Mercedes out of Marco Polo airport and headed west.

"This is a nice car," he thought. Harvey had always preferred the Lincolns. But this was a nice fucking car.

"How long's this going to take us?" Olsen asked.

"Thirty, forty minutes. Is there a rush? We can do it in less."

Olsen didn't answer. He just buried his nose in a situation report. In the back, Goliath and The Wife sat on opposite sides of the seat. After checking his appearance in the hand mirror he carried in his flight bag, the Vice President flipped through a *Sports Illustrated* and glanced at the pictures. Not a hair had been mussed on his head. He seemed pleased.

Number Two was vain, to be sure, but he wasn't nearly as dumb as Louis and the world made him out to be. He actually was the son of a coal miner. And he was a shrewd son of a bitch. He'd come a long way by letting other people believe they were a hell of a lot smarter than he was.

The Wife appeared to be wearing every ounce of jewelry she owned and was now trying to get a bracelet untangled from her sweater. Harvey wondered if she was wearing the crap to impress the Italians, or if she was afraid the Washington staff would lift the shit while she was gone. Little Audrey busied herself by playing with the liquor bottles. Harvey was the only one who bothered to look out the windows.

After Harvey had checked his cargo, he thought, "Fuck it," and decided to settle back and enjoy the drive. The German bulletproof glass had a greater fisheye effect than the American glass. It gave the

Italian countryside, with its small houses and terra cotta roofs, a much more majestic appearance. To the best of his knowledge, no one said a goddamn word for the entire trip. The intercom was off. Little Audrey might have grunted once or twice.

Harvey couldn't tell for sure.

But then again, Harvey didn't care.

As Carter Perkins stood mesmerized in the concourse of Marco Polo airport, almost in a state of shock, almost faint, holiday travelers sprinted past. But they kept their distance, as if Carter were a lost piece of luggage containing an explosive device.

Carter's flight to Calcutta had been delayed four times. Now the wretched thing was nearly six hours late in leaving. And these delays had left Carter cursing Little Randy, a cute but often over efficient secretary, for having suggested this stopover in Venice in the first place. "It will get your juices flowing" had been Randy's rationale.

Carter had just finished reading a second paperback novel of the morning. The book had been purchased in the shop adjacent to the first-class lounge. The price for this pulp had amounted just over twenty pounds. Sterling.

The speed at which Carter could devour a book was remarkable. A five-hundred-page novel could be lapped up in less than two hours. "I am nothing less than a genius," Carter was fond of saying to Randy. It always brought a smile. But the rubbish that now dangled in Carter's overly delicate left hand had been absorbed. Swallowed. And thus had become worthless. Carter had decided to return it for another. An explanation would be given: "I've already read the foolish thing." A demand for a different one would come next. It wasn't the first time Carter had executed this folly. It was a game. The practice had been honed to a glorious science.

But this new vision now forced Carter to forget the paltry volume altogether. A hundred feet away, a dream of a lifetime had appeared in the form of a gargantuan mass of steel.

"Delays have dangerous ends," Carter quoted from a favorite—Shakespeare's *Henry the Sixth, Part One.*

Carter's gaze was glued to the far end of the airport passageway. Through the thick window glass stood a massive aircraft. A Boeing 747. Silver and blue. With red and white trim. It had a large gold insignia. An eagle. Spread. A bird of prey made immortal by the United States of America. Carter calculated this mass of steel to be *Air Force One.* The President's plane. Carter watched as the creature lumbered past the window and came to a dead stop. Only a small portion of the tail section remained visible. Carter smiled a small smile and whispered, "Won't DOC be happy to hear about this turn of events?"

Carter Perkins' itinerary had just changed.

And in Carter's mind, so had the course of human events. "After all," Carter thought, "as flies to wanton boys, we are to the gods; they kill *us* for their sport."

Carter picked up the black leather carry-on bag and walked directly to the Air India first-class ticket counter. Carter glanced back at the 747 only once, but seemed to be literally drooling at the sight of the thing. The anticipation of encountering its cargo had made Carter's body damp throughout.

"I'm afraid I'm feeling rather ill and won't be able to board the flight to Calcutta," Carter said and handed the ticket envelope to the dark-skinned Air India steward. An irresistibly good-looking young man by Carter's judgment. "Would you please see that my luggage is removed from the airliner and sent back to the Hotel Malvasi—as soon as possible." This was followed with a slight wink.

"Yes, sir. I'm terribly sorry. Perhaps I can call for one of the Malvasi launches. Or would you prefer to take a car in?"

"Please arrange for an automobile. I will be in the first-class lounge. Perhaps a sherry will help. Call me once you're sure my luggage has been sent on, if you would be so kind."

"Yes, sir."

Before going to the first-class lounge, Carter made three telephone calls. One to Calcutta. One to the Hotel Malvasi. The last call went to an unlisted number in Long Rapids, Michigan. The telephone was answered, as always, by a computer-generated voice. "You've reached DOC. At the tone leave your message."

Carter waited for the tone and simply said, "It's Carter Perkins. I am at the Malvasi Hotel in Venice, Italy. I can deliver half of your article within forty-eight hours."

Carter replaced the receiver in the cradle and then moved off to exchange the book at the airport shop. This time Carter selected something that truly had been read before—many, many times. William Shakespeare's *Julius Caesar.* A line from the play floated to the very front of Carter's brain. It was accompanied by a Cheshire cat's grin.

> The evil that men do lives after them,
> The good is often interred with their bones.

Four

Inspector Lamberto Solfanelli glanced first at Louis Zezzo and then at Joe Bradlee as they slipped into his police station. He then eyed the large clock on the wall above his desk. Eleven-twenty. Solfanelli had dealt with Joe on many occasions. In many situations. He had the utmost respect for him. But this was the first time in all their encounters Lamberto could recall Joe being late. Twenty minutes late, to be precise.

The *informazione* Inspector Solfanelli had been ordered to relate to Joe didn't seem all that important. But some *capo scarico* in Roma had forbidden the information to be broadcast over the telephone. And Lamberto had no desire to chance a poor interpretation by Louis Zezzo. Additionally, the inspector didn't like the idea of being a messenger boy. No matter who the message was for. Friend or no. Thus, a certain justifiable irritation at having been kept waiting. Especially on the day before Christmas.

"Joe, sono qui," Solfanelli called across the desolate police station.

The two Secret Service agents worked their way through a maze of empty desks and stepped into Solfanelli's office. He closed the door behind them. It was now eleven twenty-one.

The office was as neat as a pin. Every paper in order. Every pencil and pen in its spot. The three photos of Lamberto and his wife and children were perfectly spaced and cocked at the exact same angle. These photos were set on a corner of his desk next to a tray reserved for pending cases. The tray was completely devoid of papers. Barren. Vacant. Lamberto Solfanelli, and Venice, for that matter, never carried a huge case load.

The inspector thought himself an average man. He was of average height and average weight. He had the standard Italian mustache. Not too big. Not too small. His clothes were unimpressive. He had what some would call labored Italian good looks. From the photos on his desk, Louis observed his wife to be no great beauty. Nice breasts, though. "Perky," Louis thought. And then found himself wondering how good she was in bed.

Solfanelli never went to the cinema. Never watched television. Never read books or magazines. Only newspapers and police reports. But despite all this he was a very perceptive man. And he loved his Venezia. He loved it with a passion.

"You should look into getting a Swiss watch, Joe."

"Was it eleven?" Louis interjected.

"Si."

"My fault, Inspector. I told Joe eleven-thirty. Which, by the way, would make us early. Eight minutes, if you think about it."

"*Si,* if you think about it," Solfanelli sighed. "*Allora,* what I have to tell you is this: Oscar Sanchez left Milano by train this morning, and an *intelligenza* report puts him on his way to Venezia."

Solfanelli gave the word *intelligenza* a slight twang. Lifted his eyebrow twice.

"I personally do not consider this report all that reliable. For one, it is from Roma. And two, Oscar Sanchez has been out of the explosives business for a number of years. A *riposo.* Retired, according to my sources. But, Joe, you must know that better than I."

He pulled a small piece of paper from the desk drawer and continued.

"But then again, money can change all things. The

man still keeps his apartment here on the Calle del Forno. In the old ghetto section. He is traveling with his present woman, Christina. But I must think, if they are coming to Venezia at all, it is for a Christmas holiday and nothing more."

"But you will put one of your men on him? Just in case?"

It was a foolish question, but Joe had to give it a try. The last thing he wanted to do on Christmas was tail Oscar Sanchez, the Mad Jewish Bomber.

"This is Venezia, Joe. It is the day before Christmas. Most of my men are not working until after Il Capodanno. The New Year."

When Solfanelli inserted these little translations, he would glance at Louis and force a smile. He handed the paper containing Oscar's address to Joe.

"If you want to look out for Oscar Sanchez," he continued, "you will have to do it yourself."

"When do you expect him to arrive?" Louis piped in.

"I do not expect him to arrive. He has no business here. But if I were to expect him to arrive, it would be on the *diretto.* The direct train. Due from Milano at two thirty-six."

"The Vice President's on his way in from the airport now. We'll pick him up at Isola Nuova. Hopefully have him at the Malvasi well before two." Almost to himself, Joe added, "Then I guess I'll go looking for my old friend Oscar Sanchez."

"*Arrivederci e Buon Natale,* Joe . . . Merry Christmas, Louis," the inspector said as he opened his office door.

Joe felt a slight case of the bum's rush from Solfanelli. But the inspector most likely only wanted to get home to his family and try to have a normal Christmas without any undue interruptions from the United States government. A thought that made Joe chuckle.

Louis and Joe stepped out of the police station and were smacked with the fresh, cold air. They stood for a second. Nothing was said. Joe looked into the sun, and another second passed. He took a deep breath.

Let it out. He then turned to the right and started to walk down the street. Louis, being a big believer in supporting any and all public and private transportation systems, couldn't believe his eyes. Joe was a walker, Louis was not.

"Yo, Joe? We're walking to Isola Nuova?"

"It's good for you, Louis. It's a nice day. You'll get to know the city better. . . . I also want to take you by Oscar Sanchez's apartment. There's ten or twelve Calle del Forno in Venice. You'll probably have to find the damn place on your own later. I want you to know where it is."

"Forno?"

"Oven."

"Who the hell is this Oscar? I should know this guy, right?"

"Not really. Before your time. He carried out a bunch of bombings in the seventies and eighties. No particular allegiance. Just whoever had the cash. A money man. I'm sure our guys used him as much as the other guys. That's why there's been no rush to jail the bastard. He was born in Argentina but now seems to spend most of his time in Milano. He's also Jewish and the main reason, I would guess, that Solfanelli thinks there's not too much to worry about."

Louis' response to all this was a look that Joe easily interpreted as Louis' "I don't get it" look.

Joe said, "The only people who are pissed off at us are Arab extremists, and Oscar won't work for Arabs. Money or not."

"Oh. Right."

They walked a little farther and Louis said, "If he's Jewish, why's he going somewhere for Christmas?"

Joe had considered this question just about ten seconds before it came from Louis' mouth. He had no answer for it.

Oscar fucking Sanchez. In Venice. "Christ," Joe thought. He had spoken to the bastard on only one occasion. It had been twelve years ago in Paris. Two-thirty in the morning. Joe'd stopped into a bar, Les

Trois Mailletz, for a beer. The place had preserved a rather large collection of torture devices and had displayed them on the walls of the cabaret in the basement. Some folks found it charming.

Joe had recognized Oscar immediately. The beard was gone, but there'd been no question. It was Oscar. In those days the Central Office handed out photos of the sleazeball as often as paychecks.

Joe took the stool next to him.

"I'll have a beer, French, whatever," he said to the barmaid.

"I take it you're having a night off," Oscar said. "I'd like to think if you were undercover, you might look somewhat more like a Parisian."

"No Sneaky Pete here."

"I can smell a policeman and his gun from a hundred meters, *monsieur.*"

"I've had too many of the damn things pinched by the hotel maids. It pays to keep it with me. . . . Besides, you never know when you might have to shoot some schmuck. By the way, you look better without the beard."

"We've met, then? Forgive me, I'm usually very good with faces."

Joe produced a small wad of photographs. All of suspected enemies of the United States government. He fanned through them until he came to the one of Oscar, *avec* beard. Slid it across the bar.

"I had no idea I had so many competitors. You're right, the beard was a foolish vanity. . . . But I'm at a slight disadvantage here, *monsieur.* You seem to know me, but I don't know you."

Oscar's voice had developed a pronounced edge.

Joe took a long, slow sip of beer and, without so much as a glance at Oscar, said, "Joe Bradlee. I'm with the American Secret Service. We're taking you in, shithead."

Though Joe hadn't been looking directly at Oscar, he was able to sense his beady eyes darting from one possible exit to the next. He'd become like a wolf in a cage. Waiting for some fool to leave the gate open.

Oscar stood. Joe grabbed his arm and squeezed hard. Like a vise on a copper pipe. He pulled Oscar back down to the stool and said, "I thought you Argentineans had a sense of humor?"

The bar girl had returned with Joe's change, and they traded a glance. She seemed soft. Steady, was Joe's quick read.

"No, we're not taking you in. But I enjoyed your squirming act. You do it well."

"You're not taking me in?"

"I'm not taking you in."

"Someone else is?"

"Couldn't say. Couldn't really give a shit. Got in today. Leave tomorrow."

"You are with the American Secret Service, though?"

Joe only nodded.

"Some would consider this a rather cruel joke."

"Well, when you compare it to the bombings of a terrorist, it doesn't seem all that cruel, now does it?"

"I'd like to point out to you, and your government, if you would be so kind to deliver the message, that no one has ever died as a result of my business practices. I intend to keep it that way. It sometimes is very difficult to live up to this standard. Believe it or not, there is an art to what I do."

"Berlin, '78?"

"The man had a heart attack, for God's sake."

"A heart attack? Holy moley. What am I thinking of? So, it's not like he's really dead, right? Christ, you're an asshole."

"We're all in the same business, Mr. Bradlee. Don't be so self-righteous. We all think we're on the right side."

"And what side would be yours?"

"That's exactly my point. You see, every side is right. Who am I to judge? I'm a businessman. . . . Would you let my arm free?"

Joe did.

"Thank you . . ." Oscar rubbed his elbow. "I have a family to feed. I don't ask questions."

"Great."

Joe always found "good guys, bad guys" conversations only slightly less depressing than talking about the war in Vietnam. With each change in administration, the agents had been asked to stand up and take a bullet with the Big Boy's name on it. This year it was Goliath and Atlas. In the past it had been Sunbeam. Or Cottonwood. Muleskinner. Warrior. And it made no difference what the politician's affiliation was or what he stood for. If anything.

It'd get worse during the election years. The agents would be asked to shield candidates with less moral fiber than a fucking ant. Stand guard at motel doors while they entertained one whore after another. One bag man after another.

Joe had seen Oscar's point only too clearly. And it had begun to depress the shit out of him. "So we'll leave it at that," Joe said. "No questions asked. None answered."

Joe'd become anxious to end the goddamn conversation then and there.

"You're Jewish, right?"

"On my mother's side. But wasn't it going to be no questions, Mr. Bradlee?"

"Joe. You can call me Joe. . . . Did it sound like a question? I meant it as a statement. A point of conversation. If you don't want to talk about it, I can understand that. Consider the subject closed. Shut. *Finito* . . . I mean, it's not like you're emotionally tied to Israel. Or Argentina, for that matter. Or any country, when you think about it . . . I've been to Israel a few times. It's got to be one of the most beautiful countries in the world. I mean, it's not Venice, or Paris, or New York, but it's a beautiful place. Well, Venice, Paris, New York, they're cities, really. Not countries. You've been there, right? Israel? . . . Right, no questions. Well, I'm sure you've been there. It'd be a nice place to settle down, plant some roots. Don't you think? Especially if you're Jewish. Jesus."

Oscar had listened to all this and emptied his glass. "Well, Mr. Bradlee, it's late, and if there isn't anyone else like you waiting for me outside, I think I'll say good night."

And Oscar Sanchez was gone.

Joe'd been relieved. A boring American could drive anyone to the fucking hills. Originally, he'd wanted to find out what made the bastard tick. He'd thought it a stroke of luck to have found him there. In the end, he'd just been glad to be rid of him.

But depression hadn't walked out the door with Oscar Sanchez. From past experience Joe knew there was only one sure way to exorcize the "good guys, bad guys" demons. Even if only for a little while.

He'd never forgotten her name. Marguerite. The girl behind the bar. He'd guessed her age to be about twenty-seven. Not much younger than he was at the time. She had possessed absolutely crystalline gray eyes. It turned out she'd needed to spend the night with someone as much as he had. And she'd become a far more beautiful woman than she'd first appeared. Neither one was depressed by morning.

It was an image of Marguerite, naked in the sunlight, dozing on the small bed in her Parisian flat, that was shattered, blown out of Joe's mind, when Louis brought him back to Italy and the here and now.

"If this guy Sanchez is Jewish, why's he going anywhere for Christmas? I mean, it doesn't make all that much sense if you stop and think about it."

"Oscar, you mean?"

Joe's attention was only halfway back. It'd stalled somewhere between Venice and Paris, and his distraction had Louis confused.

"Am I missing something here?"

"I was just thinking of Oscar . . . and Paris. We had a chance meeting. Twelve years ago. But there's nothing in it that explains a damn thing. I don't know why he's coming here for Christmas—unless it's for us."

"Us?"

"Number Two."

Louis and Joe continued walking while Venice closed down. Shop doors were locked up. People were racing to get home to their families and to their *Cele-*

brazione. No one cared about or even noticed the two Americans. They were not family. They did not belong. Like two orphaned brothers, Louis and Joe had become their own family.

Joe saw a small child cross the narrow street just ahead. He jogged for three or four steps. He thought it might have been the boy. Eubie. From the Piazza Di San Marco. Eubie and Eubie's mother. The woman with the dark glasses. And those riveting brown eyes. He was wrong. When he rounded the corner the boy was being held high in the air by his grandfather. An older woman, his great-grandmother perhaps, held a brightly colored package behind her back. There was an abundance of good-natured teasing. All in Italian.

"What's up?" Louis said when he caught up to Joe.

"Thought I saw someone I knew."

"Joe, are you okay? You seem a little out of it."

"Jesus, fuck, Louis, it's Christmas, for Christ's sake. What the hell are we doing?"

"Huh?"

"Right, shit, we're looking for Oscar's apartment. It should be over this bridge. A few blocks to the left." And after a long pause Joe added, "Sometimes I'm not all that crazy about this job. And Christmas is one of those times."

"Yeah, I know what you mean. We should be looking for toys."

"Exactly "

Louis couldn't help but point out the number five *vaporetto* stop as they passed it.

"You know it would have been real easy to get here by boat. Actually, I think this is the *five* right here. We could probably take this boat right over to where Goliath gets in from the airport. What is it? Isola Nuovo? Nuova . . . ? After you show me Oscar's, that is."

They turned right on the Calle del Forno, walked for another forty feet, and stopped. The building was as old as most in Venice. Maybe older. But it was obvious the structure had gone through some extensive renovations. All new maple doors. New wood surrounded the windows. The original window glass had been kept—glass was sacred in Venice. Geraniums were still green in window boxes. And a lone yellow canary sang in a cage dangling from a fourth-floor apartment window.

Oscar had done well for himself. Sure, his wife had finally divorced him. And it was now impossible for him to see his two children. But he was wealthy and living the good life. It was a beautiful building. A beautiful neighborhood. The old ghetto. Not fancy, but a place where the real people of Venezia lived. Joe thought, "This is the kind of address I could be very happy in."

"This is it, huh?" Louis said. "You'd think that bird would freeze to death."

"Somehow they get used to the cold."

"Or else they die."

"Right . . . Or else they die."

"Which apartment is it?"

"B."

"I can't believe someone would leave the bird out there like that."

"They're out at night too. All over Venice. You think you can find this place by yourself?"

"Sure."

Joe looked at his watch. "Olsen should have Number Two in from the airport soon. Let's go. It'd be a shame if we missed him."

"I'm worried about that bird. Maybe we should see if those people are home." Louis said.

"Forget the fucking bird, Louis."

"Semper fi."

Five

Joe and Louis arrived at Isola Nuova by *vaporetto*. As per Louis' request. A huge parking facility was the dominating structure on the island. Joe visualized thousands of snipers suspended from the building. Arguing with one another about who would have the honor of placing the first bullet in Number Two's skull.

Shortly after Louis and Joe arrived, three gleaming motor launches from the Hotel Malvasi pulled in and tied to the southwest bulkhead. Joe greeted the helmsmen, all of whom he knew by name. He thanked them for their promptness and made it well worth their while. He dealt the lira out like playing cards. Inspector Solfanelli's men had done a nice job of clearing the area. Not a sniper in sight. The police were nowhere in sight either—a Solfanelli trademark . . . and a sniper trademark.

The two Americans, agents Joe Bradlee and Louis Zezzo, now stood and watched as the huge Mercedes limousine rolled toward them. They'd put their identifying lapel pins back on their jackets and stuffed their communication devices back into their ears. They were ready. Ready for the man from West Virginia. The Vice President of the United States of America.

Joe liked to call him Number Two. The Vice President preferred the code name Goliath. However, once he'd held the office for six months, one of the Roadrunners had made the startling discovery that West Virginia was also known as the Panhandle State. From then on, the Vice President had been nicknamed The Panhandler by the advance men.

Joe gave the all-clear, and Harvey rolled the limousine up to within an inch of Joe's legs. The sedans had been following so closely behind the Mercedes, it appeared as if they'd been towed in from the airport. All the cars froze at the exact same moment. The doors of the sedans flew open. The agents poured out. Olsen and Harvey stepped out of the Mercedes.

Joe spoke first. To Harvey.

"Thanks, Brian, I owe you one."

Olsen jumped in, "Brian . . . ? Brian . . . ? I thought you said your name was Harvey."

"Well, yeah, it is. It's my last name. Harvey. Brian Harvey."

"You could've made that more clear at the airport."

"It was in the report."

Joe interjected, "I think we should get Number Two on his way to the hotel. I've never liked this place. Too open. The boats are all set."

Olsen nodded and walked to the Vice President's door. Joe headed for The Wife's. As Joe passed by Harvey, the agent said, "What an asshole," under his breath.

"Who?" Joe said.

"Olsen."

"You're just finding that out? It was in the report."

Both Mercedes' doors opened at exactly the same second. Olsen said, "We're here, sir."

On the other side of the car Joe said, "Welcome to Venice, ma'am."

"Thank you, Joe. It's nice to see you again. Merry Christmas."

"Thank you, and the same to you. How was Marco Polo, any problems?" Joe said as he helped her out of the car. A blast of cigarette smoke began to make his eyes water.

"Marco Polo?"

"The airport. Sometimes landings there can be a little rough."

"That's what they call the airport? Marco Polo?"

"Yes, ma'am."

"After the explorer?"

"Yes, ma'am."

Little Audrey had jumped out of the car on her father's side and run to Louis, who'd been standing by the first Malvasi launch. She was decked out in the same sapphire velvet dress she'd been wearing for the better part of December. The agents had guessed the dress, no doubt, had become her favorite. Little Audrey was more spoiled than any child Joe had ever known. She gave new meaning to the word *pest.* But Little Audrey thought the sun rose and set on Louis. So a lot was overlooked by Joe. And by Louis. Naturally.

"I have a Christmas present for you, Louis, but you can't have it until tomorrow. And if you're not good, you can't have it at all. What do you think of that?"

"Did you know Santa Claus comes to Venice in a boat?" Louis said as he swooped Little Audrey up in his arms and carried her on to launch number one.

The Wife asked Joe to gather the handbags from the car and was off to join Olsen and her husband. The back of the Mercedes was an absolute fucking disaster area. It reeked of cigarette smoke. All the labels had been scratched from the liquor bottles, and two gold knobs were missing from the television set.

Joe collected Little Audrey's white patent leather purse. He then grabbed a soft travel bag with a large United States of America seal on it and a badly crumpled *Sports Illustrated.* The Redskins were going to the Super Bowl. Last, a stuffed dog named Wow-Wow. Wow-Wow had seen better days. So had the fucking Cowboys.

Joe took it all down to the launch. Handed it over to Louis, who had been joined on launch number one by Olsen, The Wife, and Goliath. Joe called to Olsen:

"Jerry, I want to go over a few things with you," he said, then moved back to Harvey and the Mercedes. "I'll give you a tip about Olsen. Call him Jerome. It drives him up a fucking wall."

"Couldn't this have been handled on the boat? On the way to the hotel? I don't like this place either," Olsen said as he walked up.

"I didn't think 'your boy' needed to overhear me for one, and two, Louis is taking you to the hotel. I'm staying here."

"Louis? He doesn't even speak Italian."

"Look, everything's set, Jerry. All the men on these boats speak English. Everyone at the Malvasi speaks English. The guy who takes out the garbage at the Malvasi speaks better English than the fucking HUD secretary. There'll be no problems with the hotel staff. They've been through it before, with more important people than Number Two. Now, the deal is this: The Italians have picked up movement on a guy named Oscar Sanchez. He's before your time, so I'll—"

"Hold it. What do you mean, 'before my time'?"

"Easy. He's arriving by train in an hour or so. I'm going to the station. I'll see if I can pick him up, find out what the hell he's up to."

"What do you mean, 'before my time'?"

"Jesus Christ, Jerry, do you know anything about this schmuck?"

"No."

"Then that's what I mean by 'before your time.' "

"Well, who is he?"

"Louis will fill you in on the way to the hotel."

"Louis?"

"Louis. You better get rolling. The Wife looks a little impatient. I wouldn't want you to get on her bad side."

"Shit," Olsen said. He trotted back to the launch.

Harvey couldn't resist throwing in, "I'll catch you later, Jerome."

"Another tip," Joe said. "Don't overdo the Jerome stuff. Olsen can make life very difficult for you. . . . I'll call you if I need anything. You'd better get the car cleaned up. You're going to have to find a couple more knobs for the TV. I think Little Audrey might have liberated them."

Joe turned and headed for the train station.

Harvey let him walk a few paces and called, "*Buona fortuna, mio onorevole collega.*"

Joe flipped him the bird.

Six

Joe Bradlee never wanted to see Oscar Sanchez again for as long as he lived. In Paris he'd found Oscar to be an oily character. Just too damn smooth. Since Paris, Joe'd been put on Oscar's tail two times. They'd never made contact again, but Joe's assessment had always been the same: Oscar Sanchez was no killer. Oscar loved to destroy property. Sure. He was paid well for it. Maim a few people, why not? *So* what if they lost their feet? Part of the job. But no killer. He was an *artist*. Twice Joe had come back to the Central Office with this same report. Both times the response had been: "Stay with him, there's always a first time. The man's dangerous when big money comes out." And that was what propelled Joe onto the train station—there was always a first time. There would always be big money.

He wished he'd had time to change from his suit and into a more homespun outfit. But a few things prevented this. There was no way he could have made it to the Malvasi, change, and be back in time to meet Oscar Sanchez's 2:36 train from Milan. Also, Joe didn't have any homespun outfits to change into. He found himself wondering if this was the same damn suit he'd been wearing when he'd met Oscar in Paris.

Joe walked the short distance from the parking structure to La Stazione Ferroviaria, Venice's rail link with the rest of the world. Once inside he looked up at the mammoth information board. The train from Milan was on time. He then passed under the board and out behind the waiting room. Onto the train platforms. There were twelve platforms in all. A few were vacant, but most held trains. The trains were waiting like giant steel iguanas. They would absorb what human cargo they could and cart it to a thousand spots across Europe for the Christmas holiday. One train was unloading. Joe instinctively tried to separate the assassins and psychopaths from the everyday Italians.

But instead of his expected pandemonium he saw only reunions. Emotions ran rampant. Lovers embraced lovers. Grandparents squeezed grandchildren. Mothers greeted sons returning from faraway schools. No one was shooting anybody. Joe was again struck with that same old feeling. The one that'd hit him earlier in the day. On the Malvasi launch. How easy it would be to get on one of these steel monsters and disappear into a cloud of railway steam. The train had emptied. It now seemed to be calling his name. Beckoning him to climb aboard and rumble off. He found any sense of loyalty to the White House evaporating. "They could get along just fine without me," he thought. Number Two was in good hands. Olsen might be considered an ass by some, but if nothing else, he was overprotective. Only Oscar's arrival was keeping Joe in Venice . . . Oscar and maybe Eubie's mom. Something about this woman got to Joe. He was sure he knew her from somewhere. Sure he had met her in the past. But he had no recollection of where or when.

In the end it was Eubie's mom and her brown eyes that kept Joe from getting on the train and vanishing. Even if he hadn't known her in the past, he would get to know her now.

But first Oscar.

He walked back into the main waiting room and checked the clock. Two-fifteen. He had twenty minutes. Enough time for a bite to eat.

The only difference between the restaurant in the Venice train station and the restaurant in the old Baltimore, Maryland, train station is that the espresso is better in Venice and the employees speak Italian. Other than that they're exactly the same. The waiters are rude. The tables are Formica with aluminum edging. The ashtrays are filthy. The chairs are rickety. The paper napkins are too thin. The salt and pepper shakers are greasy and empty. The sandwiches are stale. The cups are all chipped. They don't match the saucers. And everything is overpriced.

After wasting ten of his twenty minutes waiting for the waiter to arrive, Joe left. He went outside to the *vaporetto* landing and bought a *panino* from a vendor. It consisted of a hard roll and thin slices of freshly roasted pork. Joe had a vision of the pork skipping his stomach altogether, ignoring his digestive tract, and packing itself directly around his heart. Then clamping down on his aorta like a boa constrictor. The vision eventually passed. Joe washed the meal down with a bottle of Pellegrino water and returned to the train station. He walked directly to platform number eight.

The sign read "Binario otto: Milano-Direttissimo, AR-14:36." The train was just coming into view when Joe arrived. The express was larger. Newer. Far more sinister-looking than the other trains. It slipped into the station quietly, like a dagger returning to its sheath. Joe's mind wasn't too clear on how he was going to handle this Oscar thing. He felt strangely unprepared. It would have been far easier if Solfanelli had put one of his men on Oscar. A uniformed policeman. Oscar would have immediately known he was being tailed and would have made a telling move.

If he was on the up and up, legit, in Venice only for a holiday, he would ignore Solfanelli's man. He'd let the poor bastard spend his Christmas standing in front of Taverna La Fenice while Oscar and Christina dined on roast goose on the inside. But if Oscar was up to no good, he'd try to give Solfanelli's man the slip at some point. Which would mean he'd have to be watched all the more closely. Either way it would have made Joe's job a hell of a lot easier.

The doors of the *direttissimo* opened with a long

hiss. People stepped out. They stood for a moment. Embraced the air. The scene was unlike that of any other train station in the world. Most places, New York, London, Rome, Paris, people would have scurried off. Off to their final destination the instant their feet hit the pavement. Not Venice. For these people, arrival in the City of the Lagoon was like having a ton of concrete lifted from their shoulders. They had left the world behind and moved back in time.

Oscar and Christina were no exception. They stepped down from the train and placed their bags in the center of the platform. They turned to each other and indulged in a long, passionate kiss. Oscar had not gone back to the beard. It surprised Joe how easily he recognized the terrorist. After all the years. Oscar Sanchez had changed very little. Joe guessed Christina to be in her late twenties. She had long, overly straight flame red hair. She wasn't beautiful. But something, it could have simply been her arrival in this city, or maybe the way she clung to Oscar, but something made her glow.

Joe looked up and down the platform. It was a rerun of the last train's unloading. There were more grandparents. More sons and daughters. More mothers and fathers. And Joe noticed, for the first time, the gallant attempt the stationmaster had made to decorate his domain for Christmas. The theme was strongly religious. Scores of angels. Hundreds of the little fuckers. All on wing. And although the air of the city had left a certain film on them, there was a feeling that the angels were about to swoop with the pigeons and bless the travelers with peace.

Joe'd been admiring the craftsmanship of one of those cherubic angels when Oscar and Christina passed behind him and moved off toward the boat landing. So when he brought his gaze back to where they'd been standing, the couple seemed to have vanished into thin air.

Joe darted into the waiting room. But when he realized his quick movements had drawn some attention, he came to a stop. He looked at the schedule board.

Checked his watch. A passenger late for a train. That's all.

He checked the restaurant. No Oscar. He went back out to the train platforms. They were nowhere. He checked the men's room. Nothing. He then walked to the center of the waiting room. He began to turn. Slowly. They couldn't have traveled that far.

He turned again. Slower . . .

Bang.

"Fuck. Shit."

Some goddamn kid. Some fucking kid. At that precise moment ran by. Smacked Joe square in the balls with his goddamn tent poles.

Maybe he was seventeen. A student most likely. American. The kid wore a bright red parka. Sunglasses. Blue jeans. Black combat boots. And a hat formerly owned by some Peruvian llama rustler. He was also loaded down with a backpack the size of a goddamn steamer trunk. And fucking tent poles. "Christ."

"Sorry, dude, I thought I saw my mother."

If it wasn't for the fact that Joe was trying to attract as little attention as possible, he would've grabbed the bastard, shoved his pistol in his face, and said, "Try to be a little more careful next time, okay, sonny?" Instead Joe turned and moved across the waiting room. Out through the glass doors and out onto the steps that led to the boat platforms. And there, waiting for the number five *vaporetto,* were Oscar and Christina.

Joe needed to look more touristy. A camera would do. He looked down the canal. No *vaporettos.* He ducked back into the train station and headed to the gift shop. He tried the door. The shop had shut down early. Joe then spotted the American kid.

"Hey, kid, hold up."

The student began to walk backward. He held his hands out in front of himself as a buffer.

"I said I was sorry, mister. I don't want any trouble."

"No problem. You want to sell your camera?"

"What?"

It was one of those point-and-shoot Minoltas that sell for about sixty dollars.

"I'll give you two hundred for it."

"For this?"

"You can buy another one for two hundred bucks, right?"

"My stepfather gave it to me. It's a piece of shit. Everything's out of focus. What do you want it for?"

"I need a camera. Is it a deal?"

"What do you want it for?"

"Jesus . . . Forget it."

Joe turned and started to walk away.

"No. Yeah. No. Wait. Hold on. It's a deal. Sure. Two hundred bucks? Dude man."

"Is there any film in it?"

"Sure. A half a roll. No extra charge."

"No. Jesus. Don't you want to keep it? Save your film? Save your pictures?"

"Oh, yeah. Good idea. Hold on."

As the kid took the film out of the camera, Joe fished three hundred thousand lira notes out of his pocket and pushed it toward him. The kid was horrified when he saw the money.

"No way, dude. American money."

"Jesus Christ, kid, this isn't the third fucking world. It's Italy. This is a hell of a lot more than two hundred bucks."

"American money or no deal."

Joe put the lira back into his right side pocket. He reached into his left for American money. When he did this, the kid got a good look at Joe's 9mm pistol.

"Hold up. What is this? Some kind of sting operation or something? You with customs?"

"Don't fuck with me, kid. I don't have time for this shit. Deal or no? You want to sell the fucking camera or not?"

Joe was now holding three crisp, new hundred dollar bills. It was too much for the kid to resist.

"Yeah, it's a deal."

He handed Joe the camera. Joe handed him the money.

"Merry Christmas. Don't spend it all in one place."

Joe put the camera around his neck and walked outside. The number five *vaporetto* was just rounding the corner and heading for the landing. Oscar and Christina were still waiting patiently. Arm in arm. Taking in the waterway. As Joe walked over to the ticket booth he wondered if Oscar would recognize him. He doubted it. Joe had stared at pictures of Oscar for the better part of fifteen years. Oscar had seen Joe only once.

"Uno, per Ponte Guglie, per favore," Joe said to the ticket seller and followed it with a *"Grazie."*

The *vaporetto* pulled into the dock. The first mate tossed his rope around the tie-down, and the motorman eased the boat into reverse. The *vaporetto* nestled up against the dock. The gate was slid open. Passengers poured off. Oscar, Christina, and about a dozen other people waited. Joe stood back. He let the others board and then jumped to the boat just before the mate slid the gate closed. He moved to the stern and took a few bogus photos as the *vaporetto* left the train station in its oily wake. A combination of white-gray clouds mixed with a yellow-gold light from the west made the station look far more grand than it actually was. Joe found himself wishing he had film in the camera.

The Ponte Guglie was the first stop on the number five *vaporetto* after leaving Stazione Ferroviaria. A short enough walk from the station. Joe could only guess that Oscar had decided to take the boat in an effort to keep from having to carry his bags the seven blocks. The ride took four minutes. Oscar and Christina were laughing like children when they stepped off.

Joe decided to stay with the *vaporetto* until it reached the next landing, on the off chance that Oscar'd seen or recognized him. The apartment was midway between the two stops. Joe could easily double back to catch up with the two lovebirds.

He put the camera to his face and watched the pair

through the view finder. When he did this Christina stopped, turned, and looked back at the *vaporetto.* She pointed in Joe's direction and said something to Oscar. Oscar looked back over his shoulder and set the bags down. Joe could read his lips.

"Fuck me," Oscar had said. He then picked the bags up again and continued toward the apartment.

It took three minutes for the boat to reach the next stop. Joe had kept the two in sight most of the way. The *vaporetto* dropped down to a crawl, and the docking procedure was duplicated as it had been done a billion times before. Joe jumped off ahead of the other passengers. He caught sight of the couple again as they turned onto the Calle del Forno. He trotted, turned the same corner, and got a glimpse of red hair as it disappeared into the building. The heavy door closed with a dull thud.

Joe walked back to the canal. He watched the traffic go by. He tried to untangle the meaning of Oscar's "Fuck me." He reached into his shirt pocket for a cigarette. He hadn't smoked for years. "Christ." It was always the same goddamn reaction. Sit and wait for some son of a bitch to come out of a building—reach for a cigarette. A stakeout. Here he was on another stakeout. And it dawned on him that Joe Bradlee just might be the poor bastard spending Christmas outside the Taverna La Fenice—while Christina and Oscar dined on roast goose on the inside.

"Fuck you, Oscar?" he thought.

"Fuck me."

Seven

After Jerry Olsen settled his tribe, the three gleaming Malvasi launches eased away from the bulkhead. The Wife and Little Audrey had never been to Venice, and they were swept up by the city's charm and beauty from the moment they'd stepped onto the gleaming powerboat. There were no longer any signs of jetlag in these two. They wanted to see it all. Right here. Right now. The Vice President, on the other hand, did not share their enthusiasm for a short tour of the city.

"All right, all right, we'll go by way of the Grand Canal. But let's not take all day about it. See to it, will you, Olsen?"

But the more Olsen tried to get the Malvasi helmsmen to "step on it," the slower they seemed to progress.

"It can be very dangerous, *signore,* to move the boats too quickly at a time of, how do you say? Celebrazione? Natale? Christmas? Some of the men on the other boats get into the *grappa* early."

The helmsman was playing dumb. Olsen knew it. But he didn't care all that much. He'd spoken to the man. Twice, in fact. Goliath had seen him do it. That's all that counted. Olsen's chat with the pilot had been enough to get the Vice President to stretch out on one of the leather seats. He was asleep before the Italians had cast their lines off.

The two ladies had found a spot on the rear deck of the launch. They were leaning over the rail and spitting into the water. Trying to bombard a paper cup as it passed on the port side. Louis stood next to them. Feeling somewhat chilly. Wishing he hadn't left his overcoat back at the San Marco office.

All the agents had radio communication with one another. Along with the family on the first boat were Olsen, Louis, and two other agents named Barnes and Wilson. There was a photographer and assorted aides. And the quintessential aide. Aide of all aides. The Vice President's right arm—George Strutz.

The second boat carried another two agents and more aides. The third boat also carried two agents. A few press people. More aides.

The launches eased their way down the Grand Canal, maneuvering around gondolas but always remaining perfectly spaced. Olsen was pleased. The prone Goliath could not be seen, and their floating caravan attracted no attention whatsoever as the boats began working their way back to the safety of their home, the great Hotel Malvasi.

While the ladies drooled over the sights, Louis filled Olsen in on the Oscar Sanchez mess. After he had done this, Olsen said, "I'll send two men over to back Joe up as soon as we get to the hotel. It sounds like this guy could be big trouble. Where did you say the apartment was? Porno? Forno?"

"Joe'll check in. I don't think he wants a bunch of the boys showing up unexpected. And you know he probably doesn't have his wire on. . . . Anyway, it's a tough place to find if you don't know the city as well as Joe and me. There's got to be twenty, twenty-five Calle del Fornos here. . . . Forno. It means oven. Like in glass oven. They make a lot of glass here."

"I know."

They were interrupted by The Wife.

"Louis, I wonder if you could point a few things out to us."

"Yes, ma'am. I'd be happy to. . . . Excuse me, Jerry."

Louis moved to the stern of the launch with The Wife. Little Audrey had been waiting somewhat impatiently.

"Louis, do you know all the names of these places?" the little girl asked.

"Sure do. Most of the big ones are churches. That one there is a casino."

"Casino?"

"For gambling."

"It's where people lose their shirts, dear."

When The Wife said this, she was looking Louis square in the eye, and he had the distinct feeling that she was putting a move on him. This sort of thing happened to Louis all the time, so he recognized it easily. Women putting the move on. It had just never happened to him at the executive level. That's all. It left him off balance.

"Uh, yes, ma'am. That would be the ones who lost their money. Gambling, that is, shirts and whatnot," was his snappy comeback.

"I was hoping that maybe tomorrow, after we've had a little time to rest up, you might be able to show me some spots that most of these people never get to see."

"Yes, ma'am. But tomorrow's Christmas Day. Not much will be open. If anything."

"You're right. I wasn't thinking. Maybe the next day, then?"

"I'll have to clear it with Olsen, ma'am, but there shouldn't be any problem there. No, ma'am."

"Thank you, Louis. Maybe we could see some . . . glass . . . blowing, perhaps?"

"Umm . . . Yes, ma'am. Joe says there is a lot of that done on Murano," he said without looking at her.

"Murano?"

"It's a nearby island. We'd have to take a boat to get there."

"We're taking a boat now, Louis. You have to take a boat to get anywhere in Venice. I like it, though. It kind of brings out the romantic in me. How about you?"

"Umm . . . Yes, ma'am. I guess it does."

Little Audrey saw a break and jumped in. "What's glass blowing? Where's Joe?"

"Well, dear, it's a way to make drinking glasses. I believe the Venetians invented it. We'll just have to wait to see how it's done. . . . Where is Joe? I expected him to be with us."

"He had a few things to go over with the Italian officials," Louis lied.

They were now passing San Marco. Moving out into a wider, more open waterway. The wind had picked up and the water was beginning to get choppy. With the short days of winter, the sun was already on its way down behind the island of Giudecca. The Chiesa del Redentore, on the island, was now just a black silhouette. Illuminated from behind by a huge mass of yellow-gold light. The sun's rays slid between the surrounding buildings and bounced off the white caps. Turning them strangely silver.

The Malvasi launches were well equipped to handle the swells, but that didn't keep The Wife from losing her balance. She found it necessary to hold onto Louis' arm for support

The trip could not go quickly enough for Agent Zezzo. As they passed between the tip of Giudecca and San Giorgio Maggiore, he could see through the cabin window that The Panhandler was up and about. Louis was desperately trying to figure out a way to dislodge himself from The Wife.

"I think Little Audrey might like to get a closer look at those naval boats," he said. "What do you think? If you'll excuse me, ma'am, I'll just take her up to the bow before we pass by."

Louis broke away and took Little Audrey's hand. The Wife reached out. She grabbed the back of Louis' jacket at the hem before he could take a step.

"Torcello," she said.

"Excuse me, ma'am?"

"I hear Torcello is very nice."

Louis could distinctly feel her breasts pressing hard against the back of his suit jacket.

"I believe Torcello is another island, ma'am. I'll have it checked out."

"Thank you, Louis."

"Yes, ma'am. Umm . . . I'll need my jacket back now, ma'am."

She released him. He passed the cabin door just as The Panhandler stepped out.

"Getting a little rough out here, isn't it, Louis? Not everyone can handle this sort of thing. Takes a special lot."

"Yes, sir. The hotel's just around the bend, sir. I wanted to show Little Audrey these navy boats."

"Coast Guard."

"Sir?"

"I believe they're Coast Guard boats."

"Yes, sir."

"Right. Well, I guess I'll go back to steady my wife, then. We wouldn't want to leave her with no one to hold onto, now, would we?"

"No, sir."

Eight

Where the Malvasis had come from was never very clear. But by the late 1950s they had become an institution in Venice. To say the least. The family was now the closest thing to royalty one could find in modern-day Venice. And only the Catholic church held more Venetian real estate.

There was Dennis, the eldest son and ever present smiling face at Dennis' Bar. The bar had long been a hangout for the Hemingways and Gables of the world. And to this day it catered to the who's who of Europe and the globe. If Dennis didn't greet you with, "Ciao, Poppi, long time, no see!" you might as well pack your bags and move to Iowa City. You were nobody if you weren't on a first-name basis with Dennis.

There was Locanda Malvasi. On the island of Torcello. The Locanda was a small country-style inn. It had six guest suites and a restaurant. In the winter months the Locanda was closed up tighter than a drum. Almost no one went to Torcello in December. But in the summer months even Michelangelo would have trouble getting a room at Locanda Malvasi.

Then the jewel in the crown, the Hotel Malvasi. The hotel had been built by the family in 1956 on the island of Giudecca—away from Venice proper. Without a doubt, the Hotel Malvasi was one of the finest in the world. It had the only swimming pool in Venice.

A Malvasi tennis court often had to be booked a year in advance. A decade ago the family had taken over a neighboring sixteenth-century *palazzo* and turned it into a luxury residence. They referred to it as the Palazzo Agostino after the youngest son. It had only seven suites. Each furnished with priceless antiques. Each with its own valet and maid. The *palazzo* was also closed in winter. Not enough traffic.

Except for the kitchen help, it now seemed to Olsen, every Malvasi employee stood before the grand hotel waiting to greet the Vice President. A bead of sweat had formed on his brow. He could only trust that these people had been thoroughly checked out by Joe. That their names had been run through the Watch List computer at C.O.—the Central Office. It was standard procedure to do this with hotel employees as well as with all guests. It was one of the few things Olsen liked about working with Joe. He knew it had been done and done right. Still, all these Italians waiting on this dock and lawn were just too damn excited. It looked like one big mess to Olsen.

The first boat came to rest with a bump, and Little Audrey smacked her head square on Louis' Smith & Wesson model 19. This .357-caliber pistol had been issued to Louis by the Treasury Department when he'd joined the Secret Service. It left his hip only when he was showering, or in a woman's bed. It was a big gun. His suit jacket didn't offer much in the way of a buffer, and the little girl was now in tears. Louis once again swooped her up in his arms.

"Hey, hey, hey. You can't let these Italians see you crying. You know what they say about Venice?"

Little Audrey shook her head. Louis wiped a tear away with his thumb.

"There's too much water here already."

Louis then carried her off the boat and set her on the dock. She was immediately surrounded by thousands of hotel employees. They miraculously produced handfuls of Perugina chocolates. A waiter picked her back up almost before her feet hit the deck. Another pinched her cheek and popped a chocolate in her mouth.

"Che Bella!"

Little Audrey was in good hands.

But Olsen continued to be very uneasy. He seemed to have less and less control over the situation. He grabbed Louis.

"I don't like this. Who did Joe leave at the hotel?"

"Just Reynolds. We got caught a little shorthanded. Everyone went out last night. Lightfoot got sick on something."

"The liver."

"You heard about that shit, huh? Man, I wouldn't eat liver if it came up and offered me a night with the fucking Laker Girls," Reynolds said. He seemed to have appeared out of nowhere. Which was no mean trick. Reynolds didn't look all that Italian.

Agent Reynolds had been with the Secret Service for only two years. But he was too bright for the Central Office to ignore. And in their eyes he was too valuable to be anywhere but with the President or the Vice President. Reynolds had an uncanny sixth sense when it came to sniffing out the nuts. The loonies. The Quarterlies. In two short years he had pulled five nameless faces out of well-meaning crowds. Every one had been a certifiable nutcase. And every one armed to the teeth.

But Agent Reynolds had two critical flaws. One: Nothing or no one was sacred to his irreverent sense of humor. Politicians included. And two: He was black. No Norse god here. And The Panhandler, the good old boy from West Virginia, liked his agents white. Very white. So like Louis and Joe, Reynolds was doomed to be a Roadrunner.

"I told him to stay away from the goddamn liver. You know, if you're going to go ahead and eat crap like that, you got to stick with a place like this. The Malvasi. Lightfoot had to try it in some podunk, off the beaten path, out of the way, hole-in-the-wall trattoria. Of course, I personally wouldn't go near that shit no matter where I was."

"Thank you, Reynolds, I'll try to stay away from it," Olsen said. "Have all these people been checked out? This place is a zoo. Can't we settle them down a little? At least get them inside before we get the others off the boat. . . ." Olsen spun in a complete circle. "Damn it. Where the hell did the girl get to?"

"Relax, these are my people. I'll take care of it," Louis said.

Louis could see that Olsen and some of the other agents were about to go into their pushing and shoving mode in an effort to clear some space. So Louis diplomatically began to ask the employees to open up. They'd be having five days with the Vice President. They'd all have plenty of time to see him. Louis' approach seemed to work just fine. Reynolds then escorted Olsen into the hotel.

"The guy at the front desk right now is Nelo. He's a good dude. No attitude there. A lot of these I-ties seem to have a problem with those of us of the Negro persuasion. Not Nelo. He's cool. Anyway, if you need anything at all, he's the one to see. Stay away from the other one. The one over there with the mustache. He's a real prick. Joe's had everyone checked out with C.O., including all guests that are due in the next five days. There's one dude who got sick at the airport awhile ago. Was here this morning. On his way back in, I guess. A guy named Carter Perkins. I didn't see him, but I had C.O. run him through Big Bertha. He checks. Not much on him . . . travel writer, British. Somewhat swishy, apparently . . . If that interests you, maybe we could set up a date for you?"

"I don't think so," Olsen said.

When they reached the front desk they found Little Audrey perched on top of it. Nelo was hand-feeding her chocolates as if she were a parrot.

"Nelo, this is Agent Olsen. He will be in charge of security now that the Vice President has arrived."

Reynolds then gave Little Audrey a big squeeze. "Hey-hey, how's the queen of the Potomac?"

"Okay."

"Our pleasure to have you, Mr. Olsen," Nelo said.

"I hope you will have a pleasant stay with us. If I can be of any service at all, do not hesitate to call. Your rooms are all ready. Signore Reynolds has taken all the keys."

"I've got them right here," Reynolds said. "You've got the entire top floor. Nice view."

He handed a pouch of keys to Olsen.

"Louis, Joe, and I are a floor below you. In case there's something you can't handle."

The other agents were now escorting their herd into the hotel. Olsen moved to join them.

"Grab the girl, will you?" he said to Reynolds.

Reynolds looked at Little Audrey. "Piggyback?"

"Okay."

She saddled up. They walked directly to the Vice President.

"Everything seems just fine, sir," Olsen said. "We have the top floor. If you'll follow me. It should be a very nice view."

"Good to see you again, sir," Reynolds said.

"Right . . . Jefferson, isn't it?"

"Ah, no, sir. Actually, it's Reynolds. As in *aluminum* . . . or *tobacco,* if a reference to something *brown* might help you remember." This came from the agent with a more than slight edge.

"Right. Be careful with my daughter. Make sure you don't drop her."

"Absolutely, sir. I sure wouldn't want to drop her. No, sir."

He considered letting the little girl fall from his grip. But the hoard of aides coming his way probably would have trampled her to death in a second, so he held on.

Reynolds had been an advance man for The Panhandler for over a year now. The dick never remembered his fucking name. He was constantly mistaking him for Washington. Or Jackson. Or Jefferson. There wasn't now, nor had there ever been, anyone on his detail with those names. Reynolds was beginning to think the good old boy from West Virginia was a bit of a racist.

When they reached the top floor, it was Louis' responsibility to see that it was sealed off. He'd politely stopped the hotel employees that had followed, explaining that none of them were to enter the top floor unless they were specifically called for. He tipped the appropriate people, and they went about their business. All stairways and elevators were covered by agents. Another two agents had been stationed on the roof.

Olsen set up his command post in the room next to the Vice President's. The room Joe had prepared for him. Everything was in order. The hotel had supplied the agents with two three-by-six-feet folding tables to support the masses of computers and communications gear that had been brought in. A good portion of the antiques had been removed from this "operations room" to accommodate the machinery. All that remained of the original furnishings were the bed, an overstuffed armchair, a seventeenth-century desk, and matching chair.

The Vice President, The Wife, and Little Audrey all had separate rooms. They were, naturally, the largest rooms the hotel had to offer. Reserved for foreign dignitaries and movie stars. The rooms were connected by way of the bathrooms. In fact, two movie stars had been put out because of Goliath's arrival. They'd become livid when they were unable to get their regular Christmas suites. Huge egos had labored overtime. In the end, one stormed off to the Gritti Palace and one to the Danieli. Both in a huff. Vowing they would never return to the Malvasi. The management considered this highly unlikely. Everyone returned to the Malvasi. Everyone.

After the Americans had settled into their rooms, Olsen called Louis and Reynolds into the operations room.

When they sat he said, "Would someone like to tell me where Bradlee is? And what the hell he's up to?"

Nine

Carter Perkins' airport taxicab rolled onto Isola Nuova a little over twenty minutes after the Malvasi launches had glided off with their precious cargo. Carter paid the driver and over-tipped him out of habit. Then draped the black leather carry-on satchel over a very weary shoulder, approached a waiting water taxi, handed the bag to the helmsman, and stepped on board.

"*Hotel Malvasi, per favore.*"

"*Si, signore.*"

As the boat slipped from the bulkhead, Carter looked back and counted three police cars as they rolled across the bridge and away from Isola Nuova. A soft smile formed on Carter's lips, and the bright blue eyes seemed to darken by a shade or two. Carter then settled back for the ride.

Carter would miss the recently nullified jaunt to Calcutta. That engagement had been something Carter had been looking forward to for several weeks. Actually, it was the week or two in India that would be missed most. An engagement was an engagement—some tickled Carter's fancy; some, merely work. But Carter would miss the dark, smiling faces of the Indian people and the prospect of finding a new lover. Some young handsome with skin the color of a chestnut.

Carter was most fond of young lovers and their nearly hairless bodies.

Carter had been hired by an Indian prince to do away with a small-time bookmaker. The prince had felt he'd been cheated on a bet in some fashion, and the bookmaker had refused to make good on it. So it was essential the bookmaker be done away with. Exterminated, as it were. Simple enough. The prince was wealthy, the bookmaker was not. Carter didn't always care to get involved with why people wanted others removed, or why they would come up with the extraordinary fees. But as long as they were as discreet as Carter was, and paid in cash, it made no difference. Carter remained a happy creature.

Carter had, however, felt somewhat awkward at having to postpone this Calcutta thing. Even though it would only be for a few days, it most certainly was not professional. It wasn't Carter's style. People had schedules. Punctuality was always important. Carter wouldn't be in the least bit surprised if the prince was to give this trinket to someone else. Perhaps even a local. It had become increasingly difficult to stay a step ahead of the competition. And without a decent war in the works, there were quite a few newcomers. Upstarts. Nomads. Discharged mercenaries. Low-class, bloodthirsty amateurs looking to make names for themselves.

Carter was proud of a longstanding reputation. One that covered nearly thirty years of untraceable extermination. And an extremely reliable source had informed Carter that no police organization possessed a single file that even so much as alluded to the name Carter Perkins. At fifty-seven years, Carter appeared to be more in the late forties category—a portrait of decorum and good health. A highly successful travel writer. Books and articles published in at least twenty languages. And free to travel the globe at will. No one, not a soul, could circulate like Carter Perkins.

And that was the beauty of the entire operation. Carter could glide into town—and glide out. With total justification. No one thought twice about it. Nobody ever put two and two together. No one ever suspected that Carter Perkins might not be what Carter Perkins appeared to be. Carter had a pick of young men throughout the world. The expensive suit pockets were forever lined with local currency. Carter dined and slept like a visiting monarch. Because of the travel articles, rarely did Carter pay for a meal or hotel room. And the money saved was freely handed out in gratuities. From Rome to Hong Kong to Moscow to Paris to London to Bombay there wasn't a head waiter, bell hop, doorman, or concierge who didn't gratefully acknowledge "Monsieur Perkins."

When Carter's water taxi had pulled away from Isola Nuova, the helmsman had angled south. But Carter had stopped him. Asked the man to go by way of the Grand Canal. It was one of the more visually stimulating boat rides in the world. Carter had already missed the sights and sounds. Of course, it had been seen a million times before. But one could never get too much of Venice and the Grand Canal.

As Carter's water taxi passed under the Ponte Scalzi, it came within inches of a number five *vaporetto.* The same boat that had carried Louis and Joe off to their meeting with the Vice President. And at that exact moment Carter began wondering if this move had been too hasty—running off on this unscheduled adventure and potentially destroying a superb contact in India. Childishly jumping at this opportunity to execute the desires of DOC—and fulfill Carter's own lifelong desire to make the Big Kill.

And it was just that. An impulsive whim. Somewhat out of character. Carter believed this life to have order. Finish one thing before rushing on to the next. Carter believed that the passionate impulses that stirred from within were completely under control.

Carter had slipped past bodyguards many times. Granted, not the United States Secret Service, but Carter had made it past some rather sophisticated operations. Then had disappeared neatly, without a trace.

But Carter still had never made this Big Kill.

And that fact haunted this assassin.

What had been lacking in Carter's existence was that no one, until DOC had made contact a little over a month ago, had ever asked Carter to do away with a head of state. Vanquish a truly influential being. A man capable of changing the course of world events. A man like the President of the United States. Carter wasn't getting any younger. This opportunity might never come up again. So Carter thought, "It's now or never, lovey. 'Tis the eye of childhood that fears the painted devil."

The water taxi worked its way farther up the Grand Canal and under the Ponte di Rialto. Carter looked up and recited:

> "Signior Antonio, many a time and oft
> In the Rialto you have rated me
> About my moneys and my usances:
> Still I have borne it with a patient shrug,
> For sufferance is the badge of all our tribe."

The taxi's helmsman, whose name happened to be Antonio, wasn't quite following this *Straniero.*

"Non capisco, signore."

"The Merchant of Venice."

"Ah, si, il Ponte di Rialto. Signore Antonio. Parla l'italiano, signore?"

"No," Carter lied.

Although Carter was fluent in almost every language known to man, the last thing this travel writer wanted was a guided tour of the Grand Canal by a taxi driver. A subject that had been written about more times than anyone could count. It was beautiful to see. And reading about it allowed the imagination to take over. But it was quite another thing to hear about it. It could be deathly boring. Especially if accompanied by someone's wretched home video. Carter assumed that Antonio's English wasn't up to snuff. The boatman fell silent for the remainder of the trip.

When Carter's taxi glided into the Hotel Malvasi dock, one would have thought the queen of England had arrived; that's how many employees turned out to greet their favorite guest. Carter had telephoned from the airport explaining a strange and sudden illness, and the necessity to return immediately to the hotel, but the Malvasi staff now behaved as though Carter would soon be on a deathbed.

"Signore Perkins, we were not expecting you back so soon," a doorman said.

"You will be with us for Christmas, then, Signore Perkins?" a waiter asked.

"Sí, Tito," Carter responded. "I've had a change of fortune, and passion has drawn me back to the Malvasi for Christmas. Worse things could happen to a soul."

"Senta male, signore? Mi dispiace." This time it was a chambermaid.

It seemed as though twenty hands, draped in white gloves, were extended to help the poor ailing writer from the taxi. And Carter played it up with exaggerated weariness. Putting an arm around young Roberto, a bellboy.

A blanket with the Malvasi crest seemed to appear from nowhere. "Please, please, *per favore*! Signore Perkins is ill. Make room! All of you!"

Even the luncheon chef was there.

"What is it that I can send up for you, signore? I have a lovely *brodo*."

"*Grazie tante.* I'm feeling somewhat better," Carter said. "The air. The water, perhaps. You are all such good friends and much too sweet."

Carter paid the helmsman, was escorted to the front desk and respectfully greeted by Nelo. Nelo had worked for the Hotel Malvasi for sixteen years. He was one of Carter's favorite desk clerks. He always had a smile. Was never artificial or condescending in his manner, and was eternally friendly. He treated every guest as though their stay had brightened his life just a little bit. Desk clerks around the world could learn a lot from Nelo.

"It is with pleasure and sadness that I welcome you once more, Signore Perkins. I hope you will be feeling better soon. I have one of your favorite rooms prepared. It is as if you have never left. . . . I am, however, sorry to say, we now have a diplomat with us. So please excuse any inconvenience this may cause you. Some of their security people will unfortunately have to be on the same floor as you."

"Not at all, Nelo. They shan't bother me and I shan't be a bother to them. I expect to be quiet. Read and rest." Carter patted a Nikon camera that dangled from a leather strap. "Take a few shots perhaps."

"If it is not too soon to ask, how long do you think you may be staying on with the Hotel Malvasi?" Nelo asked.

"I still have my morsel to do in Calcutta. Perhaps I can reschedule my flight for a day or two after Christmas. I hope that won't be an inconvenience?"

"Not at all, signore. The Malvasi is your home. You are welcome as long as you like."

"And who might be this diplomat be that seems to have excited everyone so?" Carter asked with a tiny wry smile.

"The American vice president."

Carter took a small step back. Almost stumbled. And then blanched slightly as the smile quickly disappeared.

"The *Vice* President . . . ? You're positive about that?" Carter said weakly.

"Si, signore. We are sorry. Are you feeling ill . . . ? Roberto!"

"No, no, not at all . . . well, my goodness. The Vice . . . President. Yes . . . Well, he's such a good-looking man. I must try to meet him."

Carter coughed twice. The sound almost resembled a laugh. "So," Carter thought, "I'll be delivering the lesser half of DOC's package. All is not lost."

Carter's smile returned.

"This will certainly be a thrilling Christmas for me. My goodness, yes. All's well that ends well. Thank you, Nelo."

"*Per niente.* Roberto! Roberto! *Vieni qui! Sbrigati!* Take Signore Perkins to his room!"

Ten

Joe Bradlee's mind seemed to be traveling on a parallel track with Jerry Olsen's. He too was wondering, "What the fuck am I doing?"

Oscar and Christina had left their apartment ten minutes after they'd arrived. They'd stayed only long enough to use the bathroom and change clothes. They'd realized that if they expected to have anything to eat for the next few days, they'd better get it soon. They were now selecting fruits and vegetables from a stand outside of their local *mercato.* And Joe stood across the street, looking into the window of an electronics shop. Displayed was the same goddamn Minolta point-and-shoot he had just paid three hundred dollars for. He could see the couple's reflection on the shop's window glass.

Again Joe thought how stupid this was. "What the fuck am I doing? These people have come here for a Christmas holiday. What else could it be?" He considered approaching the two. Introducing himself. Asking them: "What the hell are you here for? Don't you have anything better to do? What's on your schedule?" and "Just stay away from the Malvasi, okay?"

The only thing that kept him from doing it was the idea that Oscar and Christina actually were up to nothing at all. Which would mean Joe would have to go back to the Malvasi and spend Christmas Eve with

Olsen and Number Two. At least this way he was out in the open air enjoying Venice. Sort of.

So Joe followed Oscar Sanchez and his girlfriend, Christina. They filled their net shopping bags with nothing but top-of-the-line items. Prosciutto. Dark green olive oil. Provolone. Caviar. Wine. Champagne. Cannoles. Marzipan. Fresh veal. Garlic. Purple and white eggplants.

After shopping, the two lovers worked their way back to the apartment. Laughing the entire way. Joe wasn't close enough to make out any of their conversation, but it didn't take a goddamn genius to figure out what was coming next. When they closed the heavy apartment door behind themselves, Joe found himself wishing that the apartment was his. That it would be Joe Bradlee who would be getting laid for the next hour or so and not Oscar. But as a young lady had once said to him on a prom night long ago, "If wishes were horses, beggars might ride."

Joe had been right. An hour and a half later Oscar and Christina emerged from behind the heavy doors. Fully refreshed. Rosy-cheeked and ready for Venice.

They were walkers. Joe had sensed that from the beginning. He was happy Louis wasn't along. Moaning.

The couple picked their way through the Cannaregio section. Past San Leonardo. Santa Maddalena. Onto the wide Strada Nova. Joe hadn't been in this segment of the city in years. He was surprised at how unfamiliar it had become.

Oscar and Christina stopped and peered into the windows of every intriguing shop they passed. Joe was left fifty feet behind. Peering into whatever shop happened to be in front of him.

At one point, after he'd been staring, for what seemed like hours, at a dead rabbit in a butcher's window, the butcher came out and asked him if he was hungry and if he wanted something to eat. Joe hoped he hadn't looked that pathetic.

"No, grazie. Lei e molto gentile. Grazie, signore," was Joe's response.

"Prego. Prego. Buon Natale."

"Buon Natale, signore."

Oscar and Christina crossed the bridge at the far end of the Strada Nova, and Joe closed the gap. The streets were getting narrower. The city had become more maze-like. Had closed in on him. And the couple no longer looked into windows.

Joe rounded a corner. He saw Oscar glance at his watch. Then start to pick up his pace. They weren't running, but there had been a definite change in attitude. Joe considered Oscar might have become aware he was being tailed. Thus the "Fuck me." Christina had looked back. Twice. But Joe never spotted Oscar looking back. Not once.

Joe was now getting dangerously close to the couple. But he knew if he didn't stay in tight, he'd lose them in a second.

Eventually they broke into the Campo San Bartolomeo on the west side of the Rialto bridge. Joe could back off a little. The square was crowded but open. It would be much easier to keep an eye on them from a distance. There were fifteen or twenty vendors with their carts, and they offered an excellent cover.

Hundreds of people were doing their last-minute Christmas shopping. You could get it all. Right here. Neckties. Shirts. Tacky souvenirs. Incense. Pots and pans. Espresso machines. Wood carvings. Religious artifacts. Soccer balls. Art. Games. Linens. China. The works. There was a cart and a vendor for everything. Christina stopped to look at some soap. Then she tried a sample splash of perfume. Oscar stood by impatiently. Again he looked at his watch. Joe found himself playing with a self-cleaning garlic press.

Oscar tugged Christina's coat and whispered something into her ear. They moved out of the square heading south. Joe followed for a few yards. Then realized he still had the fucking garlic press. He quickly doubled back. Returned it. And caught up to the couple in the next square.

In this *piazza* the church bells of San Salvatore were so loud, echoing so raucously, people on the street had to shout to be heard by a person standing beside them. Oscar and Christina hustled through the square and quickly out the other end. They were now walking much faster. Oscar was noticeably on edge. Christina held onto his arm. Her stride wasn't nearly as long as his. She found it necessary to take extra steps to remain with him. High heels on cobblestones didn't help. Joe was also moving quickly in an effort to keep up. Everyone else in Venice was moving at a damn snail's pace. Joe had a feeling he stood out like a sore thumb and he was right.

Time to take a shortcut. Take a chance. Duck around a few blocks. Around a few buildings. And hope the hell he'd find them coming out on the other side. It was a stunt that could be pulled only in Venice. But Joe knew the city well enough. He was also sure he knew where they were going—the bridge. The Accademia bridge. It was chancy, but it was the direction they were heading. They were obviously late for a meeting. The bridge would be the logical place to intersect someone. A stranger. A man with money. A man with instructions. Information. A gun. Explosives. Whatever. The bridge would be loaded with tourists from every country in the world. No one would seem out of place. Joe was taking a calculated risk by letting the two out of his sight. It was a judgment call. His instincts were usually right.

He could now run. No one paid any attention. He was just a man in a hurry. He weaved over to the Canal Grande. Came back behind San Luca. Crossed the little bridge behind the Teatro Rossini and down two more side streets. He popped out in the Campo San Angelo on the north side. A moment later Oscar and Christina popped into the Campo San Angelo on the east. They were also running, and they were out of breath. Joe looked around the square. A lot of people were running. Not everyone. But most. Oscar and Christina jogged past him. They were now laughing. They passed within eight feet of Joe. Oscar looked directly at him and smiled. But gave little sign of recognition.

As the two angled through the crowd Joe fell in behind. They trotted around to the right side of San Stefano, up the church's front steps, and disappeared inside. Joe walked up the same steps. He stopped to study the mimeographed paper that had been tacked to the door. It read: *Chiesa di San Stefano, Concerto di Natale, Lunedi 24 Dicembre, ore 18:30; Soprano—Carla Megatti; Organo—Sergio Frari.* It went on to list a program of Bach, Handel, Frescobaldi, and Vivaldi. Joe looked at his watch as a young Asian couple pushed their way past him. Like everyone else, they were ten minutes late.

He followed the couple inside. The church was dimly lit and there was a faint smell of incense in the air. Five small altars stretched down either side of the church's interior. Each altar was adorned with a large painting depicting a particular moment in the life of Christ. Joe was convinced that all the paintings were done by one great master or another. Right again.

The high ceiling was supported by eight mammoth columns. At the far end of the church sat the main altar. It was lit only by candlelight. Chandeliers hung from the ceiling. Many of the bulbs had blown out long ago. The remaining ones appeared to have been there since Il Duce's christening. A few shards of light from the street lamps outside were forcing their way through the stained glass windows.

Between Joe and the main altar were ten rows of wooden folding chairs. They had been arranged with an aisle down the center. Each row seated fourteen. There wasn't an empty seat. The priests had set up twenty rows of metal folding chairs behind the wooden ones. These metal chairs were filling up quickly as latecomers pushed their way past him. Joe remained standing. In the back and in the dark. Near the holy water. He scanned the crowd for his missing couple.

Eventually he spotted Oscar sitting in the sixth row of the metal chairs. Off to the right. Christina was no longer with him. Oscar was fiercely guarding an empty seat. A large German woman was trying to bully her way into it. Oscar was trying to fend her off and search the area for reinforcements. Christina was nowhere.

While Oscar was distracted by the fat German, Joe moved off to find Christina. He walked down the left side of the church. Stopping before each small altar. Every painting hooked him. They'd all been there since the day the oil dried. It was impossible not to be struck by their force. They had been painted with such passion. They seemed to pour a godly energy out over the entire church. A priest, who Joe guessed was most likely Angolan, was kneeling before the third altar. Lighting a candle. The man appeared to be carrying the weight of the world on his shoulders.

Joe continued his search for Christina. He moved back to the rear of the church and crossed to the right side. Passing the confessional booths. Far to the right there was another door between the altars and leading to a small chapel. He pushed it open and walked in. There were ten more wooden chairs in the chapel and another very simple altar. A white linen shroud covered it. Kneeling at the railing were two older women dressed in black. And Christina. Joe closed the door behind him. He stood in silence. After a minute Christina looked up at the silver crucifix on the altar. She genuflected, stood, turned, and exited the chapel. Brushing by Joe on her way out.

Joe was slack-jawed at his own stupidity. Everything seemed so clear when placed in this house of God. Oscar, the Jewish explosives expert, wasn't coming to Venice for Christmas—Christina was. She was the Catholic.

Joe turned and followed her back into the main part of the church. Oscar was losing his battle with the fat German. Christina arrived just in the nick of time. She squeezed past the woman and shot her an evil eye that would have stopped a fucking combine. She then sat down next to Oscar and gave him a light kiss on the cheek.

Joe scouted the church for a seat. There weren't many left. It was basically between him and the German woman. He spotted an empty chair on the left.

Toward the back. The fat woman also saw it. He moved off to the left to approach it from the rear. She rolled to the right in an effort to get at it from the front. No competition. Joe was in the seat before the woman passed the main altar. And he stopped to genuflect as he crossed the center aisle. She didn't.

His timing was perfect. The organ was just starting in with the prelude to Vivaldi's "Domine Deus." Not that he would've known what the hell it was, but there was a program on his seat. He had, however, heard the music before. He guessed it came out a lot around this time of year no matter where you were. It was a remarkable piece. And when combined with the surroundings, it made almost everyone a believer. He settled into the metal chair as best he could. The soprano was now joining the organ. She consumed the space with her voice. It surrounded everything. Joe closed his eyes and took it all in.

But the child in front of Joe was beginning to get restless. He started to swing his legs and play with his program. His mother promptly took it away from him. Now completely bored and having nothing to play with, he began to look around the church. The grandeur of it all had obviously been lost on him. He began tapping his fingers on the metal chair. His mother put her hands over his and whispered something into his ear. He sighed and sat still for a minute. He then turned around in his chair, knelt on the seat, and faced Joe. When he spoke, there was excitement in his voice. He was also a good deal louder than he needed to be.

"Hey, Mom, look. It's the guy with the gun."

Eleven

The little boy, Eubie, was right as rain. Sitting directly behind him in the Chiesa di San Stefano was—"The guy with the gun." When Eubie's mother turned around she was stunned, to say the least. She spoke in a raspy whisper:

"Are you following us? What do you want?"

Joe said nothing. Didn't make a sound. He slowly brought his index finger up to his lips as if to politely say, *"Silenzio, calma, signora."* He then winked at Eubie, folded his arms in front of himself, and closed his eyes.

"Do you think he'd show the gun to me now, Mom?"

"Eubie, please. No one would bring a gun into a church. Not even an idiot. Now turn around and settle down."

Eubie turned around, but he didn't settle down. Every few minutes he would turn back. Check Joe out. This went on for the entire concert. One hour and ten minutes. However, Eubie's antics didn't annoy Joe in the least. Joe had his mind on the music. He considered it a blessing that Oscar had led him to this spot. He also had his mind on Eubie's mom. Every time she looked at him, he became paralyzed. Stupid.

The program ended with Pasqualetti's "Priere pour Noel." It seemed that a round of applause was in order, but this was a church. People didn't clap in church. And people didn't bring guns. Joe allowed his eyes to fall open again. The boy was on his knees and staring at him as if he'd never turned back to his seat. Or sat down.

"My mom says you wouldn't bring a gun into a church."

"And your mom's right," Joe lied. He then turned his attention to the boy's mother. "I'd like to apologize for that business earlier today. I was running late. I wasn't thinking very clearly. And, no, I'm not following you. It's just a coincidence. . . . Terrific music, didn't you think?"

"You're not Italian, then?"

"No, I'm North American."

"What does that mean?"

"I don't know . . . Just regular American, I guess."

"And you're not a mobster?"

She was smiling.

"No, I'm not a mobster. . . . Joe Bradlee."

He extended his hand. She shook it.

"You're visiting Venice or do you live here?" he said.

"Visiting. For a week. We got in on the twenty-first. Friday."

"It's a wonderful place. You've been here before, though?"

"No."

"Are you here alone?"

"No."

"Ah . . ."

"I'm here with my son. Eubie, say hello to Mr. Bradlee."

"Hi."

"Hi."

Eubie shook Joe's hand.

"You can call me Joe. You look tough enough."

Joe could see from the corner of his eye that Oscar and Christina had stood. They were moving toward the exit.

"What'd you do with your gun, Joe?" Eubie asked.

Joe had his right biceps pressed so tightly against his side that he thought his pistol would soon cut off all circulation to his fucking arm.

"It wasn't really mine," he said.

Eubie somehow bought that as an answer to his question.

Joe then looked at the boy's mother. "Listen, I know this may sound unbelievably stupid, but I'd like to make this all up to you. I wonder if you might like to have dinner with me tonight? That is, if you don't have other plans."

"Okay," she said.

"Okay? Like that. You say okay, like that?"

"Okay."

She smiled again.

"Jesus Christ," Joe thought. She was a beautiful woman.

"Well," he said, "that's great. I can explain a lot of this to you. Is nine too late? I have one thing to do. It shouldn't take long. Where're you staying?"

"Don't worry. Nine's nothing for us. At home this little guy's lucky if I get dinner on the table before ten. I paint. Sometimes I forget to stop. . . . We're at La Primavera. It's past the Accademia, on the—"

"I know it."

"You do?"

"Jesus, lady, where did you get those fucking eyes?" He didn't say it—he only thought it. What he said was, "I come here a lot."

Oscar and Christina had disappeared out the door.

"Shit."

"Pardon me?"

"Nothing, damn, sorry, I'll see you at nine." Joe smiled. "You can tell me your name then. It was nice to meet you, Eubie."

He turned and moved off after Oscar. She saw his gun. Eubie didn't.

A crowd was standing on the church steps when Joe came out. Most of the people had hustled off, but the ones that remained were just milling around. As if the concert still dangled in the air. Clutching on to them.

They seemed frightened to leave the area for fear the music would abandon them forever. Oscar and Christina were among those milling.

Joe had one thing on his mind. He'd recognized something in Eubie's mother that was good. Something he wanted to hold on to. He now needed to get this Sanchez bullshit over with. He needed to piece together a normal life. He walked down the church steps and approached Oscar.

"Oscar Sanchez?" he said.

"Yes."

"We met twelve years ago in Paris. I don't expect you to remember me. Joe Bradlee. I'm with the American Secret Service."

"Fuck me."

"Fuck you?"

Oscar looked off to his left.

"Do you know, Mr. Bradlee, I believe I do remember you. I had hoped I was wrong. This is my fiancée, Christina. But I would guess you already have that information."

"Yes. Simply put, we'd like to know what your business is in Venice."

"And what might your business be in Venice, Mr. Bradlee?"

Joe was bordering on giving up information he couldn't give up. He was trying to play it close. Tight. so, it would seem, was Oscar.

He went on, "We have some people visiting, and we'd like to make sure the streets are safe at night."

"That's very interesting. And who might these 'people' be?"

"I'm not at liberty to say."

Joe saw Eubie and his mom pass about twenty yards behind Oscar. There was a strong temptation to say, "Ah, fuck this shit," and take off after her, but Oscar's voice held him in the square.

"Let me put it this way, Mr. Bradlee. Why should anything you do, or your *people* do, concern me?" Oscar was having fun. He was going to make Joe work. "I'm sure your problems wouldn't interest me in the least bit. So . . . if you'll excuse us."

"Well, I don't want to bring up any ugly incidents from the past, and maybe we've suspected you of a few things that you didn't actually do, but for some reason the United States government has you on a watch list. Now, I could start going into this in detail if you like, but it's getting chilly out here. Have you noticed that?"

"Yes," Oscar said with a fair amount of annoyance.

"I do have the authority to take you to a police station. Where it might be a lot more comfortable. Warmer anyway. But then that would take us four or five hours. Have you noticed how the Italians love paperwork . . . ? But, see, I have a dinner engagement, and I'd rather not call it off. It being Christmas Eve and all. So, if you could just explain what you have planned for the next few days, everyone would be a lot happier. I'm sure of it."

"Yes, I do remember you, Mr. Bradlee. You're the one who likes to talk too much. However, your *people* must be convinced by now that I've long since removed myself from any international affairs. I'm here only for a holiday. The farther I stay from you and your business, the happier I become."

"I'd like to believe that."

"You have my word on it." Oscar smiled. It was almost a laugh. "I do feel somewhat bad for you. In the long run, it's the reason I moved on. Left the business, if you will. Trust. Ask yourself who you can trust. Who you can believe and who you can't. I tell you I'm here for a holiday, and I tell you to trust me. To believe me . . . But, can you do that? I don't think so."

Joe looked to his left. Watched as Eubie and his mom disappeared at the south end of the square.

"Remember, Mr. Bradlee," Oscar continued. "You can trust no one. Because that's the business you've chosen. But I tell you it's no longer mine. I can assume you will have us followed. Do so. I'd rather the person not be an aggravation—if that can be arranged. Now, we must be off. If you'd be so kind as to excuse us?"

The two brushed past Joe and headed in the direction of San Marco. Oscar then turned back and said, "But, Mr. Bradlee, do not trust anyone. You'll live longer . . . Not happier, but longer. Give my best to your 'people.' "

He laughed.

Joe stood and watched until they turned at the far end of Campo San Angelo. Oscar never looked back.

Joe crossed the square. He walked to the street they'd turned on and stopped. Watched them go off to the right. Cross the small bridge that led to the Teatro la Fenice. Joe didn't go any further. Again, it was a judgment call. For some reason he believed Oscar. He believed they had come here for a holiday. He believed Oscar was no threat. He hoped his brain hadn't been clouded by this woman in the dark glasses.

Joe would now go back to the Hotel Malvasi. Change his clothes. Have a Christmas Eve dinner like a normal human being. He looked up at the ancient street sign that had been imbedded into the corner of the stone building to get his bearings. He smiled and shook his head, and thought, "Christ, these bastards are all over the place."

The sign read:

"*Rio terra degli Assassini*"—Street of the Assassins.

Twelve

In the rugged but impeccably maintained hunting cabin sixteen miles northwest of Long Rapids, Michigan, two men sat at the ivory-inlaid poker table. Steam once again drifted from Eddie Bauer coffee mugs, and the bottle of Black Label, somewhat depleted, sat perfectly centered on the table. And Buck, the ancient yellow Labrador, found himself once more curled up as close to the fireplace as he could get.

The two men had driven Cadillacs, and had arrived separately. A hundred and forty thousand dollars worth of Detroit steel resting in the snow before a seemingly innocent cedar cabin might have looked strange to some, but there wasn't a person within miles, and furthermore, not a soul knew this cabin existed other than the other two men inside and the one man they were waiting for.

"You're sure he got the message?" the shorter of the two said.

"He got it."

"Look, Grant . . ." The voice trailed off.

Grant waited a moment, then said, "What is it, Art?"

"I don't know . . . Christ, I mean it's just that . . . Well, now that it all may be coming to a head, I'm beginning to get cold feet about the whole damn thing . . . and I don't mind saying so. At least not to you

. . . I mean, do we really want to *kill* someone?" He reached for the Black Label and poured a heavy shot into one of the glasses. Art's hand trembled only slightly, but Grant caught the movement in the corner of his eye. He ignored it.

"Don't tell me that. Not now, Art," he said. "We have all of our resources in place. We're set. We can make this work."

A sharp shot of white light from a pair of approaching headlights glanced off the icy tree branches and pried its way through the thick curtains and on into the cabin. It was followed by the sound of fat tires crunching the frosted snow down to the earth and the soft purr of yet another General Motors V-8 engine.

"There's Phil now."

After a minute Phil walked through the door and kicked the snow from his boots. The white of his hair matched the snow perfectly. He smiled and said, "Grant, Art . . . I understand we're halfway home? A very nice Christmas present, don't you think?"

Phil had waited a very long time for this day. He'd become the chief executive officer of one of the world's largest grain-processing companies before he'd turned forty, and from that day on, he'd taken nearly every penny he could squeeze from corn, oats, barley, wheat, hops, and rice and used it to back any candidate who swore to cleanse America and return her to her former greatness. For Phil, this new American purity usually took the shape of campaign banter like "Throw the commie bastards out," or "Clean up welfare—bring back the death penalty," or "If they don't like the way we do things here—nuke the fuckers."

Art and Grant were of shared political convictions and had amassed fortunes that made Phil's millions look like small change from a downtown Burger King. Art's father had done very well by creating one of the Great Lakes' largest shipping empires. Art in turn had expanded the family business far into the global market and now had his fingers on nearly eight percent of all goods imported to the United States. Grant had earned his loot from TV and radio, and had the entire

Midwest satellite television and cellular telephone markets virtually cornered. From Sunday morning gospel to Saturday night porn, it all arrived in America's living rooms courtesy of Grant. The three of these gentlemen many times boasted among friends how they could, between themselves, come up with twenty million dollars in cold cash within thirty minutes. And they could.

They had gathered around this selfsame table, twenty-nine years ago, and had come up with an acronym. DOC. It was simply the beginning letters of their last names, but when they saw it in print for the first time, it had given them an immense feeling of unity and power. Together they would conquer the world. Originally Phil had insisted that his name be up front, being oldest, but it was generally agreed that COD didn't have the same forceful impact as DOC. So DOC it was.

They did, however, keep this acronym to themselves. It was not shared with their wives, their children, or their mistresses. There were rumors that DOC existed, but no one knew who, where, or what they were. A handful of people had access to an unlisted telephone number that was answered only by a computer-generated voice. But even this was so buried in a morass of cellular and satellite whirlwinds that it was impossible even for the FBI to determine what the contents of the messages might have been, who picked them up, or who left them. Grant had made double-sure of that.

And DOC used their money to back like-minded candidates. And back causes. And push for a better America. A white America. America the way it was meant to be. No commies, no Spics, no coons, no fags, no dykes, no Chinks, and no goddamn redskins. These sentiments were not always voiced in public by Art, Phil, and Grant, or the politicians they owned. But in the back rooms, and in the hunting and fishing cabins, you were either with them one hundred percent or you were out one hundred percent. No middle ground.

On a number of occasions the voters of Michigan

and her neighboring states were frustrated enough with taxes, liberal Democrats, moderate Republicans, poor police protection, the deficit, the military, the gangs, health care, welfare, the cities, the aged, the meat packers, the farmers, professional baseball, or the group of thieves presently in Washington that they would elect one or two of the candidates DOC supported. Over the years some had made it into the governors' mansions, some had reached the U.S. Senate, and a good many had gone to Congress. But none had done as well as Lenny Hofstadtler.

For all intents and purposes, Lenny had very nicely managed to get himself lost within the governmental cracks for the better part of his first twenty-five years in office. Representing a congressional district whose constituency was ninety-seven percent white Americans, he had been reelected time and time again, having to do little more than shake a few hands and pass out a few cigars. And up until five years ago, when he had been pressured by a certain heavy campaign contributor into introducing a bill that would severely restrict law enforcement officials' ability to enter onto private property, few legislators were aware of what side of the political fence Lenny actually sat on. However, the bill didn't clear things up much. The wording was so ambiguous that most political analysts found it impossible to determine whether it was designed to protect the rights of minorities in Detroit, or to pave the way for wealthy separationists up North to built their own private armies. Many congressmen saw the introduction of this bill as incredibly misguided on Lenny's part. It seemed to have come from left field and was squashed quicker than a possum trying to cross I-75.

But the bill's failure in no way kept fellow legislators from enjoying Lenny's jokes, or his company, or his cigars. Over the years Lenny slowly had become one of the most senior congressmen in Washington. And then, three years ago, largely because he had neatly avoided creating any enemies at all, he had been unanimously elected House Minority Leader.

All of this, coupled with the fact that in the past election the balance of power had unexpectedly switched from one party to the other, added up to: Lenny Hofstadtler had become the speaker of the House of Representatives and a mere two heartbeats away from becoming the next president of the United States.

These developments had surprised DOC as much as anyone in the nation. However, they wasted no time in pursuing this shortcut to the White House. Within two months after the election, Grant had used his computer and satellite connections to obtain a rather formidable list of the best international terrorists and assassins money could buy. Through an intricate process of checks and crosschecks with easily accessed government records, this list had been pared down to five untraceable names—literally the cream of the crop. And word had gone out: Ten million dollars would be resting in a Swiss bank account for the first of these executioners to deliver the head of the President of the United States on a silver platter—seven million for the Vice President, a man surely expected to win the White House in the upcoming election.

Phil placed his navy blue Brooks Brothers camelhair overcoat neatly over Grant's hunting jacket and cleared a chair for himself at the poker table. Before he was able to get comfortable, Art started in, "I don't know, Phil, this is all beginning to seem a little rushed to me all of a sudden. I think we should hold off until after the first of the year. At least hold off until we have a confirmed presidential hit set up."

"Have a drink, Art. We all know how hard it is to get close to these bastards. It'll take them months to replace this clown. Look at how long it took Nixon to replace Agnew. We'll have plenty of time to work on the other one. We have to grab the opportunity at hand. Seize the goddamn day . . . The only real question at this point is, how good is this Carter Perkins character?"

"The best," Grant said. "I've run him through every intelligence source we have. I've siphoned the FBI and CIA computers dry. There's not a damn thing on him. And the people who recommended him say he's never missed. If Perkins says he'll deliver, he'll deliver. It's as good as done. This is an opportunity of a lifetime. And all things considered, we have to go for it here and now."

"Can he be traced to us in any way?" Art said with a slight squeak in his voice. In an attempt to cover it, he cleared his throat, but that came out squeaky too.

"Not in a million years," Grant said. "All of our communications have been virtually nonexistent. We can disappear whenever we choose."

"Okay. That settles that. We give Perkins the green light." Phil was smiling, but his mind was already on the next order of business. "That takes care of *Jeff*. Now let's clear up how and when we get rid of his buddy *Mutt*. . . . What's the present location of our other boys?"

Grant pulled a hand-held computer from his hunting jacket and punched a few keys. "Believe it or not, John Napier, our *invisible man*, is right here, in Pontiac. Salvatore DiParma; still in Milan. As of December nineteen the Lincoln woman was in New York City. But she could be anywhere by now. Communication does not seem to be her specialty. And, Oscar Sanchez, as you know, has yet to respond, yea or nay, to our initial query. . . ."

Thirteen

At the very moment Joe had decided Oscar was no threat, Jerry Olsen had been reading over a response he'd received from Washington, D.C.—the Central Office. He'd asked them to fill him in on one Oscar Sanchez. This response was their second. The first message had told Olsen to talk to Joe Bradlee about Sanchez. Bradlee would know everything. Olsen had then explained that Bradlee was out of the office. On a stakeout. Olsen needed the information immediately. This statement by Olsen, and the use of the word *immediately,* had the effect of making everyone at the Central Office assume that Oscar Sanchez was most likely in the process of lining the hallways of the Hotel Malvasi with plastic explosives.

After Olsen had finished reading the second message, he stood. Reynolds and Louis were also in the operations room.

"Well, according to C.O., this Sanchez character hasn't been active in a number of years."

Reynolds gave Louis a "we're obviously dealing with a brain trust" look, and said, "Well, Jerome, I think that's the point Inspector Solfanelli and Louis were trying to get across earlier. Guess we'll just have to wait for Joe to check in . . . Cards, anyone?"

Reynolds one-handedly fanned a deck of playing cards and reclosed it in a single fluid motion. He then performed a two-fingered cut and peeled four aces off the top. He smiled devilishly. Good agents used times like this, the slow times, to hone their card tricks. Or work on their juggling. Or magic. Harmonicas were big. Louis walked to the closet and began practicing a rope gimmick in the full-length mirror. He'd learned the trick in Bangkok from a certain young lady and was becoming so good at it, he could sometimes fool himself.

But Olsen was getting testy. He didn't consider this a slow time.

"Louis, I want you to go find Bradlee."

"What? Are you nuts?"

"Go find him. He's probably somewhere near this guy Oscar's apartment. You know where it is. Jesus, I wish the son of a bitch would check in a little more often."

"He could be anywhere. You've got Sanchez's picture. If he shows up here, we hustle him out. What's the problem?"

"Look, give him another half hour," Reynolds jumped in. "If he doesn't show we'll both go find him." The telephone rang. "That's probably him now."

Louis answered it. Listened for a second. Cupped the mouth piece.

"It's C.O. They want to know if we need any extra people."

"Yeah," Reynolds said, "tell them to send Chester Mock over. Fuck his Christmas up for a change."

Olsen shook his head and Louis said, "I think we're okay here. We'll get back to you if there's any change."

Reynolds began waving his hands frenetically.

"Wait a minute, Reynolds has something," Louis said. He handed the telephone to Reynolds.

"Yeah, this is Agent Reynolds, who's this . . . ? Doris, oh, you lovely thing, you. Listen, Doris, I was thinking, we don't know too much about this Sanchez character. I mean, if anything happens to Bradlee, no one really knows what he looks like, and these fax photos are for shit, if you don't mind my saying so. . . . Sanchez is supposed to be retired, but we don't know that for sure. I mean, what the hell is he doing here? . . . Exactly, Doris, now you've got it. . . . Anyway, my feeling is, just to be on the safe side, we ought to get someone from the Fantasy Factory over here."

Doris hated this reference to the Intelligence Division.

"Okay, okay, easy, I'm sorry." Reynolds continued, "Anyway, I was thinking maybe we ought to at least get Mock over here. He'd be a big help. . . ."

Even Olsen was enjoying this.

". . . Yeah, well, we've got a lot of respect for him, you know. I think we need someone with a little more experience. Expertise. It might be a big help. . . . Thanks, Doris, you're a sweetheart. . . . That's great. What do you think, twenty-four hours? . . . Great. Thanks." Reynolds hung up the phone. "Fuck Mock, the bastard."

"You know who's going to be blamed for this, don't you?"

"Yeah, you are . . . Jerome."

According to Reynolds, "Chester Mock had been with the Secret Service longer than Spartacus." He was sixty-five years old. He stood six foot nine inches and weighed a very lean two hundred and forty-five pounds. He had been born in Washington, D.C. He could trace his ancestry back through slavery and on into Africa. He'd hit two home runs in the 1957 World Series, but left baseball because Milwaukee was a shit hole. He also hated traveling. Washington, D.C., was Mock's city. He actually believed he owned it.

After leaving the big league he'd finished college and joined the Treasury Department. In the early sixties he'd found a friend in John Kennedy. He'd been there in Dallas in '63. He had taken it hard. Real hard.

After Dallas he'd hated the travel more than ever. He had a family and wanted to stay in Washington.

He did. He rose quickly at C.O. and reached grade thirteen in record time. Mock was as shrewd as hell and as arrogant as the day was long. He was now at grade fifteen, and he wasn't opposed to using his size or his position to get what he wanted. Nobody pushed Chester Mock around. And nobody but nobody called him Chester.

Late on Christmas Eve, Mock was awakened by a telephone call. He knew better than to answer the fucking thing, but he thought it might be his mother. She was ninety-two years old, blind as a goddamn bat, and had no concept of time. Or day or night, for that matter. As a result she had a bad habit of calling at completely irrational hours.

It wasn't his mother on the telephone. It was Doris from Intelligence Division. The Fantasy Factory. She explained to him the concerns Agent Reynolds had over Oscar Sanchez's presence in Venice. "Italy. Yes, sir." She told him that Atlas had been phoned at Tree Top, the White House. It was a tough call. But in the end Atlas had decided Mock's expertise could be critical to the situation.

"Jesus Christ, Doris, it's Christmas fucking Eve."

"Sorry, sir," was all Doris could think to say.

Reynolds, Olsen, and Zezzo were still splitting a gut over the Mock business when Joe walked into the operations room.

"Obviously I've missed the fun. Someone like to fill me in?"

"Mock's coming over. We told C.O. we needed his expertise," Reynolds said.

"Jesus, not Chester. What for?"

"No reason. We just wanted to fuck up his Christmas for a change."

"No 'we,' Reynolds. It was you. And don't forget that." Olsen was already having second thoughts about having the Big Man, Chester Mock, in Venice.

"Yeah, well, it's funny now," Joe said with a forced smile, "but keep the son of a bitch away from me when and if he gets here. Okay?"

Reynolds spied the point-and-shoot hanging from Joe's neck.

"Niiiiice camera, Joe. Did you buy that here?"

"Absolutely. Imported . . . It was cheap too."

Olsen was back to business.

"So what's up? Where the hell have you been? What's Sanchez up to?"

"I don't think he's a problem. I had a little talk with him. He checks out. Actually, the more I think about it, Sanchez wouldn't play with explosives in Venice. I've seen his home. I'd say he's got a certain amount of respect for classic architecture."

"What about blowing a boat out of the water? Ever think of that?"

"Well, Jerry, as a matter of fact, I did think of that. That's why we have people keeping an eye on the boats, isn't it?"

"I just want to be sure this guy's clean."

"He's fucking clean."

Louis could see where this conversation was leading, and it wasn't going to be fun for anyone. He stood and said, "You know, I was thinking we ought to send down for some food." He looked at his watch, "Jeez, it's almost eight-thirty."

"I'm going to get cleaned up and go back over. I told Solfanelli I'd have dinner with his family," Joe lied. "Who's got the dining room duty, Hall 'n' Oates?"

"Who else but Hall 'n' Oates? I'll be down there too," Olsen said.

Actually, their names weren't Hall 'n' Oates at all. Their real names were Barns and Wilson. They were the only agents The Panhandler could bear to have near him when he dined in public. Somehow he thought they blended in better than the other agents. As if anyone wearing ear pieces, wires down their necks, wrist communicators, and Uzis stuffed in their suits could blend in anywhere.

Hall 'n' Oates were men of few words. From a distance they looked like identical twins. Both had short-cropped sandy blond hair. They were the same height and weight. They never took their dark glasses off. They tended to wear the same suits on the same days. They were inseparable.

Reynolds had been the one who'd had tagged the two with the Hall 'n' Oates moniker. Why, or how, he came up with Hall 'n' Oates was something that was clear only to Reynolds. But the name stuck. It stuck so well that most people around the Vice President could no longer remember what their real names were. They were just Hall 'n' Oates.

Reynolds sighed and sang, in a Charlie Pride kind of way, "Hall 'n' Oates got the dining room . . . one more time." He looked to Louis. "Well, Louis old man, I guess it's you, me, and room service. Just another romantic evening in Venice, Italy."

"Things could be worse. Mock could be here already," Joe said as he slipped out the door.

He continued to the stairway. The Roadrunners had been given rooms one floor below. Basically, their job should have been over the minute Number Two arrived. If this had been a tour of Europe or some other similar bullshit, Joe would be off to the next city with Louis, Reynolds, and Lightfoot. That is, if Lightfoot was one-A. If Lightfoot hadn't eaten the goddamn liver. The *fegato*.

However, after his five days in Venice, Number Two would be heading back to D.C. And because Joe was in charge of the advance detail, and because they wouldn't be advancing anywhere, he was at liberty for a few days. He was expected to be around if Olsen needed him. But Jerry wasn't likely to call on Joe. He had Louis and Reynolds to harass.

At the end of the hall, Joe skipped merrily down the steps. His mind completely on his dinner plans. A watch agent stood on the landing. Talking with a hotel guest. Joe gave the agent a pat on the back and a "Merry Christmas." He rounded the stairwell and continued on down the steps, whistling "Good King Wenceslas" the entire way. When Joe got to the last step, the watch agent called out:

"Yeah, Merry Christmas to you . . . Hey wait a minute, hold up a second, will you, Joe? That's the guy you ought to talk to, Mr. Perkins . . . Hey, Joe, Mr. Perkins here has got a slight . . . problem."

Fourteen

Joe stopped whistling his Christmas tune. He turned and looked back at the landing and the small, delicate person alongside the watch agent.

"What's up?" he said.

The two moved down to meet him.

"This gent's a travel writer," the watch agent said. "He's doing a piece on Venice."

"Perkins, Carter Perkins."

Carter's handshake sliced Joe's skin like a razor, turning his blood to ice. He studied Carter's eyes. The devil gazed back.

The watch agent seemed not to notice this silent exchange. "Mr. Perkins here wanted to do a short interview with the Vice President, but Judy, up in the press office, is being a real pain in the butt. Got any ideas?"

"Like what?" Joe said.

"Well, I thought Mr. Perkins could meet the V.P. in the garden room or the lounge or something. Judy doesn't have to know anything about it."

"I don't buck Judy," Joe said. "It's a good way to lose your teeth."

Joe smiled at Carter. He then took the watch agent by the arm and led him back to the landing.

"Excuse us a minute, Mr. Perkins. We'll be right back."

They rounded the landing and continued to the top floor.

"Who the fuck is this guy? He's not on the guest list," Joe said.

"Sure, he is."

"He is?"

"Yeah. He was checked out."

"By who?"

"Reynolds."

"Reynolds checked this fucker out?"

"He had Perkins' name run through at C.O. He checked out. What's the problem?"

"Keep him busy. I'll be right back down."

Joe went back into the operations room. Louis was on the telephone ordering up a meal. Reynolds was doing a card trick for Olsen. When Joe entered, Reynolds barely looked at him.

"Back so soon. How was Inspector Solfanelli?"

"Fine. Who's this Perkins character? He wasn't on the guest list."

"Perkins? The travel writer guy?"

"Yes."

"He checks out. Nelo said he got sick at the airport. He stays here all the time, apparently. I checked him with C.O. He's okay, just some British lightweight. Nothing much on him. What's the problem?" Reynolds then looked to Olsen. "Was this your card? Two of heart?"

"Yeah, shit . . . How'd you do that?"

"He checked out? Perkins? You're sure?"

"Yeah."

"How'd you do that?" Olsen took the two of hearts and flipped it over. "These are marked, right?"

"I just ran into Perkins on the stairs. He doesn't seem all that sick to me."

"Maybe he got better," Olsen threw in.

"I don't like him. Something's really fucking off."

"You don't like him . . . ? Fine. You don't have to like him."

"I don't like him. Don't let him in close, okay?"

"Okay," Olsen said. He looked at Louis and

shrugged. Then to Reynolds, "How the hell did you know it was the two of hearts?"

Joe went back out to the hall.

"Semper fi," Louis called. After the door was shut he added, " 'I don't like him?' What's that supposed to mean?"

When Joe got to the bottom of the stairs, Carter was still standing with the watch agent.

"I'm sorry, Mr. Perkins, I just talked with Judy, up in our press room, and she said the Vice President would like to have this be a nice, quiet family vacation, with no disturbances. I'm sure you can understand that. It doesn't happen that often for him."

"Yes. Of course. Thank you very much for trying Mr. . . . ?"

"Bradlee."

"Yes. Thank you, Mr. Bradlee. Perhaps I'll see you around the hotel."

Before Joe moved off to his room he gave the watch agent a Look. The Look was very easily understood by both Carter Perkins and the agent. And Carter at once knew an alternative route to the top floor of the Hotel Malvasi would have to be unearthed.

Back in his room, Joe looked at his watch. He realized there was no possible way he was going to make it to La Primavera by nine o'clock to meet Eubie and his mom. He picked up the telephone and was connected to the front desk. He asked Nelo to find the number of La Primavera and call him back when he got through. He then stretched the telephone line as close to the bathroom as he could get it. He stripped and jumped into the shower. Like all the agents, Joe Bradlee was a master of the one-minute shower. Get 'em while you can. He'd gotten used to it. Long ago.

He had just turned the water off when the telephone rang. He grabbed a towel and reached the receiver on the third ring. Nelo had connected him directly to La Primavera.

"Pronto . . . Sí . . . Sí . . . Grazie . . . Vorei la camera de Signora . . . Shit . . . *Non . . . Lei e un'Americana*

. . . *Non lo so . . . Lei ha un figlio* . . . Eubie, Eubino . . . *Sí . . . Sí . . . Grazie."*

Joe breathed easier. He began to towel himself off. Eubie had obviously left a strong impression. After a moment Eubie's mother came on the line.

"Hello. It's Joe Bradlee . . . Hi . . . I'm a running a little late . . . I'm sorry, but I'll definitely be there by nine-thirty. I didn't want you to think I'd stood you up. . . . No, of course not. . . . I'll see you in a little bit . . . Right . . . Bye."

Joe hadn't felt like this in a long time. His heart was pounding when he hung up the phone. He couldn't believe he was actually going out on a date. A serious date. Not just another bimbo in the another bar. In another city.

Joe took a long look at the clothes he'd brought with him. Suits. Suits and one goddamn windbreaker. And an overcoat. He tried mixing pants and jackets. It looked like shit. He finally decided on the gray suit, threw it on, and checked himself in the mirror. Except for the bulge under his right arm he looked like any other businessman.

The bulge. The goddamn bulge had to go.

He took his jacket off. Then his holster and 9mm. Placed them both under the mattress. In a cheaper hotel someone might have noticed a lump. But the Malvasi mattress absorbed it neatly. Joe put his suit jacket back on, grabbed his overcoat, and headed for the door. The instant he touched the knob, there was a pounding from the other side. It scared the shit out of him. He took two steps back and considered sliding out the window to safety. Too far down. He opened the door to find Louis.

"Guess who just walked into the lobby . . . ?"

"Jesus Christ."

"Nope. Your old friend Oscar Sanchez."

"Fuck me."

"You want me to call Solfanelli and cancel your dinner?"

"Fuck me."

Fifteen

"How the hell do you know it's Oscar?"

Even Joe could feel the sharp edge in his voice. It was idiotic to jump on Louis just because he'd been the bearer of the bad news. But maybe, just maybe it hadn't really been Oscar fucking Sanchez who'd walked into the lobby of the Hotel Malvasi.

"It's him, all right. Olsen had so many photos of the guy faxed from D.C., I feel like I went to high school with the bum."

Joe walked back into his room. He sat down in the overstuffed armchair by the window. Then said, almost to himself, "Why did we have to come here?"

Louis followed him into the room. The man was upset. Louis had no idea how to take it. How to read Joe. He watched Joe slump in the chair. Neither man moved. Neither spoke. Finally Louis broke the ice.

"You want me to call Solfanelli?"

"Fuck me."

"I'll call him from upstairs."

Louis moved for the door.

"No, wait."

Joe said it too fast. Louis picked up on it just as fast.

"Okay . . ."

"Look, you all know what Oscar looks like. There's probably no reason for me to hang around. Keep an eye on him. I still think he's okay. No problem."

Joe knew it wouldn't wash as soon as it came from his mouth. It was completely out of character, and in reality he was no longer convinced that Oscar really was—no problem. Joe remained seated. Again it was a long time before either man spoke.

Louis finally said, "Why's he here, Joe?"

"Hell, if I know . . . I guess I'm having dinner with the boys. I'll meet you upstairs. . . . I'll call Solfanelli from here."

Louis literally backed out of the room. He had the sense that if he turned his back on Joe, he'd have a lamp smashed over his head. Joe was that dangerous in his silence.

After Louis left, Joe made his telephone call. It was much easier to get through this time. The old woman who answered the Primavera phone recognized Joe's voice immediately and was off to fetch Eubie's mother before he could make the request.

He had no idea what to say when she came on the line, so he told her everything. What he did for a living. Why he was in Venice. Why he couldn't make it for dinner. He suggested three or four restaurants where she and Eubie might go. He explained that if she mentioned his name, the management would look after them very nicely. All the restaurants were within walking distance from La Primavera. She seemed genuinely disappointed not to be having dinner with him. He was able to convince her to give him a second chance.

"So we'll make it tomorrow night, okay? Maybe earlier, say six? I'll make a reservation. I might be stupid enough to stand you up, but I wouldn't dare do it to a Venetian maître d' on Christmas."

After his telephone call, Joe started back up the stairs to the operations room. The carpeting on the steps was thick and heavily padded. It slowed his progress. He had the sense the rugs had turned to quicksand. He felt like a snail. A goddamn slug. He wanted to go down, not up. Down to the lounge on the Malvasi's lower level. Have a double vodka. Listen to the singer, Flavio, sing his sad Italian love songs. It took all of Joe's strength to climb the steps. He felt tired. Exhausted. He passed the watch agent on the landing without a word. Continued on toward Olsen's room. The operations room.

The hallway on the top floor of the Malvasi was beginning to get cluttered with the standard press corps debris. Things that proved to take up too much space in the rooms had been discarded. The members of the press were always the worst offenders. Whatever they didn't want in their rooms got chucked into the hall. Cardboard boxes. Papers. Trash. Suitcases. Sometimes the furniture. Olsen kept a fairly tight rein on the aides and staff members. There was no way he could control the press, and they took particular delight in making a mess just to irritate him. Oddly enough, the press people themselves were the ones who always ended up tripping over the shit. But it didn't stop them from doing it.

When Joe entered the operations room, they all seemed to be waiting for him: Olsen, Louis, Reynolds, and Hall 'n' Oates. The fax machine was spitting out yet another photo of Oscar Sanchez. Olsen spoke first.

"Well, Joe, I guess Sanchez saved you a dull meal."

"Actually, Solfanelli's an interesting guy. Believe me, I rather be having dinner on the other side of the canal."

"Well, I only met him once," Olsen said. "He seemed like a prig. . . . Anyway, here's the deal. Sanchez has got a woman with him. Louis says her name's Christina. C.O. confirms it. They went straight into the dining room. No reservation. I would have known they were coming, otherwise. I considered just hustling the bastard out, but hotel management's already getting testy with us. . . . Anyway, Oscar's been worked. He's clean."

"I'm still not sure there's a problem, but if you want, Louis and I will go down for dinner with Number Two." Joe then looked at Hall 'n' Oates and said, "Don't worry, boys, we'll sit at separate tables."

"I was going to suggest that," Olsen said. "Goliath

just called. They'll be ready in five. I'll be down there too."

"I just ordered something from room service," Louis said.

"Forget it. Reynolds can eat it. I want you in the dining room," was Olsen's response. It was more like an order.

But Reynolds began to panic. "Wait a minute, hold on here. What the fuck did you order, Louis?"

"Cervello."

"What the fuck is *cervello*?"

"Brains."

"Get the fuck out of here. I'm not eating that shit. It's worse than liver. I'll be dead from trichi-fucking-nosis by the time you bastards get back up here."

The other agents were able to convince Reynolds that he could cancel the *cervello* and order something else. Which he proceeded to do immediately. The kitchen was none too pleased about this change of order. But since Joe had taken care of everyone, from the head chef on down, the grumbling was kept to a minimum.

While Reynolds ordered up something more pedestrian, the other agents discussed the best way to handle Oscar Sanchez, the dining room, and whether or not to give any information about the situation to The Panhandler. Hall 'n' Oats still thought the best plan was to just throw Sanchez out on his fucking ear. Actually, they probably would have been very happy to shoot him on the spot. Given the opportunity.

Joe had always suspected Hall 'n' Oates of being extremely trigger happy. Itching to get into a real good gun battle. But then, the dining room of the Hotel Malvasi on Christmas Eve wasn't quite the time or place for it. Joe considered suggesting to Hall 'n' Oates that they could take Oscar out to the back boat dock and hose the bastard down with their Uzis. But he didn't dare mention it to them even in jest. They just might have said: "Okay, we'll be right back." In the end, they went with Olsen's plan. "Why not?" Joe thought. After all, Olsen was in charge.

The family would sit at a corner table. Olsen would eat alone at the table to the right of the Vice President. Hall 'n' Oats would sit at a table directly in front of the family. Presumably to protect them from a full-scale cavalry charge. Louis and Joe would be at the table to the left of The Wife and Little Audrey. "Lovely," Joe thought.

Louis plugged in his earpiece, threw his jacket on, and left to see that the tables were properly set up. Everyone else waited for Number Two to get hungry.

Sixteen

When Louis arrived in the dining room, the maître d' greeted him with a huge smile and, "*Buona sera, Signore Zezzo.*"

Louis handed the man fifty thousand lira.

"*Buona sera.* We have a slight change in seating. We're going to need four tables. It doesn't look like we'll have to move any of your guests. Maybe we could have this corner over here?"

He pointed.

"But of course, *signore.*"

The room was spectacular, even by Malvasi standards. Crystal chandeliers hung from the ceiling. Candles were burning in the wall sconces as well as on every table. The walls were garnished with paintings of exquisite beauty. Every table was dressed with the finest linen and sterling silver flatware. Fresh flowers were grouped in blown glass vases on each table. There were three waiters for every patron. However, the dining room was surprisingly empty. Louis attributed it to the late hour. Possibly the fact that it was Christmas Eve.

Louis and the maître d' walked to the far corner of the dining room. Oscar and Christina were seated dead center, and Louis passed within a foot. It was his first face-to-face glance at Oscar. He recognized him at once. With Olsen's seating plan, Oscar would end up having his back to the Vice President, while Christina would face the family. The two were wrapped in conversation. A bottle of wine had been served. They paid no attention to Louis as he walked by. His immediate assessment was that they were a harmless couple here for a quiet dinner.

Louis surveyed the rest of the room as he passed through. There was one party of four. Two men, two women. And three other couples. All spaced throughout the room. The situation pleased Louis. If there was any trouble at all, the chances of innocent people being hurt would be severely reduced if they were spread out.

When he reached the far end of the dining room, he chose the four tables he wanted. The maître d' made note of it. He then returned to his station. Louis walked to the kitchen door. When he got there, another agent came out and greeted him.

"We figured that's Oscar in the center," the agent said.

"You figured right."

"Looks harmless enough."

"You never know."

Louis grabbed a pear from the side stand and took a bite.

"No one's gone near those corner tables, have they?"

"Every table in the place is clean."

"Oscar?"

"We worked him. He's clean."

"Good. The Panhandler will be here in a minute. How are the brains tonight?"

"Hall 'n' Oates? They're upstairs, aren't they?"

"Not Hall 'n' Oates. The brains on the menu."

"I had the quail. They had some brains out a minute ago. They looked fine. Firm."

"Good."

Louis checked his watch. Nine-thirty. He hated eating this late. He couldn't understand why it never bothered Joe. Even when they were out on advance, Joe wouldn't eat until nine-thirty or ten. The Panhandler didn't eat until nine-thirty or ten. The President didn't eat until nine-thirty or ten. Most diplomats didn't eat until nine-thirty or ten. Louis was always hungry at six. After he finished the pear, he picked up a handful of long, thin bread sticks from a serving cart as it rolled by. Started to munch away.

Louis was on his third handful of bread sticks when Number Two and his entourage entered the Malvasi dining room. Hall 'n' Oates arrived first, looking as though they were expecting some sort of an ambush. After they scanned the room, they nodded and were immediately followed by the family and the ever present aide; George Strutz.

Strutz was detested by every agent in the Secret Service. Even agents who had never met George Strutz hated George Strutz. He was a pompous fool vaguely resembling a hog. He was hideously overweight. He had a short, fat nose. Squinty eyes. He was very, very pink. His ties always had food stains on them.

Strutz was followed by Olsen. Joe brought up the rear. It was not an inconspicuous scene. Everyone in the dining room turned to see who was making this grand entrance. Who it was that had subjected them to the metal detector search.

Number Two was recognized at once by all. It was easy to determine the political affiliation, or leaning, of the other guests by their appearances and actions. All the couples, except Oscar and Christina, kept their eyes fixed on the Americans and their child. Commenting on how lovely The Wife looked. Or how adorable the little girl was. Or how handsome the Vice President was.

But the party of four only forced a brief glance in The Panhandler's direction. Then returned to their espresso and Sambuca. The younger of the two men said something under his breath, and all four exploded in laughter. Oscar and Christina eyed the Vice President only a second longer than the foursome. Oscar also had a humorous thought. He lost it when he saw Joe Bradlee enter the room.

None of this behavior went unnoticed by Louis. In a flash he sized up the good guys and the bad guys. Who was a potential troublemaker and who wasn't. Still, he wished he could have heard what the guy had said to make the foursome laugh so much.

None of this behavior had escaped the attention of The Wife either. And she could be far more dangerous than anyone in the room. Especially after a few glasses of champagne. If looks could kill, the guy who had made the joke would have been turned to shit in a millisecond.

Louis judged that The Wife had already had a few glasses of bubbly. He could only hope the foursome would finish and leave before she had the opportunity to throw down a few more.

The maître d' led the party to the far corner of the room. Joe was the last one to pass Oscar. Oscar didn't look up. Joe didn't look down. After he'd passed, Oscar leaned in and said to Christina, "Why do you suppose Mr. Bradlee would decide to be unarmed?"

"Is he?" she replied.

"I'm almost certain of it. It's the type of thing that seldom gets past me."

When the family reached their table, the maître d' pulled the far chair out for the Vice President. Olsen pulled out the chair to the right of Goliath for The Wife. Little Audrey quickly jumped into it. George Strutz seated himself with his back to the room. Louis was left holding out the one empty chair. The Wife slowly brushed Louis' arm with her right breast as she took the remaining seat.

"It's nice to see you, Louis. I was afraid you might have left for the evening." She gave him a slow wink.

"No, ma'am."

Louis pushed the chair in for her and then moved off to join Joe.

Olsen had found his table to the right of the Vice President. Hall 'n' Oats had seated themselves at the center table. Everything as planned.

"Christmas Eve dinner with George Strutz. I can think of nothing more romantic," Louis whispered to

Joe. Then dropped into the chair next to him. "Man, I'm hungry."

Only after Goliath was seated did the situation seem to dawn on him. The setting vaguely resembled Custer's last stand, and Number Two appeared to be the last one to pick up on it. He called Olsen over.

"Why do we have all these people down here, Jerry?"

"Well, sir, we thought . . . well, what we thought was . . . well, we thought it might be a good idea. That is, I thought it might be a good idea."

"Absolutely. Christmas Eve. What the hell. Good show."

Olsen waited for more. Nothing came.

"Thank you, sir."

He retreated to his table.

The Wife and Strutz looked at each other in disbelief. Then at the three tables occupied by agents. Then back.

"What do you think's going on?" Strutz asked the Vice President. Little Audrey was trying to balance a spoon on a wineglass.

"Oh, I find it's best not to question Olsen too much about these things. I'm sure it's under control. We have more important things to worry about . . . I think a little wine might be in order."

"I'd rather have champagne," The Wife said.

"Well, we can have both, my dear."

Wine sounded good to Joe, but it wasn't going to happen. Neither was his dinner with Eubie and his mom. The idea of eating in the kitchen, gabbing with the employees, began to seem pretty damn appealing. But that wasn't about to happen either. He was going to sit and have dinner with Louis as he'd done so many times before. Usually it was more relaxing than this. Usually they weren't screening for Number Two. This screening position, this Working the Man business, was getting fucking old.

Over the years Joe's enthusiasm for standing up and taking a bullet for one of these guys had begun to wane. It wasn't a case of nerve or guts. No one could hold a candle to Joe in that department. It was more a case of good-guys-bad-guys. A few years ago he'd started to lose sight of who was what. That's why he'd started to ask for the advance work. It kept him away from direct contact with the politicos.

It had actually been six years ago. Joe'd been assigned to cover some South American dictator-drug runner who was on a visit to Miami. The man was a real fucking charmer. His henchmen butchered goats and chickens and rabbits in the hotel hallways. Then roasted them on hibachis out on the patios. They also liked to pee on the azaleas and palm trees instead of using the johns. Joe assumed it gave them a sense of purpose.

The amazing thing was, Joe was expected to stand up and take a bullet for this jackal. After all, the dictator was an honored guest of the United States of America.

But what had amazed Joe the most was, after this clown had made it safely through Miami and packed it off, back to his own country, he had been gunned down in a local whorehouse. And Joe had it on good authority that the CIA had done the job. He'd always been grateful to the boys from Langley for having decided to do the deed in the whorehouse rather than, say, Florida. Being buried with a CIA bullet in his gut hadn't been what Joe'd signed on for.

"What're you having?"

Louis brought Joe back out of the foggy bottom.

Joe looked at the waiter, "*Buona sera, Lorenzo.*"

"*Buona sera, Signore Bradlee.* How are you tonight?"

"Just fine. Bring me what's good."

"*Si.*"

Lorenzo walked off.

"Did you order?" Joe asked Louis.

"Yeah. Where were you? You looked like you were in outer space."

"Thinking good-guys-bad-guys."

"Oh boy, better save it for your dreams. Here comes one of the bad guys now."

Oscar had risen from his table and was headed directly over to Number two. Hall 'n' Oats had risen as well. As had Olsen. All three had their hands under their jackets and were ready for a major show of force. Louis and Joe were the last to get up. They both reached into their jackets at exactly the same instant. The only difference was, Louis grabbed the handle of a Smith & Wesson, Joe grabbed thin air.

Seventeen

Nelo had rung up Carter Perkins' room at precisely nine. At eight-fifteen Carter had opted for a short nap. It had been a long day, and there was a strong fear of oversleeping and thus missing a lovely dinner altogether. So Carter had instructed Nelo to ring up the room at nine. The call had naturally been placed to the room on the second. Nelo had also informed Carter that Roberto would be on his way up with a message.

Carter thanked Nelo profusely for the call and bade him a good night. Nelo had remained at the front desk an extra half hour after his shift to be absolutely certain his guest was awakened on time and that the message went out properly.

After hanging up the telephone, Carter walked over to the French doors. They were covered with lace curtains that had been stretched from top to bottom between brass rods. Carter fondled the lace between two fingers. Local. Handmade. Burano.

Carter then looked at the ceiling and wondered if the American vice president was, just maybe, standing directly above. One flight up. On the top floor. Carter smiled and pointed at the ceiling. Then twitched the index finger as though it had been on a gun trigger. Carter laughed out loud and pulled the French doors wide open. A blast of cold air penetrated the silk of the nightgown and snapped Carter back into the here and now. The temperature had dropped to just below thirty degrees. Carter thought, "Now, this is what the air at Christmas should be like," and was at once overjoyed that Calcutta had not worked out. The Vice President wasn't the target Carter had hoped for. But it was now the challenge of the hunt that thrilled the assassin as much as anything. Whether DOC wanted the deed done or not, Carter had already decided to go through with it.

"There is a tide in the affairs of men,
Which, taken at the flood, leads on to fortune;
Omitted, all the voyage of their life
Is bound in shallows and in miseries."

Carter looked out over the perfectly maintained garden and lawn at the entrance to the Hotel Malvasi. Yellow bulbs glowed in blown glass fixtures. Red and green Christmas lights had been strung throughout the topiary, and the boat slips beyond the lawn had been decorated as well. Five sparkling chrome and mahogany power launches rocked on the water. The drivers waited attentively. Ready to take the hotel guests to wherever they cared to go.

Beyond the boat slips lay the water. The lagoon. Laguna Veneta. And beyond that the Lido. Carter could see a sparkle of neon from the distant shore. It was pale blue in color, and the light ricocheted and bounced off the waves as it worked its way back to Carter's window. The beach of the Lido would be vacant and frigid at this time of year, but Carter made a mental note to visit it before leaving. Carter liked the beach in the winter. The wind would whip the Adriatic up and blow a cold mist that would give a person the feeling of being out on the sea itself.

There was a new moon lying a quarter of the way up in the sky. It reflected weakly on the water to the east. Three clouds rested between the stars. Carter tilted a now newly exhilarated head back, sucked in the night air and quoted from *Julius Caesar* once more:

> "When beggars die, there are no comets seen;
> The heavens themselves blaze forth the death of princes."

Carter stepped back into the room and closed the window. A chill had begun to set in and had hardened the nipples on what seemed an overly feminine chest. Carter shivered slightly, moved into the bathroom, donned a white Malvasi robe, and started a bath running in the oversize tub. Back in the room, Carter took the larger of two valises and hefted it up and onto the bed. There was a soft knock at the door.

"*Un momento, per favore,*" Carter called and moved across the room to open the door.

Roberto stood with a Malvasi envelope in his left hand. When the door opened he said, "Nelo did not wish to disturb you earlier, *signore,*" and handed the note to Carter.

"Not at all. You're very sweet, Roberto. Thank you."

After Carter had tipped him, Roberto turned on a heel and was gone. Carter then walked the envelope over to the desk, took up a penknife, and slit the back flap open with a surgeon's precision. The short message had been scribbled out by the switchboard operator rather hastily, but Carter had seen enough Italian handwriting not to be put off. It read: "Green light on your article. Will pay top dollar. Expect confirmation within forty-eight hours. Advise of any difficulties . . . DOC."

Carter smiled and sat on the bed alongside the large valise and stroked it as though it were a sleeping cat. The bath continued to slowly fill. This was it. It was all meant to be. For Carter and DOC a lifelong dream of grand achievement was about to reach fruition.

Carter lifted the valise open. Then skillfully removed the lower back panel with the penknife. Hidden inside the compartment were nine pieces of metal. When assembled they would become a .22-caliber Beretta semi-automatic pistol. Also in the compartment was a ten-inch dagger.

This dagger had been originally issued in 1943 to an officer in the German Luftwaffe. When Carter was much younger, a summer had been spent traveling with this former major. The two sampled the best northern Africa had to offer, and by August the dagger became a gift. When it came time for the major to be killed, Carter thought it only fitting to do it with this blade. It had glided into the man's heart with a remarkable ease.

Carter then removed from the valise a .38-caliber revolver. It was a Webley-Fosbery. It had been in Carter's family for years, having originally been purchased by a grandfather in 1903. Carter had fired this pistol on only one occasion. It had been Carter's thirteenth birthday, and a proud father had taken his favorite child out to a rye field for a lesson in marksmanship. He lovingly briefed Carter on the gun's operation. However, the revolver had made a tremendous noise and had frightened Carter and brought on a flood of tears. But Carter's father had been more than comforting that evening. It seemed a special night to Carter. One not easily forgotten. They had remained overly close until the father's death two years later.

This colossal noise, this Webley-Fosbery explosion, made the weapon completely impractical for Carter's line of work. But the gun was kept because it was the love of Carter's life and the only physical remembrance of a loving father. Carter mostly considered the revolver something to be stroked and caressed, and after that, a last line of defense.

Carter began to piece the Beretta together slowly. At any given moment this could be accomplished with eyes closed. In a matter of seconds. But tonight Carter took extra time. The sound of the filling bath was calming as it floated by. Slowly each part of the pistol was slid into its designated groove. This was a model

950 Special. The model with the 100mm barrel. The last piece, a three-inch-long cylinder, was finally fitted onto the end of the muzzle. Its purpose was to make the sound of a bullet passing through the barrel virtually inaudible. A silencer.

Two clips of ammunition were the last items to be removed from the compartment. Carter slid one clip into the Beretta, chambered a round, and brought the hammer to rest in the uncocked position. Then engaged the safety. This was all done in one graceful motion. Carter raised the gun, pointed it at the reflection that bounced back from the mirror, and said, "Bang, bang, bang." Carter then set the pistol on the bed and closed the hidden compartment. The dagger and the two guns were left on the bed while Carter retreated to the bath.

A twenty-minute soaking followed, and Carter emerged from the bath perfectly refreshed. Ready to go. Carter then wallowed in three different colognes and a lady's bath powder that had been a special gift from Randy. Randy was more than a simple houseboy, he did it all: secretary, research assistant, wonderful cook, and all-around good lay. Randy was particularly fond of watching Carter apply this bath powder to a freshly washed body. One of the annoyances of being on the road was that Carter was forced to handle all these things alone. Sole. Back in London there was Randy, always Randy. Everything would have been carefully prepared. But alas, there would no Randy this evening. There would be no young thing in Carter's bed tonight.

Carter pulled a gray gaberdine suit from the closet along with a white handmade shirt and dark blue bow tie. After everything was in place, it was decided a little more color was needed, and a red cashmere V-neck sweater was added. More Christmasy, Carter thought.

Last to be donned were the shoes. Peales were selected. A pair of black loafers with gold tassels. Carter walked over to the bed, sat, and slipped each shoe onto a very dainty size six foot.

Carter turned on the bed, picked up the Beretta, and removed the ammunition clip and chambered round. Then slid the bullet back into the clip. Carter put it all, including the dagger and Webley-Fosbery, back into the valise. The case was locked tight and placed back in the closet. Carter returned to the room. A small crimson carnation was plucked from the vase on the desk and pinned to the suit's lapel. Carter patted it twice, picked up the room key, and left.

When the elevator door opened, Carter was standing directly before it. The only occupant was a room-service waiter. The waiter spoke first.

"*Buona sera, signore.*"

"*Buona sera.*"

Nothing else was said. Actually, it would have been difficult for the waiter to have said anything. He was holding his breath. Carter's blend of cologne and powder smelled exactly like the waiter's maiden aunt, who now lived in Florence. By the time the elevator arrived at the lobby the man was close to being doubled over in pain from lack of oxygen. Carter stepped off the elevator when the doors opened. The waiter allowed the doors to close without getting off. He then gasped for air, slid to the floor of the car, and rolled over twice in a fit of uncontrollable laughter.

Carter took the room key to the front desk and handed it to the night clerk. Nelo was off. Gianni was on. Gianni greeted Carter politely and put the key in the appropriate slot. Carter then walked to the dining room. Before entering however, Carter was stopped by the same Secret Service agent that had been spoken to earlier. On the steps. The watch agent.

"I apologize for the inconvenience, Mr. Perkins, but if you don't mind, we'll have to check you with a metal detector before you enter the dining room."

"Oh, is the Vice President dining with us tonight?"

"Yes, sir. I know it's annoying, but it's a precaution we have to take."

"I don't suppose Judy from the press office is here tonight?"

"No, sir."

"That's too bad. I'd like to talk to her."

"Yes, sir."

The agent held up the metal detector and moved it to Carter's side. It was a black cylinder about thirteen inches long and two inches wide. Carter looked at the metal detector, back at the agent, then smiled and winked.

"Please be gentle with that thing, lovey. This is my first time."

Eighteen

As Oscar Sanchez made his cross to Number Two, Joe realized it was a touch late to scoot back up to his room, rummage under the mattress, grab his 9mm, and duck back down to the Malvasi dining room. But he also realized that the likelihood of a shoot-out here, on Christmas Eve, was slim, to say the least. Plus, Hall 'n' Oates were carrying enough firepower to take out the better part of the Turkish army.

This was of no comfort to Joe. He was naked. If guns were to come out, he'd be empty-handed. An inexcusable position to be in. Reason enough to be summarily discharged from the service. Right on the fucking spot. Additionally, the odds of getting some quality time in Leavenworth were very good. Joe decided a chat with Oscar was the only way to go. He told Louis to stay put. Moved to intercept Oscar before he got to Olsen. Or worse yet, Hall 'n' Oates.

Joe jogged around three tables and caught up to Oscar a second before Olsen arrived.

"Mr. Bradlee . . . *Buona sera.*"

"*Buona sera.* Is there something we can help you with?"

"Yes, as a matter of fact, I would like to buy your Vice President a bottle of champagne."

"I'm sure that can be arranged. If you care to order

one from the wine steward, I'll be happy to give him any message you like."

"Perhaps I could have a word with him."

"I don't think so," Olsen said as he moved up next to Joe.

Both men kept their hands out of their jackets. The situation was not sizing up to be dangerous. Procedure called for the agents to be shields. Not gunslingers. Oscar had been carefully screened with a metal detector before he entered the room. At this point both men saw him as no great threat. But they also saw no reason to let him sidle up to Goliath.

"Well, who do we have here, Jerry?" Number Two said as he squeezed between Olsen and Joe.

"A Mr. Sanchez, sir. He's offered to have a bottle of champagne sent to your table."

Oscar extended his hand. Joe diverted it neatly.

"It's a pleasure to meet you, Mr. Vice President. I am a great admirer of the present administration."

Oscar was having a ball. Joe knew it.

"Well, thank you. I'm a great admirer of your country as well," Goliath said.

"So, you have been to Argentina, then?"

"Er . . . yes, actually I have been to Argentina, but I was referring to Italy. Argentina was nice too, though. Lots of horses, I recall."

"Yes. And sheep. We have many sheep."

"Is that so? Well, then . . . Thank you for your offer. My wife has ordered a bottle of champagne, but I'm sure a second one wouldn't go to waste. It was nice to meet you."

This time Number Two extended his hand. They shook.

"And a pleasure to meet you. Please give my best to your president . . . *Arrivederla.*"

Oscar bowed slightly and left to rejoin Christina. Joe and Olsen escorted Number Two back to his table. Louis was standing by The Wife. Strutz was slurping down soup. Little Audrey was finishing off a shrimp cocktail. Hall 'n' Oates were still standing at their table as if they were expecting some more terrorists, perhaps Oscar's reinforcements, to climb in through the windows.

After he was seated, Number Two looked at Joe and said, "I thought it was supposed to be '*arrivederci*?' "

"Yes, sir, but '*arrivederla*' is the formal."

"I see . . . Anyway . . . Well, Jerry, make a note of his name so I can mention it to the President when we get back to Washington." He looked at his wife as he sat. "A very nice man . . . from Argentina."

"Sir, I don't think he actually knows the President," Olsen said, and he returned to his table. Louis and Joe did the same.

None of this exchange went unnoticed by Carter Perkins, who had just been taken to a table by the maître d'. It was by far the nicest table in the room. Overlooking the gardens. Whenever Carter stayed at the Malvasi, this table was held. Reserved strictly for "Signore Perkins". But when the maître d' had pulled Carter's usual chair out, the writer had opted for another. One facing into the room. Not out. The maître d' had found this a bit unusual. In all the past years Carter had sat in the exact same chair for every meal. All the man could think was: perhaps Carter wanted a better look at the American vice president. He was absolutely right.

Carter was amazed at how easy it had been for this other guest to get an audience with the Vice President. At first Carter thought perhaps the two men were acquaintances. The Secret Service agents seemed to know the man. And there was something very familiar about him. But as Carter had watched the conversation progress, it became obvious the man was a perfect stranger. He had just walked right up. Carter opted for a more diplomatic approach, and the maître d' was summoned back to Carter's table.

"*Sí, signore*?"

"I'd like to send a bottle of champagne over to the Americans. And a note as well. If you would be kind enough to bring me some paper and the wine list."

"*Sí, signore.*"

When the paper arrived, Carter scratched out a note and then picked up the wine list. It was bound in blood red leather with gold-leaf trim. It carried a selection of wines from every corner of the globe—ranging in price from very expensive to outrageous. Carter Perkins never had a problem spending money on Carter Perkins, but always choked a little when it came to spending money on others. The less deserving people. A very uncomfortable hole had now been dug. There was no desire to spend three hundred thousand lira on a bottle of wine, but alas, it seemed the only way out. The wine steward was now hovering over the table like a hungry falcon. Carter's only option was to go ahead and order the blessed stuff.

Carter pointed at a spot on the list and handed the man the note with a tip of fifty thousand lira. Then did some quick international mathematics. Three hundred fifty thousand lira. Three hundred eighty marks. Two hundred fifty dollars. A hundred and sixty-five pounds. Thirteen hundred francs. Carter looked to the window and the wavy reflection that came back and said, "This better be worth it, love bird."

The steward retreated to the wine cellar with Carter's note and returned with the chilled champagne Oscar had ordered. He headed directly to the Americans' table and presented the bottle to the Vice President.

"Compliments of Mr. Sanchez, *signore.*"

"Well, I approved the last one, Strutz. Why don't you have a look at this one?"

"Certainly, sir."

The Wife diverted the steward.

"I think I have a better eye for these things."

She glanced at the label.

"It looks just fine."

The steward nodded somewhat politely. He placed new glasses on the table and served the champagne. Little Audrey considered this champagne not nearly as tasty as the last bottle. The new stuff was paler and didn't taste as much like ginger ale. But it did fizz better when she dropped a sugar cube in it. There was a bright side to everything.

The steward had moved back to the Vice President.

"*Mi scusi, signore,* the gentleman by the window would like to send over to you another bottle of champagne. And there is this message for you."

Strutz intercepted the note and said, "Thank you, I think we have plenty to drink."

"I think another bottle would do just fine. Thank you, waiter," The Wife said. "After we've finished this one, of course."

As soon as the steward had left, she switched her gaze to Strutz.

"Don't be such a putz, George. It's Christmas Eve, for Christ's sake. What does the note say?"

He looked at the Vice President. "Sir?"

"Sure. Go ahead. Read it."

" 'Dear Mr. Vice President, I was so pleased when I—' "

Strutz stopped reading. He turned and looked up. Olsen was directly over his shoulder.

"What is it, Jerry?"

"I believe these things should go through me first . . . George." Olsen said the word George as if he were crushing a cigar butt with his heel.

Strutz was fuming. He had as little use for the agents as they had for him. He believed that the combined intellect of every agent on this detail was less than that of a postage stamp. For his money, Olsen was the worst. But there wasn't a damn thing he could do about it. He had no control over them. He knew it. They knew it.

"Here."

Strutz handed the note to Olsen. Olsen read it. Handed it back.

"Thank you, George."

Olsen then walked over to join Joe and Louis.

"You know, sir, I think you could do a lot better than Olsen. He doesn't handle himself well in these social situations," Strutz said—well before Olsen was out of earshot.

"Oh, he's just doing his job. Jerry's been with me almost since the beginning, and when I think of all—"

The Wife interrupted her husband, "What the hell does the note say, George?"

"Right . . . 'Dear Mr. Vice President, I was so pleased when I walked into the dining room this evening and—' "

"Mommy, I have to go tee-tee."

When Little Audrey said this, Strutz snapped his jaw closed so quickly and so tightly, he thought he might have crushed a filling. The girl started to repeat herself.

"Mommy, I have—"

"Yes, dear. Let's let Mr. Strutz finish what he's reading. I think maybe it's time for bed, anyway, don't you?"

"Nooo."

"Well, we'll see when we get upstairs. Now, let's hear the note, okay?" The Wife came back to Strutz. "George?"

The muscles in Strutz's jaw were sticking a good quarter of an inch out from the side of his face. Which was a mean trick considering the flab. It appeared as if he was concealing two marbles in either corner of his mouth. He sucked in a deep breath.

"Okay, one more time . . . if that's okay with everyone:

> 'Dear Mr. Vice President,
> I was so pleased when I walked into the dining room this evening and saw that you and your lovely family were here for dinner. Please accept my warmest wishes for a very happy Christmas, and may this bottle of champagne make this night one of your brightest.'
> And it's signed: 'Sincerely, Carter Perkins.' "

Number Two looked over to Carter. Smiled. Waved.

"Carter Perkins? Do I know a Carter Perkins?" he said to Strutz.

"Not that I know of, sir."

"Well, it was very nice of him, nonetheless."

"Mommy—"

"Yes, dear. We're going."

The Wife got up. She went behind her husband and took Little Audrey's hand.

"I'll be right back. Save me some champagne, will you?"

She then walked over to the three agents.

"Jerry, I'll be taking Little Audrey up to bed now."

"Yes, ma'am, Joe can go with you," Olsen said.

"Oh, Louis'll be just fine. Besides, I believe Little Audrey has a Christmas present for Louis, don't you, dear?"

"Yes, but it's not Christmas until tomorrow, Mommy."

"Well, he'll have to wait for your gift until tomorrow, won't he? Shall we go, Louis?"

"Yes, ma'am."

The three moved off, and Olsen and Joe picked up their conversation from where it had been interrupted.

"I don't think I'm with you on this one," Olsen said. "You think Oscar Sanchez's no problem, and this fruitcake of a travel writer is. It doesn't make all that much sense, if you ask me."

"I'm probably wrong. I just get a feeling sometimes."

Olsen sat down in Louis' seat.

"Jesus, what the hell did Louis have to eat here?"

"Brains."

"Jesus Christ, he eats this shit?" Olsen sucked in his breath and continued, "Perkins checks out. We've run the name backward and forward through Big Bertha. Nothing. Clean as a whistle. He is what he says he is."

Olsen waved for the busboy to remove Louis' plate. The waiter watched patiently as the busboy cleared the entire table. After the boy left, he approached. Olsen ordered a coffee. Joe asked for an espresso. The waiter then gave Joe a message. From Oscar.

"Jesus. Now what?" Olsen asked.

Joe scanned the note and said, "Oscar. He wants a talk . . . when he leaves . . . In the lobby . . . alone."

Nineteen

Little Audrey asked for a ride, and Louis swooped her up as if she were an eight-week-old puppy. She was asleep, dead to the world before they'd gone ten feet. They walked silently through the lobby. The elevator doors eased shut behind them. The Wife stepped back and pressed her weight seductively against the railing. Louis kept his eyes front. It was the longest elevator ride of his life. He could feel her glances through the back of his suit and hoped he was misreading the entire situation. He wasn't. After what seemed like an eternity, the doors opened and Louis leapt out into the hallway.

"Whoopsy-daisy. Wrong floor," he said and turned to get back onto the car.

But two men had ducked into the elevator behind his back and had swiftly positioned themselves on either side of The Wife. As the doors began to inch their way closed, Louis lunged his left leg into the opening. The champagne was having its effect on The Wife, and she made no attempt to get at the control panel. And the two men seemed far more interested in her than in helping Louis. As he began to lose his grip on Little Audrey, the doors banged three times on his thigh. Hard. Then finally opened. He was relieved to see The Wife's jewelry still intact. Louis reestablished his grip on the little girl and stepped back into the car. With his free hand he pushed the button marked A to hold the doors open.

"This car's going up," he said.

The two men just looked at him. Then back at The Wife.

"*Salire. Di sopra.* Up," he said.

This time they didn't even look at him. Louis switched Little Audrey high onto his left shoulder. Opening up access to the pistol on his hip.

"Hey, you two, we're going up here. Move it."

He took his finger off the A button and pointed at the ceiling of the car.

"Up. *Alto.*"

The door started to close again. He jammed his finger back onto the A button.

"Fellas. Hey, fellas, let's go. Out. Now."

Louis stepped between the elevator doors and put his foot at the base of the left side door. The move managed to take the attention of the two men away from The Wife.

"Let's go. Out, fellas. This car's going up."

He pointed once again.

"Maybe they're going up, Louis," The Wife said.

"I think it's best they wait for another car, ma'am. What floor are we on, anyway?"

Louis leaned into the car and looked up at the lighted numbers above the door.

"No, the only floor left is the top floor. Let's go, fellas. Out."

Again they just looked at him with blank expressions. Louis wasn't buying it. These men weren't as dumb as they appeared.

"Exit. Outo. You fellas speak any English?"

The taller one pointed down and gave Louis a phony confused look. Louis again pointed his free index finger skyward.

"No, no, up. We're going up. And you're not. Out. Now."

He then waved for them to come off the elevator. One stepped off. The other remained.

"Let's go, you too, fella."

The remaining man then pointed up and said, "Okay?"

The Texas accent shot blood to Louis' eyes.

"No, it's not okay . . . Listen real closely, pal: I'm going to say this slow: You've got three seconds to move . . . Clear?"

The tone in Louis' voice could have been easily interpreted by anyone. Into any language. Even Texan. It was the last drop of politeness Louis was going to give this cowpoke. The next step would be for Louis to help him out of the elevator. Even if he had to do it with one hand. And Louis was more than capable of doing it. The man used his three seconds wisely and stepped off to join his friend.

Louis removed his foot from the elevator, and as the doors began to slide closed, the shorter of the two men said, with his twang, "We just wanted to see what the hullabaloo on the top floor was all about, bubba."

Their howling could be heard for the remainder of the elevator ride. Louis made a mental note to dump these two cowboys into the nearest canal. First opportunity.

"I think you handled that very well."

"Thank you, ma'am."

Louis moved Little Audrey back onto his right hip. The elevator doors opened onto the top floor, and the howling from the two yokels below subsided. Louis and The Wife stepped off into the quiet hallway. They were greeted by the agent on duty. They then walked directly into Little Audrey's room.

Louis placed the girl on the bed. Through the entire ride, all the way from the dining room, she hadn't stirred in the slightest. The Wife took hold of Louis by the forearm and turned him. So that they faced each other. She stepped in close. Looked into his eyes. She then put her arms around his waist. He made a halfhearted attempt to step back. The bed blocked his path.

"Be careful, I wouldn't want you to wake my daughter."

She then placed her lips on his and gave him a very

long, deep, passionate, wet kiss. Louis hadn't been with a woman in quite a while. Two weeks by his count. So he probably let the kiss go on a lot longer than he should have.

The idea of pulling this off excited Louis to a certain extent. But he wasn't absolutely positive that taking this big of a toss was entirely on the wise side. Not to mention the fact that the concept of a sexual romp with the wife of the Vice President of the United States of America just generally seemed somewhat inappropriate. He stumbled for the right words.

"I don't think we should be doing this . . ."

But Louis couldn't let it go at that. After four seconds he added, "Here." He then silently cursed himself for having said it.

She took his hand and said, "You're absolutely right. Come with me."

She led him through the door that connected Little Audrey's room to her own.

"I don't think this is such a good idea," was Louis' last halfhearted protest. He also dragged his feet some. Not that anyone would have noticed.

"This is just a starter."

She locked the connecting door behind her.

"The boys are expecting me back downstairs to help them finish off that champagne."

She knelt down in front of Louis and looked up. Smiled at him. Undid his belt and trousers. The weight of his Smith & Wesson model 19 pulled everything to the floor in an instant. The hardness of the weapon made a rather loud thud as it met the soft carpeting. Louis thought of making one last protest. But he couldn't quite find adequate words to stop her from sliding his shorts to his ankles. "Besides," he thought, "what the heck. It has been over two weeks."

There was no turning back. Not now. He leaned back against the door for support and enjoyed it. He made a feeble attempt to control himself by thinking of his favorite Grimm's fairy tale. "The Dog and the Sparrow." It had always worked like a charm for him in the past. This time it didn't work that well. In fact, it didn't work at all. It was over much too quickly.

After she'd finished having her way with him, The Wife stood and said, "Well, I hope you enjoyed that as much as I did."

"Yes, ma'am . . . maybe I could return the favor?" he said.

He pulled his trousers back up.

"It's very sweet of you to offer, but I don't think we have the time for that right now. Maybe later. We'll have to see how things work out. Now, if you'll excuse me, I should put my daughter to bed, and rejoin the others." She smiled. "Thank you, Louis." She kissed his cheek.

"Yes, ma'am."

She slipped back into Little Audrey's room and closed the door.

Louis looked around The Wife's room. He'd seen them all. The best rooms in the best hotels. This suite was no exception. The paintings alone were worth more than the entire South Philadelphia neighborhood he'd grown up in. The furniture was priceless. The carpeting was priceless. Even the glass table lamps probably cost more than he made in a year. He went over to the bed. Put his hand on the linen sheets. The bed had been turned down. Obviously by one of the two chambermaids he'd interviewed the day before.

"What a job," he thought. He was looking at this fantastic bedroom setup and wondering whether the person who turned down the bed at night had the proper security clearance.

He then wondered how suspicious it was going to look when he stepped out of the door and into the hallway. He tried to visualize who was out there. One, maybe two agents on watch. Hopefully none of the drunken press people. Coming home early. At least George Strutz was accounted for. The more Louis thought about it, his presence in The Wife's room most likely only looked unusual to Louis Zezzo.

In the end he decided the best plan was—just go for it. He opened the door. Stepped out to the hall.

Reynolds was just returning from the press room as Louis closed The Wife's door.

"Anything up?" Reynolds said.

"Nothing much. The Wife just brought Little Audrey up to bed. She'll be going back down in a while." Louis considered what he'd just said and added, "To the dining room, that is." Then looked to the ceiling and turned red.

He was happy. Reynolds wasn't in the least bit suspicious.

"You want me to take her back down? It's a little dull up here," Reynolds asked.

"That's okay. I didn't get to finish my dinner."

They walked down the hall together. Toward the operations room. As Reynolds opened the door he cocked his thumb over his shoulder and said, "You ever wonder how many famous people have gotten blow jobs in those three rooms alone?"

Twenty

"Well, you look refreshed, my dear."

When the Vice President said this, it was the first time in ten minutes George Strutz had looked up from his notepad and his random jottings. Conversation had deteriorated to the "This is a lovely brandy, don't you think" level, and Strutz had decided to make a few notes for his memoirs before heading back to his room. However, now that The Wife had finally returned, there was a strong possibility things might pick up. Strutz certainly didn't want to miss any potential fireworks.

"You two clods finished the champagne? I wasn't gone that long," was the first thing out of her mouth.

"Actually, dear, we passed on the third bottle and opted for a little after-dinner drink. This is quite a lovely brandy. A private stock for the Hotel Malvasi, I believe."

"Not for me. Where's the waiter? Champagne's the only way to wash down a good meal. George, be a dear, go find him."

"Yes, ma'am," Strutz said in a borderline flippant tone.

He didn't have far to look. The wine steward was a mere eight feet away. The man had been waiting for a nod from anyone in the dining room. Strutz lifted his hand. He was there in a flash.

"We'll take that other bottle of champagne now."

"*Si, signore.*"

The Malvasi dining room had emptied out entirely except for the Americans, Oscar and Christina, and Carter. Hall 'n' Oates were splitting a piece of chocolate truffle cake with extra whipped cream.

Louis had found his way back to his table and had joined Olsen and Joe. His dinner had been removed some time ago. Olsen explained how he'd found the brains annoying to look at and had the busboy hustle them off. "Sorry, Louis."

As a result of this, and his little workout up in The Wife's room, Louis was now finding himself unbelievably hungry.

There was nothing left on the table. Not a crumb. Joe and Olsen were drinking coffee. And neither had been civilized enough to order dessert for Louis.

So Louis started looking around the dining room. Half expecting some food to drop from the ceiling. He watched Hall 'n' Oates finish up the last fragments of their truffle cake. Christina had eaten only half of her *spuma di cioccolata.* Louis strongly considered going over to her table. Asking if she was planning on finishing the thing. He glanced over to The Panhandler, but The Wife intercepted his glance. Gave him another slow, seductive wink. His face again turned beet red. His eyes shot back to Christina's dessert.

The kitchen was closed. Louis had picked that up from the maître d' on his way back into the dining room. The employees had been released for Christmas Eve. Sure, the waiter would bring him dessert if he wanted one. Or get him some eggs if it was a real emergency. But Louis didn't want a dessert or eggs. He wanted a steak. Maybe some potatoes. The only solution was to go into the kitchen himself. See what he could scrounge from the clean-up man. He sat at the table drumming his fingers and looking at the kitchen door. It finally drove Olsen nuts.

"Okay. I don't see any reason for all of us to hang around here. I can cover this with Hall 'n' Oates.

Louis, why don't you go check the kitchen and call it a night? You look like you could use a bite to eat. Joe'll be waiting for Oscar to roll out. Apparently Oscar has some words of wisdom to impart. I'll be around if you need me. I'd like you two to stay in the hotel tonight. If you would. Okay?"

They nodded. Olsen stood. He moved off to impart some wisdom of his own to Hall 'n' Oates. Louis said "Adios . . . semper fi" to Joe and left for the kitchen.

From his vantage point Joe could see both Oscar Sanchez and Carter Perkins very clearly. Carter was directly across the room on the far side. By the window. Oscar's table fell directly between Joe's and Carter's. It was getting late, but no one seemed to be tiring.

Joe wondered if the lounge would be open on this night. This Christmas Eve. He found himself wondering if Flavio had worked up a few holiday songs or if he was planning to stick with his standard Italian love songs. Either way, if the others turned in, it seemed a good place to spend an hour or two.

Across the room Oscar was now paying his check. From the number of times the waiter bowed and said, "*Molto grazie*," Joe guessed Oscar had made it well worth this man's while to have shown up for work. Oscar then looked at Joe and made a head gesture toward the lobby. He placed his napkin on the table. Christina took his arm and they walked out.

Joe stood and followed. He nodded to the maître d' as he passed. He continued into the lobby and joined up with Oscar and Christina in front of the darkened gift shop. Closed since four in the afternoon.

"Something I find interesting, Mr. Bradlee. I haven't been involved in this political business of yours for a long time, but it seems very odd that you would be protecting such an important man and choose not to carry a weapon."

"There were more weapons in that room than you think."

"I'm quite sure of that. I was only thinking what a shame it would be if you had lost yours."

Joe lied, "We like to keep one agent free—unarmed. To wrestle the loonies to the ground. I'm hoping that's not the reason you called me out here."

"No." Oscar continued, "Believe me when I say, I would rather not see you, or your friends, for a long time. Our meeting tonight was a complete, and unfortunate, coincidence. Your Vice President holds no interest for me. I would like to have a peaceful and restful time in Venezia. I am no assassin. I ask you to believe that."

"I almost do."

"Then how can we avoid running into one another?"

"Short of me giving you his schedule, I don't think there's much we can do."

"Surely you can give me some hints as to where not to be?"

"I'm afraid not."

The two men looked at each other for a long time. Christina turned and stared at the items in the darkened shop window. She sighed. No one seemed to have a solution to the situation. She just wanted to go home and be done with these people.

"Well, we'll all just do the best we can, then, won't we?" Oscar finally said.

Joe nodded. Then said, "I don't suppose you know the older gent? The little guy back in the dining room?"

"The one sitting alone?"

"Yes."

"No. I did feel I had seen him before . . . But I assumed he was one of yours."

"No. His name is Carter Perkins. Mean anything?"

"There's an individual who does travel pieces. Is that him?"

"Yes."

"Well then, you know as much as I do . . . Good night, Mr. Bradlee."

Oscar took Christina's arm. They strolled out into the night. Walked silently through the front gardens and over to the waiting motor launches. A helmsman directed them onto his boat. They stepped down and entered the cabin, away from the night air. As the helmsman cast his lines onto the dock, Oscar kissed Christina and said, "You wouldn't know it from the outside, but the odd one, Carter Perkins, is quite different from the rest of us . . . on the inside . . . A truly dangerous individual."

Twenty-one

Joe stood at the gift shop window until he was certain Oscar and Christina had left the hotel. He then walked across the lobby. He couldn't bring himself to crawl back into the dining room. The emptier the room became, the closer the air got. Olsen had dismissed Louis. Joe could assume he'd been dismissed as well. He decided to look up Reynolds. Mull over this Carter Perkins thing. Despite Reynolds' goofball attitude and card tricks, he was sharp as a tack when it came to sniffing out the bad guys. There was also this little matter of his pistol. Joe knew he was playing with fire as long as he remained unarmed. He opted to swing by his room. Pick up the 9mm. First.

When he arrived back in his room, he stripped off his jacket and went directly to the bathroom. He leaned his entire weight on the sink and stared at himself in the mirror at length. He felt he could actually see his beard pushing its way out from his skin. He decided to shave. He didn't need a shave. What he needed was to splash water in his face. A shave seemed the logical follow-up.

He removed his shirt and tie and tossed them onto the bed. The bed had been turned down. Hotel employees had been asked to stay out of the agents' rooms unless specifically told to go in. But Joe's bed had been made. Turned down. He was suddenly reminded of his facetious words to Oscar back in Paris. About hotel maids stealing guns. He smiled. Then froze. There was always a first time.

He slid his hand under the mattress. Felt nothing. He swung his hand up to the head of the bed. Nothing. Then, so quickly to the foot of the bed that when his hand hit the pistol, he thought he might have cracked the knuckle on his thumb. Louis must have cleared a chambermaid. Louis had a reputation for clearing chambermaids. Joe dragged the gun and holster out from under the mattress. He hefted the weight in his hands. Then threw the whole mess back onto the bed.

Although Joe had felt naked in the dining room without his 9mm, he found he was growing to like the nakedness. It was something he could get used to. It'd been years since he'd last walked around unarmed. He hadn't liked it back then. Tonight he had. It was a new latitude.

While Joe was shaving, Louis was in the kitchen having the meal of a lifetime. He'd dismissed the agent at the door. Taken the place over. The chef had been on his way out when Louis walked in and had basically told the clean-up man to give Louis whatever he wanted. The clean-up man happened to be an aspiring chef himself. So . . . He and Louis took this opportunity to sample just about everything the kitchen had to offer. From antipasto to dessert to espresso.

They were like two kids in a candy shop. Louis knew he'd be feeling like garbage in the morning. But this possibility in no way slowed him down. On occasion he would throw in a "please, please, no more," but the clean-up man would stroll into the huge walk-in refrigerator and come out with one of those "look what I found" expressions. Then hold up some Bulgarian sausages or something. He'd then grab a skillet and say, "*Uno momento, Signore Luigi.*" And presto, Louis would be on to yet another course. Never in his life had he eaten so much food.

Carter Perkins, on the other hand, was, and always had been, a light eater. The one day of the year Carter would overindulge, food-wise, was Easter Sunday. It was a favorite holiday. Carter loved the flowers. Loved seeing people of all types dressed up in their finery. Children racing about. It was a fabulous, festive time throughout all of Europe. Carter would wait for Easter to have a feast. Overeating was considered a sign of very poor self-control.

Carter was now sipping a cappuccino and scanning the dining rom. Other than the six Americans—three heavily armed Secret Service agents, two politicians, and a wife—Carter was the only one left. And Carter watched. Closely. After a few minutes Carter's mind wandered back to the last couple to leave the room. Who knew or cared who the girl was, but the more Carter thought about it, the identity of the man began to crystalize in Carter's brain.

It had been years ago. Many years. Oscar Sanchez had had a beard back then, but Carter would never forget those eyes. Beard or not. It had been in Beirut. Carter had just removed the unwanted suitor of a Lebanese businessman's daughter. Actually, the young man had been very much wanted by the daughter. It was, naturally, the businessman who had placed the youth into the unwanted category. The boy had been found shot. Three times. In the back of the head. Small-caliber. It had been in the bathroom of his hotel room. The daughter had been the one to find the boy. She also found her jewelry missing. An obvious robbery.

The hotel guests had been assembled in the breakfast room the following morning by the local police for routine questioning. And also a mild warning—"There may be a thief on the loose." The guests had then been released.

Oscar Sanchez had been one of those guests. He'd taken one look at Carter, and Carter had known that Oscar's eyes knew all truths. Right down to Carter's connection with the businessman. At the time Carter had felt sure that Oscar was an undercover policeman. But a month later a bellboy had been arrested for the crime and shortly thereafter executed. No murder weapon had been found.

After Beirut, Carter had followed, as closely as possible, the career of Oscar Sanchez. Oscar's photo would appear in a newspaper every now and then. A suspect in one bombing or another. But when the authorities would finally catch up with him, he was never convicted of a blessed thing.

Now back in the Malvasi dining room, Carter wondered about two things: If Oscar was this suspected bomber, how had he been able to gain an audience with the Vice President of the United States? And more important, had Oscar recognized Carter from Beirut—from all these years past? The agent Bradlee had followed Oscar out of the dining room. Obviously to question him. What had they discussed? Oscar Sanchez? Or Carter Perkins?

A small drop of sweat had formed on Carter's brow. Carter pulled the Malvasi napkin up and dabbed at it. Then dropped the cloth back down and glanced uneasily at the damp spot. This assassin enjoyed the thrill of the hunt. The excitement of it all. But now there was a feeling of being outnumbered. Possibly Carter had moved too far out of an element that was comfortable. There were too many variables. Too many surprises were surfacing.

"Men prize the thing ungained . . . more than it is," Carter murmured.

For a long time Carter sat and considered calling off the entire escapade. DOC could find someone else. Surely Carter wasn't the only assassin they'd contacted. And after all, it was only the Vice President. Did anyone care other than this elusive DOC? "However," Carter's mind hammered on, "coupled with a presidential assassination, the course of world events would be rocked to the core. I have a golden opportunity to be a part of this glorious history." And like a drug, these thoughts consumed, and eventually took control of, the assassin's brain.

It was at that moment Carter decided this would be the last thrust of the dagger. The last trigger pulled.

After this one person was eliminated, it would be travel writing and nothing else. Carter would stop. Be free. It would be over.

"Just this one more."

Twenty-two

At the Vice President's table, The Wife was downing the last of Carter's champagne. It seemed to have no effect on her. But for fear she might order some more, keep the dining room staff on duty until three in the morning, Strutz stood and said, "I understand the hotel has a very nice piano lounge on the lower level. Maybe we could all head down for a nightcap?"

Number Two was quick to pick up on Strutz's exaggerated facial expressions. He glanced at his wife's champagne glass and jumped up as well.

"That sounds like an excellent idea, George. What do you say, my dear?"

"I think I'll pass. It's getting late. I have some overdue business to take care of upstairs. You boys have fun."

She stood and tossed her napkin onto a dessert plate.

The activity at the table did not go unnoticed by the three remaining Secret Service agents, Olsen and Hall 'n' Oates, and the entire dining room staff. Everyone in the room, except for Carter, descended on the table. In a flood. Chairs were pulled out. Many "*grazie*s" and "thank yous" were thrown about. And many employees were politely moved to a more respectable distance by the agents.

"Are you turning in, sir?" Olsen asked.

"No, I think we're going to duck down to the lounge for a nightcap. My wife will be going up, though."

"Yes, sir. I'll see to that. The other agents can go to the lounge with you gentlemen."

The Wife stepped in almost too quickly. "Jerry, I believe Louis is in the kitchen. If you don't feel like going up just yet, he can go with me."

"I've given Louis the evening off, ma'am. He looked like he could use a little rest."

"Well that's a shame. . . . I guess I'll go up alone, then." She looked at her husband. "I'll see you in the morning."

She turned, walked ten paces, and turned back.

"Oh, yes . . . Merry Christmas."

She turned once more without waiting for a reply and walked out. Olsen was forced to trot to keep up.

Strutz and the Vice President stood and watched as she crossed the dining room. When she passed the maître d's desk, the Vice President said, "A lovely woman, don't you think, George?"

Strutz searched for some sarcasm in the Vice President's voice. He wasn't positive he had detected any, so he decided to play it safe.

"I would have to agree with you, sir."

The two men walked across the floor. Following the exact path of The Wife. When they were abreast of Carter's table, the Vice President stopped He peered down at the well-manicured travel writer.

"I'd like to thank you for that wonderful bottle of champagne. I'm afraid my wife drank most of it, but it was very thoughtful of you to send it over." Then from his best file of political banter, he pulled out, "I'm sure we've met before. Maybe you could refresh my memory?"

Carter stood. Hall 'n' Oates stepped in close. Carter extended a hand.

"Carter Perkins, at your service. I'm afraid we haven't met, but I've always considered you a fine representative of the United States of America. It is indeed a pleasure to meet you. Might I add, you're much more handsome in person than the photos we seem to have published in our British newspapers."

Carter did everything but click heels. Hall 'n' Oates let the handshake go through.

"Well, Mr. Perkins, you seem to be the only one left in the dining room. Maybe you'd like to join Mr. Strutz and myself in the lounge for a nightcap?"

"My goodness . . . It would be my pleasure."

Carter then asked for the check and eyed the champagne charge. "A lovely meal. Worth every penny." No need to sign it. It was Carter Perkins' table. This was the Hotel Malvasi. Carter simply placed the bill on the table, and the three revelers headed off to the lounge, Hall 'n' Oates in tow.

It was just about that same time that Joe walked in on Reynolds in the operations room. Reynolds was smoking a cigar and leaning back in a chair—his feet propped up on a desk that had been made in the early eighteenth century. The chair a few weeks later. But they matched very nicely. Olsen was also there. Having just returned from dropping The Wife off in her room. Not one word had been exchanged between Olsen and The Wife during their entire trip to the top floor. It was all Olsen could do to keep up with her.

Reynolds blew a smoke ring and looked at Joe. "Louis turn in?"

The door opened again. Louis walked in.

"Jeez-o-kameezo, I'm never eating another thing as long as I live," Louis moaned. "I feel like a stuffed pig. I wish one of you bums had been there to stop me . . . why do I always do this to myself? Man, oh, man. I feel like Strutz looks. . . . Look out, I gotta lie down." Louis collapsed on the bed.

"Where're Mom and Dad?" Joe asked.

"Strutz and Goliath are down in the lounge with Hall 'n' Oates. I put The Wife to bed," Olsen said. "She's a real cold fish. I don't envy Goliath in the least. Do you think he ever gets laid?"

Louis put a pillow over his head and groaned.

"Who knows? Did Perkins pack it in?" Joe asked the room in general.

"He was still eating when I left," Olsen answered.

"Can we throw Perkins' M.O. around a little?"

It was the best way for Joe to get Reynolds' opinions on Carter without offending Olsen.

"I know all of you think I'm being hard on him, but I don't like the son of a bitch. Something's way off with this guy. Reynolds, what's your read?"

"I don't know. I've never seen him."

"What?"

"I've never seen the guy. I haven't left this fucking floor since we got here."

"You checked him out, didn't you?"

"Yeah, on the computer."

"Tomorrow. Get a read on him. I'd like to know what you think."

A long, exaggerated groan came from the bed. Louis rolled to one side like a beached whale. From under the pillow he said, "Give the little guy a break, will ya, Joe? You're being a touch homophobic, don't you think?"

"Thank you so much for your input, Louis," Joe said and threw another pillow at the whale.

"Seriously, Joe, I've run this guy through and through. I know how you feel. I just think you're wrong this time." And Olsen definitely had checked Carter out. Even after Reynolds had. He trusted Joe's intuition, but Joe was wrong this time.

Reynolds started flipping cards through his smoke rings. Not once did he break a ring. Fifty-four smoke rings. Fifty-four cards. Including jokers.

After Reynolds had finished, Joe said, "Well, as entertaining as that was, I think I'm going downstairs and listen to Flavio. Have a vodka or two. How long's Number Two planning to be down there?"

"Couldn't tell you," Olsen said.

Louis moaned and rolled over one more time.

As Joe walked to the door, he muttered to himself, "Damn, I wish our boy wasn't down there."

"Yeah, well, wish in one hand, shit in the other. See which one fills up first," Reynolds said as he picked his cards up from the floor.

Twenty-three

Joe walked slowly across the lobby toward the lounge. He could hear Flavio singing "*Dove Sta Il Poeta.*" The piano man's favorite. Flavio managed to work it into his repertoire at least five or six times a night.

When Joe entered the room, Flavio gave him a slight wave that more resembled a salute. Joe saluted back and surveyed the lounge. Flavio sat at a jet black baby grand piano with a microphone bent over to his mouth from the left. If the mike had been any closer to his lips, he could have brushed his teeth with the thing. In front of the piano was a small parquet dance floor. A couple was dancing slow and close. Scattered throughout the room were twelve small tables. Each with a flickering candle and a lone carnation.

One entire side of the room consisted of floor-to-ceiling sliding glass doors. In warmer months these doors were opened onto the gardens. Now the gardens were decorated with tiny white lights. Occasionally one or two of the lights would blink off. Then back on again. The effect was like gazing at a starry night in August. Reflections of the paintings on the opposite wall jumped in the glass doors.

The only other people in sight were an immaculately dressed couple. He in black tie and dinner jacket. She in a vermilion satin ball gown and weighted down with enough diamonds and rubies to sink a tugboat. They were seated at a table against the windows. The moment Joe looked at them, they leaned into each other and exchanged a long kiss.

Toward the rear of the room was a half wall. It divided the space into two sections. Joe assumed that Number Two, Strutz, and Hall 'n' Oates were either behind the partition or had turned in. Whatever. He was glad he couldn't see them. And equally glad they couldn't seen him.

He sat at one of the small tables under an oil painting of the Castel San Angelo in Rome. The painting was of a stormy evening. The moon pushing its way out from behind black clouds. Two shafts of lightning illuminated one of the seven hills.

When the waiter came, Joe ordered a double vodka on the rocks and asked the man if Flavio could sing "Perdere L'Amore." He then settled back in his chair. The waiter moved off.

Flavio had a phenomenal way with a piano. His music filled every inch of the room. His voice blended perfectly with every chord he played. The two couples spoke in hushed whispers. Making an effort not to intrude on the music. Joe could feel himself finally begin to unwind.

The waiter, on his way back with Joe's drink, stopped and spoke to Flavio. The piano man looked at Joe, smiled, and gave another one of his wave-salutes. When the drink arrived, Joe raised the glass to Flavio. He took a slow sip of his vodka. It had been a long goddamn day. It was finally over.

Flavio began with the first few notes of "Perdere L'Amore." The vodka had a smooth burn as it slid into Joe's gut. And the stuff created the same effect on his brain as it always did. Taking him to another place. Another time. Detroit, Michigan, and a national convention.

Her name had been Holly. She'd been working for one of the network news teams. Joe'd been in charge of setting up the advance security for the hall and the convention floor. She'd organized the advance news coverage. She was from North Carolina and had an accent that was as Southern as a damn pecan. And young. Twenty-six. Six years younger than he had been at the time.

In the past Joe'd never had any use for the press people. They always wanted too much fucking information. And they wouldn't leave you alone until they got it.

"Hey, Joe, when's So-and-So arriving?"

"Hey, Joe, what ramp's the governor using?"

"Hey, Joe, where's the senator's chair going to be?"

"Hey, Joe . . ."

Holly had been no different.

"Oh, Joe, just one more thing . . ." or "Before you run off, let me ask you . . ." or "It would really help if I knew . . ."

She'd never stopped badgering him. It always ended with: "Thanks, Joe, you're such a love," and a flirtatious glance from her coal black eyes. What a pushover he'd been back then.

All the agents had a favorite press person. It was a thing. They'd give out tidbits of information. But Joe'd never gotten in to it. At least not until he'd met Holly. They hit it off from first meeting.

Joe had nixed one of the network cameramen from the convention floor. Holly had come to Joe's office to argue the man's case. The guy had been a founding member of Vietnam Veterans Against the War. C.O. actually had film footage of the little fucker lighting a Molotov cocktail on the steps of the Capitol building back in May of '69. But at this point Joe remembered him looking more like Mr. Peepers than anything else. A far cry from his 1969 photo with his fu manchu mustache and V.V.A.W. armband. And that had actually been the crux of Holly's defense:

"That was years ago. Jesus, Joe, the war's over."

Joe pretty much agreed with her, but it was the wrong time for him to take a chance on anyone. The cameraman was trashed. Joe's word was final.

"There's nothing like starting off a relationship with a good argument," he said.

"I'm going to be getting into trouble with you for my entire time in Detroit, aren't I?"

"Christ, I hope so."

She smiled. Joe decided he'd give her a break. They ended up eating nearly every meal together.

Having four hours of free time in twenty-four doesn't leave much for a love affair, and when the delegates and politicians arrived they barely saw each other.

After it was all over, and the big fish had returned to their small ponds, Joe walked down to the convention floor. A congressman by the name of Lenny Hofstadtler had given him a box of cigars. Joe'd been looking for someone who might actually want the fucking things. He found a man stacking folding chairs just below the podium—where eight hours earlier another man had accepted his party's nomination for president of the United States.

"You smoke cigars?"

"Sure do," the chair folder said.

"God bless America," Joe said and handed the box over. He then heard his name called from the podium. It was Holly.

"Jesus, I was afraid you'd left. Come on up here. The view's to die for."

He went back behind the podium and climbed a ladder he'd installed three weeks earlier. Strictly for Secret Service use. When he got to the podium he said, "I was afraid you'd left too."

"Not hardly. It seems somebody thought I did a good job of picking up some inside information. They gave me a week off. . . . 'Course, I don't know what the hell to do with it. I love North Carolina, but the idea of spending a week with my mother doesn't exactly appeal to me. Not right now."

"If you can wait forty minutes, I know a nice little dump in St. Lucia. It'll be hot, though."

They'd ended up spending six days and nights in St. Lucia. And it was hot. But television news had seeped too far into Holly's blood. She flew back to New York City on her own. Joe thought he might have loved her. But it wasn't about to happen. Not then. Not Detroit. Not St. Lucia.

Back in the Malvasi lounge, Joe took another sip of vodka and wondered why his brain had taken him to Detroit and the convention. He tried to make some sense of it. How it fit into Venice. He searched the Detroit episode for a clue. He ran it over again in his head. He felt his left wing was trying to tell him something. Something had happened in Detroit. It would happen again in Venice. He was sure of it. There had been only one scare at the convention. A man had charged the podium with a dagger. It had been during the benediction. But the Michigan troopers had ushered him out easily enough. A disgruntled Shakespearean actor turned religious nut. Nothing more.

The duo on the dance floor had retired to their table. The couple at the window had left. Flavio had taken a break. The only audible sound was coming from the men tucked behind the partition. A sort of low mumble that Joe determined was Number Two and Strutz. The two men were capable of staying up to all hours. Talking about the good old days when they were roommates at Princeton. Or Harvard Law. Or the time they played eighteen holes in the dark at the Big Club. With no fucking clothes on. And how they'd lost their balls.

Joe was just beginning to feel a little sorry for Hall 'n' Oates when he heard one of Strutz's overly loud belly laughs. To say it shattered the mood of the room would be a goddamn understatement. Even the usually cheerful Flavio had an annoyed look on his face. Joe heard the sound of chairs sliding on carpet. Guessed the boys were finally calling it a night.

He was right. Hall 'n' Oates were the first to emerge from behind the partition. They passed Joe without looking down.

"Nighty-night, fellas," Joe said but got no reaction from either one of the agents. They were soon followed by Strutz, Number Two, and the damn travel writer—Carter Perkins.

Joe was spooked when he saw Perkins. He'd heard

nothing that even resembled Perkins' voice for the entire time he'd been in the lounge. He found himself wondering if the little bastard had spoken at all. Possibly Perkins hadn't been at the same table as Number Two. Maybe just following him. Whatever, Joe got up and fell in behind Carter.

When they reached the lobby, Carter, Strutz, and Number Two stopped to say good night.

"It was a sincere pleasure to spend so much time with you. What sights do you have on your schedule for Venice?" Carter asked.

Joe walked over and mumbled something to Hall 'n' Oates in an effort to eavesdrop.

"My wife would like to go out to Torcello. It's a nearby island. I suppose we'll do that tomorrow."

"I doubt if any boats will be running to Torcello on Christmas," Carter said.

Number Two, having no use for public transportation, let alone having to rely on it, looked genuinely confused. He thought, "Do I have to explain to this foreigner that I have my own boats?"

"But of course, you have your own boats. How foolish of me. However, I'm sure you'll find the island somewhat desolate in the winter. The hotel has a lovely spot on Torcello. Locanda Malvasi. But I'm certain it's closed in December. A shame."

"Well, if anyone can get these people to open the place up, it's my wife."

They all chuckled politely.

Carter glanced over at Joe. Then turned back to the Vice President.

"Well, gentlemen, I must say good night." Then in a somewhat louder voice Carter added, "I look forward to our little interview. You say I should speak with Judy in your press room to arrange a time?"

"Yes. Ask her to set it up for the day after tomorrow," Number Two said. "Well, good night, Carter. It's been swell."

"The pleasure has been all mine. Have a wonderful time on Torcello tomorrow," Carter said.

They all shook hands. Carter said good night to

Strutz. Then left for the elevator. After the doors pinched closed, the Vice President looked to Strutz and said, "What a pud knocker."

They howled.

Joe didn't howl. He walked back to the lounge and finished his vodka. He ordered another. It was at that point that Joe Bradlee decided Carter Perkins was exactly what everyone else said.

No threat.

TUESDAY

One

Christmas attacked Venice like an explosion. For the lucky ones, the ones who'd been up before the sun, it seemed as though they'd been living in the dark of night one minute and the blinding bright light of day the next. The rays of the sun bounced off the tile roofs and windows. Ricocheted from building to building until they finally rested on the narrow walkways and canals.

Not a single cloud graced the sky. Paler in the east and growing darker and darker as it stretched over to the west. A sliver of platinum moon still hung above the Italian mainland. A cloudless day was unusual for this city. The meeting of sea and land almost always made its mark on the sky. Much to the delight of the local painters.

Little Audrey had been worried sick from the moment it had been announced the family would be in Italy for Christmas. How would Santa Claus be able to find her in a place like Italy? In Venice? All the streets flooded with water? Would there be snow for his sleigh? Besides, how could he ask for directions if he got lost? There's no possible way he could speak Italian.

But all of these fears were quickly forgotten on this bright morning. As if by magic, the green and red stocking that her Auntie Kate had knitted for her appeared at the foot of her bed. She tore her way through the colorfully wrapped gifts. Stopping every now and then to throw down another Perugina chocolate-covered hazelnut. Within minutes the floor was littered with a dozen silver and blue candy wrappers.

There were three tiny dolls in the stocking. A redhead. A brunette. A blonde. The dolls were immediately given the names of Cindy, Becky, and Lorie. Outfits for each of them were mixed in among the Peruginas. Little Audrey also found a miniature set of colored pencils. A small rubber disc that when dropped on the floor bounced nearly to the ceiling. A stuffed zebra. A stuffed elephant. And at the very bottom, two sacks of gold coins with chocolate fillings. By the time her mother entered the room, nearly all the chocolate had been consumed.

"Merry Christmas, darling."

"Look, Mommy, Santa Claus did find me! This is Becky. She's my favorite. Her hair is the same color as yours."

Little Audrey's mother considered informing her daughter that at various points in her life, she'd worn a hair color that matched each of the dolls. But decided against it.

"I saw Santa last night, dear. He left you another present in my room, and said that there were even more gifts waiting for you back in Washington."

"When can we go back? Wait, I want to open the present in your room first, and I have a present for Louis too. I almost forgot. Is Louis in your room, Mommy?"

"No, dear."

"Well, I think we should go into your room so I can open my other present. Is it big?"

"Like this."

Her mother held her hands out to indicate a package of about eighteen inches square.

"Let's go."

The Wife took her daughter's hand and led her into her room. She thought it somewhat ironic that Little Audrey had wrapped up a gift for Louis and none for her husband or herself. Everyone seemed to be giving Louis gifts. She smiled. It would be a Christmas Louis wouldn't forget for a long time.

When the two ladies entered The Wife's room, Little Audrey spotted the gift. She raced across to tear it open. Paper and ribbon flew in all directions. But the cardboard box under the paper proved more difficult. It'd been taped shut. She was forced to ask her mother for some help. The Wife ran a fingernail along the seam, and the tape split. The girl grabbed the box from her mother. Flung it open. Pale blue and pink tissue paper still hid the contents from Little Audrey. She tore the paper and tossed it aside.

"Be careful, dear. It may be fragile."

This warning didn't slow Little Audrey down for a second. She pulled and tugged at the remaining tissue paper. Then, after what seemed like an eternity, she lifted her prize from the box.

"Oh, Mommy, it's the most beautiful doll in all of the world."

It should have been. The Wife had given Judy, in the press office, seven hundred dollars to spend. Judy had done well. The doll had long, flowing auburn hair. Her dress was made of white velvet. It had been adorned with braided gold trim, and tiny gems were sewn into the hem and sleeves.

"Oh, Mommy, she's so beautiful. She looks like a queen. I think I'll call her Queenie."

She held the doll up to the mirror so she could view herself with her new friend. She was unable to see her mother twist an eyebrow and mouth the word, "Queenie?"

Unaware of the festivities in the room next to him, Goliath stood at his French doors watching the moon fade on the horizon. He needed a plan. The last thing in the world he wanted to do on Christmas Day was get on a goddamn boat and ride out to goddamn Torcello with his goddamn wife. He was already tired of boat rides. The ride to the hotel had been enough for him. He cursed George Strutz for picking this damned hotel. The famous Malvasi. A hotel where you had to get on a goddamn boat to go anywhere. Even if it was just to Saint Marks.

But Torcello? It was ridiculous. From the looks of the map on his desk, Torcello had to be at least an hour away. He wasn't going. That's all there was to it. There was nothing on Torcello, anyway. Just some old goddamn church. According to Judy.

Right. Goliath needed a plan. But, just as he'd done for his entire political career, he sighed and eventually said to himself, "A solution will come to me. I'll just jump in with both feet, and to hell with a damn plan."

The Vice President passed through the connecting bathroom and tapped twice on his wife's door. He waited for a response and walked in.

"Daddy, look what Santa brought me. Her name's Queenie. Isn't she beautiful?"

He looked at his wife, twisted an eyebrow, and mouthed the word, "Queenie?"

She shrugged and said, "Merry Christmas."

"Yes, and to you . . . Now, I was, well, thinking about this Torcello business—"

His wife shot him her executioner's look. He stopped in mid-sentence. She turned her back on him. Said, "You don't have to go. You can stay here, for all I care. I just thought it would be nice to be in a quiet place for a little while today."

"Now, you see, I was thinking just the opposite. I was thinking . . . well . . . more festive. That's what I was thinking. I was thinking, it's Christmas. We should stay closer in. Be around people."

"We've been around *people* for seven years, my dear."

"Well, you know what I mean."

"Actually, I don't think I do."

"I was thinking . . . Saint Mark's. Maybe go to church there."

"There's a church on Torcello."

"Yes, but it's old, from what I understand."

"And Saint Mark's is new . . . ?"

Little Audrey was trying to keep up with all this.

She appeared as if she were at Wimbleton, watching a tennis ball fly back and forth.

"Of course Saint Mark's isn't new, but I think it's newer. There's probably more art and gold and what not. I mean, it's a bigger church. We have to see it sometime."

The Wife sighed.

"Listen, I have a plan. Why don't you go to Torcello this afternoon? We can arrange a boat for you. And I'll take Little Audrey to see Saint Marks. That way we'll only be apart for a few hours. How does that sound?"

"Fine."

"Well, you don't have to say it like that."

"Like what?"

"That."

She sighed again.

"I'll have George set it up."

"Fine."

It was George Strutz's job. He was the Vice President's top aide and adviser. He would have to confront Olsen. Actually speak to the man. Pass the plans for the day on to him. Strutz knew Olsen didn't like changes. Olsen never complained, but you could see it on his face every time. He hated changes.

This was one of the things Strutz despised about having stuck it out with the Vice President for so long. Having kissed his ass for so long. He hated dealing with the damned Secret Service agents. They seemed to think of him as a lower life form. They never gave him the respect he felt he deserved. It was, however, a small price to pay for the up side of the job. The travel. The expense account. Mixing with the right people. The power. Power was the best. Power was always good.

But he had no power over these gun-toting goons. And the Vice President was no better with them than he was. Neither one of them seemed to be equipped to cope with these glorified bodyguards. So Strutz, being the one who wasn't the Vice President, was always sent off to "handle it."

Strutz found Olsen alone in the operations room listening to a cassette recording of Christmas music by the Mormon Tabernacle Choir. Olsen had just flipped the cassette over to side two. The first notes of "O Come, All Ye Faithful" were beginning to roll out of the seventeen-thousand-dollar piece of high tech, U.S. government "spy" equipment when Strutz stepped into the room.

"I didn't think you could play music on that thing," was George Strutz's attempt at being friendly.

Olsen turned the machine off.

"What do you want, George?"

"Well, there's been a slight change in plans . . ."

"Fuck me."

Two

Joe Bradlee was feeling good. Real good. For the first time since Number Two's arrival, he felt comfortable. He'd slept well. It was a perfect morning. He was in Venezia. The job portion of his time here was done. Over. If it had been a normal workday, he would've been on his way to the airport and on to the next city on the Vice President's itinerary. Or back to Washington, D.C. But it wasn't a normal workday. It was Christmas. No flight arrangements had been scheduled for Joe and Louis and Reynolds and Lightfoot on this day. They would return to Washington on the twenty-sixth. A day off in Venezia. No one could ask for a better Christmas present.

Joe shaved one more time. He took a shower, dressed, and placed his pistol back under the mattress. This was his day. He was ready for it. No guns. The past three days had been long ones. Nineteen hours each. Joe was going to take this one day and behave like a normal human being if it killed him.

He checked his pocket for cash. Cash was all he needed. He had enough to get by. Fifteen hundred dollars in a mix of Italian and American currency. He could disappear in this city in the blink of an eye. No one would find him. He had dinner plans set. He was as free as a bird.

He grabbed the camera he'd bought from the kid

with the high hopes that Nelo would be able to supply him with a roll of film. He dropped it into his overcoat pocket. He threw the latch on the door. And he opened it.

Bang.

Joe Bradlee found George Strutz, Beelzebub him-fucking-self, standing with his right hand up beside his fat goddamn face poised to knock.

Joe turned his back on Strutz. He walked back into his room and said, "Fuck me."

"Is everything okay, Joe?"

"Fuck me."

"Joe?"

"What is it, George?"

"Is everything okay?"

Joe sat on the bed. From below the mattress he could feel his 9mm poking him in the ass.

"I'm off today, George. What is it?"

"Well, that's just it. It seems the Vice President and the missus are splitting up today. She wants to boat it out to Torcello. It's an island—"

"Thank you, George. I'm aware of what the fuck Torcello is."

"Anyway, you'll have to go with her."

"When?"

"Around noon. The hotel is making her a lunch for you to take along. Apparently they have an annex or something out there—"

"Locanda Malvasi."

"Right. Anyway, they're going to have one of the rooms opened up for her."

Joe did a little quick math. An hour's ride out. Lunch, one hour. Stroll around for two hours, max. An hour back. Five hours. He'd be back by five. If he was lucky. But he wasn't about to take a chance on being lucky.

"I'm afraid I'm going to have to pull a little seniority on this one, George. Go ruin Reynolds' day off."

After a long pause Strutz said, "I don't think the Vice President's going to go for that, if you know what I mean."

"No. I don't think I do know what you mean, George."

"Well, and this is just between you and me, I don't think he wants the Italians seeing his wife riding around Venice with a black man."

"Jesus Christ. Fuck both you assholes."

"That's a pretty crappy position to take. There's a lot more to your job than being a hired gun. Appearances have to be considered at all times. And if you ask me, I think you'd better take a good look at where your loyalties lie. Believe me, I'm very serious when I say, Reynolds will not be going to Torcello today."

"How's Lightfoot? Has he rejoined the living?"

"No."

"Then it's Louis."

"Louis?"

"Louis . . . Go ruin his day off."

"Why do you insist that this is ruining someone's day off?"

Joe didn't bother to look at Strutz or answer the question.

"Can I trust Louis?" Strutz said as though he were pondering the fate of the world.

"You've been trusting him for three years now, George."

"Okay, it's Louis, then." Strutz covered himself. "I didn't know he was available. Forgive the intrusion."

He started to leave, but when he got to the door he turned back and said, "You know, Joe, I think you, and for that matter all of the Roadrunners, could improve your attitudes quite a bit. And I don't mind saying so."

"Fuck you, George."

He was gone.

Joe breathed a sigh of relief.

He waited two minutes exactly, then stepped out into the hall. There was a great temptation to run, run, run out of the Hotel Malvasi before he got caught again. But he walked. It was far less conspicuous. As he passed Louis' room, he could hear Strutz's voice and a very weary Louis putting up a very lame argument.

Joe stopped at the elevator and stood for a second waiting for the car. From behind the sliding doors he could hear the whine of the elevator's motor and the tired cables slapping one another as they passed in the shaft. It seemed to be taking forever for the damn thing to arrive. From the far end of the hall he could hear a lock being unlatched on one of the guest room doors. It was time to disappear.

The stairway was another twenty feet to his right. He ducked down and out of sight just before Reynolds stepped into the hall. Neither man saw the other. Joe flew down the flights of stairs. Free. No holster banging into his ribs. No pin on his lapel. No wad of plastic in his ear. No cable down his neck. Free.

The only potential trouble spot would be the lobby. There was no telling who could be waiting in ambush. Who else would be hiding? Lying in the weeds. Poised to jump out in an attempt to trash this day off. He could've avoided the lobby altogether, but he wanted that roll of film. The lobby was the only place to get it. He'd paid enough for the damn camera. Might as well use it. And it was highly unlikely a camera store would be open on Christmas.

Joe darted across the lobby as if he were stealing second base. When he reached the front desk he felt a strong temptation to slide. He was greeted with one of Nelo's smiles and a hearty "*Buon giorno, Signore Joe.*"

He showed the camera to Nelo, who promptly outfitted him with a roll of film. Joe then ducked back across the lobby, down four short steps, and through the kitchen.

The chef was on the verge of beating the clean-up man senseless with a loaf of Neapolitan bread for having placed an onion on the meat side on his sacred walk-in refrigerator. Joe picked up a pear and two Venetian rolls on his way through.

He passed the pot washer and the dish washer. He held the back door open for Massimo as he struggled with a garbage can. He brushed past two waiters who had slipped out back for a cigarette. Then almost skipped down the narrow alleyway to the iron gate that opened to freedom and the Fondamenta delle Zitelle. He strolled thirty-five feet to the Zitelle *vaporetto* stop and counted his blessings. The United States government would not see hide or hair of Joe Bradlee until he wanted them to.

Three

Let Hercules himself do what he may
The cat will mew and the dog will have his day.

How often had a cock broken a new dawn, in countless countries, in countless cities, in countless hotel rooms, and then discovered Carter Perkins strolling to an opened window, looking out into a new morning, with those words from *Hamlet* resting in an overly slumberous head? Certainly Carter had no idea. It was a lovely, lovely day. It was Carter's day. A day of life and death. Just like any other.

A Venetian breakfast had been sent up to the room. Carter hated dressing early and loathed mingling with strange people in the morning. It was bad enough to have to do it in the afternoon. There was nothing worse than watching a cluster of overweight Americans insisting on well-done bacon or oatmeal. Or something equally as repugnant. They seemed to think that the louder they asked for something, the better their chances were of actually receiving it. Honestly, oatmeal in Italy? Where did they think they were—Disneyland?

Carter detested these people. And was more than positive they would be befouling Venezia like river rats today. In their blue jeans and white tennis shoes.

Parading in and out of San Marco. Taking flash photographs of the Christmas Mass. At least it wasn't summer. Hopefully they wouldn't be in shorts. Shorts that were too short and too tight. Their fat thighs straining to escape from under the hem of their Day-Glo splotched bicycling shorts. America was the one country Carter had never ventured to, absolutely refused to go, and often wondered if they even sold neckties there.

Carter sat at the small table that rested by the French doors and sipped morning tea and nibbled on the long white rolls that were particular to Venice. Americans hated these rolls. The rolls were too dry and were never served with butter. Americans complained about them bitterly. Incessantly. Which of course made the rolls all the more tasty. Carter's nose twitched. Americans seemed to be plaguing the little travel writer on this Christmas morning. Carter tried to remove all thoughts of all Americans from an already overly cluttered mind. All except one thought of one American. Yes, this would be Carter's day. Carter's greatest day.

The previous night the Vice President had simplified things a great deal for Carter. He had mentioned his plans to visit Torcello with his wife. So Torcello would be the spot.

The island would be virtually empty. Carter liked that. Carter liked being in control of the elements. Assassins in crowds were fools. They were destined to be apprehended. Carter would never be apprehended. Largely because this would be the last skirmish. "Makes a swanlike end, fading in music," Carter thought. This would be a swan song. And what a glorious way to retire. What an accomplishment. The Vice President of the United States. The coup of all coups. The toppling of America.

Carter wondered if it was too early to implement the first step of the plan. If it was too early to call Judy in the press office. Set up an interview with the Vice President for December twenty-sixth. An interview that would never be. A day that would never be. Carter felt warm and damp with anticipation and glanced down. Then checked the time. Barely ten. Not yet. Too early.

For the one hundredth time Carter mulled over the rest of what was a very simple scheme. The Vice President undoubtedly would have arranged for one of the Malvasi motor launches to take him and his wife to Torcello. And Carter knew full well there were a number of hotel employees out at Locanda Malvasi this very moment. Opening up one of the summer suites for these Americans.

Carter was more than familiar with Torcello and Locanda Malvasi. Having spent a week there last July with a member of Parliament. The inn was a perfect place for those sorts of assignations. Torcello was as secluded as one could get in Venezia. The suites were all on one level. Six *in toto.* The building itself resembled a country inn more than a hotel. Each suite had a number of windows at ground level. A few had both front and rear doors.

Locanda Malvasi had its own restaurant, and there was only one other restaurant on Torcello, simply called Frutti di Mare. They served fabulous local dishes. Carter remembered fondly a seafood *frito misto* that had been nicely served up this past July. The ingredients of which had all been happily swimming in the Adriatic Sea only an hour before Carter had sucked them down.

This restaurant would also be closed in winter. The only tourists to be found on Torcello this December would be true Italophiles. Coming out to visit the old church. Or lovers returning to remember. And this being Christmas Day, Carter guessed that even these people would have better things to do.

The original plan had been to leave for Torcello early. Find the suite the Americans would be using and crawl into the bathroom. Then lie in wait. As in Beirut, the Beretta's accuracy could be relied upon only for a distance of ten feet. If Carter's target was any farther away, the gun could not be counted on to do a proper job. It would be necessary to be in close.

Bathrooms were small and private places. Perfectly suited for this kind of job. People often didn't come out for hours. Sometimes not at all.

Escape would be a problem. It always required careful planning. Escape was the largest consideration with any form of eradication. And this killer was the master of escape. It was the single reason Carter had lasted so long in the business. The life.

In this original plan, Carter would have left the Locanda by way of the bathroom window after completing the mission. Or possibly through the suite itself. That is, if the Vice President entered alone. To use the toilet. Carter guessed that the alone part would be more than likely, considering the cold shoulders the American couple had been given each other the night before. Carter suspected things weren't going smoothly for the two. In any case, the Secret Service agents would be watching only the front door. As wrong as this concept was, this was how Carter had calculated things would happen.

After the task had been completed, Carter would retrace the route back to the small dock on the far side of the island. There a water taxi would be waiting, and a quick escape would be made. Even if a dash-for-it needed to be improvised, Carter had only to make it to the boat dock to be home free. The Secret Service agents would be left behind, stuck on land, with their Malvasi launches far away on the other side of the island.

As was usually the case with overzealous political assassins, the excitement of the Big Kill would cloud their judgment. Carter had now become a political assassin. Judgment was clouding considerably. Among many other things, what Carter hadn't realized was, the Secret Service would have gone over the suite on Torcello with a fine-tooth comb long before the Vice President would set foot anywhere near the island. Carter would have looked somewhat foolish when the Big Boys found the Little Imp standing behind the shower curtain, Beretta in hand.

But all of this didn't matter, and for two reasons.

One, the Vice President wasn't going to Torcello with his wife, Louis was. So the Secret Service wouldn't be checking out the suite at all. Of course, Carter didn't know this. There was a more personal reason. Reason number two. Which was, Carter was uneasy—not knowing how many Secret Service agents would be with the Vice President was far too chancy. Carter wanted to determine exactly what the odds would be—before leaving for Torcello.

So Carter altered the plan, and would now wait by the window and watch. There was a perfect view of the boat docks from this window. Carter would wait for the Americans to leave. Then ascertain exactly how many agents would be taken along. The assassin would be much more comfortable with this information at hand. Carter could slide into the bathroom of the Locanda Malvasi suite at any time. Also, there was no guarantee the Vice President would even use the bathroom. In which case plans would have to be adjusted once again. On Torcello.

After the Americans had left for the island, Carter would construct a much more elaborate route to Torcello, but remain somewhat close behind. Carefully changing boats. Carefully covering the trail. Even if Carter was caught on the island, there was time enough to call it all off and not look at all suspicious. It would just be a coincidence. Carter would be only another tourist.

The assassin checked the time once more—10:31—then picked up the telephone and asked to be connected with the American vice president's press office.

"I wonder if I might speak to Judy . . . it's Carter Perkins, she should be expecting my call."

After a bit Judy came on the line.

"Judy, I was told to speak with you in order to set up a little chat with your vice president." Carter listened for a second. Continued, "Well, I spoke with him last night, and he assured me he would have some free time tomorrow."

Judy was playing dumb. Carter knew it.

"You do expect him to still be around tomorrow, don't you?"

A thin smile formed on Carter's lips.

"He told me you were most efficient. 'His favorite,' I believe were his exact words."

It worked.

"Yes, eleven-fifteen will be just fine . . . And that would be in his room on the top floor, I expect? . . . Oh? . . . Well, the lounge it is, then. Thank you. I look forward to meeting you tomorrow as well . . . Yes, thank you, my dear . . . Good-bye."

Carter hung up the telephone and poured some more tea. Then passed a very wet tongue over the tip of a slender Venetian roll . . .

> . . . cloy the hungry edge of appetite
> By bare imagination of a feast?

Four

Louis wasn't a complainer. At least not today. Anyway, what else was he going to do on Christmas? Who knows? It could be fun. He'd never been to Torcello. According to Joe, it was supposed to be a decent place. But then again, Joe liked some pretty strange places.

He had once dragged Louis out to the wire fence that separated Hong Kong from the communists. On the Hong Kong side of the fence cats had been chasing rats, and the dogs the cats. They'd kicked up so much of the dusty street, Louis could barely see his shoes. How they'd kept from getting run over by the cars and trucks was anybody's guess.

On the other side of the wire fence there had been hills covered with deep forests. The contrast between the different shades of green had been unbelievable. Louis and Joe had stood in silence for fifteen minutes. Finally Joe spoke.

"I could live here," he'd said. Then turned and walked away.

Louis never did find out which side of the fence Joe had been talking about. No matter. Neither side appealed to Louis. Too many Chinese no matter how you sliced it.

At any rate, Torcello had to be better than the wire fence trip. That's what Louis was thinking when he walked in on Olsen and Reynolds in the operations room. Reynolds was just finishing up yet another classic Reynolds tale of conquest:

"... Man, I'm telling you, my dick was harder than Chinese arithmetic ... Hey, Louis. What's up?"

"Not much ... Actually, I was just thinking about China."

"What?"

Reynolds had used the old Chinese arithmetic line so many times, he'd now forgotten that there could possibly be any connection between it and a country somewhere.

"Six months ago? Remember? China ... ? The country? Not plates. Hong Kong ... ?"

"Right. Man, there was some good lookers in Hong Kong. Hey, Olsen, did you ever get to that place? You know, the one I told you to check out, Momma Lo's, up by the—"

"No . . . So, you all squared away on Torcello, Louis?" Olsen said, getting back to business. And not wishing to be reminded of the excursion to Hong Kong. Or Momma Lo's, the place Reynolds had recommended so highly.

"I guess so. Who all's going?" Louis said.

"Just you and The Wife."

"What . . . ? Just me? What's everybody else up to?"

"Louis, we're shorthanded here. Lightfoot still isn't over that liver crap, and Bradlee escaped. Hall 'n' Oates and I are going to be with Goliath and Little Audrey all day. Anyway, it's a one-man job," Olsen said.

Reynolds threw in, "Count your blessings, pard. I'm stuck in this fucking room for the goddamn duration."

"You'll be using Vittorio's launch. It's Malvasi launch number four. Vittorio's a good man for an Italian. He speaks pretty good English."

"Yeah, well, so do I ... For an Italian, that is," Louis said.

"You know what I mean. Jesus, Louis ... Anyway, we've loaded the boat up with some goodies, but I want you to carry one of the Uzis in your overcoat. Like it or not."

"Can't. I left my overcoat back at the Saint Marks office."

"You're going to freeze your fucking ass off, bucko. Torcello's close to an hour on the water."

Reynolds tossed this in without much sympathy and followed it with a diabolical chuckle.

"He's right . . . Well, you're not going anywhere, Reynolds, so let him use yours," Olsen said and went back to his desk and papers.

Reynolds and Louis looked at each other and shrugged.

Reynolds then got up and walked over to Louis. He stood an inch away from him and called over to Olsen. He spoke as if he were teaching a class of first-graders.

"Excuse me . . . Jerome? If we could have your attention for just one minute here? I think we might be able to clear something up."

Olsen turned in his chair. Louis was five inches taller than Reynolds and probably outweighed him by sixty-five pounds.

"Thank you, Jerome. Now, what's wrong with this picture? Which one of these men is bigger? Is it Agent Zezzo . . . ?"

He pointed at Louis.

"Or is it Agent Reynolds . . . ? Anybody . . . ? That's right, Jerome It's Agent Zezzo. Now, who here thinks that Agent Zezzo could fit into Agent Reynolds' overcoat? Nobody . . . ? And you're probably right, class, but let's just say, for the fun of it, that Agent Zezzo, after a lot of work, was able to squeeze his beefy butt into Agent Reynolds' overcoat. Okay? I mean, just for the fun of it. Bear with me here, will you?"

Reynolds pulled an Uzi out from behind his back.

"Now, kids, where the fuck would he hide this big fucking gun? In his fucking Jockey shorts?"

"Thank you, Reynolds. Once again you've been more than helpful," Olsen said. "Looks like you're going to freeze, Louis."

"Here, you can use my prayer shawl."

Reynolds threw a red, green, and white scarf to Louis. When stretched out full length, the scarf read, BUON NATALE.

"Thanks."

"Oh, by the way, Reynolds"—Olsen gave the word Reynolds a particularly strong emphasis—"when Chester Mock gets here, he's going to be bunking in with you."

"Get the fuck out of here."

"You're the one who called C.O. and told them we had to have him here."

"Get the fuck out of here. He's a bigger fucking racist than all you fucking Mormons put together."

"He's black, for Christ's sakes."

"That doesn't mean shit. Just because he's *black*, that doesn't mean he has to like *black* people. Have you ever seen his wife? Lady Godiva? She makes Nancy Reagan look like Aunt fucking Jemima."

"Sorry, Reynolds. He stays with you. No more rooms."

"I don't believe that shit for a second. The bastard can sleep in here. He won't want to be too far from his precious hot line to D.C., anyway."

"I'll feel him out when he gets here."

"Pray tell me, when that will be?"

"He'll be in by six."

"F-14 or commercial?" Louis asked.

Louis was always curious as to what mode of transportation the top men in the Grid opted for in an emergency. And Mock was one of the top men. And definitely under the impression there was an emergency at hand.

Mock had three choices. He could take the next available commercial flight to Venice, but there were no direct flights from Washington, and that really wasn't Mock's style. Another option would be for him to go scramble up an air force F-14.

"Never marine or navy. Can't trust those bastards," Mock was known to say. "Who knows where the fuck you'll end up?"

But the problem with that was, the jets really

weren't all that comfortable. They had no johns. And more important—no scotch.

His third option would be to beat it out to Dulles airport. Have one of the commercial carriers fuel up a 737 or 757 and scare up a crew. Mock carried a government checkbook at all times. Just in case things like this came up. In the long run it was actually cheaper on the taxpayers than the F-14 route. Louis often had fantasies about when he would reach grade thirteen and get one of those magic checkbooks.

"Commercial," Olsen answered. "You know, Reynolds, that's something you didn't think about when you called the fucker over here. Not only did you fuck up his Christmas, you fucked up ours. And also some poor Delta Airlines saps who most likely would have been very happy to stay put in Virginia."

"Bullshit. They were probably looking for something to get them the fuck out of the house. It's either that or put together their goddamn kid's new bicycle—"

Before Reynolds had completed his sentence, the door to the operations room had been opened.

Hall 'n' Oates entered as though they were expecting snipers to be hiding out behind the paintings. It could mean only one thing. And sure enough, The Panhandler was right behind them. Along with him, the Vice President had Little Audrey, George Strutz, and Judy from the press office. The three agents stood when he entered.

"Good morning, gentlemen. Feel like a little sightseeing?"

"Good morning, sir. Absolutely."

Olsen answered. Louis and Reynolds only nodded. Slightly.

"I think George explained what my wife has planned."

"Yes, sir. I have it all taken care of."

"Thank you, Jerry. But before we get started, Little Audrey has a Christmas gift for you, Louis. And we all can't wait to see what it is." Goliath looked at his daughter. "Honey?"

Little Audrey shyly stepped forward. She had her new doll Queenie tucked under her arm. In her hand she held Louis' gift.

The gift had been wrapped in a crumpled piece of the same paper Santa had wrapped Queenie in. It was about the size of a small lemon. All eyes were upon her. It was obvious to everyone that there was a big-time crush going on here.

She marched slowly up to Louis and said, "Here."

"Thank you very much. That's a beautiful doll. Did Santa give it to you?"

"Yes. Her name is Queenie. Open your present."

Behind The Panhandler's back, Reynolds twisted an eyebrow to Olsen and mouthed the word "Queenie?"

Louis carefully unwrapped his gift. Inside the paper were two similar-sized objects. Both covered in silver and blue Perugina candy wrappers.

"That paper is made of real silver," she said proudly.

"No kidding?"

Louis, careful not to tear the candy wrappers, eased them off and laid them flat on the desk. He held his gifts out on the palm of his hand for everyone to see.

"They're very pretty."

"They're solid gold," she said with even more pride.

Reynolds resisted the temptation to say, "What the fuck are they?" and instead said, "They're really quite handsome, Louis."

"Yes, they are. Thank you very much, Audrey."

When Louis said this, omitting the *Little*, the Vice President straightened up and shot Louis a look that was intended to kill. Nobody called his *Little* girl anything but *Little* Audrey. It was not intended for *Little* Audrey to grow any older. The Vice President would have to have Strutz speak to Louis.

The look was completely missed by Louis. He continued with the girl.

"I'm sorry I don't have anything for you, but I tell you what. When I'm out on Torcello today, I'll look for a seashell for you. How's that?"

"Okay," she said and ran back to her father giggling.

"I wasn't aware that Zezzo here would be taking my wife to Torcello."

"Well, if you'd rather Reynolds, sir, it's easy enough to switch." Olsen knew exactly what he was doing when he said this to the Vice President. "Put Goliath on the carpet," he thought. "Let him call a spade a spade. If he has it in him."

"Well . . . no . . . I mean . . . well, I thought Agent Bradlee would be going, that's all."

Strutz now piped in as if awakened from a deep sleep.

"No, sir, I explained all that to you. You see—"

"Yes. Thank you, George. So you did . . . Well, why don't we leave it as it stands? No point in confusing the issue."

The Vice President took in a deep breath. He looked around the room hoping for an ally. A friend. Even George Strutz seemed to have deserted him. Finally he made eye contact with Judy from the press office. As ever, she was feeling sorry for this poor misunderstood man. He was back on track in an instant.

"Well, what do you say, boys and girls? Shall we be off? There's a beautiful city out there just waiting for us."

"Yes, sir," Olsen said as he slipped into his overcoat.

Hall 'n' Oates led the way out, followed by Judy, George Strutz, Little Audrey, the Vice President, and finally, Olsen. Olsen turned and gave Reynolds and Louis an exaggerated thumbs-up signal. Then closed the door behind himself.

"Onward, Christian soldiers, marching off to war . . ."

Reynolds sang this loud enough to be heard by everyone in the hallway. Out of politeness it was universally ignored.

"Well, Louis, old man, this is how I like it. Not a damn thing to do but answer the phone."

Louis looked at his watch. Eleven-thirty.

"I guess I don't have time to get something to eat," he said.

"Relax, they're putting some lunch on the boat. I assume they'll be enough for two. You want me to check with the kitchen?"

"Nah, that's okay."

"Say, what the fuck were those gold things Little Audrey gave you?"

"Knobs."

"What?"

"TV knobs. She must have lifted them from the set in the Mercedes. The one that brought them in from the airport."

"Fuck me."

Five

Joe was waiting patiently at the Zitelle *vaporetto* stop when the Malvasi motor launch carrying Number Two and his troupe sped through the channel that separated San Giorgio Maggiore from the Hotel Malvasi grounds. The boat had been overly loaded with superfluous personnel and was riding somewhat low in the water. And when it broke through into the Giudecca canal, the tide turned against it. Joe could hear the engine struggle and groan as the boat cracked each new swell.

But these launches were more seaworthy than Noah's ark, and the men who piloted them were masters. Joe had no concern for the safety of the boat's cargo. Pietro was at the helm. He was the best. But it wouldn't be a fun ride for anyone. Anyone but Pietro, that is. Already Strutz was hanging over the port side. Passing his breakfast onto the octopi. This had to be bringing a bit of joy to the helmsman. A man forced to work on Christmas Day.

Of course, the reality was, they were all working on Christmas Day. For Number Two it was an eight-year job, not counting the campaign. And every day was twenty-four hours long. He might be touring San Marco with his daughter, behaving as though he had a day off, but he knew better. He'd be recognized. He was an ambassador of the United States of America.

He was working. Strutz was working. Hall 'n' Oates were working. Olsen was working. Judy was working. Except for Little Audrey, all the other useless people on the motor launch—were working.

And Joe was working. It was hopeless. Every eye contact, every sound, every smell, every sight, was still being analyzed by his brain like a cornucopia of unwanted computer drivel. He couldn't turn it off. He watched as the number eight *vaporetto* pulled into the dock. He tried to force himself to think of his dinner plans. His meeting with Eubie's mom. But he found himself counting the passengers on the boat. Thirteen. Analyzing them for any potential danger. Any neuroses they might carry with them. Dissecting their personalities with only the information their faces were willing to give up. He jumped onto the boat. The only normal people appeared to be the helmsman and the first mate.

Joe took a seat. Alone and in the back. He rationalized this not as paranoia, but as a more comfortable place to sit. Which of course was bullshit. He knew it. From the stern he'd be able keep an eye on everyone.

The stern, open to the air and the sun's warming effect, eventually began to lull him into a better sense of security, and finally he stopped training an eye on everyone. His thoughts drifted. Although he loved this city, he was finding it difficult to imagine what he would do to occupy his time until his six p.m. dinner date. He watched the city pass. Hoping for inspiration.

The boat pulled in and out of the dock on San Giorgio Maggiore and came to rest at the Zaccaria. Joe switched to the number one *vaporetto* and headed down the Grand Canal. The number one stopped at San Marco. Salute. Santa Maria del Giglio. Then pushed on to the Accademia bridge.

Joe was half nodding off in the sun. He found himself wondering if he was going to spend the first half of his Christmas riding up and down the Grand Canal. If so, it was going to be a long six hours.

Then, out of the blue, he heard his name called from the bridge above him. It was the boy. Eubie.

Waving frantically. His mother was by his side. Also waving but not quite so frantically. Her smile was as warm as the sun. And the sun's rays seemed to be illuminating only these two. At first Joe thought they were a mirage as they hung over the railing and peered down at him. The *vaporetto* began to pass under the bridge. A second before they disappeared from view, Joe raised his arm and waved. He called out to them:

"Wait for me. Stay right there."

The *vaporetto* glided under the bridge and came to rest at the dock thirty feet beyond. Joe was the first one off the boat. Turning his back on all the potential psychopaths who chose to remain on board. He trotted off to his left. Up onto the Ponte dell'Accademia. Eubie ran to meet him.

"See, Mom, I told you it was him. You need new glasses."

Joe greeted Eubie and they walked back to his mother together. The sunlight made her radiant. A slight breeze had kicked up and had blown her brown-gold hair across her face. She struggled to keep it in place. She still wore dark glasses. Joe found he was a bit disappointed. Unable to see her brown eyes. Her eyes were what he'd remembered most from their meeting in the church. He found he'd missed them already. They were magnetic. It wasn't a beauty in the Madison Avenue sense. It was truth and honesty. So much so that she stood out in this crowd.

"Merry Christmas," she said as Joe approached.

"And a Merry Christmas to you too."

"I wasn't expecting to see you until later."

"First things first. My government says I can't talk to you anymore unless you tell me your name."

She smiled.

"Your government?"

"Well, it's your government too. If you want to get picky."

"It's Nina."

"You're kidding."

"No. Why?"

"When I was twelve years old I had a dog named Nina."

"Thanks."

"I loved that dog. She went with me everywhere. Well, almost everywhere. She died eight days before I got back from Vietnam."

Joe looked up at the sky. He couldn't believe this shit was coming out of his mouth.

"Well, there's a nice bright note to get things started on. Do you have a last name?" he asked.

"Yes."

"Would this be some information you might like to share with me?"

"I don't know. What was your dog's last name?"

"Same as mine. Bradlee."

"Hey, Joe, let me see your gun."

Eubie was getting bored. Joe opened his jacket, exposing his shirt. No gun.

He turned, lifted his coat, and said, "Nothing behind my back. Nothing up my sleeves."

"Wallace."

"Pardon me?"

"Wallace. That's our last name."

"Nina Wallace. Any relation to George?"

"It's not my maiden name."

"Yes, well, I was going to ask you about *Mr. Wallace*, but I thought I'd save it for later."

"That's okay."

By this point Eubie had deemed the conversation intolerably monotonous. He moved off to watch two teenagers playing with the same type of bouncing disc Little Audrey had found in her stocking that morning. These discs seemed to be very popular in Venice this Christmas. With Eubie out of earshot, his mother continued.

"Mrs. Wallace divorced Mr. Wallace three years ago. He liked to put the money he earned up his nose. It didn't seem like a sound investment to me. He now lives in Los Angeles, but we haven't heard from him since the divorce. He produces a television sitcom and lives with the show's star. Someone named Jodi Alsop.

I don't watch television, so I couldn't tell you if Jodi is a man or a woman."

"She's a woman."

"Well, good for him."

"She's not very good-looking. Well, a bimbo, sure, blond, big breasts and all . . . She likes to show them off. For some reason her breasts make the studio audience laugh uncontrollably. But she's not my type. . . . The shows not that funny."

"You watch the show?" A fair amount of disbelief rang in Nina's voice.

"Olsen loves it. He's one of the agents. He never misses it."

"You could leave the room."

"Generally I do. What's your maiden name? Sounds like you should go back."

"Lake."

"It's something to think about. Going back, I mean. I like Nina Lake better. . . if it matters."

"Thanks. Maybe I will."

"Lake."

She removed dark glasses and smiled at him. He smiled back.

"Listen, this may not sound like much fun, since it happens to be December, but if you two don't have any plans, how'd you like to go out to the Lido? You'd be surprised what a beach in winter has to offer. It's magical sometimes."

Before she put her glasses back on, she said, "I'll bet it is."

She then called to her son.

"Eubie, come on. We're going to the beach."

Six

The beach and the Lido were the furthest thing from Louis' mind when he tapped on The Wife's door exactly at twelve noon. He had no idea where this was going to lead, but he knew it would be an experience, to say the least. There was no response to his first knock. He considered turning away and telling Reynolds he thought she'd changed her mind, but he knew it wouldn't wash. Louis knocked once more and the door opened.

"Louis, what a pleasant surprise."

"Yes, ma'am. Whenever you're ready, I'll be right here."

"Don't be ridiculous. I'll only be a minute. Come on in. Nobody's here."

He did. He went in. He closed the door. The room looked different in the daylight. It had a stupendous view that stretched across the lagoon. The sun lit up the sea and flooded back in through the windows, giving everything in the room an extraordinary contrast. Christmas wrapping paper littered the floor. The bed hadn't been made.

"I like to leave the papers on the floor all day long. I love Christmas. I love giving gifts. It makes me happy," she called from the bathroom.

Louis stood in one spot. In a minute she came out.

She selected a navy blue camel hair overcoat from the closet, and Louis helped her slip it on over her suit.

"Thank you . . . I'm sorry about the bed. I should have let someone come in to make it, I know, but I didn't want the company."

Louis was seeing her differently now. It was a side of her he was completely unaware of. It was the side she kept behind the doors.

"I didn't make my bed either," he said, and they laughed.

She walked over and pressed herself against him. He put his arms around her, and they kissed for a long time.

"I'm looking forward to this trip," she said. "I'm looking forward to getting away from all of them." They kissed again. "Shall we go?"

They walked out into the hallway looking very official. When they got to the lobby, Nelo greeted them. A boy held the door open. Nelo found it necessary to place his hands on his papers to keep the blast of cold air from sending reservation slips flying into the dining room. The Wife stopped. She grabbed Louis' arm.

"You're not going out to Torcello without a coat, are you?"

"Yes, ma'am."

"No, you're not."

"I left mine at our office on the other side. It's okay. I'll be warm enough."

"You will not."

"It's not a problem, honestly."

"Well, wear someone else's."

"It's really okay. Besides, everyone my size is out. It's okay."

"It's not okay. I won't have it. What size are you?"

The boy had been holding the door open throughout all of this. Nelo was slowly losing control of his papers. But not once did he show any irritation toward the Americans. Nelo was a prince.

"Forty-six regular."

"You can wear one of my husband's. He has too many, anyway. You have the key to his room, right?"

"Reynolds does."

"Good."

She pulled Louis back to the elevator. The boy closed the door. Nelo put his papers back in order.

Upstairs, Louis picked up the key from Reynolds.

The couple now found themselves standing inside the Vice President's closet.

"Christ, can you believe the clod brought three overcoats?"

"Four," Louis said.

"Four?"

"He's wearing one."

"You're right. Four. Here, take this one. He wore it yesterday. He won't miss it for two more days."

Seven

Long before the Vice President had left for San Marco, Carter Perkins had grown very comfortable upstairs at the small table near the French doors. And had remained there all morning. Carter had sipped tea and chewed Venetian rolls and watched as the American Secret Service agents loaded what was obviously extra armament onto Vittorio's motor launch. Malvasi launch number four. The helmsman had kept a close eye on the Americans. He'd wanted nothing to mar his highly polished mahogany or cut his leather seats.

Because it was Christmas, the management of the Malvasi had put only two launches into service. Three additional boats sat covered in their slips. The other boat on duty, captained by Pietro, rocked back and forth with the waves. Uninterested in the goings-on in the next berth.

Pietro had been sitting on the bow of his boat for as long as Carter had been looking out the window. He'd been watching the commotion on Vittorio's launch. And he'd tossed in *helpful* comments whenever he could. Each of these comments had been followed up with one of Pietro's caustic laughs. And then followed by an obscene hand gesture from Vittorio. Carter had felt as though this was becoming an evening at the theater. The animation had been absolutely divine.

After Vittorio's boat had been loaded, the agents returned to the hotel, and Vittorio and Pietro walked off for a smoke. It was at that point that Carter had decided there would be enough time for a quick shower. Not much would be happening. Not for a while.

The shower had warmed the body. And Carter soaked for a long time—too long—and stepped out feeling like a new person, refreshed and ready to go to work. Anxious to go to work. After toweling off, Carter strolled back over toward the window, stopped once along the way to admire the nude physique reflected in the room's full-length mirror, then covered up in a plush Malvasi robe and moved on to the French doors to recheck the situation at the boat landing.

Carter's heart nearly stopped cold when it became clear that there was now only one Malvasi launch remaining. And an eruption of panic in the brain made it difficult to focus on which of the two boats had departed. Carter flung the doors open and bent out over the railing for a better view.

The robe fell open to the waist, and from below Carter heard Vittorio shout, "*Buon giorno, Signore Perkins.* You should be careful not to catch a chill. You must have a big hairy chest like mine for this weather."

Vittorio smiled broadly, then ambled back to his boat and lit a cigarette.

Carter closed the French doors. It was embarrassing to have been seen in a half-opened robe at the window. Chest almost fully exposed. But Carter was much relieved to know that it was Pietro's boat that had departed and not the one with the guns. Not Vittorio's. Not launch number four. The window would not again be left for more than a second.

Carter darted to the closet and quickly selected clothing for the day. Pink shirt. Gray tweed suit. Blue-black tie. Dark gray overcoat with black velvet lapels. The overcoat had a long pocket stitched into the left side. This pocket was designed to neatly accommodate the Luftwaffe dagger.

Carter stacked the clothing on a chair by the French doors and glanced outside once more. Vittorio was still sitting alongside his launch smoking his cigarette. Carter then scurried over to the dresser and selected hose and underclothing and darted back to the chair. No problems. Carter slowed the pace and began to dress.

After fussing with necktie and hair in the mirror, Carter placed the Beretta, the silencer, two clips of ammunition, and the dagger on the small table. Carter was pleased. They had served well. Today would be their day of retirement. After just this one more job, they would be in their final resting spot at the bottom of Laguna Venezia.

Carter slipped the dagger into its custom-fitted pocket inside the overcoat and placed the silencer in the right side pocket. Then looked down at the two clips of ammunition. Each were loaded with five rounds. The clips could accommodate seven, but Carter had always felt that putting too many rounds in a clip wore the springs out. This probably wasn't true, but five was a very nice number. What's more, no more than three bullets had ever been used on any one function in the past.

Once again the assassin slid an ammunition clip into the pistol and chambered a round. It was a motion Carter was particularly fond of. Slowly the hammer was released. The safety put on. Then the gun was placed in an alligator holster that had been attached to a lizard belt and then positioned at the small of Carter's back. Everything was ready. Carter went back to the window.

At noon, a couple walked out of the hotel. They headed across the lawn to the motor launch. They had their backs to the hotel, but Carter guessed they were Japanese from the way the sun highlighted their coal black hair. Vittorio tossed his cigarette into the water. He stood to greet them. After a short exchange they were sent back into the hotel. Undoubtedly to call for a taxi. This boat was taken.

Five minutes later, a water taxi arrived. The couple came back out and were whisked off to see the sights of Venice. Carter waited. Vittorio smoked another cigarette. Nothing happened for ten minutes. Vittorio lit a second cigarette from the first.

At twelve-fifteen, another couple emerged from the hotel. They followed, almost to the letter, the same path the first couple had taken. Carter's initial reaction was to discount them as well, but when The Wife turned back to see what two angry starlings had been squabbling about, Carter recognized her immediately. The Vice President was wearing the same overcoat he'd had on the day before, and she was clutching his arm as though she were afraid of falling into the lagoon. It was obvious the couple had long since forgotten whatever it was that had made them treat each other so coolly the night before.

"Where in God's name are all the aides? Press people? More important—Secret Service agents?"

The question flew around and around in Carter's brain like a rabid bat. A yellow jacket. Carter could barely see straight. On the one hand, there was elation at seeing that the Secret Service wasn't going with the couple. On the other hand, there was complete and utter panic. Why couldn't any bloody agents be seen? Were they in the bushes? Under the dock? Already in the boat? It felt as though there was a tornado thrashing about within Carter's skull. The adrenaline shot created from this sight—these babes strolling in the open, so virginal, so unprotected—had made Carter's body go completely orgasmic. Vision blurred. All control seemed lost.

Carter watched in a trance, as the Vice President spoke a few words to Vittorio, patted the helmsman on the back, and then helped his wife onto the launch. The man never once looked back, and the couple disappeared into the cabin.

Carter stood mesmerized as Vittorio cast his lines to the dock and eased his boat out into the lagoon.

Once in open water, the helmsman increased power. The exhaust billowed above the white wake. The stern of the launch dipped low and the bow lifted. They were off. The American white knight and his bride. Off to spend Christmas day on Torcello. Alone. It was the *alone* that now worried Carter the most.

As the boat disappeared around to the left, Carter's head began to clear. It had all happened much too quickly. If only Carter had been paying closer attention. Waited until a little later to take the shower. Or not taken such a long one. The first boat. Pietro's boat. Who had left on that boat? Only some tourists? Or had it been a group of advance men? Advance Secret Service agents? Sent out to Torcello to check things out? To set up a defense? Would they be lying in the weeds? Waiting? Carter had to know where these men were. Where they had gone. It would be a gamble. Carter reached out. Picked up the telephone. Waited.

"Yes, would you be kind enough to connect me with Mr. Bradlee's room? . . . He's one of the Americans. . . Thank you."

Carter let the phone ring until the operator came back on the line. "I see. Well, maybe you could try their security room?"

Reynolds answered the telephone.

And Carter said, "Yes, I'd like to speak to Mr. Bradlee. . . . Carter Perkins . . . I see . . . And he isn't expected back until tomorrow, then? How about Judy? . . . I see . . . No, I don't think you can help me. I'll call again tomorrow. . . . Thank you."

Carter hung up the telephone. Reynolds' smart-alec replies had been, "Hey, Mr. Perkins, some agents can get Christmas off," and "Judy's gone off to see the sights of San Marco. Lucky girl."

Carter was relieved. It was doubtful that there would be no agents on Torcello, but at least they wouldn't all be there. A good portion of them obviously had a day off. The one that had been the most suspicious of Carter, the agent Bradlee, was most definitely out of the way.

Carter donned the overcoat, tapped the side with the dagger, and headed out the door.

Once in the lobby, Carter approached the front desk and greeted Nelo warmly.

"*Buon giorno, Nelo. Buon Natale.*"

Nelo looked up from his papers.

"Signore Perkins. Good afternoon. How can I help you today?"

"I see your motor launches are occupied. Would you be kind enough to call for a water taxi for me?"

"But of course. Where will you be off to today, signore? The taxi drivers insist on knowing before they come out to our island. What can we do?" He shrugged politely.

"Nelo, they are the same all over the world. I'm only going to the Dorsoduro. I have some friends there."

"It should not take more than five minutes to have a boat here for you. I apologize for the inconvenience."

"That's quite all right, Nelo. God only knows, I'm becoming a very patient soul."

Eight

A crisp December morning in northern Michigan can sometimes make a person feel closer to God than anything in the world. However, of the three men now reassembled around the poker table seventeen miles northwest of Long Rapids, only the baby, Art, was vaguely aware that there might be any God at all. Which was strange in itself—Art had not slept a wink in the past twenty-four hours. Grant and Phil had slept soundly—despite the numerous interruptions.

It was Art who had insisted on ruining everyone's Christmas by forcing this second unscheduled meeting in two days. He had called the others no less than ten times throughout Christmas Eve, and Grant and Phil had become significantly annoyed—and eventually even more significantly concerned that Art might say something unfortunate over a phone line that had little or no guarantee of being secure.

Phil's El Dorado was now up to its hubcaps in a mixture of ice, snow, slush, and mud due to an evening of freezing rain and softening earth. And if the cold snap the weathermen had predicted came through on time, the car would remain frozen like a fucking lawn jockey by the cabin's front door until Easter—front-wheel drive or no. Art and Grant had arrived later, surmised Phil's dilemma, and parked their Caddies on higher ground.

Inside, Buck, the ancient retriever, was cowering in the far corner of the cabin. He hated loud voices. He hated swear words.

"Goddamn it, Art, if I can't get that fucking car out of that fucking mud, I'm going to make you pull the motherfucker out with your goddamn motherfucking teeth. I swear to fucking Christ."

"Take it easy, Phil. We'll get it out. Right now we have something more important to deal with." Grant was the glue that held this troop together. "Now, Art, we can talk here. It's safe. Take a nice deep breath, and tell us what the problem is."

Art did not take his allotted deep breath. "It's too soon. It's just too damn soon." His hands were shaking uncontrollably. "If we hit the Vice President now, they'll close in around the President like a pack of wolves. It's too early. We have to wait, damn it. We have to get the President first. Don't you see?"

"Jesus fuck, Art. First of all, it's probably too fucking late to call it off, and second of all, it's probably already over and done with. You can be such a fucking pussy sometimes. I can't fucking believe you," Phil said—without much compassion for Art's condition.

"It's not over. It's not done. I would have heard about it on the radio on the way out here if it was. Damn it, Phil, it's too much of a spread. We have to wait. If the Vice President turns up dead in Venice, the Secret Service, the FBI, the CIA, the DEA, and probably the damn FDA, all of them, they'll build a cage around the President that no one gets through. Not even his mother. It's too damn early, Phil."

"Why didn't you bring this up last night if you had all these goddamn reservations . . . ? Christ, stop shaking, will you? You're starting to make me nervous. Have a goddamn drink. Fuck."

"All right, all right. Let's work this all out," Grant interjected. "Art, why don't you take Phil's advice. Pour yourself a drink."

Art found the Black Label and filled a highball glass nearly to the top. "Anybody else . . . ? Phil?"

"Yeah, shit, pour me one. But not so much. And try not to spill it, for Christ's sake."

"How about you, Grant?"

"I'll pass," he said and looked up at the rafters. Then added, "Consider this, Art: If we knock the President off first, the V.P. becomes president. We're then left with trying to get through the much tighter presidential web a second time. And it will be tighter than ever, you know that. Remember how they closed in around Johnson? And that was well over thirty years ago. No, the more I think about it, the more this order makes sense. Two goes before One."

Art absorbed it. Returned to the table with the scotch and proceeded to topple his glass over and dump the entire contents out onto the green felt.

"Jesus fucking Christ."

"That's okay, Art. Just relax. Get yourself another one. Don't fill it so full this time."

Art moved off and Grant scrawled a quick note. Passed it to Phil. It read: "Time to move on. No more Art."

Art returned with his new drink and sat. He was now crying.

"Okay, Art . . . ?" Grant continued, "Get a hold of yourself . . . Calm down . . . Listen." He took a deep breath and pushed it back out through slightly flared nostrils. "Maybe you're right about this. Maybe it's too soon. I'll make contact with Perkins. We'll put all of this off until January. We'll work on getting the President first. How does that sound to you?"

"What . . . ? Are you fucking nuts?" Phil's vocal level made Buck leap to his feet, pace twice in a counterclockwise circle, and then press his mammoth head deeper into the corner.

Grant held his left hand up to Phil. The gesture said, "Wait, I have this under control." He then turned his attention back to Art.

"Now, Art, I hope you didn't keep your wife up to all hours with these constant phone calls?"

"No, she went to bed early," Art managed through his sobs. "I used the phone in my den."

"Well, good. I like Frances. She's a nice lady. I hate to see her overly concerned about anything. You did tell her you were coming to meet with us, though, didn't you?"

"No. I don't think she knows I left."

"Well, she must know by now. Won't she be worried about you? I mean, it's Christmas morning, after all."

"No, no, it's okay. She'll figure I went over to my sister's to exchange gifts."

"That's good. I feel a lot better about that. . . . Actually, speaking of gifts, Art, I have a little something for you."

Grant turned his back to Art and lifted his canvas jacket from the chair to his left. He rummaged through the side pocket for a second, then dropped the jacket onto the floor. In his right hand he held a semi-automatic pistol. He quickly chambered a round with his left hand, brought the weapon around to meet Art's forehead, and sent a .32-caliber bullet straight through his brain and out the back side of his skull. The twisted piece of lead continued across the room and lodged into the far wall two inches above Buck's tail.

"Jesus, fuck, fuck, fuck, Grant, Jesus fuck." Phil jumped to his feet and looked down at Art's lifeless body. "Jesus, Grant, Jesus Christ. Why the fuck did you do that? Jesus, you dumb bastard. We needed him. Christ, he's our friend, for God's sake. Are you nuts? You can't just do that to a friend. What's wrong with you? Jesus fucking Christ."

"He had become a liability. He couldn't be trusted anymore. It was time to move forward. Not backward . . . Take it easy, Phil."

"Take it easy? Christ. Look at him. Jesus, Grant . . . Listen, okay . . . okay . . . That's it. Okay . . . ? This is too much. Aw, God, What are we going to do with him? Christ, I've gotta think. We've got to slow this shit down. This is getting out of hand."

"Relax, we'll make it look like a suicide."

"A suicide? You're fucking crazy. That's my fucking

car that's stuck in the mud out there, just in case you've forgotten. We've gotta do something. We've got to slow the fuck down. Art's right. We've got to call this hit off. Regroup. Get back on track in January. He's right . . . It's too damn early. Christ almighty, I need a drink."

"We're not calling it off, Phil. Nothing gets called off. Nothing. Everything continues as planned. We nail this bastard while we can. We have plenty of time to set something up for the President. Nothing changes. Art or no Art."

"Aw, God, look at poor Arty. Jesus."

Phil stumbled over to the Black Label bottle and filled his glass nearly to the top. His hands were shaking violently, and the liquid slopped out over his fingers. He threw the scotch down his throat and refilled the tumbler. The bottle then slipped from his hand and smashed on the floor.

"God, look at him." Phil began to cry softly. "This has all gotten out of hand. Jesus, God, Grant, what are we going to do? How are we going to cover this up? . . . What about Art's dog?"

After a moment Grant said, "Oh, I think things will work out just fine. Suicide's the way to go with this. Stop shaking. Take a nice deep breath and calm down. There's absolutely nothing to worry about. . . . By the way, by any chance did you tell your wife you'd be with me today?"

"Christ, no. Why would I do that?"

"Just curious . . . So, that settles that. Suicide. It's so simple. We move forward." As Grant said this, he brought the pistol up to meet Phil's right-side temple.

Nine

"I thought you smoked," Louis said as the powerful launch banked to the left and began its hour-long trek to Torcello.

"Well, sometimes I do, and sometimes I don't."

The Vice President's wife had placed herself alongside Louis. She had pressed her body tightly against his from ankle to shoulder. Her arm was once again entwined with his. He was relaxed. So was she. He had grown to like this woman. He knew nothing could come of a relationship. And she knew it too. They had both understood that back at the Malvasi. There was no need for either of them to talk about it. No need to make believe things were different than they were. They both knew the position the other was in. They were simply two lonely people with not a soul to talk to on Christmas Day. Why not be together?

"Well, you shouldn't do it."

"Do what?"

"Smoke."

"Thanks."

She meant it.

"For what?"

"For giving a shit whether I smoke or not. I'm not sure anyone else does."

The launch sped across the wide channel. It crossed directly over the route Joe's taxi boat had taken only ten minutes earlier. On its way to the Lido. A little sooner and the wakes of the two boats would have made a perfect X in the water. Vittorio guided his launch down the narrow Rio del Arsenale. Past the huge decaying naval arsenal. In no time they were out into the open spaces of the lagoon. Full throttle to Torcello. Louis and the Vice President's wife yakked like children the entire way.

They passed to the south of Cimitero San Michele. The tiny island would be somewhat of a final resting place for many Venetians. Burial spaces were limited. After twelve years the not-so-famous would be reinterred communally. Those who had made a name for themselves stood a better chance of hanging on to their place in the sun a little longer. Vittorio pushed on.

"That's Murano, right?" The Wife asked.

"Right."

"It's where they blow glass, right?"

"Right."

She knew what she was doing. Her look made Louis blush. But he smiled.

"I'm happy it worked out this way."

"Yeah, me too."

They didn't know how far they could go with Vittorio looking on. They would glance back at him more times than they needed to.

But Vittorio had seen it all before. More times than he could count. With more important people than these two. What they were *up to* had been more than obvious from the moment they came out of the hotel. Discretion was part of his job. The hotel would have dismissed him in a second if he was known to possess a loose tongue.

That's not to say Vittorio held on to what he knew. He was one of Inspector Solfanelli's men. Not a stoolie. Not a snitch. But a member of the Forza Pubblica. Vittorio was a cop.

It was an ideal place for Solfanelli to have one of his men. No self-respecting drug dealer, money launderer, or politician would consider staying anywhere but a five-star hotel. Vittorio was there to eavesdrop. He spoke eight languages fluently. He was an expert marksman. And, like Agent Reynolds, a master of the slight-of-hand and magic tricks. The last being the skill he was most often called upon to use. And then usually to entertain children on the hotel dock while their parents asked, in pidgin English, "Can-you-take-us-to-Saint-Marks?"

Still, after all the years, after all the times he'd ferried Carter Perkins to this place or that, neither Vittorio nor Inspector Solfanelli had ever picked up on anything unusual. Other than the apparent *omosessuale* businesses. And Vittorio had set Carter straight on that shit from day one.

As Vittorio guided his boat past Murano, he glanced again into the cabin and his cargo. He chuckled to himself. No one sat that close together unless they were lovers. The two were laughing and enjoying each other only as lovers do. Vittorio found himself wishing he were home with his wife and son. Having a normal Christmas like the rest of Venezia. The rest of the world. He shook his head and brought his face back up to meet the cold air and sea spray. He was a policeman. He was working.

The cabin had become warm. Maybe too warm. They both took off their heavy coats.

"Are you hungry?" she said.

"I'm starved. What have we got? Is there enough for two?"

"I haven't looked. But I'll make it enough."

She opened the basket the Malvasi staff had prepared for her. There wasn't enough for two. It was a lunch for one. With a split of champagne. She held up the small bottle.

"Somebody's keeping an eye on me."

"I'm not really that hungry."

"Here, open this and shut up."

She handed Louis the bottle and a glass.

"You don't mind drinking out of the same glass, do you?"

"I'll take you up on half of the sandwich, but I can't drink any of this."

"Louis, don't be such a goody-goody."

"I'd love to, believe me, but I am on duty here, remember."

"Thanks a lot."

"You know what I mean."

"It'll always be that way, won't it?"

"Probably."

They looked out on the water and were quiet for a while. Then Louis said, "Should I still open it?"

"Yes. I'm very happy."

"Good. I am too."

They pushed on. And the boat was happy. It was happy to have its motor at full throttle. It was happy to be on the open water. Blow some of the carbon out. Scare a few fish.

They were approaching Burano. Another tiny island known for its lace work. Lace work so fine and delicate that many of the women who produced it went blind at a very young age from working so closely with their eyes. Louis passed this information on to his companion.

"That sucks. Why do they do it, then?"

"I don't know," Louis said. "They start young, according to Joe. I guess they don't know what else to do. Where else to go or how to leave. So they're stuck."

Again they were quiet.

"How much longer?"

"Torcello's that island over there. I think. I'll check with Vittorio."

She grabbed his arm. "No. Don't bother. We'll get there when we get there. Sit back down."

He did.

Vittorio banked around Burano and eased off the throttle a bit. He could see Torcello's long dock in the distance. About a mile or so out in front. The dock seemed overly large for an island so sparsely populated. However, the main vessel, the one that supplied regular service to the island, was much larger than a standard *vaporetto*. It was more like a small passenger ferry. It would travel almost empty in these winter months, but when summer arrived, with its onslaught of tourists, it would be impossible to find a seat.

From Vittorio's vantage point Torcello looked completely deserted. Only the birds were here for Christmas. Gulls flew high overhead while snow white egrets fed among the marshes.

The helmsman allowed his craft to drift into the dock. When he was close enough, he jumped to the landing with the bow line between his teeth and secured the launch to the piling. His passengers had already put their coats back on. They stepped out of the cabin and onto the open aft deck.

"This is beautiful," Vittorio heard the woman say. She turned her face to the breeze and tilted her head back. She spread her arms out wide and said, "Nobody else is here."

Then with a magician's gesture, and as if to say, presto, Vittorio smiled, faced the island, bowed and said, "Ladies and gentlemen, I give you Torcello."

The couple stepped off the launch.

"Thank you, Vittorio," Louis said. "I guess we'll be an hour or two."

To which The Wife smiled and added:

"Maybe three."

Ten

Joe and Nina and Eubie had arrived on the Lido a half hour before Vittorio had secured his launch to the Torcello dock. The Lido was a seven-and-a-half-mile-long island. A narrow stretch of sand that separated Venice's lagoon from the Adriatic. It was like any other beach community in the Northern Hemisphere on Christmas Day. Empty and closed up tight. After jumping off their water taxi the three walked down the main street. Gran Viale Santa Maria Elisabetta. Eubie found the name to be ridiculous. He pointed out that he lived on Fourth Street in New York City. It was a much more sensible name for a street. Easier to remember. Easier to spell. Especially if you used only the numeral 4.

They stopped at every shop window along the way. Looking into every one. Crisscrossing back and forth across the wide boulevard so as to not miss a single window. By the end Eubie had changed his tune about this street. The stores had on display every tacky beach toy imaginable. From buckets and shovels to kites and water guns. All stamped out of some electrically charged shade of Day-Glo plastic.

And there were balls. Beach balls. Soccer balls. Golf balls. Baseballs. Basketballs. Footballs. Rugby balls. Handballs. Tennis balls. They had them all. They also had nondescript balls of all kinds. Balls for just plain everyday general use. Whatever you wanted. If you needed a fucking ball—this was the place to come. Of course, every store was closed. And that's what made the Lido so appealing to Joe. It also appealed to Nina. But it sure didn't sit well with Eubie.

"Well, when will they be open?"

"Maybe tomorrow," his mother said.

"Can we come back?"

"We'll see."

The stores that didn't sell toys sold clothes. Mostly bathing suits, towels, hats, and beach cover-ups. Eubie showed very little interest in these shops, and when they slowed down to gaze into the window of one, he would run up to the next toy store and shout, "Hey, guys, come here, quick. Look at this neat stuff." As if it all might disappear.

Joe walked with his hands in his pockets. Nina stayed at his side. But never getting close enough to touch. There wasn't a need. They could feel each other. Both were aware of a closeness. A feeling they'd known each other for a long time. When Eubie was out of earshot, they talked like old friends. When he was near, their tone became more like parents.

"I've never seen him take to anyone like this. I hope it isn't your gun. They say five-year-olds are fascinated with them."

"Yeah, well, I hate to tell you this; but so are eighteen-year-olds. Some people never outgrow them."

"Like you?"

"I've been thinking a lot about that. I think I actually outgrew them ten or twelve years ago. It's only catching up to me now."

"Ten or twelve years? Hmm . . . a quick learner. So why don't you quit?"

Joe watched Eubie kick an Orangina can up ahead.

"I plan to," he said.

"You're kidding?"

"No. When I get back to the States . . . I have a contract. They won't like me quitting. But they won't make me stay on if I don't want to. I won't be any good to them. They don't want people who don't want them." Without looking at her he added, "You're a very pretty woman. . . . But I'll bet you know that."

"Thanks."

They reached the end of the wide boulevard and came to the Lungomare. The long street that ran the length of the beach.

Stretched out before them was the Adriatic Sea in all its shining glory. The arm of the Mediterranean that kept Italy separated from what was formerly Yugoslavia. The wind had increased from the north, and small grains of sand blew into their faces. They turned to the right. To the south. They walked slowly and kept the wind to their backs. Up ahead they could see the grand hotels that lined the more fashionable section of the beach. Most were closed down for the winter. Their clientele opting for the warmth of the Sinai. North Africa. Rio.

When they reached the first hotel, Joe found three lounge chairs that had been left out to cope with December on their own. He dragged them through the sand and positioned them next to one another facing the sea. Eubie sat in the middle. Protected from the wind by the larger adults.

"Let's have a squnch," Eubie said.

"A what?"

"A squnch," Nina answered for him. "It's when everyone kind of squeezes together in a pile."

"And that's a squnch?"

"Yeah," Eubie said. He threw himself at Joe. Nina slid over. The boy was pinned between the two of them, giggling. They both then began to tickle him unmercifully. He squealed like a pig.

"Tickle torture, tickle torture."

"Stop. Stop. I'm going to pee my pants. Stop."

They let go of him. He fled six feet, collapsed in the sand, and howled with laughter.

Eubie's absence left Joe and Nina sitting alone and touching each other for the first time. They were laughing along with Eubie. But the energy that was passing between them penetrated to their bones and made them oblivious to anything the boy was up to.

She took off her dark glasses. Joe followed suit. They looked at one another for a long time. Each trying to find something in the other's eyes. Considering Eubie's presence, the timing seemed inappropriate to kiss. But that's exactly where they were headed. The boy called to them and saved the day.

"Hey, guys, look what I found."

Eubie was now twenty feet away and holding a dead eel high in the air.

"It really stinks," he said.

They got up and walked over to him. They weren't in any great rush. Eubie was right. The fish stank.

"I think we should leave that here, angel. It would be a nice dinner for the seagulls."

"Nicely put," Joe said under his breath.

Eubie reluctantly dropped the eel. Joe produced a handkerchief. He wiped Eubie's hands off. Then was left with no place to put the reeking cloth.

"Well, let's smell those hands and see if we got it all."

Joe bent down and put his nose to Eubie's hands. Nina guessed, by the way Joe recoiled and almost fell over, that perhaps he had not—got it all.

"Well, I think we men should look for a place to clean up a little. The Hotel Des Bains might be open for the holiday. Maybe we can duck in there." Joe pointed. "It's that one. The big one."

They continued down the beach.

"What kind of stuff do you paint?"

"I'm sorry, Joe. You're going to have to give me a little breathing room."

She waved her hand in front of her nose.

"Or keep downwind. One or the other."

The wind had died down some. It meant they wouldn't have it in their faces on the walk back. But it was of little help now. There was no downwind.

"The wind's gone. We'll keep our distance."

They moved fifteen feet closer to the water.

"What kind of stuff do you paint?" Joe shouted.

"Watercolors mostly," she shouted back. "How did you know I painted?"

"You told me. Back at San Stefano. After the concert . . . Do you make any money at it?"

"I do pretty well. I'm having a show in March. At the Holt Gallery."

"New York, right?"

"Soho."

They were still shouting.

"I've had shows there before. They seem to like my stuff."

They were then quiet for a bit.

"What are you going to do if you quit the service?"

"I'll go back to New York."

"Back?"

"I was born there . . . in an elevator."

"Somehow that doesn't surprise me."

When they arrived at the Hotel Des Bains, the terrace on the beach side was looking very much closed up. The umbrellas had been put away. The tables and chairs had been stacked up against the building. And it might have been Joe's imagination, but he was getting the distinct feeling he and Eubie had been followed by a small consortium of seagulls.

Joe was wracking his brain, trying to come up with an alternative spot for the men to wash their hands, when a waiter came out of the hotel's double doors with a bottle of wine and two glasses. The man scurried off to one of the cabanas fifty feet away on the beach.

"Jesus. They're open."

Joe and Eubie headed for the double doors.

"You two go. I'll wait here. I want to see where that wine's going," Nina said.

"Romantics, no doubt. Don't get too close. It could be contagious."

Joe and Eubie passed through the doors.

They were back out in five minutes. Smelling like one of those goddamn Giorgio ads in *Vanity Fair.*

"You should have come, Mom. The place is really cool inside. They had a guy in the bathroom that hands out towels. And he sprayed my hands with perfume too. Smell."

"We needed it. I let him keep my handkerchief. Sport that I am."

Joe knelt down to Eubie's level. "Did you know a very famous writer, Thomas Mann, wrote a book that takes place in this exact same hotel?"

"So? Who cares?" Eubie said.

Not being much into literature, Eubie took off for the water and shouted back, "Let's go, you guys."

"*Death in Venice* was here?" Nina asked.

"Bingo. You should do a game show."

Eleven

When Carter Perkins had informed Nelo a water taxi must be summoned for a little trip to the Dorsoduro, it was the absolute truth. It would be only the first stop on a somewhat roundabout journey to Torcello. There was no telling how long the Vice President and his wife planned to stay on the island, but two hours would be a safe guess. Carter had calculated the couple would have no need for the loo at the Locanda until they were ready to leave. Thus Carter would have more than enough time to reach the island by whatever route seemed the most secure.

The ride from the hotel to the Dorsoduro had taken twelve minutes. Carter had jumped off the boat at the Zattere *vaporetto* stop only a hundred yards from La Primavera—the *pensione* where Nina and Eubie had their room. And from there walked the short distance to the other side of the Dorsoduro. After a wait, another taxi was hailed. The driver was told to go directly to the train station. Another twelve minutes. Carter had then entered the train station, looked at the departure board and waited for this last taxi leave with another fare. Carter then came back out onto the dock.

Two additional water taxis were now waiting at

the train station landing. One driver would have Christmas dinner with his family. The other—never again.

Carter opted for the older of the two drivers.

The man's boat was older as well. It needed sanding. Paint. Varnish. And judging from the green growth at the water line, a bottom scraping was also in order. But Carter chose this man because he was small and looked like a friendly sort. A man who liked to talk.

Carter stepped down onto the launch, smiled sweetly, and said, "I'd like to go to Torcello, please."

The driver rolled his eyes to the sky after hearing the request, but a hundred thousand lira note seemed to magically appear in Carter's hand and they were on their way.

The old man eased his boat down the Cannareggio canal. He passed under the Ponte Guglie. And by the Calle del Forno, where Oscar and Christina were lounging in their apartment, sharing a bottle of Christmas wine.

Carter moved up next to the old man.

"I've always had a soft spot in my heart for powerboats. I keep one on the Thames, back in London, and I miss her terribly."

It was enough. The driver never stopped talking for the entire trip to Torcello. He explained all the gauges to Carter. How the winch, the lights, and the air horn worked. He showed Carter the operation of the gear box. The throttle. He discussed his theories on how to approach a dock without so much as a tap. How to judge the tides. What side to take the buoys on. He actually let Carter have the helm for a short period of time.

As they approached Torcello, Carter told the driver to avoid the main landing and pull up to the small dock on the far side of the island. Enough money had changed hands that no questions were asked. When they arrived, Carter produced a five-hundred-thousand lira note.

"Please wait for me here." The note was passed to the driver. "I shouldn't be more than one or two hours."

"*Grazie mille, signore.* Be careful. There are snakes in the grasses on Torcello. Even in winter."

Twelve

Torcello had sprung to life long before the city of Venice was anything more than an uninhabited swamp. Civilized folks had built a community on the island as early as the seventh century, and by the twelfth they had shipyards. Palaces. Churches. A respectable population. They had nobility. And with that nobility some very noble laws. What could be better?

The island was marshy. Food was plentiful throughout the year. From the land. The sea. The air. And in summer, like all marshy places, Torcello had mosquitos. Mosquitos have an annoying way of getting around. And with all the trade with the Far East, it wasn't long before malaria arrived on the island. It came through the grasses with a vengeance. And now, in the twentieth century, all that was left on Torcello was a smattering of houses and two churches. One, Santa Maria Assunta, a stone cathedral, finished in the year 639. Still standing strong. The stones having been somewhat oblivious to the mosquitos. The other, Santa Fosca, was pure Byzantine.

The path from the *vaporetto* dock to what remained of the town was less than a half mile. It was a footpath. For most of the half mile it lay next to a narrow waterway. It more resembled a stagnant brook than a real canal. A few small boats were lashed to poles along the banks.

The Wife and Louis strolled silently along the scraggly path. When they could no longer see Vittorio's launch, and Vittorio could no longer see them, she reached out and took Louis' hand. Not a soul was out in the Christmas air. Not a single tourist. The island belonged to these two alone.

Only one small footbridge crossed the meager canal. When the couple reached it, they walked to the arch. They stood at the center. The bridge had been made famous by countless photographers and painters. It led nowhere. It only crossed to the other side, where nothing but a low, crumbling stone wall struggled to stay alive. A wall that once had a purpose. Centuries ago. But now supported only vines and weeds. In a few spots trees had grown straight up through the middle of the barrier. And without their summer leaves the trees looked like the skeletons of a long-departed nobility.

The Wife and Louis came back down from the bridge. They continued on to the center of the town. They passed Locanda Malvasi. It stretched along to their right.

"I have the key to suite five if you need it," Louis said.

"Not yet."

In the center of the tiny town they found two boys kicking a brand-new soccer ball. No doubt a Christmas present. From the similarity in their faces, it was obvious they were brothers. The older kept barking out the rules of the game. The younger kept changing them. The ball was kicked hard. It flew by the smaller boy, and the older one called out in disgust.

"*Christiani! Attenzione!*"

The ball rolled to a stop in front of Louis. He picked it up and tossed it back.

"*Molto grazie, signore. Lei e molto gentile. Grazie.*"

Their faces beamed in the sunlight.

"They suggest forcibly that the best assurance of happiness in this world is to be found in the maximum of innocence and the minimum of wealth."

The Wife said this in almost a whisper.

"That's fairly deep," Louis said.

"Well, it's Henry James. He was a fairly deep guy."

For an hour they walked the small paths that laced Torcello. Other than the two boys and a spectrum of birds, they saw no signs of life. They passed the cathedral and moved on to the smaller church. Santa Fosca. They sat for a minute on one of the wooden benches a caretaker had placed in the sun. The caretaker had long since gone home for Christmas.

"You know what I'd like to do?" she said eventually.

"No. What?"

"I'd like to take a nap."

"Okay."

"With you."

"Okay."

They stood and headed back to Locanda Malvasi. Each could feel their pulse increase from the anticipation of what was to come. When they arrived at the inn, Louis slipped the key into the lock of suite five and opened the door. The suite had been prepared by the hotel staff as though it were the height of the summer season. As if the island were in full swing. Cut flowers were in the vases. The bed had been made. Fresh towels arranged in the bath. Louis instinctively checked the place out. Not as a lover. As a Secret Service agent.

The first thing he did was pick up the telephone.

"Phone works. Anyone you want to call?"

She smiled. Said, "I don't think so, Louis, but thank you all the same."

He then checked the closet. Under the bed. Under the dresser. Under the desk. He could feel her warmth as he moved past on his way to the bathroom. He stopped and kissed her.

"I'm sorry. It's procedure."

"I understand."

Once in the bathroom he checked under the sink. The cabinet above the sink. He pushed the shower curtain back, away from the tub. He opened the large double windows. Looked out onto the view behind the inn. The view of a large meadow. The grasses were high and gold-green. He looked to the left and to the right. The low sun flooded the room and warmed it. It gave the bath a feeling of springtime. When he was happy everything checked out, he returned to the bedroom. The Wife had removed her coat, her jacket, and her blouse. She now stood naked from the waist up.

"I didn't want to get things wrinkled."

Louis put his borrowed overcoat, his jacket, and his Smith & Wesson .357 on the chair by the desk. He walked over to her.

"I hope you're not going to get me into trouble," he said.

"Louis, I think you're the one getting me into trouble."

They kissed another long kiss.

She stepped back for air.

"Holy mackerel," she said and took a deep breath. "I'm going to the john for a minute. Don't go away."

She was gone for eight minutes.

When she opened the bathroom door she stood before Louis completely naked.

She was ten years older than Louis and ten years younger than her husband. She'd had two children. The first had been stillborn. Little Audrey was her second. And that birth had been endlessly complicated. At the last minute the obstetrician had decided to go in with a C-section. For all intents and purposes, the dickhead botched the job. Then he'd deemed it necessary to perform a hysterectomy. Her child-bearing days were over.

To the doctor's credit, he'd done a fabulous job in closing. Very little of the trauma of her two pregnancies was visible—from the outside. The cesarean scar was barely noticeable. Her stomach was flat. Her breasts were firm.

Louis had used the eight minutes she was gone to lock the door, turn the bed down, and remove his own clothes. He was now lying in the bed with the covers up over his waist.

"You saw the view out of the bathroom window?" she said.

"Nice, huh?"

"I'll say. And so peaceful. I just stood there. Naked. Letting the sun warm me . . . That's what took so long."

She came over. Slid into bed next to him.

"I'm excited as hell," she said.

Louis rolled over and they kissed. Again.

"What if we fall asleep?" she asked.

He pulled his left hand out from under the covers and pushed a button on his stainless steel wristwatch. A small electronic beep pierced the room.

"What time do you want to get up?"

"Four-thirty?"

"Four-thirty it is."

He pushed two more buttons. The watch made two more beeps. They kissed. And without breaking, Louis rolled over and they made love like lovers who hadn't seen each other in five years. After they finished, they sat up in bed and gabbed for twenty minutes. Venice might well have been on the other side of the earth.

"You know he's next in line for the number one job? No one can stop him. We could conceivably keep this thing up for another eight years—"

"What *thing* might that be?"

She smiled. Said, "What if we never go back?" Then positioned herself on top of Louis and started the lovemaking all over again. From the beginning. The second time was more intense than the first. It almost lasted forever.

After this turn they fell into a sound asleep. She on her back with her head on the down pillow and facing the ceiling. Louis on his chest. His left arm draped across her breasts and his head half stuffed under the pillow. Their breathing was heavy. Deep.

Thirteen

Vittorio wasn't a stupid cop. He was a smart cop. If he had been a stupid cop, Inspector Solfanelli would have never placed him undercover at the Hotel Malvasi. Driving a motor launch. It was a spot where a lesser man would have been tripped up long ago. The crooks that stayed at first-class hotels were not stupid crooks.

But Vittorio now found himself caught between a rock and a hard place. His police instincts told him something was wrong. Something was in the air. Something was up. He couldn't put his finger on it. He couldn't determine what the hell it was. But it was there. A voice in the back of his head. It was telling him to find the Americans. Stuff them back into the boat. Leave Torcello and return to the Malvasi.

Vittorio wasn't sure if the cause of his concern was here, on the island, or back at the big hotel. But like Joe Bradlee, he'd learned to listen to these voices very carefully. Whatever it was, this thing that was jabbing at his sixth sense, he had to find it and deal with it one on one.

But his problem was this: If anyone was to see him walk away from his boat, his cover was blown. No Malvasi pilot would ever abandon his launch. Leave it unattended. Leave his baby sitting alone where anyone could put their greasy fingers on it.

Vittorio lit another cigarette from his previous one and tossed the old butt into the water. He looked down and counted. "*Tredici.*" An old tire floated near the dock. Inside it floated thirteen cigarette butts. Not once had he missed his target.

He looked at his watch. Three-fifteen. He'd been waiting for over two hours. Maybe he was just bored. Maybe boredom was what had been stabbing at his gut. Maybe he just wanted something to happen. Anything. Something to liven things up a little. So Vittorio decided to get closer.

He started his boat's engine and pulled in his lines. He swung around and headed up the slender canal that led to Locanda Malvasi and the small town. It'd be risky. The canal could silt-in in winter. There'd be no telling how deep the water was. The tide was high. It helped. But it wouldn't stay high forever. Time would make it impossible for him to bring the launch about in this narrow canal. When he did leave, he'd most likely have to back out.

He eased his way under the small footbridge Louis and The Wife had stood on earlier. The high tide brought the top of his cabin dangerously close to scraping the underside of the low bridge. He needed to guide the boat through hand by hand. Once free he increased speed slightly. He passed a few houses. A dry-docked gondola out for the winter. Another thirty yards. He found himself abreast of Locanda Malvasi.

Vittorio's thinking was to continue into the town and search for the couple. However, he was stopped by something he saw on a door to one of the suites. Suite five. He smiled and cut his engine. Then secured his launch to the nearby landing. He looked back over to the Locanda. He lit another cigarette. Smiled once more. Hanging on the doorknob to suite number five was a pink and green sign. It read, NON DISTURBA.

Fourteen

Carter Perkins was out six hundred thousand lira to the ancient taxi driver. That is, if the man didn't wait at the small dock on the far side of Torcello. This worried Carter some, but there wasn't much that could be done but trust the old man would wait. If the taxi driver did remain at the dock—Carter would have the money back in jig time.

Carter angled up the footpath toward the small town. The grasses were knee high on both sides, and Carter began wondering if the old man had been telling the truth about snakes. The assassin opted to keep eyes peeled. Just in case. Carter was also keeping a keen lookout for Secret Service agents. They were somewhere. And they most likely would be harder to find than any snakes. Every forty feet or so Carter would stop and scan the horizon. No agents could be seen. Not now. Not yet.

The plan was to be casual at first. If an agent was to spot Carter, it should cause no concern, and not look in the least bit suspicious. The writer was simply on Torcello for a visit like anyone else. If not detected, once close enough to the Locanda, Carter could determine what suite the Malvasi people had set up for the Vice President, and proceed accordingly.

The walk from the dock on the far side of the island to Locanda Malvasi was close to a mile. Most of the island consisted of marshy fields. A few ancient stone fences, in various stages of disrepair, trailed throughout these fields. Some of the fences, slowly sinking, had all but disappeared into the marshes. There wasn't a portion of the path that had remained straight. Over the years it had evolved into an obstacle course. Bending here to avoid a marshy swamp. Bending there to avoid a stone wall or fallen tree. In some spots small walls had to be stepped over in order to continue on the path.

Carter soon passed to the front of the cathedral and decided to stroll in. A solo priest was giving his Christmas afternoon Mass to no one. Carter exited and continued to survey the vacant town.

To the left was the smaller Byzantine church. It slightly blocked Carter's view of the wide path that led to the main dock. But it also hid the assassin from anyone at the Locanda. Anyone who might be glancing in the direction of the church. Carter now had a clear view of the other half of the small town. There wasn't a soul in sight. A new soccer ball was set on a small wooden table behind one of the houses. Two doves pecked at some crumbs in front of the Byzantine church.

Carter knew if even one step was dared from behind the church, there would undoubtedly be someone at the Locanda pointing a finger. Someone would surely put two and two together, and all would be back at square one. Carter sucked in the crisp air. Then watched the steamy breath as it escaped into the chilly afternoon. It was now or never. The final commitment had to be made.

And Carter made it.

From this point it was essential to become invisible. Essential to blend with the breezes. The grasses. Carter could not afford to be seen by a soul from this moment on. The writer was no longer just a visitor to Torcello. The writer had become the political assassin.

And Carter was a master. A master of invisibility. There had been nearly thirty years of practice. No one was better. Carter moved to the north side of the old church and slipped down the wall. When the corner of the building had been reached, Carter was able to get a quick glimpse down the wide dirt road that led to the Locanda. Vittorio could be seen sitting on his shining launch in the narrow canal. He was smoking a cigarette. Vittorio would recognize Carter in a instant. Something that couldn't be chanced. Not now.

Carter pulled back behind the church, took the Beretta from its holster, eased the silencer into place, and crept around to the back side of the old structure. And again looked in the direction of the inn.

The church and Locanda Malvasi were somewhat parallel in their layouts, and from Carter's vantage point the rear of the inn and the fields that stretched out behind it could easily be seen. The sun hung low in the sky. Its radiance was warming on the skin, but the hot rays stung the interior of the killer's eyes. Carter withdrew to the safety of shade.

Still no agents. Still no Vice President.

Carter pulled farther back and took stock.

It was clear that Vittorio was the only person out in the open air. The helmsman was obviously waiting. Which meant the Americans had not left. And there were just two public buildings remaining. The Americans could only be in the Locanda—or in the Byzantine church.

Carter slipped the Beretta back into the overcoat pocket, and tried the ancient wooden side door of the church. It was unlocked. Carter stepped in and found a tiny room where folding chairs had been stored. It was damp. Dark. It had a chill that made one feel as though a tomb had just been invaded and that the Grim Reaper had made his escape.

There was another door on the opposite wall. Carter opened it and looked out on the septum. The church was unlit except for two large candles. They stood guard beside a small altar. Carter found it hard to see more than ten feet. The space was frighteningly still. There wasn't a sound.

Carter instantly became conscious of heavy breathing and an urgently beating heart, and ducked back outside much more quickly than was necessary. A lone beetle scurried to avoid the killer's footsteps. Carter reached for the Beretta and trembled slightly. The feeling that death itself had just made a visit shook through to the soul.

"The sense of death is most in apprehension," Carter tried to joke. But then felt compelled to finish the Bard's words. They were spoken in a faint whisper with eyes closed.

"And the poor beetle, that we tread upon,
In corporal sufferance finds a pang as great
As when a giant dies."

Carter's eyes opened slowly. The beetle was found scratching for traction on the loose gravel. A shoe was placed over the insect and the hard leather held the bug pinned to the stone walkway for nearly fifteen seconds. The creature struggled to get free. Carter grinned. Then pressed down. Slowly. Until the weight finally cracked the hard shell of the animal. The sound was that of a small twig breaking, and it gave Carter a tremendous feeling of relief.

Carter was now positive. The Vice President was inside one of the suites. And the Secret Service agents were obviously in the suite as well. Or possibly using one of the nearby rooms. Carter cursed silently for failing to bring the second ammunition clip. What if it was needed for self-defense? What if it was necessary to eliminate an agent to get at this target? There was always the German dagger. But these agents were big men. Any one of them could easily overpower the slight assassin. Carter's head twitched sharply in an attempt to clear the brain. More information was needed. Carter had to know who was where.

"Get in closer, lovey."

Carter began to inch down the back side of the church. Two vacant houses were passed, and before long Carter was standing on Malvasi property. Carter glanced down the length of the Locanda. All the suites had large windows that looked out over the fields.

And a few had doors that opened on to small terraces. One suite had a window wide open. Everything else was closed up tight—a fact that never worried Carter. Any door or any window could be opened from the outside. And it could be done in a second, without making the slightest sound.

Carter continued down the back side of the hotel. Listening more than looking. Creeping below the windows and passing the doors quickly. Americans were loud people. They'd be heard long before they'd be seen. Carter passed the first, second, and third suites. All empty. Then on to the fourth. Empty. Two remained.

Carter came to the fifth suite. The window to the bathroom had been left open, and Carter cautiously peered in.

The bathroom was empty. The shower curtain had been pushed to one side. A single washcloth and large towel had been used. The towel had been draped over the side of the tub. The washcloth lay beside it. A small bar of Malvasi soap was perched beside the sink. The wrapper had been tossed in the direction of the wastebasket but had missed the thing altogether. It rested on the floor. There was a square piece of tissue floating in the toilet. The tissue had spread itself flat on the water's surface. In its center was a crimson ring.

Lipstick.

This was the room.

This was the Vice President's suite.

Carter still could not explain the lack of noise. The lack of voices. Where in blazes were these people? The assassin instantly, and somewhat intuitively, decided to go back to the original plan. Obviously this room had already been checked out by the agents. Carter would enter the bathroom and wait. Confident the Vice President would have to use the toilet at least once before he returned to Venice. From there Carter's escape route would be clear sailing.

The assassin vaulted up, over the window ledge, and landed on the bathroom floor without a sound. Once inside, Carter instinctively bent down, picked up the soap wrapper, and placed it in the wastebasket. Hung up the towel and washcloth. Looked about. The door to the bedroom had been left slightly ajar. However, it was impossible to see any of the room through the small crack.

The Beretta dangled in the right hand. With the left Carter tapped the dagger as though it was expected to be lonely and in need of love. Then Carter eased the door open another half inch. Listening for a noise. A noise from the door. A noise from anywhere. Carter hadn't expected the Locanda Malvasi to have squeaky doors, and it didn't. The door made no sound at all. It was then pushed farther open.

The couple had been asleep for a little over twenty minutes. Their breathing was still very deep. They were dead to the world. The woman slept on the side closest to the bath. She'd rolled onto her back. In her sleep she'd pulled the blanket up to cover her unclothed body. The man had wedged his face into the darkness and safety of her down pillow. He had left only the back of his head exposed to the fading light of day.

Carter was elated but again confused. Was this the same couple who had seemed so distant the night before? Perhaps. Carter remembered having a similar relationship. Years and years ago. It had been with an actor. The two of them would constantly fight like hens. But when it would come time for them to make up, the lovemaking had been pure bliss. Carter guessed this couple had almost the same type of relationship.

As thrilling as this good fortune was, Carter knew the Secret Service agents could not be far away. Most likely in suite number six. There was still the need to be deathly quiet. And no time to dally. Silently Carter moved around the foot of the bed and found a position on the man's side. Carter then tucked the Beretta beneath the flap of the overcoat and eased the safety to the off position. Not a sound could be heard. Carter brought the pistol to arm's length and placed the silencer within a half inch of the back of the man's head. Carter smiled. It was not expected to be this easy.

There was a strong temptation to wake them both up. Give the Vice President one last look at life before he tasted death. Carter smiled once more. Lord, this was fun. The thought of bringing this sweet anticipation to an end was almost too much. It should last longer. It should be prolonged. It should be more like a glorious sexual encounter. But there wasn't time. Carter could wait. The sexual encounter would have to come later. Carter gently squeezed the trigger.

The Beretta sent one round into the man's skull. The bullet exited through his right eye and forced its way into the mattress.

Whether Louis felt anything, no one will ever know. But it was quick. Damn quick. His left leg kicked twice. They were not violent kicks. They more resembled a dog chasing rabbits in his sleep. The Wife sighed a low sexual sigh. She smiled, but she never woke.

"Glamis hath murdered sleep, and therefore Cawdor
Shall sleep no more, Macbeth shall sleep no more!"

It was said in less than a whisper, and besides the obvious, Carter suspected this bit of Shakespeare had come to the lips by way of the old lover, the actor. The child had flown into a furry anytime Carter would say the word Macbeth.

"It's fucking bad luck. Don't you ever say that fucking word around me again, you bitch" had been the actor's usual response to the Word. Carter had enjoyed saying the Word as often as it could be logically worked into sentence. And Carter strongly doubted if it really had been bad luck. After all, the actor had gone on to be knighted.

Carter dropped two more bullets into Louis' brain.

A small-caliber pistol like a Beretta makes very little noise even if no silencer is used. But with the silencer it was virtually inaudible. It was not in the least bit surprising to Carter that the Vice President's wife did not wake up.

Carter walked back toward the bathroom, around the foot of the bed, and stood. Silently. Only eighteen inches from the woman's face. Carter stayed there for two full minutes. There was a strong temptation to wake her. To show her her dead husband. But Carter found blood repugnant. Abhorrent.

Now a stronger desire had swept in. Carter wanted to see her naked body. Wanted to see her breasts. Her pubic area. Her navel. Her nipples. Carter had never slept with a woman. It just wasn't something that turned this killer on. Men did. Women didn't. But now Carter wanted to look at this woman. That's all. Just merely look. Compare physiques. See if they were at all similar. See what this woman had to offer that this man considered so wonderful. Carter had no time or interest for anything else. Just a comparison. However, she must be eliminated first. Carter brought the pistol up to arm's length once more and placed the silencer a half inch above the woman's right eyebrow—the soft part of the skull.

This time there was a pang of sexual arousal. A musky dampness from below that came as a complete surprise. Carter massaged the damp spot and took a deep breath. Then squeezed the trigger slowly.

Nothing.

Nothing happened. Carter squeezed harder. Then harder. Carter's hand began to tremble. Then shake violently. Carter had never killed a woman. Both hands shook. Carter had never been in this position before, and now all power seemed to be on a path of desertion. The knees were turning watery. The heart was racing more and more. Out of control. Carter pulled the pistol back and held it tightly. Then scraped it into an extended and hardened chest. The woman stirred and Carter stood motionless.

Another minute passed. Carter looked down at the Beretta. After the three rounds had been fired into the man's head, Carter must have put the safety back on. Of course the damn thing wouldn't fire. The assassin smiled at this stupidity and was immediately back in control. The safety was flipped off and the gun put back to the woman's head. But this time the trigger wasn't pulled. Instead Carter grinned a small grin and let the pistol dangle by the nightstand. And thought for a moment. There was no more excitement. Carter was now calm.

"Let this bitch wake up and find her husband dead at her side. Let her carry that around for a while," Carter thought. Besides, only two rounds remained. There still might be Secret Service agents to deal with—hopefully, no more than two.

The assassin left the same way the assassin had come. Through the bathroom window. Carter retraced the path along the back side of the inn and the two vacant houses. Past the Byzantine church. Carter then took a quick look back at Vittorio and his Malvasi launch. The helmsman was still smoking a cigarette. A fresh one, no doubt.

Carter had done it. Had pulled off the impossible. And would sleep like a baby tonight.

Fifteen

Oscar Sanchez was in the mood to give out Christmas presents. Possibly. Or he was attempting to convince Joe Bradlee he was no longer in the terrorism business. Another possibility. Then again, maybe it was just the wine he'd been drinking all day. Whatever it was, something made him pick up the telephone at three-thirty on Christmas afternoon and dial.

"Operations. Reynolds here."

Reynolds was bored. He'd answered the thing on the first ring.

"No, sir, Agent Bradlee isn't here. Some of the lucky ones get Christmas off. I'd be happy to give him a message. Who should I say is calling? . . . Mr. Sanchez? The famous Mr. Sanchez? Oscar? . . . I suppose I should be honored. I'm not. I'm bored and you're not helping. What's the message? . . . That's it? . . . You wouldn't care to go into any more detail than 'He's a very dangerous individual,' would you? Well, what am I supposed to do with this? How dangerous is he?"

Reynolds' last question was left stranded in the telephone wires somewhere between the Hotel Malvasi and the old Ghetto section. Oscar was off the line.

Reynolds had never seen Oscar Sanchez. Or Carter Perkins, for that matter. However, he did know that Joe felt Sanchez was no potential threat and that something was definitely wrong about Perkins. So when Oscar told him, "Carter Perkins was a very dangerous individual," Reynolds figured it probably wasn't completely bullshit.

His first call went to Carter's room. No answer. Next he called the front desk and asked to speak to Gianni. Reynolds knew full well that Nelo wasn't about to release any information on a Malvasi guest. Reynolds also knew Gianni detested Carter. When he got Gianni on the line, Reynolds asked the desk clerk if he'd seen Mr. Perkins. Gianni gave it up. He told Reynolds that Carter had left by taxi at twelve-thirty, headed for the Dorsoduro.

Reynolds then contacted Olsen. By radio. The Panhandler and Little Audrey were having cookies and ice cream at Florian's on the Piazza San Marco. Reynolds repeated Oscar's warning about Carter and also told Olsen that Carter might not be far at hand.

"Three hours ago he headed out right behind you. To the Dorsoduro. He could be anywhere."

Olsen didn't share Reynolds' enthusiasm or paranoia with regards to Carter Perkins. He considered Oscar's warning to be something of a hoax. Maybe even a smoke screen of some sort. However, he was a professional. He took the necessary precautions. The information was passed on to Hall 'n' Oates. This excited the bejesus out of the two boys, and they now considered it to be open season on the little British travel writer.

After contacting Olsen, Reynolds went back to the telephone and attempted to call Joe. It as a long shot, but Joe just might be in his room. He wasn't. Reynolds opted not to call Louis. If Perkins truly was dangerous, he wouldn't be after The Wife. He'd be after bigger game. Even if Reynolds had called Louis, he would have been too late. Louis was dead and gone.

Sixteen

By three-thirty it had gotten chilly on the I
wind had kicked back up. On their walk
dock Nina told Joe she'd never seen the gr
Malvasi. As reluctant as he was to go near th
Joe broke down and conceded to give Eubie and
a little tour of the place.

Getting a water taxi proved to be impossible. But it wasn't long before a *vaporetto* chugged into the Santa Maria Elisabetta landing. They jumped onto the boat and found three seats at the bow. Eubie sat at the railing. In a matter of seconds he was asleep in his mother's arms. Nina sat in the middle. Close to Joe. The bow was open to the fresh air. As the boat pulled out, the wind stung their faces.

"I'd like to come back here," she said.

"I thought I saw you eyeing an orange soccer ball back in one of those shop windows."

"Not tomorrow, I mean in the summer. When it's warm."

Joe thought her reference to temperature might be an invitation for him to put his arm around her. He didn't. His heart was behaving strangely. He found himself not knowing how to respond to the situation. He was afraid to push. He didn't want to do anything that might scare her off. On the other hand, he thought, "Jesus, who the hell is she? What do I know about her? Christ."

"The Lido's nice in the summer. Colorful, to say the least. You could paint," he said.

"Exactly."

"You know who did some great watercolors in Venice?"

"John Singer Sargent?"

He laughed.

"Yep . . . You've got to do a game show. Call your ex-husband. He could probably get you on one."

"I'm sure he could. But then I'd have to talk to him, wouldn't I?"

"More than likely."

They sat quietly for a minute. The boat steadily pushed the salty water out of its path. The entire city seemed reflected in her dark glasses.

"If you left the Secret Service and moved back to New York, what would you do?"

He hadn't thought that far ahead. He only knew he wanted out. "I've saved a fair amount, and assuming I don't screw things up, I should be eligible for some decent money when I leave."

"That doesn't quite answer my question. You don't seem the type to sit around the house reading Kipling and drinking tea."

"Believe it or not, Kipling's one of my favorite writers."

"Who would have guessed?" Her sarcasm could have been cut with a knife.

"Have you ever read 'Tommy'?" he said

She lowered her voice and put on a phony English accent: " 'I went into a public-'ouse to get a pint o' beer—' "

"Never mind."

"I had a feeling you'd be attracted to something like that." She looked down at her sleeping son. "It's also one of his favorites. Number two request at bed-time. Number one is 'If,' if you can believe it. Kipling. Jesus, Joe. Grow up, why don't you?"

They exchanged a look. He wanted desperately to

kiss her just then. Kipling aside. But again he pulled back. He looked out at the water.

"Let me try this one more time," she said. "If you move to New York, what—"

"What will I do?"

"Right."

"Have any ideas?"

"Become a cop?" she said.

"My father was a cop. I think I'll give that one a miss."

"I know, become a private detective."

Again her sarcasm was just too damn thick.

"Thanks again."

"You have to answer this question before we get off the boat."

"Says who?"

"I do."

"Okay, I'll answer the question."

"When."

"Now."

He didn't.

"Well?"

"Christ, you can be a real pain, you know that?"

She put her hand on the back of Joe's head and turned his face to hers. She brought her lips to his and they kissed. It ended up becoming difficult for them to separate. Eventually they did.

"If you move to New York . . . ?"

"Jesus. What if I don't know?"

"Then just say so."

"Okay. I don't know."

"That's not good enough."

"I didn't think it would be."

He sat for a minute. Then stood and went to the far end of the bow. He took the point-and-shoot camera out of his coat pocket and set the automatic timer. Then placed it on a chest containing life preservers. He pushed the button and ran back to his seat. Just before the thing went off he kissed her. It was another long kiss. It lasted well past the click of the shutter.

"I'll become a photographer. I have a camera. What more do I need?"

"Kodachrome."

They laughed as the *vaporetto* swiped into the San Marco landing. The ride was over. Joe approached a waiting water taxi.

"Sí, signore?" the driver said.

Joe said, "Hotel Malvasi, *per favore,*" and helped Nina and Eubie onto the boat.

Nina looked off at the dark clouds that'd formed in the east.

"Looks like we're in for nasty weather," she said. "Welcome back to reality."

Seventeen

Not a single Secret Service agent had been seen by Carter on the way back to the waiting taxi boat, left nestled at the far side of Torcello. Or anyone else, for that matter. And Carter had a good deal of trouble suppressing a desire to run and skip and sing through the marshy countryside. After all, Carter had done it. Had pulled it off smooth as pie. Had done away with a major political figurehead. The vice president of the United States of America—The next president. And picked up a cool seven million along the way. A life-long dream had been achieved. Carter was on cloud nine. Only one more killing and this assassin would be out of the life for good. A shadow of *Macbeth* tagged along behind.

> ". . . that but this blow
> Might be the be-all and the end-all here,
> But here, upon this bank and shoal of time,
> We'd jump the life to come."

To blazes with *Macbeth*. It would be over in thirty minutes. Carter wondered how difficult it would be to quit. It seemed doubtful it would be easy. This was too much blessed fun.

When Carter came upon the waiting water taxi, the old pilot was sound asleep in the cabin. Carter jumped down onto the rear deck, and the man woke with a frightened start.

"Mi dispiace, signore. Ero assonnato."

Carter froze. This mind was not spinning in Italian. It was wallowing in Shakespeare. *Assonnato* sounded too bloody much like *assassino*—assassin. Carter's face turned to stone. A black evilness shot from the killer's eyes. Bore deep into the helmsman's soul. Carter's right hand moved to the Beretta, still resting in the overcoat pocket. The words flew from Carter's mouth like fireballs.

"What did you say?"

The old man took a step back. Carter's rage had put the fear of the devil into him.

"*Ero assonnato.* I was sleepy. I am sorry to have gone to sleep. Please, *signore,* where can I take you?"

Carter slowly sat on the weathered seat in the taxi's stern. Without once removing the hand from the coat pocket. Or taking it away from the Beretta.

"We'll go back to San Marco now."

The old man started his engine. He then cast his lines off and directed his boat back toward the city. As far as he was concerned, he couldn't get back soon enough. Death seemed very close behind.

After a mile or so, they were out of the channel and back into the open spaces of the lagoon. The driver gave his weary boat full throttle. Something he hadn't done in years. And like Lot's wife, he was petrified to look back. And this fear was easily perceived by his passenger.

Carter pulled the Beretta from the coat pocket, looked at it, and now wished notches had been placed in the pistol's handle, just like the gunslingers of the old American Wild West. Carter truly did not know how many men had been eliminated with this gun. Now there was a yearning for the information. This was a burial at sea. There should be a eulogy. The weapon's accomplishments should be spoken of.

Two bullets remained in the pistol. Carter brought the Beretta up to arm's length, pointed it toward the back of the driver's head. Held it there for a minute or more. Then lovingly brought it back down. No. To kill this man, with this gun, would only serve to lessen its last accomplishment. Carter held the Beretta out over the water in a limp right hand and looked up at the sky. Then let the pistol slip and fall into the Venetian lagoon. This old man would be saved for Carter's other pet.

Carter then stood and pulled the Luftwaffe dagger from its custom pocket. In one single, silent motion it was removed from its stainless steel sheath and the scabbard flung overboard. It came to rest on the bottom only forty feet from the Beretta. Carter took three steps forward. Then with surprising strength, pushed the twelve-inch blade up and through the helmsman's thick coat. Through his sweater. Through his shirt and undershirt. It pierced the man's skin between his second and third rib and continued on up and into the left ventricle of his aging heart.

The driver's back arched ever so slightly. As if a moth had been trapped within his sweater. He then dropped. Carter removed the dagger as the man crumpled to the deck of his weatherbeaten boat. The dagger was switched to the other hand. Carter took the wheel, eased off the throttle, then held the dagger out over the lagoon in a slightly bloodied palm.

"Will all great Neptune's ocean wash this blood
Clean from my hand?"

Carter chuckled—then continued.

"No, this my hand will rather
The multitudinous seas incarnadine,
Making the green one red."

Carter let the blade fall.

"Lady Macbeth and her dagger. Bad luck indeed. Macbeth. Macbeth. Macbeth. They can all sink for all I care."

Carter said all of this aloud and laughed again. This time like a child who had just won a hand of Go Fish.

Carter had always considered Lady Macbeth a role model. She was the one with the backbone. A great woman she was.

Carter brought the boat to an idle and let it drift. Then bent down and took the six hundred thousand lira from the old man's pocket along with whatever else he had. And counted it. As if there was some expectation the man might have stolen a portion of it. After reclaiming the cash, Carter dragged the corpse into the cabin and covered it with a blanket.

Carter had remembered well the lesson on seamanship and boat handling the old man had passed on a few hours earlier. The timeworn taxi responded nicely as it was swung around back toward Venice. However, Carter lacked the confidence to give it full throttle. The helmsman knew how much this boat would take. Carter did not.

Even without full throttle, good time was made and the old taxi was passing San Michele, the cemetery island, within three shakes of a lamb's tail. As a joke Carter toyed with the idea of tossing the old man's body onto the dock for the caretaker to find in the morning. But the risk of being seen was much too high. Nonetheless the thought did bring a chuckle.

Carter first brought the boat to the northernmost part of the city, just off the Cannaregio—the old Jewish ghetto. Then he slowly started to work the boat to the southeast and began to search the streets along the waterway. Carter needed a dock. An empty dock. A place to leave this old boat with its old man. A place where there would be no witnesses. No overly curious Italians.

But every location seemed populated. A child with a new Christmas toy. People arriving for dinner. People leaving for dinner. A man testing a new fishing pole. Two lovers waiting for a water taxi. The couple seemed bewildered when this taxi did not stop to pick them up.

Just as Carter was about to give up and move off to another section of the city, an opening appeared.

It was just past the Celestia *vaporetto* stop. In the

Castello district. A small dock on the Fondamenta Case Nuove. Not a soul in sight. It would be inconvenient as the devil, but the assassin was now in no position to be choosy. Carter pulled in and lashed the boat to a piling. Then jumped ashore and ducked down a narrow street.

It was a long walk to the other side of the Castello district. A boat would have made it in a quarter of the time. But Carter couldn't take a chance on standing around the waterfront looking for another taxi. Furthermore, a public phone needed to be uncovered. So the distance was walked. It felt good.

Within four blocks, Carter stumbled upon a telephone and made another call to the unlisted number in Michigan. After DOC's computerized voice had finished and the tone had sounded, Carter said, "It's Carter Perkins. My article is finished. It should be in every major newspaper by morning."

Carter hung up the phone and continued walking. It took much longer to cross the city than it should have—having little or no concept of the quickest route. But the sun was followed, and eventually Carter popped out on the Riva degli Schiavoni, just to the east of the Piazza San Marco.

Carter approached a waiting water taxi and stepped down onto the deck.

"Sí, signore?"

"The Hotel Malvasi, *per favore.*"

"Sí, signore."

Eighteen

At three-thirty on the afternoon of Christmas day, at London's Gatwick airport, the Big Man, Chester Mock, sat paralyzed by a snowstorm. He was one very pissed-off government employee. Italy is an hour off GMT. Three-thirty in London is four-thirty in Venice.

At four-thirty in Venice, Joe Bradlee had just finished giving Nina and Eubie the grand tour of the Hotel Malvasi. The tour had started with the gardens and finished with the dining room. And that was where Joe had left them. Nina with a cappuccino. Eubie with a bowl of ice cream. Cherry-vanilla.

Being the good trooper he was, and against his better judgment, Joe went up to the operations room. According to Reynolds, everything was "calm as a dead man's dick." There had been two phone calls. One from Carter Perkins. No message. One from Oscar Sanchez. Saying that Carter Perkins was a very dangerous individual.

"Figure that one out. I know you don't like the little fucker, but how dangerous could he be?" Reynolds said.

At four-thirty Vittorio still sat on the bow of his launch, tied to a pole in front of Locanda Malvasi's suite number five on Torcello. He lit another cigarette.

At four-thirty Carter Perkins was on yet another

water taxi. Halfway across the Canale della Giudecca on the way back to the Hotel Malvasi.

At four-thirty Olsen was paying the Vice President's tab at Florian's, as Goliath, Strutz, Little Audrey, Judy from the press office, and Hall 'n' Oates warmed themselves in the sun on the Piazza San Marco.

And at four-thirty, inside suite number five of Locanda Malvasi, the alarm on Louis Zezzo's wristwatch beeped sixteen times. His left arm was still draped over The Wife's bare breasts.

"Louis, turn that damn thing off, will you?"

She laughed and reached for his wrist with her right hand. The second she touched him she knew she'd been sleeping with a dead man. From the moment Carter's small bullet had entered Louis' brain, his body temperature had dropped almost twenty degrees.

She slipped out from under Louis' arm and stood. She pulled the blanket back. Blood soaked the sheet under Louis' head. At the back of his skull, by the hairline, were two tiny holes. One slightly larger that the other. The skin was burned to a black-brown around the holes. There was a small amount of dried blood on the back of his neck. After thirty seconds the alarm on Louis' watch shut off. Automatically.

"Shit, Louis, goddamn you . . . Goddamn you. Fuck."

She said it quietly and slowly as tears began to flood from her eyes. They fell down across her cheeks and dropped onto her bare chest.

She wasn't the type to scream hysterically. Or run from the room. Run outside. Completely exposed. Out into the winter air. But she could cry. And she did. She tried to force herself to stop, but she couldn't. She sat. Naked. On the floor. Beside the bed. She leaned her weight against the mattress. She cried for seven minutes. She did not wipe the tears from her face. She let them fall across her breasts, onto her lap, and drench her thighs. Then she stood and walked to the bathroom. She looked at her backside in the mirror.

Louis' blood had been matted to her skin from her

spine, across to her left shoulder, and on down to an inch above the small of her back. The blood had begun to dry. It was thick. Wrinkles had been left in her skin from her heavy sleep. The blood had settled into the grooves and was coagulated and darker along those lines. She took a washcloth, ran it under water, and tried to wipe the blood away. She dropped the cloth three times.

She was beginning to lose her composure. Beginning to get frightened. As events soaked in, so did a form of shock. She turned the shower on and stepped in. Fear kept her from closing the curtain. The water and blood mixture sprayed out and onto the white towels. Onto the tiles.

The floor was saturated with water and blood by the time she stepped out. She nearly slipped and fell when she reached for the towel. She found it necessary to grab the sink for support. She was shaky. After she had dried herself, she dropped the towel onto the floor and went back to the bedroom. She pulled the blanket up, placing it over Louis' head. Covering his bloody body completely. She dressed slowly. Methodically. And only then did she pick up the telephone.

Nineteen

Although The Wife was a bit incoherent, and sounded more like a zombie than anything else, the switchboard operator at the Hotel Malvasi was able to discern that she wanted to be connected with her husband's security office. And when she heard the familiar voice on the other end of the line, she began to feel her composure return. But only slightly.

"Operations, Bradlee."

"Joe. Thank God."

"Yes, ma'am."

Joe recognized her voice immediately. But it was irregular as hell. Something was wrong.

"Is everything okay?"

No answer.

"Ma'am?"

"Jesus God, Joe."

The Wife was now crying heavily. Sobbing. She had lost control instantaneously.

"Where are you?"

". . . I'm in the room."

"Yes, but where?"

"The hotel."

Joe kept his tone even.

"This hotel? You're in this hotel? The Malvasi? You're in your room?"

He cupped his hand over the mouthpiece and motioned to Reynolds.

"Check The Wife's room. Be careful. Somebody might be with her."

Reynolds pulled his Smith & Wesson, chambered a round, and bolted out the door.

"No, I'm still on the island," she said.

"Is Louis there? . . . Ma'am? Can I talk to Louis?"

"I can't . . . I can't . . . No . . . He's not here . . . He's gone . . . He can't—"

"Okay. Just try to relax a little. Okay? Try to calm down. Where did Louis go?"

Reynolds came back into the room shaking his head. Joe cupped the telephone again.

"They're still on Torcello."

He pointed at the other telephone.

"Get on the line."

Reynolds picked it up.

"Joe?"

"Yes. I'm still here."

"Goddamn it, Joe."

"I'm right here."

"Somebody killed Louis."

Bradlee and Reynolds reacted as if someone had just slammed cinder blocks into their chests. All oxygen seemed to evaporate from their lungs, and their stomachs shot hot acid into their throats.

"Jesus, you're sure?"

"Oh, God. Joe . . . I need help."

Joe let the phone drop to his side for a split second. He took an overly deep breath and swallowed the wad of saliva that had formed in the back of his mouth.

Reynolds turned his face directly into the far wall and kicked the baseboard hard.

And Joe pressed on.

"Okay, now listen to me closely. Try to be calm. I know it won't be easy. Is there someone in the room with you? . . . Someone in the room now? Is someone holding you in the room? Keeping you there?"

"No."

"You're sure? You don't see anyone?"

"No."

"Okay, where was Louis"—he had trouble getting the word out—". . . killed?"

"Here. In the room. We were both . . . asleep."

Joe looked at Reynolds to see if he could shed any light on what the hell was going on. Reynolds had yet to turn back and face him.

"And there's no one in the room with you right now?"

"No. No one."

"Okay. Now, there's some things I want you to do. It's important to be careful. . . . Look in the closet and behind the shower curtain. Look behind all the doors. Look under the bed. Look out of the front window. Then the back window. Do you have all that?"

"Yes."

"Okay, do that and come back and tell me if you see anything or anyone."

She put the telephone down. Joe cupped his receiver once again.

"What the hell is going on?"

"I don't know. Why would someone kill Louis and not kill her? And not take her as a goddamn hostage or something?" Reynolds said. As an afterthought he threw in, "And why would anyone kill Louis? It doesn't make any sense. He was a fucking saint."

Joe could see that Reynolds' eyes were beginning to fog.

"Don't lose it, goddamn it. Shit. Don't you dare lose it on me. I need you."

After a minute The Wife came back on the line.

"Joe?"

"Yes. I'm here."

"The room is empty. Except for Louis . . . and me."

Her voice cracked. Joe let her take her time.

"There's nobody out back. But the bathroom window is open. . . . The man who brought us out here . . . is sitting on his boat . . . out front. I couldn't see anyone else."

"Okay. Go lock the bathroom window. Make sure

all the other windows are locked. Now. The man on the boat . . . ?"

"Yes?"

"His name is Vittorio. He's a very good man. He's an Italian policeman. You can trust him. He speaks English fluently. After you've locked all the windows, go out, tell Vittorio what happened, and bring him back to the phone. Be sure you stay with Vittorio. Do not let Vittorio out of your sight. Do you understand all that?"

"Yes . . ."

She put the telephone down. Then brought it back to her face.

"Joe . . . ?"

"Yes?"

"I'm sorry. God, I'm so sorry."

She put the phone down again.

Joe looked at Reynolds. He cupped the mouthpiece.

"Call the police station. Tell them to patch you through to Solfanelli. Most likely he'll be at home. I'm going to need a helicopter."

"I don't know if my Italian is good enough."

"Make it good enough. '

After a minute, Vittorio came on the line.

"Joe?"

"Yes. Vittorio, what the hell is going on out there?"

"You got a fucking mess here, Joe."

"What happened?"

"I don't know. I did not hear a thing. It looks very professional. Two, maybe three slugs to the back of the head."

"Jesus."

"I think whoever did it is long gone. A lot of the blood has dried."

"Look after the woman, will you? . . . And Vittorio?"

"Si?"

"Do me a big favor? Don't call your people until I get there. I'll try to be out in twenty minutes."

"I will give you twenty minutes."

"Thanks. Put the woman back on, would you?"

Vittorio handed the phone to The Wife.

"Joe . . . ?"

"Listen. Stay with Vittorio. Do whatever he tells you to do. I'll be there in twenty minutes. Okay?"

"Thank you, Joe."

They both hung up the telephone.

Joe walked to the window and looked out at the setting sun.

"Let me know when you get through to Solfanelli," he said to Reynolds. He never turned around.

All the Marine Corps bullshit and semper fi crap aside, Louis was the closest thing to a younger brother Joe had ever had. And he was gone. It all made no sense. Why would someone want to hurt Louis?

Joe could feel his teeth digging into the flesh on the inside of his lower lip. He could feel and taste the warm, salty blood as it rolled out and over his tongue. But he bit down harder. He would not let his eyes mist over. He had learned this trick years ago on a sand dune in Vietnam. He had always hoped he would never have to use it again. "God fucking damn it," he thought. "Why Louis?"

"Got him," Reynolds said. He handed the phone to Joe.

Joe explained nothing to Solfanelli. Other than he had an emergency and he needed a chopper right away. Solfanelli assured him he would have a helicopter at the Hotel Malvasi in ten minutes.

"I'll be waiting out front," Joe said to Reynolds after he hung up the phone. "I want two men to go with me. I don't care who they are. I want you to stay here. Contact Olsen. Brief him. But tell him to keep it from Number Two until we have The Wife back at the hotel. Safe. What's going on with Mock? Wasn't the bastard supposed to be here tonight?"

"Oh, shit. I forgot. He called too. From the plane. They had to put down in London. The weather's fucked."

"There's a break. Do something for me, will you? When he does get here, try to keep him away from me, okay?"

"I'll do my best."

Joe opened the door, and Reynolds said it again, "Jesus, Joe, who would want to kill Louis?"

"I don't know. But I'll tell you one thing. I'm going to get the son of a bitch. You can fucking count on that. I'm going to get him and tear his fucking head off."

Joe walked out. Closed the door. Went to his room. Threw the mattress off the bed. It landed on the side table. The glass lamp fell to the floor. It shattered. He didn't notice. He strapped his holster on. Slammed a clip into his 9mm. He stuffed the weapon under his arm. Then headed directly to the dining room.

When he entered the Malvasi dining room, Nina could see by the look on his face, by the way he moved, that there was a problem. A big problem. But the thing she noticed most was that he had strapped his gun back on.

"I've got to talk to you."

"Sure. Sit down. Want some ice cream? I don't think Eubie can finish it all."

"Let's go outside."

Nina and Eubie got up. They all walked out. Out onto the hotel's front lawn. Silently.

"I can't have dinner with you tonight. Something's come up."

He never looked at her.

She put her hand on his arm and forced him to face her. He resisted. Finally she said, "Listen. There's a problem. I can see that. I'm not stupid. I can deal with it. I'm an adult in case you haven't noticed. So, there's a problem. But don't close me out. That I can't deal with. Don't just walk away from me. Talk to me."

She waited. Then she tightened her grip on his arm. He didn't look at her.

"Don't do this, Joe."

"I have to go to work."

"Bullshit."

"It's not bullshit."

"I want you to quit. I want you to quit right now. I want you to walk away from them. Don't look back.

Take the gun off. Throw it into the damn water. You don't need them."

She got no reaction.

"Can you hear me . . . ? Give me a nod or . . . something."

Joe was biting his lip again. Again he could taste blood.

With her free hand Nina reached up and took her dark glasses off. She handed them to Eubie, and then she reached up and took his off. She could see his eyes were beginning to water. They stood like that for some time. Finally he put his arms around her. He held her tightly. She could feel him trembling.

"Jesus, Nina, I can't talk. Trust me . . . I can't talk."

They held each other until the sound of an approaching helicopter had Eubie squirming to get a closer look.

"I guess that thing's here for you, isn't it? Well, Christ." She looked out at the Lido and the grayness. "You gotta go, you gotta go. We'll wait here," she said. "We'll have dinner here. Take care of yourself. Come back. We'll be here."

"Charge dinner to me. If you're tired, get a room. Charge it to me. I'll be back."

She could barely hear his last sentence as he walked off. Joe jumped onto the helicopter with two other agents. It lifted back into the sky. The dark gray sky becoming black. The noise was monstrous. The machine swooped out over the hotel and disappeared to the north. Eubie waved the entire time the helicopter remained in sight.

Nina and Eubie then walked back to the hotel. They fell in directly behind a funny-looking little person who had just arrived by water taxi. When they got to the door, Carter Perkins turned. Smiled. And held the door for them.

"After you, my dear," Carter said.

"Thank you," Nina said.

Twenty

The Venetian police helicopters were white. They had the green, white, and red Italian flag displayed on both sides of the tail section. The seal of the police department decorated the doors. Except for one lowly chopper, the entire fleet was brand spanking new. Their interiors were handsomely trimmed. Leather seats. Telephones. The works. They rode as smooth as silk and were mostly used to ferry dignitaries about. The one not-so-new helicopter, the lowly one, was Inspector Solfanelli's baby. It was an Agusta-Bell 212. It had been made in Italy in 1973 under a licensing agreement with the Bell Aircraft Company of North America. It was basically a reworked Bell 205. A UH-1. It was a fucking Huey.

It was a beast. It was too old. The paint was chipped. It had seven visible bullet holes on the underside. It rode like one of those cabs that had gone one on one with too many New York City potholes. But Solfanelli kept it around for a number of reasons. It could carry a bunch of people. It could get him where he wanted to go in a big hurry. And it carried enough firepower to take the island of Torcello clear off the fucking map. Inspector Lamberto Solfanelli was waiting in his baby when Joe and the two other agents boarded. He had to scream to be heard.

"Vittorio filled me in as best he could. This looks like a real mess, Joe."

"I asked him not to call you for a while."

"He works for me. Not you. You'll be gone tomorrow. He won't." Solfanelli was all business.

"Any ideas?" Joe said.

"I've got a few."

"Like what?"

"Were they lovers?"

"I don't know. It would be a hard thing to keep from the rest of us. . . . No, I don't think they could have been. Louis tells me"—Joe corrected himself—"Louis told me everything."

"He is in the bed. He has no clothes on. Vittorio says the sheets indicate they were lovers."

"I'd like to have a look for myself."

"Call it my Italian blood, but I think we may have a jealous husband on our hands."

"Her husband was nowhere near Torcello."

"Joe, this was professional. A hired gun. And I'll bet you, when we find the weapon, it will be Italian. Small-caliber. A Beretta most likely. And belonging to a local hood."

"I'll have to look for myself."

"Remember one thing, Joe. This will be my investigation, not yours."

"Louis was an American. I want the bastard who killed him."

Joe could feel the blood pounding in his temples. It was the goddamn helicopter. The noise. The whomp, whomp, whomp of the rotors. The bumpy ride. The canvas seats. The red cross on the medical box. The rocket pods. The M60 machine guns hanging out the doors. The two other agents with their Uzis at the ready. The strain in his throat from screaming. The crackle of the radio. The whine of the fucking Pratt & Whitney engine. The damn thing was taking him to a place he never wanted to go to again. And again he bit into his lip. Hard.

No one spoke a word for the remainder of the trip. Joe was burning. He wanted Louis back.

After ten minutes the beast dropped and landed with a smack on an open spot in front of Santa Fosca, Torcello's Byzantine church. The four men got out. The pilot shut down. It seemed deathly quiet when the rotors eventually ground to a halt. A few of the locals poked their heads out to see what the commotion was. But it wasn't enough for them to forsake their Christmas dinners.

The men walked to Vittorio's launch. He was sitting on the bow with a pump shotgun across his lap. Smoking a cigarette. The Wife was down in the cabin. The men exchanged greetings, and Joe went below.

"Joe, thank God," The Wife said without standing.

"How are you holding up?"

"Okay."

"I'm going to look things over in the room. I'll be right back. Then we'll get you out of here, okay?"

"Thank you, Joe."

After five minutes, Joe returned to the launch with the inspector. They stepped into the cabin. Joe spoke first.

"This is Inspector Solfanelli, ma'am. He's with the Italian police. Do you feel up to a few questions?"

"Can we wait? Can we do this tomorrow?"

Solfanelli answered, "Well, *signora,* if we do wait and ask these questions tomorrow, at the Hotel Malvasi, your husband will most likely want to be present."

It seemed the most diplomatic way to confirm whether she and Louis were lovers.

"I see. Perhaps we should go through it now," she said.

"Then you were lovers?"

The Italian still had to hear her say it.

"I guess we were. . . . Jesus, Joe what are we going to do?"

Joe didn't like that word *we*. But on the other hand, he'd known enough to be discreet. He'd kept the other agents out of the suite. And they hadn't caught any of his conversation on the chopper. So The Wife had been right when she'd said *we.* She and Joe were the only ones who knew the truth. Still, he had no answer for "what are *we* going to do?"

"We'll figure out what's best, ma'am," he said. "How long have you and Louis been . . . together?"

"Only today."

Solfanelli rolled his eyes. She caught him.

"Well, and last night too. But it wasn't . . ." She began to cry.

"That's okay," Joe said.

"Take your time, *signora.* I know this is difficult. We are only looking for a motive. Please, tell us what you saw."

"Nothing . . . I saw nothing."

"Did you hear anything?" Joe asked.

"No . . . How could this happen?"

"Do you think your husband knew about you and Louis?" Joe said.

"No."

"Can you be so sure?" Solfanelli pressed her.

"The inspector thinks that maybe the Vice President could be the jealous type."

Joe did not want to take credit for this theory.

"It was only today. That's it," she spat at Solfanelli. "And the thing last night. Okay, that too. But how could my husband know? You think he killed Louis? Jesus Christ. Listen, mister, this isn't the first time I've done this. And I've been caught before too. And nobody got killed over it."

She turned on Joe.

"What do you think he's doing with that bitch in the press office? What's her name? Judy or something? If anyone deserves to be killed, it's that slut, not Louis."

She was back to her old form. But she was having trouble holding on to it.

"Yes, ma'am. Maybe we should take a break."

"No. I want to get out of here. Let's get this over with."

"*Signora,* please. *Mi dispiace.* Can you tell us everything? From the time the two of you arrived on Torcello?"

She settled back on the seat and closed her eyes. But the move didn't slow her tears.

"We got off the boat at the dock back there. We walked around the island for about an hour. Then we went into that room over there"—she pointed. "And we fucked. We fucked twice if you must know. And we went to sleep. I woke up. And Louis was dead."

She turned and looked back at Locanda Malvasi.

"I like Louis."

Her voice began to break up again.

"It may sound stupid to you two, but in one day . . . he . . . he touched me. There was almost something there. And some bastard killed him like a fucking dog. . . . It's not fair. It's just not fair."

More tears came to her eyes.

"I didn't see anybody and I didn't hear anybody. Can I go back to the hotel now?"

"Yes, ma'am," Joe said. "I think we're all at a loss here. It doesn't make sense. Can you think of any reason why someone would want to kill Louis? Anything at all?"

"I can't . . . I can't."

The tears made her inaudible.

"My husband won't . . . be able to handle this."

Joe went to her. Put his arm around her.

"I don't think we have to tell him everything. We'll take you back now."

Joe looked at Solfanelli. The Italian nodded his approval. The Wife and Joe stepped off the boat. They walked with the two other agents to the helicopter.

"These men will take you back."

He helped her onto the chopper. She then turned and faced him as if possessed by a spirit.

"Cawdor."

"Cawdor?" Joe asked.

"Cawdor . . . I don't know what it means. It just came into my head."

"Get some rest when you get back. I'll brief your husband. Don't worry."

"Thank you, Joe."

He walked to the two agents.

"Tell Olsen things are secured here. Tell him that and what you've seen. Nothing else. I'll fill in the details when I see him. Tell him he has to boost things. I think Number Two should consider leaving earlier than planned. Cancel his meeting. Get back to Washington. This could be a lot deeper than it looks. Tell Olsen that too. I'll come back on the launch. It'll be a few hours."

The two men jumped onto the helicopter. Joe backed off. He signaled the pilot, and the beast lifted into the sky with a familiar whomp, whomp, whomp.

"Leave the dead. Take out the wounded."

Joe remembered being twenty years old and yelling those words to an even younger door gunner as the kid struggled with a corpse. Every time Joe heard a helicopter it was the same old crap.

Joe looked to his left. He found himself standing next to Solfanelli.

"Why don't you get rid of that piece of shit?" he said.

"She's a beauty, isn't she?"

Solfanelli smiled as he watched as his baby cut across the blackening evening sky.

Solfanelli and Bradlee then ambled back to the Locanda. Vittorio jumped off his boat. The three men walked into suite number five together. Joe sat in the chair by the desk and surveyed the situation. Louis' lifeless body was on the bed. Face down. Covered once again by the blanket. Solfanelli opened the bathroom window.

"He came in through here. We have some good marks in the grass outside."

Joe called to him, "It was open. She told me that on the phone."

Solfanelli walked back into the room.

"The lock was not forced. . . . I have one of my teams coming out. They should be here in a half hour. Would you like Louis taken to the consulate after we're finished?"

"Thanks. You know the CIA boys will want to be in on this. It's just too damn sharp."

"Do you think he was involved in something?"

"He was a good trooper. Clean as a whistle. A saint. Nothing. You have my word on that."

"I believe you." Solfanelli tugged at the bedroom window. Locked. "You don't have to stay. Vittorio can take you back. You know damn well the man who did this is not still on Torcello."

"I'll stay for a while. Something might come to me. You don't suppose she did it, do you?"

"The thought had occurred to me."

"And?"

"Where's the gun?" Solfanelli said.

"Christ, she could have had it in her purse for all we know .. But why would she do it? That's the big question."

"Ricatto?"

"Blackmail? I don't buy that."

"Maybe he had threatened to tell her husband."

"I don't buy it. That wasn't Louis . . . And if she did do it, that was a hell of a performance she just gave us."

"Never underestimate the powers of a woman. They can be much slyer than you think."

"No, I don't think she'd have it in her."

Joe sat quietly in his chair. Looked at the clump on the bed that was Louis. Solfanelli poked around the room. Lifting this and that with the tip of his pencil. Vittorio lit another cigarette. Joe reached over and picked up the telephone with his handkerchief. He asked the switchboard at the Hotel Malvasi to connect him with the Americans' security room.

"Yeah, Reynolds, this is Joe. Is Olsen back? . . . No, I don't want to talk to him. Tell him The Wife is on her way back by chopper. She should be there in five minutes or so. They boys on the bird will fill him in. I'm going to stay with Louis for a while, okay? . . . No, it's confusing as hell. Look, I want you to do me a favor. And you better be as good a pickpocket as you claim . . . Go down and meet The Wife. Help her off the chopper. Before she gets into the hotel, I want you to go through her purse. . . . I don't care how you do it. But don't get caught. . . . No, you're not looking for anything in particular, but if you find anything unusual. Anything that doesn't fit. Doesn't belong there. I want you to take it. Hold on to it . . . For me . . . Okay?"

Reynolds' response to all this was, "You mean like, if I should find a fucking gun in her purse, I should keep it for you, right?"

"Right, smartass. If you find a gun, hold it for me. And Reynolds, this is just between you and me, okay?"

"I'll tell you one thing. If I find a gun in her purse, we're going to have to flip a goddamn coin to see which one of us gets to flush her ass down the toilet."

Twenty-one

Joe arrived back at the Hotel Malvasi at eight p.m. on Christmas. He had remained at Louis' side. He'd helped the Italian police put Louis' body into the plastic bag. He'd pulled the zipper closed himself. Helped them carry it to the police launch. Joe had stayed put throughout Solfanelli's entire investigation of the scene. Hoping to pick up something. Anything. Desperately trying to piece it all together.

In the end, they'd all been left with the obvious. Whoever killed Louis had arrived on Torcello by boat and had tied up at the small dock on the far side of the island. The murderer had then walked to Locanda Malvasi, coming at it from the back side. He had slid in through the bathroom window. Shot Louis. In the back of the head. Most likely three times. Then left by the same way he came. Solfanelli's lab would confirm how many bullets had been put into Louis' brain.

One bullet had been found in the blood-soaked mattress. The inspector had seen enough small-caliber Beretta slugs to be positive of the weapon, but the lab would have to confirm his suspicions.

Joe had come back to the Malvasi on the hotel's launch with Vittorio. The two men had run through it all a dozen times. By the time they'd finished their fifty-minute trip, they had resolved nothing. They were still at square one.

Joe jumped off the launch and onto the hotel dock. As Vittorio steadied his craft, the policeman said, "*Per favore,* Joe, I think my cover is still good. The inspector would like to keep me here as long as he possibly can. You can speak to the woman, yes?"

"Yes."

Joe reached into his pocket and handed Vittorio a twenty thousand lira note. To make it look clean.

"Grazie, signore. Lei e molto gentile."

Joe entered the hotel. He walked straight through the lobby and into the Malvasi dining room. About thirty people had come to the room for Christmas dinner. There wasn't a familiar face among them. Joe went back to the front desk. Nelo had left. Gianni was still on.

"Good evening, Joe."

"Hello, Gianni. Mrs. Wallace, Nina Wallace, did she check in with her son? Possibly under the name of Lake?"

"I'm sorry, Joe. The problem was, the hotel is booked up."

"Shit."

"I am sorry. It was impossible . . . But . . . She is a very forceful woman. You must know that?"

"And?"

"I gave her a key to the laundry room. They are in there."

"Thanks, Gianni. *Sono in un debito di gratitudine.*"

Joe went to the house phone and asked the operator to connect him to the laundry room.

"Nina, it's Joe . . . Fine . . . No, really, I'm fine . . . I have to bring people up to date. It'll take about a half hour. Pick up a key for my room at the front desk, okay? . . . I'll be there soon. Are you okay? . . . You're sure? . . . Good. I won't be long."

After Joe hung up the telephone he arranged for a key for Nina and went up to the operations room. All the agents were there. Olsen. Reynolds. Hall 'n' Oates. Even Lightfoot, who had returned from his bout with the bad liver.

The room was quiet. Joe looked at the other men.

The feeling was that of a newly formed posse. Maybe a lynch mob.

"Jesus, I feel sorry for the poor son of a bitch if he runs into any one of you bastards."

It cut the tension a little. Not much.

"Reynolds, did you find anything?"

"She was clean."

Olsen was confused. "Would you like to share this with the rest of us, or at least me?"

"It was a long shot, but The Wife was the only one in the room with him. . . . You never know," Joe said.

"So, was he fucking her or what?"

This comment from Olsen sent a bristle up Joe's spine. But he couldn't ignore it. He had to decide, here and now, who could know about Louis and The Wife. And who couldn't.

"I don't think so," he said.

He wasn't any good at this. He knew they could see the truth on his face. In his eyes. He was too close to these guys. Also, he was going to need their help if he wanted to find out who the hell had killed Louis. He walked over to the window and looked into the darkness.

"How'd he get it?"

Joe wasn't sure who'd asked the question. But to come up with a decent lie seemed harder than figuring out the truth.

"Joe? You okay?"

This was Reynolds.

Joe turned back to the others.

"Yeah."

Then after a pause.

"They were in bed together . . . but let's not let it get out of this room, okay?"

"Wait a minute. They were in this room balling, and she doesn't know who did it?" Reynolds said.

"They were asleep."

"She says . . . She didn't wake up?"

"I believe her. I saw a different person out on Torcello. I don't think she's a good enough actress to be faking this."

Joe looked at Olsen.

"What's Number Two know?"

"He's been briefed. I put a little scare into him. I told him that someone had mistaken Louis for him. That Louis died saving his wife. He bought it. But he's scared shitless. He won't come out of his room. We're taking your advice. Going back to D.C. tomorrow. We'll fly Cardinal out at one p.m."

"All things considered, I think it's best. Solfanelli had a jealous husband theory. Did you pick up anything like that from Number Two when you told him what happened?"

"It's hard to say. I wasn't looking for it. But off the top of my head, I'd have to say no. He seemed concerned about Louis . . . of course, not as concerned as he was about himself."

"Hey. Come on. We all know the guy. He's got balls the size of rat turds. We could've all been fucking her, and he wouldn't have done anything."

"Reynolds is probably right," Joe said. "So what does that leave us?"

"Well, unfortunately, it leaves us our jobs."

Olsen was sounding too damn official for Joe's liking.

"We're going to have to leave it to the Italian police," Olsen said. "I'm sure State and the CIA will get into it too. But we don't have the time or the manpower for it, and you all know that. Our job is to Work the Man, and that's what we'll do."

Joe knew there was no way he'd be getting on Cardinal the following afternoon. He wasn't going anywhere until he got the fucker who killed Louis. He also knew he'd be able to have Solfanelli hold Louis' body as long as he needed him to. So he tried a bluff.

"Well, somebody's going to have to take Louis home. It might as well be me."

"The boys at State will take care of that. I've already spoken to them about it. We're going to need everyone we have."

"Goddamn it, Jerry. I'm not leaving Louis here, with a bunch of wops down at the morgue, waiting for the assholes at the State Department to get their shit together."

Joe knew this was the kind of reasoning Olsen could understand.

"Well, we'll leave in to Mock. He should be here by morning."

A synchronized groan spread through the room.

"I forgot about him. Keep the son of a bitch away from me, will you?"

"What about this Oscar Sanchez character?" Reynolds asked.

"Solfanelli and I batted that around. The whole thing's not Oscar's style. . . . I told Solfanelli that Oscar'd called here. He'll be able to have the phone line checked. See where and when he made his calls. What time was it, anyway?"

"It's in the log. I think it was around three-thirty or so."

"If he was calling from his apartment, there's no way he could have been on Torcello. Solfanelli will have the phone crap tomorrow."

Reynolds shook his head, "Yeah, but that's not my point. You said Sanchez wasn't a threat yesterday. I was thinking more of what he said to me this afternoon. He said, 'Carter Perkins is a very dangerous individual.' Where was Perkins today? And how dangerous is the bastard?"

Reynolds looked at Hall 'n' Oates.

"Hey, if you boys feel you'd like to add anything pertinent to this situation, get involved in some way, don't let me stop you. Speak right up."

They both stood and moved toward Reynolds. Olsen stepped between them.

"Okay, okay. Let's everyone settle down here."

He then focused on Reynolds.

"How dangerous is he? He's a fucking faggot, for Christ's sake. You think some fucking queer's going to hotfoot it out to Torcello and get the drop on one of my men?"

They all bristled at Olsen's use of the term *my men.*

"No fucking way. And why would Perkins do it?

Answer me that, will you. Why . . . ? Christ, sometimes I wonder about you, Reynolds."

"Do me a favor, Reynolds," Joe said. "Contact C.O. and have them run Nina Lake Wallace through Big Bertha. Let me know what they come up with."

"Right."

"Hold on. Is this something else we should all know about? Who the hell is Nina Lake Wallace?" Olsen asked.

"I'm having dinner with her. I just need a history."

"The Wife doesn't know shit, then, huh?" Reynolds said to Joe. And Joe was happy to get off the subject of Nina so quickly.

"No. The Wife's too rattled. Maybe tomorrow. Something might come to her. Where is she?"

"They're all locked in. They had their dinners sent up . . . separately," Lightfoot said.

Reynolds couldn't let this pass untouched.

"Did you tell them to stay away from the calf's liver?"

"Fuck you."

Twenty-two

The assassin was still floating on cloud nine. After arriving at the Hotel Malvasi, Carter had gone back to the room and soaked in a bath for an hour and a half. Let the hot water run slowly for the entire time so as to keep the temperature up. Carter had taken a book along to the bath and finished it long before the soaking. Four hundred and seventy-nine pages.

Carter stepped out of the bath and toweled off. And once again admired the nude figure in the full-length mirror, and the hardened nipples. They'd become overly enlarged. Carter thought, "What I need most, right now, is to have some bronzed thing to spend the night with. A young one that could keep it coming all night long." Of course, that would be impossible. The clubs where Carter's favorites spent their time would not be open on Christmas. Plus, Carter wanted to be here, in the Hotel Malvasi, when word of the Vice President's death spread.

Carter guessed it was going on right now. The top floor of the Malvasi should be buzzing with hysteria. By this time every American of importance—the President, senators, congressmen, ambassadors, and moles—must all know that their second in command has fallen. The White Knight. The handsome prince. Found in a pool of blood lying next to his ever loving wife on the island of Torcello. On Christmas Day.

And DOC will have known about it long before any of them. Whoever DOC was—he, she, or they—must be in seventh heaven by now. Halfway home. "Glorious," Carter thought.

The Secret Service would be found lacking in their duties. Unable to protect the American prince. The news would leak out eventually. The press would get it quickly enough, and lastly it would sift down to the poor women and men on the street.

Carter had made a dinner reservation in the hotel dining room for nine o'clock. Forty-five minutes to go. There seemed little point in waiting. The news must be out. It surely must be a madhouse in the lobby by now, and this assassin didn't want to miss a thing.

Carter skipped to the closet and threw on a favorite holiday suit—the one saved for special celebrations. It was black velvet, with black satin piping adorning the lapels. A vermilion bow tie finished the ensemble off. Carter went back to the bathroom and admired the reflection in the mirror one more time. And smiled at what bounced back from the silvered glass.

". . . let the devil wear black, for I'll have a suit of sables."

Carter took the revolver, the .38-caliber Webley-Fosbery, the last line of defense, and dropped it into the holster that had been slung under an accommodating left arm. And once again went to the mirror. Even the most carefully trained eye would see no sign of a bulge. And there would be no metal detectors in the dining room tonight. There would be no need. The prince was dead. Carter cackled like a child, did a tiny pirouette, snatched the room key, and danced out.

The elevator seemed to take forever to arrive. And then take an eternity to get to the ground floor. When the doors finally opened, Carter stepped out into a very serene lobby. On the one hand, there was a strong feeling of disappointment, but on the other, relief to know nothing had been missed. The Americans were doing an unbelievable job of keeping everything under cuffs.

However, it didn't take long to become impatient.

Carter wanted the news to break, and break now. This wasn't bloody fair. This was Carter's day. There should be fireworks.

Carter went to the house phone and asked to be connected to the Americans' press room. It took eight rings before it was answered.

"Yes, would this be Judy? It's Carter Perkins, my darling. How are you this evening? . . . Lovely. I just wanted to confirm my appointment with the Vice President for eleven-fifteen tomorrow. . . . Really? . . ." Carter was getting somewhat excited. "Well, I don't quite understand. Why must he cancel? I was so much counting on this. . . . I see . . . And you can't go into any more detail than that? . . . Don't get snippy with me, young lady. Travel writer or not, I am a member of the press, and if there is a problem, I feel I have a right to know."

Judy hung up.

This was another surprise. Carter had expected Judy to be a tad more upset than she was. By all appearances, she surely had a crush on the Vice President. She might even have been having an affair with him. It was difficult to tell. Whatever the case, her reaction to the events of the past few hours was definitely not what Carter had hoped for. This killer was looking forward to seeing the whole world cry. Starting with Judy.

It would happen. It would come. If it would happen in the middle of Carter's dinner, so be it. The dining room would erupt. Become a fantastic volcano of emotions. And Carter would have a front-row seat.

"*Buon Natale, Signore Perkins.* I have your table all ready for you," the maître d' said when he saw Carter.

"Thank you. Christmas can be such an exciting time of year, don't you think?"

Twenty-three

Joe was exhausted. It had been the simple truth and he'd said so. They all were. But Joe had been the one to sit with Louis for two and a half hours. He was the most drained. It showed.

"Call it a night. We'll pick it up in the morning" had been Olsen's suggestion. Joe took it. He now found himself in the strange position of having to knock before he could enter his own room.

"Yes?"

"It's me."

Nina opened the door. She was wearing a white terry-cloth Malvasi robe. Her hair was wrapped turban-style in a towel, and she was still wearing her dark glasses. Eubie was asleep on the bed.

"Didn't I see you in a Fellini movie last summer?"

She smiled, took her glasses off, and kissed him.

"I was worried about you."

She put her glasses back on.

"Sorry, I can't see a damn thing without them."

"Hey, it's a look."

"How are you doing?"

"Okay . . ."

She put her arms around him. "This room was a mess when I got here. Someone had thrown the mattress off the bed. The lamp was broken."

"It was me . . . I like this look on you. It should go over big in the dining room."

"I had to take a shower. I needed the distraction. I also felt a little grungy. I guess I wasn't thinking too far ahead."

"Hey, it's a look."

"Well, I just couldn't put the same clothes back on. I'd rather not. We can have dinner sent up, can't we?"

"Are you nuts? I promised you a Christmas dinner, and we're going to do it right."

He picked up the telephone and was connected to the press room.

"Judy it's Joe . . . Yeah, me too. He was a good man. . . . You know this business about Louis isn't a press item, don't you? . . . Good. Listen, I need a big favor. Can I borrow a dress? . . . It's not for me, I have a friend here with no clothes. . . . Yes. No, I mean no . . . it's not what you think. It's confusing. It's been a long day. . . . Here, I'll put her on. She can explain it to you." He handed the telephone to Nina.

While Judy and Nina got the dress mess straightened out, Joe took a shower. It was a long one. By the time he came out of the bathroom, with only a towel around his waist, he found Nina dressed and ready to go.

"Sorry, I'll only be a minute. I need to get some clothes from over there."

He pointed, then walked sideways like a crab to the closet door.

"Hey, it's a look," she said.

"Thanks."

"We have to work on our timing. Get our looks coordinated," she said. She then came to him and they kissed.

"That's not going to expedite things much." Joe held Nina back and looked her up and down. "Nice dress."

"Pink's not really my color."

"Goes great with your shoes."

"Have you ever looked down at Judy's feet? Her shoes could double for gondolas. Come on, get dressed, I'm starved. I'll work on bringing Eubie back amongst the living."

She could feel Joe deflate.

"Damn. I'm sorry, Joe. Judy told me about Louis. I sort of squeezed it out of her. I'm sorry . . . Tell me to shut up anytime you want."

When they arrived in the Malvasi dining room, it was still well over a third full. Each table had been decorated with holly branches and a small poinsettia plant. There seemed to be no other colors in the room except red and green and the white of the table linen. People were happy. The noise level had become much higher than usual. The maître d' took them to a corner table, and in a rare move Joe sat with his back to the masses. He let Nina and Eubie look out to the other guests and take in the great room. He never noticed Carter Perkins sitting at the table by the far window.

The maître d' handed out menus and a wine list. The waiter served a bottle of Pellegrino water. The water wasn't something they did without asking, but the waiter knew Joe. He knew what Joe liked.

"*Signore Joe,* it's good to see you. Your friends seem to have deserted us for Christmas."

"They had a change in plans."

There was no real smile from Joe. The waiter knew better than to press the subject further, and he backed away from the table.

"This is the best Christmas I've ever had," Eubie said almost loud enough for the entire dining room.

"Me too. I can't think of anyplace I'd rather be right now," Joe replied. He glanced at the chandelier and wondered who he was trying to fool.

"Me three," Nina said. She had taken her dark glasses off to read the menu. She held it about three inches from her nose and had to squint to see Joe. He smiled. All things considered, Nina and Eubie probably were the best things for him at the moment. Nina put her glasses back on and looked beyond him.

"Do you know this person?"

"What person?"

Carter Perkins was walking directly toward their table.

"Mr. Red Bow Tie. He's coming our way," Nina said.

Joe turned. Sure enough, Carter was parading over for a chat.

Nina had recognized Carter as the person who'd held the door for her earlier. She remembered feeling a hideous chill invade her bloodstream as she and Eubie passed Carter by.

"Some people give me the creeps," she said.

Joe looked back to her and said, "Do you know him?"

"No. He held the door for us this afternoon. Creepy, creepy that's all. There's something very strange about him."

End of conversation. Carter had arrived.

"Good evening, Mr. Bradlee, and a Merry Christmas to you all."

"Thank you. Is there something I can help you with?"

Joe did not stand.

"I just wanted to offer you, and your guests, a bottle of champagne, to add to your celebration, if you will." Carter was desperate to get Joe to blurt out some news on the Vice President.

"Thank you, but I think we'll pass."

"Oh, but it is a day for celebration, don't you think?"

"Nice tie."

Carter didn't pick up on Nina's sarcasm.

"Thank you. I purchased it in Berlin several years ago. I only wear it on Christmas."

"So we've been sort of blessed to see it, then?"

"You might say that. I don't believe I've had the pleasure?"

"Carter Perkins, this is Nina Wallace and her son, Eubie." Joe took a breath. "Now. Mr. Perkins, at the risk of sounding rude, we're trying to have a sort of family-type dinner here. If there's something I can help you with, let me know. Otherwise, would you please excuse us?"

"As a matter of fact, there is something. My meeting with your Vice President, the one I had scheduled for tomorrow morning, has been canceled. I was wondering if you might be able to shed some light on what the problem might be?"

"His plans have changed. He won't be seeing anyone for the remainder of his time in Venice."

"Is there something wrong?"

"No. Plans have changed. Now, if you'll excuse us."

"No explanation? Mr. Bradlee, I needn't remind you, I am a member of the press. If something's wrong, then I have a right to know."

"I have nothing more to say to you, Mr. Perkins."

"Well, obviously something is rotten in the state of Denmark, and I am entitled to know what it is."

"Excuse me for a minute, will you?" Joe said this to Nina and Eubie. He then stood, took Carter by the elbow, and walked the worm to the maître d's desk.

"Now, let me make something crystal fucking clear for you. If you come over to my table one more time, if you say one more word to me, or my guests, I'm going to stand up and rip your fucking throat out. Are you with me on that?"

Carter adjusted the lapels of the velvet jacket and raised nose and chin to meet Joe's glare.

"Steed threatens steed, in high and boastful neighs."

This confused Joe a bit.

"Whatever . . . Just stay out of my way."

When Joe returned to his table, Eubie and Nina had already decided on dinner. The waiter was patiently waiting for Joe.

"We're both having goose," Eubie said. "I've never had it before."

"Sounds good to me." He handed his menu to the waiter. "Let's make it three. . . . Sorry about that guy. I thought he was just a travel writer. Now all of a sudden he thinks he's Jimmy Breslin."

"Doesn't Perkins seem strange to you?" Nina said.

"That's an understatement."

"No, I mean beyond the clothes and whatnot. Isn't there something way off?"

"I know I don't like him."

"Well, it's too bad, whatever it is. Free champagne would have been nice."

"Hey, you want champagne? You got champagne. . . . Lorenzo, *per favore* . . ."

Twenty-four

When the champagne arrived, it exploded with a crack so loud, the entire dining room turned to see who the lucky people were. Nina raised her glass.

"An' it's Tommy this, an' Tommy that, an' anything you please, An' Tommy ain't a bloomin' fool—"

Eubie jumped in and finished the verse: ". . . you bet that Tommy sees!"

They laughed and downed their champagne. All three of them at once. Eubie burped. They laughed again.

"Listen," Joe said. "I'm sure they could find you a room if you want to stay here tonight."

"All our things are back on the other side. Thanks. I couldn't wear this dress another day."

"You're sure?"

"I'm sure."

The dinner was fabulous. Eubie devoured the goose. Whenever Joe would slide into thoughts of Louis, or the work piled ahead him, Nina would pull him up. Keep him from slipping. She'd bring him back to the table with a joke or a story. Or simply say, "It'll be okay, Joe. Don't worry, it'll work out."

Before they knew it they'd finished their espresso and dessert and were on their way back to Joe's room. They picked up Nina's clothes, then headed down to the dock. They found Pietro waiting by his launch. Nina stopped.

"Damn, I still have the key to your room."

She pulled the key out from her purse.

"Keep it. It doesn't make any difference."

"Well here, you can drop it off when you get back inside."

She handed the key to Joe. He handed it back.

"Just keep it, okay?" He pressed the key hard into her hand. "For me."

"Okay."

Nina didn't get it. Neither did Joe. He just wanted her to have the key.

The three then jumped down on the Malvasi launch and were off into the darkness. On their way to the Dorsoduro and La Primavera. Small shots of lightning illuminated the water's surface every minute or so, but no rain or snow fell from the sky.

When they arrived, Eubie was once again sound asleep. Joe picked him up in his arms. He seemed like a forty-pound sack of rice. He didn't move a muscle. Joe hefted him like he was checking a watermelon for bruises.

"Eubie, huh. After Eubie Blake?"

"Who's Eubie Blake?" she said.

"Who's Eubie Blake?" A look of absolute disbelief covered Joe's face.

"Yes . . . Who's Eubie Blake?"

"The composer . . . ? You've never heard of Eubie Blake?"

"No . . ."

" 'I'm Just Wild About Harry' . . . ?"

"It was my husband's idea. He named him after Eubie Brooks."

"Who the hell is Eubie Brooks?"

"He used to play for the Mets."

"That's *H*ubie. With an H. *H*ubie."

"*H*ubie . . . ? It's *H*ubie Brooks? His name is *H*ubie?"

"Yes."

"What an idiot . . . Jesus, Hubie . . . ? Now you see why I divorced the blockhead."

They laughed. Joe called to the helmsman.

"Can you wait for me, Pietro? I shouldn't be too long."

"It is not a problem, Joe. Take your time."

"Eubie Brooks . . . Christ."

The main entrance of La Primavera had been locked for the evening. They needed to ring for the night clerk and ask him to open the side door. Nina led the way up the curving stairs to their room. She unlocked the door. Joe put Eubie down on the folding cot that had been placed in the corner for him. He went to the window and opened the shutters.

"This is nice," he said. "I've only seen it from the outside."

"It could use a little more heat, but other than that I like it."

"There are a lot of innovative ways to warm up," he said.

She came over to him. They kissed.

"It's not tonight, Joe. Not here. The timing's just not right."

"I know it's not. I didn't really mean it that way. I didn't say what I meant. Maybe I was thinking more of the future. Or maybe . . . Hell, just wear socks to bed."

"That's good. It's something to think about—the future."

"I like you."

"That's good too."

"I don't know anything about you."

"No, you don't." She kissed him again. "Now leave. I'm whipped."

"I'll call you tomorrow."

He walked toward the door but stopped at the dresser. He picked up a glass figure. It appeared to be a man with a lance. Possibly a knight. It was difficult to tell. The craftsmanship was a bit crude. It was bright red. The color of a cherry soft drink.

"This is a nice piece. Nice color." It was Joe's turn for sarcasm. "What the hell's it supposed to be?"

"Be careful with that. It's very fragile. It's Eubie's glass man. He bought it yesterday. We watched the man make it. If you break it I'll kill you."

"Don Quixote?"

"I guess so. It's hard to tell. Put it down. You're making me very uneasy."

"It's heavy as hell."

"Please. Will you put it down?"

"I won't break it."

"Will you put it down?"

Joe set the glass man on the dresser and continued on to the door. Again he stopped and turned.

"Does the word Cawdor mean anything to you?"

"Cawdor?"

"Cawdor."

"You mean like the Thane?"

"The Thane? What the hell's a thane?"

"The Thane of Cawdor."

"What's the Thane of Cawdor?"

"It's a who."

"Okay. Who's the Thane of Cawdor?"

"Macbeth."

"You mean the Shakespeare guy?"

"Yes. The Shakespeare guy . . . Good night."

She pushed him out the door and threw the lock.

WEDNESDAY

One

When the Big Man, Chester Mock, walked into the operations room on the top floor of the Hotel Malvasi at nine on the morning of December twenty-sixth, one thing was painfully obvious to the Secret Service agents present: He was one very, very pissed-off government employee.

Mock had done exactly as Louis had predicted. He'd kissed his wife and family late on Christmas Eve, driven to John Foster Dulles International Airport, walked up to the Delta counter, whipped out his magic checkbook, and said, "Get me a plane and a crew, I need to go to Venice, Italy—now."

The look in Mock's eyes had been easily translated by the flight attendant. Not one question had been asked. In twenty-five minutes the Delta people had supplied him with a gassed-up 737, a crew, and enough Chivas Regal to last ten hours. Again, just as Louis had predicted.

By midnight they had become airborne and were headed north. The polar route.

"Maybe we'll see Santa Claus. What do you think?"

The pilot had said this as a gesture of friendship and in an attempt to open a dialogue with the agent. Mock had glanced up from his scotch and thought, "If it wasn't necessary for this putz to land this fucking plane safely in Italy, I could take his head off right fucking here and now." The pilot had interpreted Mock's expression perfectly. He slinked back to his cockpit and never said another word for the entire flight.

Things had begun to get shaky over the pole. Mock still hated to travel, and airplanes were the fucking worst. This time the co-pilot had been sent back with the bad news.

"Excuse me, sir?"

Mock had been asleep.

"Sir?"

The co-pilot nudged Mock as though he were touching a napping rattlesnake.

"What the hell is it?"

The co-pilot jumped a good two feet.

"Jesus, can't you bastards smooth this fucking thing out?"

"Well, that's just it, sir. There seems to be a slight storm kicking up over Scotland, and I'm afraid we're going to have to put down at Gatwick for a short time."

The man had considered running back into the cockpit. Bolting the door behind him.

"You push this fucking plane through this fucking storm, or I'll throw all three of you bastards out on your goddamn asses and fly the fucking thing myself."

It sounded good, but in the long run it couldn't work. They were being thrown around the sky like a piece of popcorn. And after some very clever maneuvering, the pilot banked his plane sharply, dropped his gear, and bounced down at Gatwick International Airport. England.

A rolling stairway had been pushed to the side of the 737. Mock stood. Waited for the hatch to be opened. The door to the cockpit had been left ajar. The three men inside scratched notes on clipboards and sang the first chorus of "White Christmas." They seemed to put an unusually strong emphasis on the word *white*.

Mock could have killed them all right there on the spot. It would have been easy. He was armed. He had plenty of bullets. Instead he pushed his head through the door and said, "I'll be in the first-class lounge—sleeping. I want to know the minute you bastards can get this piece of shit in the air again."

It took eight hours to get the piece of shit in the air again, and Mock slept like a child for every one of them. So, not only did he appear very pissed off to the agents on the top floor of the Hotel Malvasi—he was well rested.

"Would one of you fucking dickheads like to tell me what the hell is going on here?" were his first words. It was going to be another long day.

In the room with Mock were Olsen, Reynolds, and Lightfoot. Olsen was the fucking dickhead who answered.

"Well, sir, we have a lot of questions and very few answers. Zezzo seems to have been killed by a professional. We're sure of that. But it's the why we can't get a handle on."

"I don't give a rat's ass about Zezzo. He was a good man. I'm sorry he's dead, but our job is to keep the man down the hall alive. We make sure he gets back to Washington, D.C., without any further bullshit. Is that clear?"

There was a grumble of "Yes, sir."

"It's State, it's State, it's State. I don't want to have to say that again. Everyone get it? The State Department will look into Zezzo's death. If I catch one of you bastards trying to poke around on your own, I'm going to be one pissed-off motherfucker. And you shitheads can count on that."

"Sir?"

"What?"

It was Olsen.

"I've set Cardinal up for a thirteen-hundred takeoff. The Italian police are supplying us with three personnel helicopters and a Huey gunship. We'll be picked up here at noon. There will only be seating for The Panhandler—ah, sorry, sir . . . Goliath, that is, The Wife and child, and agents. Everyone else goes out by boat at eleven."

Joe walked in and groaned audibly at the sight of Mock.

"Bradlee. Where the fuck have you been?"

"I was checking on a few things."

"Well, you missed out, mister, so I'll say it one more time. I don't want you bastards *checking on a few things.* I want you to work the Man and that's it. Nothing else. Clear?"

"I was seeing if The Wife was up to traveling."

Mock stumbled some.

"Good . . . Great . . . I'm glad one of you shitheads is on the ball. Where the fuck are Barnes and Wilson?"

"Who?" Reynolds said. He'd been calling them Hall 'n' Oates for so long, he too had forgotten their real names.

"Barnes and Wilson," Mock roared.

"Hall 'n' Oates." Joe helped Reynolds out. "They're in your boy's room. He won't let them out of his sight. He's a very frightened man."

"Okay. Olsen, I want to go over this step by step. I don't want any more bullshit, understand?"

Mock turned to see Joe walking out the door.

"Hey. Bradlee. Where the hell do you think you're going? We've got business here. I want you in on this."

"Listen, Chester—"

Mock gave Joe a look that would have torn the lungs out of a lesser man.

Joe ignored it.

"Somebody's going to have to take Louis back to Philadelphia. It might as well be me."

"You're not going anywhere, mister. State will take care of Louis."

Joe was very quiet when he spoke. It took a moment, but when he did speak, everyone heard it.

"I'm going back with Louis."

"What . . . ? Am I talking to a fucking wall, here? You'll be on one of those choppers just like the rest of us."

Olsen tried to save the day.

"Excuse me, sir. You're planning to go the airport with the rest of us, right?"

"Olsen, are you aware that you bastards have royally screwed up my entire Christmas? I'm not staying in this waterlogged hellhole one more second than's necessary."

"Well, my point is, sir. If you're getting on one of the choppers, somebody has to be bumped off. It might as well be Bradlee."

"Bullshit. I'll squeezed his skinny ass on one of those birds if he has to sit on my fucking lap. And that's final."

"Well, Chester, I'm afraid not." Joe still spoke softly. "One, I'm staying with Louis, and two, I'm going to find out who killed him."

"You fuck with me, mister, you're fucking with the wrong man. I'll take you back to Washington in chains if I have to."

Joe decided to call Mock's bluff.

"So be it."

He turned and headed for the door.

"Lightfoot . . . ?" Mock barked. "Cuff the son of a bitch."

Lightfoot balked.

"Now."

Lightfoot went to Joe. He shrugged and pulled his handcuffs out.

"Sorry, Joe."

He took Joe's 9mm from its holster and handcuffed Joe behind his back.

Joe looked at Lightfoot and said with a shrug, "You do what you gotta do."

"You're in big trouble, buddy," Mock said. He took Joe's pistol from Lightfoot. "What the fuck is this? How long have you been carrying this non-issue piece of shit?"

"Since '77."

"You're in big trouble, buddy."

The telephone rang. Reynolds picked it up.

"Yes, ma'am. Let me see if I can reach him."

He cupped the receiver.

"It's for Joe."

"Well, who the fuck is it?"

Mock said this loud enough for the better part of the Hotel Malvasi to hear.

"The Wife."

Mock lowered his voice a bit.

"See if she can talk to someone else."

"Maybe I can help you, ma'am," Reynolds said into the phone. "I see . . . Yes, ma'am." He cupped it again. "She won't talk to anyone but Joe."

"Jesus Christ. Bradlee, see what she wants," Mock whispered.

Joe walked over to the telephone, and Reynolds held it to his ear.

"Yes, ma'am . . . I'll do that. I'll see that he gets it . . . No, ma'am, there'll be no problem. . . . Yes, ma'am, everything's according to schedule. . . . That's right. Noon . . . Yes, ma'am."

Reynolds hung up the telephone. Mock bore down.

"What did she want?"

"Nothing much."

"Out with it, mister."

Joe was still very low-key.

"Louis had apparently borrowed one of Number Two's overcoats. She wanted me to be sure to get it back."

"Well, what the fuck did he take one of the boss's overcoats for?"

"Maybe he was cold."

"Don't you push me, Reynolds. I'll lock your ass up too."

"Yes, sir."

Joe walked to the overstuffed chair by the window. He crouched and brought his handcuffed wrists down behind his knees. He sat. He then lifted his legs and pulled his wrists out from under his feet so that his hands were now in front of him. Mock glared at him.

"It's a lot more comfortable, Chester," Joe said. "Something tells me this is going to be a long fucking day."

Two

Throughout the elongated night, Carter Perkins had not slept well. And any explanation for this sleeplessness had not been forthcoming. It surely couldn't have been because another human being had been eliminated. Another life snuffed out. Carter had done that many times in the past and slept like a baby afterward.

Carter had suffered horrendous dreams throughout this endless night. One in particular, where the assassin's naked body had been staked out on the ground, a small brown bird, possibly a sparrow, pecking relentlessly at the arms and legs, had returned time and time again. Eventually this bird would move on to the eyes and feast like a starved vulture. At the dream's end the bird would fly down the throat, and Carter would cough and gag until wide awake. Sitting straight up in bed, hands clawing at the sheets.

The dream had returned many times. All night long. And Carter would continually jolt upright in a cold sweat. Choking. And there was always a feeling that the bird was still there in the room. Hiding. Staring down from the darkness. The dream had become so frightening, that by three a.m., Carter had turned on every light. And had left the bulbs burning until the sun came up. It hadn't worked. The persistent brown bird always came back.

At nine Carter slipped out of bed and dressed. Exhausted and shaky. The news of the assassination must be in all the morning papers by now. Carter would not have breakfast in the room this morning, but would venture to the dining room. Would risk having to hear Americans cry for their well-done bacon just to have the opportunity to see them cry over the death of their prince.

But after arriving in the lobby, Carter was once again jolted. There was no flurry of activity. There was no panic. No mass hysteria. There were no tears. Only Nelo's smiling face. Carter crossed to the front desk.

"*Buon giorno, Signore Perkins.* You are having your breakfast with us on this beautiful morning? This will be our pleasure. Did you sleep well?"

"Yes. Thank you, Nelo," Carter lied. "It seems rather quiet this morning, don't you think?"

"Many guests have not come down yet."

"Anything interesting in today's newspaper?"

"The feast of San Stefano, Signore Perkins? You surprise me. Nothing happens in Venezia."

"And how about the American vice president? Is he down for breakfast this morning?"

"Signore, I haven't seen him since yesterday noontime. He seems to have become . . . I'm sorry . . ."

Nelo looked at the ceiling as if the word might appear there.

". . . *scarto?*"

"Shy?"

"*Si.* Shy."

"Quite . . . Has some problem arisen?"

"They are a very secretive bunch, the Americans. But I think there is no problem. No, signore."

Carter thanked Nelo and continued on into breakfast.

The Malvasi dining room was empty except for one table. At that table were seated three people. An older woman and, most likely, her son with his wife.

Carter guessed them to be Americans. Californians, no doubt, from their attire. The couple wore blue jeans, white tennis shoes, and synthetic sports shirts with Mickey and Goofy embroidered on the back. The older woman was grossly overweight. She sported a pink velour sweatsuit with red piping and a blue ball cap with two large white letters on it—LA.

It was time to stir the pot. Carter approached their table.

"Excuse me?"

"Yes," the son answered.

"You're Americans, aren't you?"

"Yes, we are, as a matter of fact. How did you know?"

Carter grumbled slightly, then said, "Did you know that your vice president is here at the hotel?"

"Yes, we saw him yesterday morning. He's so handsome," the mother said.

"Indeed. I was wondering if you had heard of any trouble."

"What kind of trouble?" she said.

"Well, I'm not altogether sure. I was in the elevator with two of the Vice President's security men, and . . . Well, I heard them mention something about a shooting. I only wondered if you had heard any news."

"A shooting? No, we didn't hear anything like that."

The woman took a large bite from her breakfast roll.

"God, these are dry," she complained. "Say, you don't speak Italian, do you?"

"Some."

"I can't seem to get this damn waiter to bring me any oatmeal. How the hell do you say oatmeal in Italian?"

"Madam, the waiters in this hotel speak fluent English. They may very well speak better English than you and your entire family. Perhaps they don't have any . . . oat . . . meal."

Carter spun on a heel and returned to the table by the window.

The fat woman's final remark was, "I think he was a fairy, don't you, Rusty?"

Carter slumped in the padded chair and gazed out the window. The waiter was there in a second.

"Coffee," was all Carter could say.

"Sí, signore."

The coffee was also there in a second. Carter continued to gaze out the window. It all made no sense. "Why are the Americans keeping everything so quiet?" Carter barely whispered.

"Excuse me. Carter Perkins, isn't it?"

Carter almost jumped a foot from the chair. But then, after turning and regaining a touch of composure, said, "Well, my goodness, the Moor of Venice . . . before my very eyes."

"My name is Reynolds, sir. I'm with the American Secret Service. Do you mind if I join you?"

"Not at all. An attractive young man like yourself. Please be my guest." Carter was instantly in love.

"Thank you."

Reynolds sat with his back to the window—facing Carter.

"I wanted to meet you, ask you a few questions, if you don't mind."

"Not at all. I hope I'm not being suspected of some horrible misdemeanor. Would you care for some coffee?"

"Thank you, no. There's been no horrible misdemeanor, Mr. Perkins. It's just part of our job to check out everyone who might come into contact with the Vice President. I'm sure you understand."

"Quite . . . I hope you don't mind my saying so, but I believe you're the most handsome man I've ever seen."

"Thank you . . ." Reynolds cleared his throat and was back on track. "I received an interesting telephone call yesterday from a man by the name of Oscar Sanchez. I don't suppose you know him?"

"No. I don't believe I do."

"He made a name for himself in the explosives business. Some would call him a terrorist."

"Not *the* Oscar?"

"Yes. Then you do know him?"

"Well, only from the newspapers. He's been in the news quite often. But, of course, that was years ago. Probably before your time. You must be very young."

"Well, Oscar seems to know you."

"Really?"

Carter shifted in the chair. The acid from the coffee was beginning to work and chew on an itchy and empty stomach. And again Carter began wishing the night hadn't been so fitful.

"Yes, really," Reynolds said. "Would you like to hear what Oscar had to say about you?"

"I don't think so. I don't know the man and he doesn't know me. So whatever he has to say could hardly be of any interest."

"He said, 'Carter Perkins is a very dangerous individual.' " Reynolds let that soak in a little, then continued. "Why do you think he would say something like that? About you?"

"I have no idea. I don't know the man. But if you are so worried about me, a harmless travel writer . . . if you feel I am of some threat to your precious vice president, I suggest you throw me in chains. Keep me as far away from him as you can. Perhaps in your own room. It could be very interesting . . . for both of us. I could surprise you."

Carter held both wrists out to Reynolds and winked at him.

"The chains won't be necessary, but under the circumstances, I am going to ask you not to approach the Vice President. Or his family. Again."

"So, now they are worried about his family," Carter thought as the wrists were withdrawn. It wouldn't take much to get to the wife and daughter. It could be done right in the lobby when they walked out. Turn them to powder with the Webley-Fosbery. But of course, Carter would have to go down with the ship. No . . . no public assassinations for Carter. It would mean certain apprehension and this killer wasn't about to let that happen. Not now. Carter was having too much fun. Except for this latest attack of insomnia.

Nonetheless, Carter still couldn't help but wonder

how the Americans were able to keep the news so quiet.

"And what exactly are these circumstances, Mr. Reynolds?"

"It's not something that would be of much interest to you."

"Well, I was talking to those nice people over there." Carter pointed at the Californians. "They're Americans, you know. And they seemed to be very concerned. They haven't seen their vice president, or any of your countrymen, for that matter, since they left for Torcello yesterday. Whatever these circumstances are, I'm sure they would be of great interest to all Americans. I feel it's my obligation as a member of the press to keep the public informed, my dear."

"Well, Carter . . . you don't mind if I call you Carter, do you?"

"Not at all. We can be friends."

Reynolds leaned in.

"Well, Carter, I don't care if you and your fucking *obligation* get on a goddamn train and go to Istanbul. Just keep your candy-ass away from my people, and you'll live a long and happy life."

"Well, my goodness . . . If you'll excuse me, Mr. Reynolds . . I'm afraid I now find you rather boring."

"I thought you might."

Reynolds stood and walked toward the lobby. And Carter called to him:

"Keep up your bright swords,
for the dew will rust them."

Reynolds turned back. "You know, Carter, this may surprise you, but I played Othello. It was in high school. It was an all-black school, so some of the subtleties of the play were lost. But believe me, I will keep my goddamn sword up."

And Reynolds left. He went back to the operations room. When he got there, he found George Strutz and Chester Mock having a little heart-to-heart.

"In all my time in the service, Georgie, you've got

to be the biggest fucking pain in the ass I've ever run across. You're worse than fucking Haldeman. And you know what? I've got a hot condition right now. So blow it out your fat ass. The only people going on those choppers are critical personnel, and you haven't been critical since the day you popped out from your mamma—take the fucking boat."

"We'll see about this."

Strutz almost knocked Reynolds over on his way out.

"What did you find out?" Mock asked Reynolds.

"Well, Joe's right. He's an odd one. But I don't think he's a threat to our man."

"He's a fag, right?" Mock said.

"Well, he didn't actually ask me for a date, if that's what you want to know. He's a creepy person, what can I say? I think we should keep someone on him when we move. Just to be sure."

Mock looked around the room.

"Lightfoot, that's you."

"Check."

"You know, Mock, you may not want to find out *who* killed Louis, but you better try to figure out why."

It was the first thing Joe had said for nearly twenty minutes.

After a pause he continued, "It was a pro. So who actually did it isn't that important. It's who hired him. And why. That same person is probably after Number Two. If we found out who killed Louis, we'd know who we're looking for."

"We work the Man, and that's it. We carry on no investigations. We get Goliath back to Washington in one piece."

"Jesus."

"Don't get in my way, Bradlee."

Joe held his cuffed hands out in front of his chest.

"Chester, have Lightfoot take these things off. I'm not going anywhere. They're uncomfortable as hell."

Mock turned to the computer monitor and ignored Joe's request.

"Chester?"

No answer.

One more time.

"Chester?"

Still no answer.

"Hey. I'm talking to you, you fuck."

Joe said it loud enough to be heard throughout the top floor of the Hotel Malvasi. Everyone in the room froze. Mock turned slowly and smiled one of his big smiles.

"Lightfoot, take him down to his room and chain him to the fucking bed. If he says anything, stuff a roll of toilet paper in his mouth."

Lightfoot walked over to Joe and said, "Come on, let's go."

The two men walked out and Lightfoot shut the door.

"Anybody else have a problem?"

There was a murmur of "No, sir."

"Now." Mock took a deep breath. He was calm. He spoke slowly. Almost methodically. "Correct me if I'm wrong, but we all seem to be forgetting something. Somebody woke me up on Christmas fucking Eve, and said, 'Oscar Sanchez is on the loose in Venice, Italy.' We have a certifiable Quarterly on our hands here, a loony tune, a terrorist, for Christ's sake, and as far as I can see, we have nobody, not one fucking soul, keeping an eye on the son of a bitch. Now, does any one of you brain trusts have a suggestions as to what the fuck we're going to do about this?"

Three

After the two agents entered Joe's room, Lightfoot unlocked the handcuff on Joe's left wrist and escorted him to the bedpost. Joe balked.

"Hook it on the other side, will you? I might want to make some phone calls."

"You don't know when to stop, do you?"

"Should I?"

"Look, Joe, we all want this bastard as much as you do, but Mock's right. The State Department has to take it. . . . And you pushed the Big Man too far. You have to know that."

"State doesn't give a damn about Louis. They'll write it off quicker than shit. A good man, killed in the line of duty. That's it. Tough luck. Send a medal to his mother. You know how it works."

"We'll follow it up. We'll keep an eye on them."

"Bullshit."

Lightfoot closed the handcuffs around the bedpost on the telephone side.

"There. Make some calls. See what you can do."

"Listen, I've got an idea."

"Forget it. I know what your idea is."

"You haven't heard it yet."

"Okay, shoot."

"Take the cuffs off."

"Forget it."

"Listen. There's no way Mock's going to look for me before those choppers come in."

Joe looked at his watch.

"That gives me almost two hours. I can cover a lot of ground in two hours. I'll be back before noon. No one will be the wiser."

"Can't do it."

"Fuck me. Why not?"

"You may want to burn your bridges with this agency, I don't. I'm on thin ice with Mock over this liver crap in the first place. I've got a wife and kid. I'm not going to get canned for you or for Louis. You want to end up a private dick in Mineola, that's your business."

"He'll never find out, for Christ's sakes."

Lightfoot could see the look in Joe's eyes. He knew Joe was getting dangerous. The agent backed up and stood a good six feet away from the bed.

"You said it earlier, Joe. I gotta do what I gotta do. Make some phone calls."

Lightfoot was gone.

Joe sat on the bed and gave his cuffed wrist a jerk out of frustration. One end scraped hard against the mahogany bedpost and left a three-inch gouge in the finish. The other end dug into the skin above Joe's hand. He sat for a long minute. Staring at the closed door. Then he called after Lightfoot.

"What if I have to take a leak, you shithead?"

Lightfoot was too far gone to hear.

Joe's first call was to Nina. She and Eubie had just returned to their room from breakfast.

"It's me. What are you two up to today? . . . Well, I've got a little problem here. . . . No, not unless a bird drops from the sky with some handcuff keys. . . . They're going to fly me out of here at noon. I think I'm under arrest, but I'm not sure."

He went on to explain the better part of the situation to her. She offered to come out to the Malvasi.

"Absolutely not. I don't want you anywhere near this place, you understand? It's too dangerous for you—and for Eubie. I don't know what's going on.

But something tells me it's bigger than we think. You have to stay away. . . . Stay put. . . . Don't worry about me. I'll find you. I'll find you in New York. . . . In a week . . . Don't worry . . . A week. No longer. I give you my word on that."

Joe's second call was to Inspector Solfanelli. He was away from his desk. He would call Joe back. Next Joe called the State Department.

"This is Joe Bradlee, I'm with the Secret Service. Let me speak with someone at the CIA desk."

Eventually he was connected.

"This is Joe Bradlee, I'm with the Secret Service. We had an agent killed yesterday. I'd like to be brought up to date on your investigation. . . . Well, who is in charge of it? . . . Can I speak to him?"

After a three-minute wait, Joe was put through.

"Yes, this is Joe Bradlee, I'm with the Secret Service. One of our agents, Louis Zezzo, was killed on Torcello yesterday. What have you found out? . . . Well, when do you people plan to get started? . . . No kidding? . . . Well, when is Mr. Moody expected back from his *holiday* in Rome? . . . I see . . . This isn't going to prove to be an inconvenience for you folks, is it? . . . No, I'm not being smart. That's the last thing I'd want to do with the State Department. Be fucking smart. But you know what I was thinking? I was thinking that if any of you people possess any goddamn gonads—I'm talking about testicles here—someone should come over, cut the little fuckers off, and chuck them into the Grand fucking Canal."

Joe dumped the receiver onto its base.

"Assholes."

The telephone rang immediately after it had come to rest in its cradle. Inspector Solfanelli. Joe explained his situation. Solfanelli gave Joe what he had. It wasn't much.

The lab had confirmed that Louis had been killed with a Beretta. He had been shot three times. Not two. Marks in the earth showed that the killer most likely had arrived and departed, by boat, from the dock on the far side of Torcello. The locals had all been questioned. Not one had seen a thing. Solfanelli added that he considered the whole job just too damn clean. The person who killed Louis could not have come from Venezia. Men like this killer did not live in the lagoon. He must have come from Milano. Or perhaps Napoli. And again, both Solfanelli and Joe were left with the question—why?

The inspector kept coming back to his jealous-husband theory. And Joe kept telling him to forget it. He knew Louis and the Vice President too damn well. It was out of the question. But Solfanelli pushed it.

"It's not going to be pleasant, Joe. I am aware of that. I have no authority to hold a diplomat, but when I find the assassin, I will find who hired him, and I will come after that man, no matter who he may be. On that you can count."

There was a long pause. Joe had nothing to say. Solfanelli continued.

"There are two other things. The footprints in the earth were very small. It is possible this killer was a woman. We will know later. The second thing may be related, it may not. About an hour ago, a water taxi was found near the Celestia *vaporetto* stop. The driver had been murdered. Stabbed in the heart with a knife. Or possibly a piece of pointed glass. It wouldn't be the first time. We believe he's been dead for over twelve hours. My lab will be able to tell more accurately. The driver was an institution around the train station. We will check to see who his last fare might have been. Perhaps he ferried our killer to Torcello. But the man had been robbed, so there may be no connection at all. I will keep you posted. *Ciao.*"

"One thing before you go. Check all your records for anything on a Carter Perkins. British. Older. Late forties. Fifty maybe. I don't know what I'm looking for, but there might be something there . . . Thanks. *Ciao, Lamberto.*"

Joe hung up the phone. And again he wrenched his handcuffs against the mahogany bedpost.

"Fuck a goddamn duck," he said.

Four

When Lightfoot walked back into the operations room, the discussion on what to do about Oscar Sanchez was winding down. Mock was standing at the window with his back to the rest of the agents. Staring out toward the Lido. His hands in his pockets. He was beaten.

"So, not one of you knows where the fucker lives? You're supposed to be an advance team. Team to me means that information is shared every now and then."

"Well, sir," Reynolds said, "Louis and Joe were on him. The rest of us were handling other stuff. Obviously Louis is no help, but I could go to his room. Go through his things. Maybe he wrote it down somewhere—with some directions."

"We don't have time for that shit."

"The Italians know where Oscar's place is," Olsen piped in.

"I'm not fucking around with any of these goddamn wops."

Mock turned and watched Lightfoot as he closed the door. Mock groaned. It was more like a low growl. He then sat down at the desk and lit a cigar.

"Go back and get him."

"Sir . . . ?" Lightfoot said.

"Go get Bradlee. Bring him back up here. Keep him cuffed, though."

"Yes, sir."

It took only three minutes. They used the stairs instead of the elevator. Joe walked in first. His hands chained behind his back. Procedure. Lightfoot wasn't taking any chances. He wasn't dumb. Mock spoke first.

"It's against my better judgment, Bradlee, but I'm going to uncuff you and give you your piece back."

He nodded to Lightfoot. The agent removed the handcuffs and handed Joe his 9mm. Joe rubbed his wrists and stuffed the pistol back in its holster. Mock continued.

"I want Oscar Sanchez shadowed until we get everyone out of here safely. You'll be able to find him quicker than any of us—and that's the only reason I'm doing this. Clear . . . ? Now, let's get a few things straight—right off the bat. I won't put up with any more bullshit. You have an assignment. If you fail to stick with Sanchez for the next two to three hours, I will consider it a treasonous act, and I will see that you hang for it, and that's no lie. Clear?"

"Yes."

"Next. You will be at Marco Polo airport by thirteen hundred hours. You will be on Cardinal before it takes off for Washington. You still have some charges to answer to. Is that clear?"

"Yes."

"Okay. As long as we understand one another. Get to work."

Joe moved in the direction of the bathroom.

Mock said, "Where the hell are you going?"

"I've got to take a leak."

The telephone rang. It was The Panhandler. He wanted to speak to Mock.

"Mock here . . . Yes, sir . . . Yes, sir, I'll take care of it. As a matter of fact, one of the agents won't be going out on the choppers, after all, so there will be room for Mr. Strutz. . . . Yes, sir, I'll see that Mr. Strutz gets on a helicopter."

Mock hung up the telephone.

"Of course, I might kick the fat fuck out at three thousand feet . . . Reynolds?"

"Yes, sir?"

"Looks like it's your skinny ass that'll be on my lap."

"Yes, sir."

Five

When Joe came out of the bathroom, no one paid much attention to him. They had work to do. So did he. He slipped out the door quietly. When he was ten feet down the hall, someone called, "Joe."

It was Mock.

"Maybe you'll get lucky. Maybe Oscar Sanchez killed Louis. Find out. Louis was a good man. We're all going to miss him."

Joe wished he could get lucky. He wished it were that simple. It wasn't. Oscar Sanchez hadn't killed Louis. Joe knew it. Mock knew it.

"We'll see," he said.

Joe trotted down the stairs to the lobby and went directly to the front desk. Nelo smiled.

"Nelo, I need a powerboat and a driver. Not a Malvasi launch. Not a taxi. A plain boat. With someone I can trust. I'll need him all day."

"Let me call my sister's husband, Ricardo. He has a good boat. He is a good man."

"Thanks, Nelo. I'll wait out at the dock."

Joe next went to Vittorio's launch. The helmsman-policeman was still holding the extra weapons the Secret Service had loaded onto his boat. Joe removed a pump shotgun. Checked to see if it was still loaded. It was. He stepped back up to the dock. And he waited.

It took fifteen minutes for Ricardo to show up with

his boat. He was a large man. Had an oversize handlebar mustache and was missing a tooth. He was heavy. Round. He was a happy man. He came from a happy family. Joe was a friend of Nelo's; Joe was, at once, a friend of Ricardo's. He greeted Joe like a brother.

Joe jumped onto the boat before Ricardo could toss him a line. He handed Ricardo the shotgun.

"This is for you, Ricardo. A gift from the United States government. I need to go to the Ghetto section."

"I am at your service, Signore Bradlee."

"Joe."

"Okay . . . Joe."

They swung out into the open water. The engine was loud. Joe had to lift his voice to be heard. He pointed at the shotgun.

"Do you know how to use that?"

"I do not think I want to learn. I am not a coward. I am a man of peace. I have no use for guns."

He handed the shotgun back to Joe. Joe took it by the barrel and threw it high into the air. Out past the stern of the boat. It sailed in a wide arc like a stick being tossed for a dog. It landed with a colossal splash in the Venetian lagoon.

"Nelo was right. You're a good soul, Ricardo."

Joe told his driver exactly where in the Ghetto section he needed to go. It seemed unlikely that Oscar would be lounging around his apartment. But it was a place to start.

At this point Joe was no longer thinking about the Service. He didn't care about getting back to Cardinal in time for takeoff. He didn't care about Number Two. He didn't care about Olsen. He didn't care about Mock. He cared about Louis.

Joe knew Mock was in the position to make his life miserable when he did get back to the States. That was one reason why he would try to find Oscar. But not the main reason.

They swung down the wide canal that separated Giudecca island from the Dorsoduro. They passed a cruise ship and ducked down the Canale Scomenzera.

In no time they popped out at the train station. The brightly colored poles where the taxi boats had been tied up were now draped in black cloth. Three taxis had black ribbons tied to their stanchions. The drivers wore black armbands.

"A driver was killed yesterday. It was a murder . . . unusual for Venezia," Ricardo said as he motored by the station.

"Did you know the man?"

"Yes. He was an old man. A gentle man. Nico. He had been driving a taxi boat since the war. He loved Venezia. He loved the water."

"I'm sorry . . . It's tough to lose a friend."

They were soon past the train station. Joe never noticed Solfanelli's police launch slip through Ricardo's wake and tie up at the Ferroviaria landing.

"Why do you think your friend was killed?" Joe asked.

"It's senseless. A robbery perhaps. But again, that too is unusual in Venezia. There is no explanation or reason for taking another man's life."

The remaining five minutes of the trip were spent in silence. Joe jumped off at the Ponte Guglie. Ricardo secured his boat.

"Wait here. I'll be back."

Joe jogged down the narrow Calle del Forno. The street of the oven. He could hear the roar of a glass furnace coming from the depths of the building next to Oscar's. He scanned the door buzzers. Sanchez. B. On the second floor. Front. Joe looked up and pressed the button.

Christina came on the intercom. *"Pronto?"*

"Christina, it's Joe Bradlee. I need to speak with Oscar."

Oscar came on.

"Is it that important, Mr. Bradlee, that you must disturb me in my home?"

"It's extremely urgent. I have to talk with you. Let me in."

"Very well."

The buzzer sounded, and Joe yanked the door open.

He trotted up the steps. Oscar was waiting in the doorway of the apartment. He was wearing a robe. Christina stood behind him. Also in a robe.

"We were about to make love. So you will excuse me if I don't seem overly hospitable?"

"Can I come in?"

"If you must."

Oscar stepped aside. From the outside of the building it was impossible to conceive the modern splendor Oscar had created on the inside. He occupied the second and third floors. He had gutted the entire place. The central room had twenty-five-foot ceilings. A circular stairway led up to what had once been the third floor. It had been transformed into a large sleeping loft.

Light flooded in through the original window glass and reflected brightly off varnished hardwood floors. Kitchen appliances lined the back wall. A mass of white marble and stainless steel. The kitchen opened into a dining area. Then into the huge expanse of the living room. All the furnishings were extremely modern—extremely Italian. Joe thought, "I want this place." It was obvious in his tone.

"Nice place you have here."

"I hope you haven't come to discuss architecture or interior decorating. It bores me."

Oscar sat on a low white leather couch. Joe remained standing.

"I came to talk about Carter Perkins. He baffles me."

"I told your man Reynolds everything I know."

"I don't think you did. You said he was dangerous. So are crosswalks. That doesn't tell me shit."

"We have a code on my side, Mr. Bradlee, as I am sure you have a code. Most policemen do. I've already told you too much about Carter Perkins."

"Well, one code I have—and some folks consider it a rather crude code—is that I'm liable to beat the crap out of somebody until he"—Joe looked to Christina—"or she tells me what I want to know."

"A threat?"

"Abso-fucking-lutely."

"I don't threaten easily, Mr. Bradlee."

Joe walked over to Oscar and grabbed the lapels of his robe. He lifted Oscar straight up off the white leather couch. He then brought his knee up to meet Oscar's groin and threw him back onto the couch.

"So much for your afternoon of lovemaking. Now, maybe you'd like to tell me what the deal is on Perkins? . . . Take your time. Catch your breath. I'm not going anywhere."

Out of the corner of Joe's eye he could see Christina edging her way to the telephone. Without turning he said, "Go ahead, sweetheart. Call. The police are on my side. Remember?"

She backed away from the phone.

"One more time, Oscar. Tell me something about Perkins."

Oscar truly was out of breath. He struggled with his words.

"I've been handled . . . by worse than you . . . Mr. Bradlee. I'll tell you nothing."

"Maybe I'm moving a little too fast here. Let me explain what the situation is. Yesterday, Christmas day, one of my agents takes the Vice President's wife out for a day on Torcello. At about three-thirty in the afternoon someone puts three slugs into the back of his head. Then disappears. The killer doesn't touch the woman. My problem is this: I don't know who did it. And I have a feeling you might be able to shed some light. Tell me about Perkins."

Oscar said nothing.

"You're the second person who's ignored me today. I don't like it. The other person was lucky. I was wearing handcuffs at the time. It's too bad really. The next step will involve some blood. Might be a little messy on that sofa."

Joe stepped closer. He grabbed Oscar's throat with his right hand. With his left hand he removed his pistol and pointed it at Oscar's kneecap. Then cocked the hammer.

"Tell me something I want to hear."

Time passed.

Oscar wasn't going for it. He knew Joe's type. The trigger wouldn't be pulled. And Christina wouldn't be touched either.

More time passed. Oscar was right.

Joe removed his hand from Oscar's throat.

"As I said, Mr. Bradlee, I've been worked over by worse men than you."

Joe put his pistol back in its holster. He walked around behind Oscar and sat on the back of the couch. Surveyed the room.

"You know, maybe I'm barking up the wrong fucking tree. All this time I've been thinking Carter Perkins is the bad guy and Oscar Sanchez is just here for a little holiday. My man"—Joe corrected himself—"my friend Louis was killed with a Beretta. You wouldn't happen to have a Beretta around here, would you?"

"Don't be ridiculous. I'm sure you know me better than that. Berettas are used by women."

Joe pulled out his handcuffs. He grabbed Oscar's left wrist and chained it to a heavy brass standing lamp. The lamp was bolted to the floor and arced out over the couch. The bulb was shaded by a globe made of a yellow-amber glass. Joe talked as he closed the handcuffs tight.

"Well, I'd feel a lot better if I knew you didn't have that fucking gun. . . . And because you're not in a talkative mood, I guess I'll just have to look for it."

Joe walked back around to the front of the couch. Oscar had a large coffee table. Maybe four feet square. It was low. Standing on short legs that resembled teak railroad ties. The surface rested only seven inches above the floor. A highly polished piece of burl maple.

On the table were four glass sculptures. Joe picked one up and held it to the light. It was solid glass and weighed close to fifty pounds.

"This thing weighs a goddamn ton. . . . What is that? Inside there? A fucking baby?"

It was. It was a molded glass fetus that had then

been incased in another thick layer of clear glass to resemble a womb.

"Yeah, it's a baby. That's really something. How the hell do they do that?"

Joe looked at the bottom of the piece and read the signature.

"Livio Seguso . . . The Old man, or the son?"

"The father," Oscar said.

"It must be worth a goddamn fortune. Solid glass, huh?"

"Yes."

"Well, I guess there's no way you could hide a Beretta in this fucking thing, is there?"

"No. It's solid."

"But, there's no harm in checking."

Joe held the piece of glass above his head and let it drop. Oscar screamed. He struggled to save it. But was jerked back to the sofa by his handcuffed wrist. The sculpture landed with a loud smack and broke into six large pieces.

"Christ, you'd think it would've shattered," Joe said. "Well, fuck. No gun in there."

"You're a madman."

Oscar lunged at Joe. Again the floor lamp held him tight. The yellow-amber globe spun off and crashed to the floor.

"A kind of a terrorist, wouldn't you say?"

Joe picked up another glass sculpture. This one was sea green. It was a Pegasus. A winged horse with flared nostrils and outstretched legs. The horse was in flight. It was supported from the underside by a shaft of engraved sterling silver. The shaft was in turn connected to a base. The base was a solid block of glass the color of an overripe plum. The horse was crusted in spots with what appeared to be white and tan salt deposits. Joe lifted it into the air.

"What the hell's this white shit? Salt? Is this thing really old, or is this crap faked? Just put on here to make it look old?"

"It's a reproduction," Oscar lied.

"You know, Oscar, I look at you and say, 'This isn't

the kind of guy who would buy a reproduction.' You're too fucking classy. Too smooth."

Joe let it drop to the floor. Oscar lunged again. Christina screamed and turned her back. This one did shatter. Into millions of pieces.

"Nope. No gun . . . Hey, you two better put some goddamn shoes on. This place is becoming a real mess."

Joe eyed a third piece of glass. It was a vase. The glass was almost paper thin. It had a narrow neck and base and was a rich eggplant color. Joe picked it up. He tried to put his hand into it.

"Jesus, I can't even get my hand into this piece of shit. Hard to believe someone could get a gun in here. Oh, well, let's just see. Shall we?"

Oscar strained at the handcuffs.

"No. no. Not that one. Please, not that one . . . Okay, okay . . . It was Beirut."

Joe held the vase at arm's length.

"What was Beirut?"

"Carter Perkins. It was years ago . . ."

Joe slowly set the piece down and Oscar continued.

"It was a long time ago. I'm not sure when. A Lebanese businessman approached me. His daughter was having an affair with singer. The man was afraid they were planning on marriage. To elope. He contacted me. Wanted me to kill the boy. I refused."

"What does this have to do with Perkins?"

"Perkins was there. At the hotel. The boy was killed two nights later. Shot in the back of the head. Three times. Small-caliber. They never found the gun."

"What makes you think Perkins did it?"

"I can recognize a killer. I can see it in the eyes. The morning after, in Beirut, I saw the look in Carter Perkins' eyes. Perkins had killed the boy."

"That kind of evidence is a little flimsy, if you ask me. But if you felt that strongly about it, why didn't you turn him in?"

"We have our code, Mr. Bradlee, you have yours."

"Never mind, I'm sorry I asked. One more question. Do you think Perkins killed my friend?"

"Given the information you've presented to me, I'd say there's no question about it."

"But why?"

"That's two questions."

"You've got a hell of a lot more glass here, fella."

"I honestly can't answer that. Perkins is a professional assassin. I am certain of it. The why doesn't lie within the assassin, it lies within whoever hired the assassin."

Joe looked at Christina.

"Go put some shoes on. Bring a pair for fuck face here."

When she came back, Joe double-looped his handcuffs around the floor lamp and locked both Oscar and Christina to it.

"I want you two to stay here for at least two hours. Fuck all you want, I don't care, but the cuffs have to stay. I can't take a chance on you being seen in Venezia until the Vice President leaves. I'll call the police. They'll come to release you in two hours. You have my word on it. Sorry about the glass."

Joe looked at his watch. Eleven-fifteen. He ducked out of Oscar's apartment and down the stairs. He ran through the narrow street. Dodging strolling pedestrians. When he came to the end of the street he jumped off the dock and onto Ricardo's waiting boat.

"Back to the Malvasi, Ricardo. How fast will this thing go?"

Six

Ricardo's boat was not fast. It couldn't be encouraged to do any more than it'd done earlier. The trip from the Hotel Malvasi had taken a half hour. It would take a half hour for Ricardo and Joe to get back.

Joe considered radioing back to the Malvasi with what he had on Carter Perkins. Passing it onto Olsen, Mock, and Reynolds. But a few things stopped him:

There was a standing order not to let Perkins anywhere near the Vice President. Joe was more than confident the agents would red-flag Perkins. And in reality, Solfanelli's jealous-husband theory was beginning to seem the only logical explanation for Louis' death. Carter and Number Two had had drinks together in the lounge the night before. Who knows what went on? Anything was possible. Number Two would be in no danger from Perkins if he'd hired the bastard to kill Louis.

But the stronger reason for not radioing the hotel was: Joe wanted to be the first one to speak to Carter. To confront Carter. Mock and Olsen weren't exactly known for their tact. They'd only give Perkins time to think. Worse yet—disappear. There wasn't a shred of evidence to hold Carter. Not for a second.

Ricardo eased his boat back into the Grand Canal. Traffic had increased considerably. Holiday travelers were flooding to the train station. Vacations over.

When Ricardo reached the station, things had become chaotic. Power boats, gondolas, and *vaporettos* were all jockeying for space at the Ferroviaria landing. Screaming was followed by yelling. Italian bravado was being thrown from boat to boat like hot hand grenades. Taxi boats in particular were having a difficult time getting to their designated dock. Ricardo pointed this out to Joe. Along with an explanation.

"Polizia . . ." He shook his head. "They can make a mess of almost anything."

Joe looked, and sure enough, a police launch was parked in one of the slips reserved for taxis. Two taxis circled like hungry sharks waiting for a parking slot to open. Their drivers shouting obscenities to each other and then to the police. Finally a man emerged from the police launch. He threw his arms in the air, as if to be chasing moths away. He shouted back.

"Basta! Tappati la bocca! Andate!"

Solfanelli.

Joe motioned to Ricardo.

"Circle around. See if you can get me close enough to jump onto the police launch."

Ricardo joined the circling sharks. On his first pass he failed to get close enough. Joe was tempted to go for it, but a voice said, "Don't be jumpy Joe." The voice was right on. He would have ended up in the canal. Joe thirsted for wings. He called to Solfanelli on his way by.

"I have to talk to you." He looked down at the murky water. "Shit . . . hold on."

Ricardo circled about a second time. This time he got so close to the police launch, Joe was able to step up to the boat easily.

"Circle, Ricardo. I should only be a minute or two."

Solfanelli shook Joe's hand.

"I thought you had become a permanent guest of the Malvasi," the inspector said.

"Things change."

"So I see."

"I'm almost positive Carter Perkins killed Louis. What have you found out here?"

"Perkins is the Englishman, correct?"

"Correct."

Solfanelli pointed at a taxi driver sitting in the rear of the police launch.

"This man says that the murdered driver left with an Englishman yesterday afternoon. He thought he heard the man ask to be taken to Torcello. But he cannot swear to it."

"Can I talk to him?"

"Si."

Joe believed Solfanelli. Still, he had to hear it first-hand. He listened as the taxi driver described Carter Perkins to a T. The man wouldn't swear that Carter had asked to go to Torcello, but he was almost certain that had been the request. Joe came back to Solfanelli.

"Can I use your phone, Lamberto?"

"Si."

Solfanelli motioned to a uniformed officer, who in turn handed Joe a cellular telephone. Joe called the Malvasi and asked first to speak to Gianni at the front desk. He needed information on Carter. Gianni was most likely the only employee who would give it up. Gianni was off duty. Joe opted to give Nelo a try.

"Nelo, can you tell me if Mr. Perkins has left for the day? . . . I know, I understand that, but this is very important. . . . I see . . . No, I understand. Could you have the switchboard ring his room for me? . . . Thank you."

There was no answer in Carter's room. Joe switched the telephone off and handed it back to the policeman. Nelo was, of course, right. Supplying the whereabouts of hotel guests was something that was never done at the Malvasi. Certainly not by Nelo. And in the long run, Carter was surely a bigger tipper than Joe. Carter liked privacy too much.

"Is he there?" Solfanelli asked.

"They won't say."

"Should I call?"

"I don't think it will do any good."

"You are right. I know these Malvasi people. They need to be persuaded in person if you want them to respond. Sometimes one must use less subtle methods. We will go out to the hotel, then."

"Wait . . . I need to talk to Perkins alone."

"I have had two murders in my city. I do not want a third. You look much too dangerous, my friend."

"You can't arrest him. You have no evidence."

"Like you, I want to talk to him."

"Lamberto, give me two hours. That's all I ask. You can block the airport. The train station. I can get some evidence. I swear I can. I'll get the gun. Or the knife. I can bend a few rules that you can't. I can get into Perkins' room. If he sees the police, he'll panic. He'll cover his tracks. He's too damn good. We'll never find him . . . I won't kill him. You have my word on that."

It was a good argument. Solfanelli bought it.

"Two hours. Not a minute more."

"Thanks, Lamberto."

Joe waved to Ricardo, who was still circling out with the other sharks. The helmsman pulled his boat back around. This time to within a foot of the police launch. He was getting good at this shit. Joe stepped onto the boat. Solfanelli held up two fingers.

"Two hours. Not a minute more."

Joe turned to Ricardo.

"The Malvasi."

"And step on it . . . ?"

"No, take your time. I don't want to get there before noon."

Definitely not before noon. After Joe'd left Oscar's apartment he'd let his emotions cloud his judgment. All he'd wanted was to find Carter. Tear the little piece of garbage limb from limb. Now he was thinking more clearly. He wanted those helicopters long gone before he returned to the hotel. Joe was still supposed to be with Oscar Sanchez. If Mock spotted him at the Malvasi, he'd shoot first and ask questions later.

Seven

Nina Wallace, formerly Nina Lake, had never been the type of woman to waste time thinking things through. Ever. She did what she wanted to do—when she wanted to do it.

This trip to Venice was a perfect case in point. Her best friend, Gaye, had scheduled the trip for herself and her husband, Tony. Gaye had purchased the plane tickets. Had made all the reservations. Even gone so far as to go to Deak and Perrara and pick up two thousand dollars in Italian lira.

On December eighteenth, two days before they were to leave, Tony broke his leg. According to Gaye, "A goddamn, motherfucking, son-of-a-bitching, New York fucking City taxi knocked him off his stupid ass fucking bicycle." Gaye had undoubtedly felt sorry for her husband, but when she called her good friend Nina, on December twentieth, to ask if Nina and Eubie could be on a plane to Italy that night, Gaye still had no intention of ever speaking to Tony again.

Nina had hung up the telephone and said to her son, "Guess where you're going tonight?" And that was that. Twenty-four hours later they were floating down a Venetian canal.

Now, at eleven a.m. on December twenty-sixth, Nina found she had been thinking things through. At least long enough. As far as she knew, Joe was still handcuffed to his bed at the Malvasi, soon to be hauled off to Marco Polo and flown back to Washington. She had to see him one more time. She had to get to the Malvasi before the Vice President left.

Nina, however, strongly considered one thing Joe had said earlier:

"It's too dangerous for you—and for Eubie."

She wasn't about to jeopardize her son for anything—or anyone. She scooped him up and ducked down to La Primavera's front desk.

The old woman working there was a close friend of the lady who owned the *pensione.* She'd been coming to Venice for over forty years and spoke her English with a heavy Scottish accent. She had become such an institution at La Primavera that she now took shifts behind the reception desk.

"Yes, ma'am?" she said when Nina approached.

"I was wondering if I could leave my son here with you for about an hour. I'm going to the Accademia, just to see a few things, and he gets bored so easily in museums."

"Oh, you won't find the Accademia open today, ma'am. It's the Feast of San Stefano."

"Of course. You're right. I wasn't thinking. Feast of San Stefano, is it?"

"Yes, ma'am."

"Is anything open?"

"Mostly just the churches and cathedrals, ma'am."

"San Giorgio Maggiore would be open, then?"

"Yes, ma'am."

"Well, I guess I'll go there. He hates churches too. I'll only be an hour. I need a little time alone. Can you watch him for me?"

Nina took a moment and then shook her head slowly.

"I'm sorry . . . I really need your help."

The old woman could see the strain in Nina's face.

"Of course, dear. Take your time. Do what you must. He'll be safe with me."

"Thank you."

Nina walked Eubie behind the desk. As the Scottish

woman took his hand he said, "Hi. My name's Eubie. I'm five years old. How old are you?"

Nina moved halfway to the front door but stopped and turned back.

"Can I use a pen and paper?"

"Yes, dear."

She spoke as she wrote.

"This is the telephone number of Eubie's father in California. If for some reason I should get into an accident or something like that, you can phone him. We can only assume he has brains enough to know what to do."

She then darted out to the boat dock. She combed the canal for a water taxi. Nothing. She ran down the street to her right, but something made her stop dead in her tracks and turn around. And there, coming out from under the small bridge that spanned the Rio di San Vio, was a taxi. She had lived in New York City too long. She had developed an excellent nose for hacks. The helmsman easily saw her waving and pulled his boat around to meet her. He helped her down onto his craft. Nina looked at him and smiled.

"I'd like to go to the Hotel Malvasi, please . . . *per favore.*"

Eight

Carter Perkins had finished breakfast in silence. Had sat in the Malvasi dining room for over two hours drinking coffee and eating Venetian rolls. And had methodically studied every guest that had entered the room—every guest that had left. Looking for a spark. Anything. Some little molecule that would indicate that news of the assassination had broken.

The waiter had brought every newspaper the Malvasi had to offer, and Carter had read them all—from cover to cover. The English paper. The American paper. The German paper. The French paper. The Italian paper. There was excitement all over the world. Bombings in London and Paris. An earthquake in Bombay. A plane crash in Madrid. Nine inches of snow in New York City. There was a murder-suicide involving two high-powered millionaires in a Long Rapids, Michigan, hunting cabin—it had all been reported by a dog named Buck. A sniper had claimed four in Sacramento. Another had claimed two in Berkeley. One more had been shot dead in Dallas. But nothing, not a single thing, was happening in Venezia. Venezia was as peaceful as a stone.

"Scusi, signore, mi dispiace."

The waiter had filled Carter's coffee cup for the fortieth time and accidentally let a droplet fall to the linen tablecloth.

"I am as poor as Job, my lord, but not so patient."

"Signore?"

Carter's speech was trancelike, "The second part of *Henry the Fourth,* act one, scene two—Sir John Falstaff."

"Sí, signore."

The waiter backed away as though he'd spoken with a Martian.

Carter stood. Then threw the German paper onto the table and reached for one last sip of coffee. By this point Carter's hands were trembling so uncontrollably, and so violently, that the hot liquid splashed over the lip of the cup. It scalded Carter's fingers. The cup was released. It fell to the table. Collided with the saucer. Broke into a dozen pieces. The coffee flooded the table, leaving a vast brown stain on the starched cloth.

A bellboy approached from the lobby. He carried a Malvasi business-size envelope. He handed it to Carter and backed away from the table. Not wishing to wait for a tip.

Carter's stomach had now begun to churn in violent spasms from the quantities of consumed caffeine. The acid scraped and clawed at the assassin's liver and kidneys. The envelope was torn open. The paper ripped from inside. Carter unfolded the note and let the envelope fall to the floor.

"No news is bad news . . . DOC."

Carter tossed the paper onto the table, spun around, and scurried out of the dining room, across the lobby, and into the men's lavatory, feeling as though the coffee would soon burst an already overextended bladder. Carter flew through the men's room door, nearly knocking the attendant to the floor, and arrived at the last stall in the nick of time. Then sat on the toilet for three full minutes. Head in hands.

When finished, Carter stepped out of the stall and walked a few paces. Then turned abruptly to the right and ducked into a second stall—and vomited. The acid from the coffee burned as it came back up past the throat and nostrils. Carter could feel the revolver, the

Webley-Fosbery, digging in on the left side. There was a strong temptation to use it for a quick suicide, right then and there. End this misery. The heaving continued until nothing remained inside.

When Carter exited the stall, the attendant was waiting with a warm, damp towel. Having taken the last of Carter's dry heaves and the flushing toilet as his cue.

"You are not feeling well, Signore Perkins?"

"I'm fine," Carter said and snatched the towel from the attendant. "Cologne. I need cologne. Here."

The attendant watched as Carter bent over the sink and gestured to a spot at the nape of the neck.

"Cologne. Now," Carter ordered once more.

"Sí, signore."

The man stepped forward with trembling hands. Then nearly dumped an entire bottle of Givenchy on Carter's head. Carter gruffly pushed the man aside and stormed out of the men's room and into the lobby.

Carter crossed to the house phone and tore the receiver from its cradle.

"Yes, connect me with the Americans' security room."

Far in the background there was a thin sound of approaching helicopters.

Nine

When the telephone rang, Reynolds could hear the faint sound of Solfanelli's helicopters approaching from the north. He assumed the phone call was from Hall 'n' Oates. Informing him that the Vice President was prepared to leave. "Goliath is prepped." That's what Reynolds had expected to hear. But it wasn't Hall or Oates or even Goliath himself. It was Carter Perkins.

"Mr. Perkins, your timing couldn't be worse. We're working on a very tight schedule. I'm afraid I'm going to have to ask you to get off this line. I need to keep it open. . . . No, you cannot reschedule your meeting with the Vice President; that would be impossible at this time. . . . Mr. Perkins, nothing could be further from the truth. . . . Sir, you are becoming a pest."

Reynolds hung up the phone. It rang again almost immediately. This time the call was from The Panhandler's room. The Vice President, The Wife, Little Audrey, and of course, George Strutz, would be ready to move whenever their helicopter was in position. Hall 'n' Oates would ride with them. The other helicopters would carry the remaining agents.

Everyone else had left by boat earlier in the morning. They had stripped their rooms of everything they'd brought. They'd come and gone like locusts. The computers and large communications devices in the operations room had left by way of an Italian coast guard launch. There was nothing remaining. The press people had picked up all of the remaining Malvasi soap, shampoo, hand lotion, shoe shiners, and shower caps.

The two agents on the roof had sighted the choppers. There was constant radio communication between Olsen, Mock, the roof agents, Hall 'n' Oates, and another two agents stationed on the front grounds. The Malvasi lawn would not be large enough for all four helicopters to set down at once. The three diplomatic taxis would come in one at a time while the Huey circled. Looking for potential trouble spots.

The roar of the choppers attracted the attention of everyone in the Malvasi. Guests and staff alike. Most of the noise was made by Inspector Solfanelli's baby, the Huey. The other three seemed quiet by comparison. The kitchen staff appeared to take the greatest interest and pleasure in these birds. They crowded out of the rear door in order to have a better look at *gli elicotteri.* The effect was to leave the waiters floundering in the pantry unable to pick up their luncheon orders. The scene was accompanied by a tremendous amount of swearing.

Within moments the first helicopter had set down on the hotel lawn. Gusts of wind whipped the multinational flags into a frenzy. They stretched out in the opposite direction of the breeze. Dust and grit attacked the facade of the Hotel Malvasi. The doorman and porters stood by every door. Insuring that they would not be blown open by accident.

This first chopper would wait there, on the lawn, for its precious cargo. The pilot would keep his engines running. The blades would turn slowly like a crippled fan. Making the atmosphere as pleasant as possible for these special passengers.

In the lobby Carter approached Nelo.

"What's all the excitement?"

"The Americans are leaving."

Carter smiled and said, "This I must see." Then Carter walked over and sat on a dark green velvet divan on the far side of the lobby near the elevator doors. And waited.

Upstairs, Reynolds picked up the telephone and dialed. It rang once in the Vice President's room. When it was answered, Reynolds only said two words.

"Let's move."

He hung up the telephone and walked out into the hallway with Mock and Olsen. It was Mock's show from here on.

All the other agents had left a few minutes earlier, securing the route the Vice President would take from his room, through the hotel, and down to his waiting helicopter. Every agent had an assignment. Every agent had carried his assignment out—except Lightfoot. He had missed Carter Perkins when the writer had ducked into the men's room. Lightfoot had assumed Perkins had left the hotel for the day, and had then taken up a position with the two agents on the front lawn. Lightfoot had botched it once more.

Mock, Olsen, and Reynolds were joined in the hallway by Hall 'n' Oates, Goliath, The Wife, Little Audrey, and George Strutz.

The Wife was a wreck. She was shaky. Her eyes were bloodshot. Puffy. Still teary. She was in a daze. It was obvious she'd been heavy into prescription drugs and would need to be supported the entire way back to D.C.

Reynolds moved toward The Wife but was held back by Olsen.

"Better let me do it," he said in a whisper.

Olsen took her arm. Reynolds backed off.

"It's a heck of a day out there, sir, looks like we're going to have some real smooth flying weather," Mock said as he approached the Vice President.

"That's great. I just want to get the hell out of here before there's any more trouble."

"Yes, sir. No chance of that. We have this place tighter than a tick. If you'll come this way, I think we'll take the stairs. I'd like to stay together. The elevator won't handle nine people."

"Certainly," the Vice President said.

The nine of them rolled down the stairway like a flock of roaches. Mock led the way followed by Hall 'n' Oates. Olsen held onto The Wife.

But Little Audrey was now insisting on being carried. Reynolds was bringing up the rear. It would be too risky for him to have the little girl in his arms. He might have to move quickly. That left Strutz and the girl's father. Strutz was sweating heavily. He sensed trouble, and was beginning to wish he had taken a boat to the airport like everyone else. Strutz also hated kids. He wasn't about to carry this one. Not on this day. Strutz would take care of Strutz. Which left The Panhandler to carry his daughter.

"Thank you, Daddy," she said as she was lifted by her father. She poked her finger into his bulletproof vest. "Your tummy is hard."

"That's the vest I have on under my shirt, dear. It's very stiff."

"What's it for?"

"It's just protection."

"Protection from what?"

"The cold."

"Why don't I have one?"

"You're too young. They don't make them small enough. When you're a big girl you can have one."

"Does Mommy have one?"

"No, dear."

"Why not?"

"I'll explain it all to you when we get on the airplane."

"Daddy . . . ?"

"Yes?"

"I think Mommy and I should have a vest."

"Please be quiet, honey."

"Where's Louis?"

"Honey, please."

"Mommy . . . ? Where's Louis? We can't leave him behind."

They had reached the last flight of stairs. Mock was the first to step out into the lobby.

Ten

Carter Perkins had never seen Chester Mock. But it was more than obvious that this huge, dark man was a Secret Service agent. Another Venetian Moor, Carter mused.

This Moor was followed by two other agents. Carter recognized them as the trolls from Christmas Eve. Next came the faithful aide. George Strutz. The obese man with the annoying laugh and filthy neckties. The Vice President's wife followed. Being supported by the other agent from Christmas Eve. The blond one.

The woman was a mess. The death of her husband had obviously hit her harder than Carter expected. Maybe it was only the idea that she'd been so close to death. All the blood. Carter smiled. She must have been covered with masses of blood.

The next to come out of the stairway was the little girl. She was carried by another agent. Carter could not see the man's face. The girl had her arms around his neck. She seemed to be holding on for dear life. Her small frame covering the man's broad chest.

Last to come was Reynolds. The handsome Moor. The young one. The agent who had bothered Carter so much at breakfast.

But no sign of the Vice President.

They would have some explaining to do.

Carter stood and prepared to approach Olsen and

The Wife. Again the revolver pinched the skin under Carter's left arm. And again Carter thought how easy it would be to wipe the entire family off the face of the earth. The assassin grinned sadistically once more, looked beyond the little girl, and made eye contact with Agent Reynolds.

Reynolds' moves were instantaneous and catlike. He pushed by the Vice President and Olsen. He passed Hall 'n' Oates and moved directly up to Mock.

"That's Perkins," Reynolds said. "Lightfoot must have missed him. I'll take him. Cover your ass."

Mock was a pro. He knew the routine better than anyone. He stepped back and told Hall 'n' Oates to flank the rear. Mock then positioned himself directly in front of the Vice President and Little Audrey.

"I think we should move a little quicker through the lobby, sir," Mock said. "Nothing to worry about. I just think the hotel would like us to get that helicopter off their grass as soon possible."

"Is there a problem? What's the problem? Mock? Mock . . . ?"

It was Strutz.

The Vice President answered for Mock.

"Shut the fuck up, George. You either walk with us or have your fat fucking ass left behind."

Mock simply said, "Thank you, sir."

Reynolds reached Perkins before Carter had a chance to recognize the man who was carrying the little girl. The agent wasn't much taller than Carter, but as he approached he seemed to expand. He seemed to blow up like a balloon. The effect made it even more difficult for Carter to see exactly what in blazes was going on.

But Carter knew all too well, if too much aggression was shown, Reynolds would get physical. Carter would be escorted out. And at that point the agent would easily establish that Carter was armed.

"Mr. Perkins, I asked you earlier not to come near the Vice President. I'm going to have to ask you to come with me. Into the dining room until he leaves," Reynolds said.

"The Vice President? I don't see any Vice President, young man. And as a member of the press, I demand to know what's going on."

"Mr. Perkins, please step into the dining room. I'm prepared to carry you if I have to."

"I demand to see the Vice President."

"You don't demand shit, pal."

Reynolds reached for Carter. Carter stepped back.

Then from behind Reynolds came, "Carter? Carter, I didn't get a chance to apologize for cancelling our interview."

The Vice President had stopped, turned to Reynolds and Perkins, and had then taken two steps in their direction.

Mock quickly grabbed Goliath's arm.

"Sir, we don't have the time for this right now. I'll have the press people contact Mr. Perkins for you."

Mock literally pushed the Vice President and his daughter toward the exit. All the while keeping his large frame between Goliath and Carter.

But Carter had seen a ghost. Had seen a dead man appear from nowhere. A dead man walking. Talking. The dead man was carrying a little girl. Carter's body immediately began to tremble and twitch in strange places. The thought that the wrong man had been killed had never entered Carter's head. Three pieces of hot lead to the brain, and this man was up and walking about as though bullets had not the slightest effect on him.

Carter felt weak. Hot, then cold. Dry and then damp. Carter's knees seemed to be turning into water. A side table was reached for, but misjudged, sending a glass ashtray to the floor. It smashed onto the marble. Carter's eyes burned and then blurred. And this betrayal of vision gave the Vice President an even more ghostly look.

"Are you all right?" Reynolds asked. "Step into the dining room. You can sit down there."

"It's an imposter."

Carter was barely audible.

"What? Let's go. Move it. Now," Reynolds said. He

put his hand out. The writer stepped back and out of reach.

Carter considered pulling the revolver then and there and doing the job right. Putting three more rounds into the Vice President. Carter's right hand began to inch and jerk its way up toward the Webley-Fosbery. But there were these two larger-than-life blackamoors in Carter's way. Also the little girl was protecting the Vice President's chest. Carter had never killed a woman. But this wasn't a woman. It was a small girl. Should she be sacrificed? Would the bullets even pass through her? Carter would never get this close again. A dream was disappearing. Floating away in a foggy hallucination.

"She's . . . a . . . child. . . ." Again Carter's voice was only a whisper. "He's dead . . . She's . . ."

"What?" Reynolds said.

"He's dead. That's an imposter. That's not the Vice President."

Reynolds took another step forward, and Carter abruptly turned and ducked to the floor, appearing to be doubled over in pain. Reynolds stepped in closer. He bent down and placed his hands on Carter's shoulders.

Reynolds almost shivered at the touch. A chill shot out from his palms and into his fingertips. It then reversed and traveled back up through his veins and arteries. It continued through his arms and found his lungs. It shook his stomach and liver until it finally settled deep within his heart and turned it icy cold. Reynolds released Carter and took two steps backward. His right hand instinctively went to the pistol on his hip, but he didn't draw it. There was no logical explanation. Reynolds' face became almost ashen.

Carter stood and turned to face him. And smiled weakly. "You Americans . . . what have I done to deserve you?" Carter then spun once more. Walked into the dining room. Went to the customary table and sat down in a heap. Exhausted.

Reynolds followed. He was almost stammering when he caught up. "What's all this about . . . ? What imposter . . . ? Carter . . . ? What the fuck's going on here?"

"I need a minute. I'm not feeling well. I didn't sleep well last night."

Reynolds sat at the table and stared at Carter for a long time—without saying another word. He studied Carter. He studied Carter's eyes and hair and hands and neck and ears and nose and mouth. After three of four minutes Reynolds slowly formed his lips into a broad smile and said, "Well, I'll tell you what, Carter old sport. We're going to sit here for a while. That's what we're going to do. Maybe get to know one another a little better. We're going to sit here and yak until I get the word that that helicopter has taken off. Then you can do whatever you please." Reynolds began to play with a butter knife. "Now, since we have this time to kill, who's dead . . . ? And who might the imposter be?"

Carter was beginning to regain some composure, but there was no question about it—Carter Perkins had been beaten.

And Carter's speech dragged. It was broken. Slow. Almost labored to the point of incoherence.

"This morning . . . the three Americans from California . . . that were sitting at that table . . . over there?"

Carter pointed.

"Yes . . . ?" Reynolds stretched the word out.

"They told me . . . that they had heard two of your agents . . . talking in the elevator."

"And . . . ?"

"They told me that your Vice President had been been shot . . and killed."

"And you believed them?"

"They were very . . . convincing."

"Do you honestly think that a Secret Service agent would talk about something like that in public? In an elevator? Did you never consider that the Americans might have been pulling your leg?"

"The seeming truth which cunning times put on/

To entrap the wisest."

"Right, whatever you say, Carter. Or is it now Bassanio?"

Carter squinted at Reynolds.

"Don't look so surprised, Carter. I read a lot of Shakespeare. Some people even think I'm sort of a bright guy. Who knows? Maybe they're right—maybe they're wrong. But all that aside, you don't seem the Bassanio type to me, for some reason. Didn't he spend most of his time sniffing around Portia?"

"You bore me, Mr. Reynolds."

"I thought I might." Reynolds looked at his watch. "Well, I'm not going to have time to talk to these cruel American pranksters for you, Carter. The ones that seem to have given you this misinformation. But I'll tell you what I will do. I'll pass the information on to the U.S. State Department, and they'll give those Californians a little talking-to for you. How's that?"

"That's hardly necessary."

"Oh, I insist. So think about it, Carter. Better cover that little ass of yours. Because I will catch up to those Californians. I will check you out. There's no telling what I might find." Reynolds smiled broadly once again, "Or might not find."

"I have no idea what you mean by that."

Reynolds glanced down at the mess that had been left on the table, and then back at Carter, " 'No news is bad news . . . DOC.' Having some physical problems, Carter?"

Carter snatched up the note and crumpled it into a small ball. "That message was confidential. You have no right—what I mean to say is . . . Yes, it's from my doctor . . . however, it's a highly personal matter."

"I gather as much."

The roar that came from the Vice President's helicopter as it lifted into the air could be heard throughout the dining room. The cypress trees outside seemed caught in a violent windstorm. They scraped and bashed against the dining room windows. Reynolds put a finger to the molded piece of plastic in his ear.

"Well, my man is gone, Carter. He's home free. And unless I want to miss my ride, I'm going to have to excuse myself. It's been swell."

Reynolds stood. Looked down at Carter.

" 'Time's glory is to calm contending kings
To unmask falsehood, and bring truth to light . . .'

Just watch your ass, Carter."

Reynolds turned. He walked out of the dining room, through the lobby, and out of the Hotel Malvasi. And off to a waiting helicopter.

Carter slumped in the chair. The sleepless night, the quantities of coffee, the shock of seeing the Vice President alive—and this agent, this Reynolds, it was all getting to be too much.

The waiter arrived. Carter ordered a glass of milk.

"Milk, *signore?*"

"Milk."

The man headed for the kitchen.

Eventually the last of the helicopters lifted off. And after a minute the cypress trees settled down. The engine noise then diminished to nothing. All was quiet at the Hotel Malvasi. All was back to normal. The Americans had left.

The milk came and was sipped at slowly. Carter's head was clearing more and more with each sip, and when the milk was finally finished, a second glass was ordered. It was now obvious this assassin had killed the wrong man. But who had been killed? Carter was baffled.

A man was dead—Carter was sure of that. And there most certainly would be an investigation. Would Reynolds talk to the State Department as he had threatened? More than likely he would. Carter sensed that above all Reynolds' smart-aleck behavior, there existed a dedicated professional. A man that could be counted on to be a royal nuisance.

If the dead man turned out to be an Italian gigolo, the only interest the American State Department would have would be to cover it quickly. They would not crave any unpleasant press. They'd let it all be handled by the local police. And they were no match for Carter. There was no evidence whatsoever. If the dead man had been an American, there was still little the State Department could do. Carter had covered things too well. Reynolds may have some suspicions, but that's all. Suspicions would get him nowhere.

Carter then pondered Reynolds' last words. It most certainly had been a bit of Shakespeare, but Carter couldn't place it. And this writer took pride in knowing all the plays by heart. But it wasn't from one of the plays. And Reynolds' words were not from a sonnet. The form wasn't right. Maybe a poem. Shakespeare's poems began to sift their way through Carter's exhausted head. "Venus and Adonis?" "A Lover's Complaint?" "The Passionate Pilgrim?" None of them had quite the right ring. The waiter arrived with the second serving of milk. Carter brought up the liquid and licked the rim of the glass. Then looked up to the waiter, smiled, closed one eye, and said,

" 'The Rape of Lucrece.' "

Eleven

Nina shielded her eyes from the sun and looked at the four helicopters as they headed north. Out toward Marco Polo airport. Her water taxi was just passing San Giorgio Maggiore when the last chopper lifted above the Hotel Malvasi. She had missed Joe. She guessed he'd probably been handcuffed for his walk through the lobby and would remain that way until they'd safely placed him on the airplane. She considered having her driver turn about and head for the airport. But the Vice President's airplane would be long gone by the time she arrived. She had missed her chance.

"You can take me back to La Primavera, if you would, driver. I'm too late."

"Sí, signora."

The helmsman swung his boat wide and came completely around.

"Wait. I'm sorry. There may be a message for me at the Malvasi. Go back."

"Sí, signora."

He swung his boat about again. His wake formed an almost perfect circle in the lagoon. Within four minutes, he had secured his craft to the Malvasi landing. He helped Nina off the boat, and she quickly disappeared into the hotel.

Nina went straight to the front desk, where she found the ever courteous Nelo.

"Sí, signora?"

"I'm a friend of Mr. Bradlee's. Nina? Nina Wallace? I was wondering if he had left a message for me."

"No, *signora.* I haven't seen Signore Bradlee since he left this morning. There have been no message."

"He didn't leave with the helicopters?"

"No, *signora.*"

"When did he go? Where did he go?"

"I'm sorry, *signora.* We can not give out that kind information regarding our guests. I'm sorry."

Nina fished through her purse as she spoke.

"I'm not thinking. I should be the one who's apologizing."

She pulled the key to Joe's room out of the purse. She showed it to Nelo.

"Actually, Mr. Bradlee is my husband. I never changed my name when we got married. It seems foolish now, but my father was in tears at the wedding. I'm sure you know how it is."

"Mrs. Bradlee?" Nelo slowly raised his left eyebrow.

"Well, he gave me a key to his room. That should count for something . . . Please . . ."

Nelo said nothing.

"Please, I have to find him. It's urgent . . . Please?"

Nelo stepped from behind his desk. He took Nina's hand. She trembled slightly. Nelo thought for a moment and sighed. He was a sucker for a good-looking woman on the edge of tears.

"Mr. Bradlee is with my brother-in-law and his boat."

"And was he handcuffed when your brother-in-law took him?"

"Handcuffed?"

Nina made a gesture with her wrists.

"Oh, no, *signora.* He was not handcuffed."

"Your brother-in-law is a policeman, though?"

"No, he is only a man with a boat. He makes deliveries."

"When will they be back, do you know?"

"Mr. Bradlee hired my brother-in-law for the complete day, so I cannot say."

"Well, I guess the best thing for me to do is to just wait for Mr. Bradlee in *our* room."

"Sí, signora. In your room."

"When Mr. Bradlee comes in, would you please tell him I'm here?"

"Sí, signora."

Nina picked the key back up from the front desk, crossed the lobby, and disappeared into the elevator. Three minutes later, Joe walked into the Hotel Malvasi. Nelo called him over.

"Buon giorno, Joe."

"What's up, Nelo?"

Nelo smiled.

"Mrs. Bradlee is waiting for you in your room."

"Mrs. Bradlee . . . ?"

"The Mrs. Bradlee with the dark hair and sunglasses."

"Fuck me."

Twelve

"Well, if it isn't Mrs. Bradlee," Joe said as he walked into his room. "Was there something I missed last night? Like a fucking wedding or something? I hope you at least had the smarts not to bring Eubie with you."

He threw his key onto the dresser.

"No, I left him at La Primavera. . . . I'm sorry about the Mrs. stuff. It was the only way I could get the man at the desk to tell me anything. It didn't seem to fool him much. He knows you too well."

Joe did his best to glare at her.

"Jesus, Joe, for all I knew, you were on your way back to Washington."

She came over and placed her hand on his arm. He pulled away and walked to the bed. He sat.

"You shouldn't have come out here. Did you think I was kidding when I said it was dangerous? Two people have been killed here already."

"I can't be worried about you?"

"No. You can't."

She sat next to him.

"Let me fill you in on a few things," he said. "And just because I might appear to be pleasant, don't think I'm not pissed off."

"You don't appear all that pleasant. Don't fool yourself."

She placed her hand on his thigh. Then her eyes bore into him. They fell back onto the bed in a long and deep kiss.

"Goddamn, I wish you hadn't come out here," he said when they broke.

"Thanks a lot."

"You know what I'm talking about. You couldn't wait for me in New York? That would have been too hard?"

"You said you were handcuffed. As far as I knew, your next stop was going to be Leavenworth, Kansas. I wanted to see you again. I don't think I want to lose you."

"Thanks . . . You won't."

He stood, walked a few paces, and pressed his weight against the dresser.

"Here's the situation. And just because I'm now sounding a little cold and professional, I'm not shutting you out. Believe me. I don't want to lose you either. That's why I told you not to come out here. But you're here, so the situation is this: The odd guy that came over to our table last night—"

"Carter Perkins?"

"Very good. Perkins killed Louis. I know that for sure."

"Can't you arrest him?"

"The Italian police or State Department would have to do that. If they could. But there isn't any evidence."

"So what makes you so sure Carter killed Louis?"

"I just know he did it."

"Well, there you have it. That's enough evidence for me. Let's just go shoot the little bugger."

Joe ignored the sarcasm.

"Don't think I haven't thought of it. . . . No, a man named Oscar Sanchez was nice enough to give me some insight into Perkins' personality. I'm convinced Carter killed Louis. There's no doubt in my mind. Believe me, I'm right about this."

"If you repeat something that many times, there's got to be some doubt."

"I need the damn evidence."

"Like what?"

"The gun maybe? A taxi driver was also killed yesterday. He was stabbed. His last known fare was Perkins. Maybe I can find the knife."

"This is all well and good. But—and I know this is probably going to sound like an incredibly stupid question—but why would Carter kill Louis?"

"He's actually a professional hit man."

"Well, hey, that explains a lot. Doesn't exactly answer the question, though, does it?"

"I don't know if I like this sarcastic side of you."

"Sorry, you're going to have to live with it. Why did Carter kill Louis?"

"The Italian police think that Number Two might have been jealous. So he hired Carter. The two of them were together the night before."

"Which two?"

"Carter and the Vice President. Pay attention, for Christ's sake."

"Oh, wait . . . Hold on . . . You mean, Louis was"—Nina made a gesture with her hand—"with the Vice President's wife?"

Joe nodded.

"Wow, that's hot. You didn't tell me that."

"There wasn't any point."

"Thanks."

"Jesus."

"This is a bad way for us to start out, you know that, don't you? Keeping things from me? But forget it . . . Do you actually believe that? Do you actually believe the Vice President of the United States would put a contract out on someone?"

"Not really."

"So, here we go again. Why did Carter kill Louis?"

"I don't know. Maybe there'll be something in Carter's room."

"And . . . I suppose now you're off to Carter's room to get your evidence?"

"I've got to nail this guy, Nina. Louis meant too much to me."

She came to Joe and put her arms around him.

"I know that. Just be careful, that's all."

"I will."

Joe walked to the telephone. He asked the switchboard to connect him to Mr. Perkins' room. It rang six times. The operator came back on the line and asked Joe if he wanted to leave a message.

"Non, grazie."

Joe hung up the telephone and moved to the window. He watched as a *vaporetto* worked its way to the Lido.

"Well . . . ?" she said.

"He's not in his room." Joe turned. He went to the door. "I'm going to search it. Hopefully I'll find something. I want you to stay in this room and don't go anywhere. And I mean that. When I told my dog, Nina, to stay, she stayed. She stayed put. I'm going to give you credit for being somewhat brighter than a dog."

"Thank you."

"Perkins' room is across the hall. It's the second one from the elevator. The only reason for you to come out of this room is if you're in danger of losing your life. If the phone rings, answer it. But do not leave this room. Okay?"

"Okay."

"Give me your word."

"Jesus, Joe, I'm not a child."

"Give me your word you won't leave this room."

"What if there's an emergency?"

"I explained that—only if you're in danger of losing your life."

He waited.

"Is it really that hard for you to give me your word on this?"

After an even longer pause Nina said, "Okay, I give you my word."

"That wasn't very convincing."

"What do you want . . . ? Jesus. Okay, I promise I won't leave this room."

"Thank you. I'll be back in ten minutes. Max. Lock the door behind me."

Joe kissed her lightly and stepped into the hallway.

He then stood by his room until he heard Nina throw the lock. He jogged down to Carter's room, pulled a credit card out of his wallet, and tried to jimmy the lock. Nothing doing. This was the Malvasi. It wasn't going to be that easy.

Joe found himself wishing Reynolds was with him. Reynolds was the master. He could get into any room, in any hotel, in any country, in a matter of seconds. Joe stood two feet back from the door and considered his options. If he found the gun in Carter's room, he'd never have to explain why he'd kicked the door in. He decided to go for it.

Joe stepped back another eighteen inches. He lifted his left leg and shot his foot out to the center of the door just below the numbers. It worked. In fact, it worked too well. Instead of splitting the jamb on the lock side of the door, the screws on the hinge side ripped from the wood. The entire door swung into Carter's room, spun once, and landed with a sharp crash on the floor.

It was too late to turn back now. He'd have to work fast. Anyone could have heard the noise. And anyone might be walking by the room. Decide to look in. They'd easily see that Joe was up to no good. Plus, there was no telling when Carter would return.

He started with the dresser to the left of the doorway. He threw the top drawer open and tossed handfuls of silk undergarments out of his way. The gun had to be in the room somewhere. He moved onto the next drawer.

But this approach was taking too much damn time. Joe started pulling the drawers completely out of the dresser and dumping the contents onto the floor. He kicked at the clothing. Nothing.

"What do you think you're doing?"

Joe's heart almost jumped from his body when he heard the voice. If he hadn't recognized it so easily, he probably would have pulled his pistol and fired an entire clip. But it was Nina.

"Fuck me . . . Jesus Christ, what are you doing

here? Can't you do one simple goddamn thing? I told you to stay put."

"I heard a crash. Besides, the Italian inspector called."

"Solfanelli?"

"I think you screwed up here, Joe. He said a woman killed Louis."

Joe took a step backward and put his right hand up to his temple. His breath seemed difficult to come by. Taxed.

"That's . . . bullshit. It was Carter. I know when I'm right. . . . That's all Solfanelli said? He didn't explain anything?"

"He wants you to call him. He wants you out of Carter's room."

"It's bullshit. The gun is in this room. I know it is. I'll find it if I have to rip the goddamn wallpaper off." His eyes drilled into Nina. "Get out of here. Right now. Go back to my room and lock the door."

"I can't. I left both keys in the room. It's locked. We're locked out."

"Shit."

Nina stepped over the fallen door and looked around the room.

"Jesus, you're making a mess of this place."

"Open your goddamn eyes, will you? Open your ears. This isn't a game. Christ . . . Go down to the lobby. Wait at the front desk. I'm serious. This man's a killer. Don't you understand that?"

"You're making a friggin' mess. How are you going to put this place back together?"

"It doesn't matter. I'm in too deep. Look at the door, for Christ's sake. . . . I've got to find that gun. Carter could be back any minute. Now get out of here."

"I'll help you. I'll work in this direction and meet you on the other side."

She pulled the drawer out of the small table to the right of the doorway and dumped the contents onto the floor.

"Are you nuts? Will you get the fuck out of here?"

"You're wasting time, Joe. What does it look like?"

She kicked through the stuff on the floor.

"Shit . . . Shit . . . Goddamn it . . . Shit . . ."

"Well?"

"Shit. Shit. Shit . . ." He looked at the ceiling lamp. "Fuck . . . It's a gun, for Christ's sake. You find a gun, any gun, a goddamn water gun, bring it to me . . . And a knife. You find a knife, bring it to me."

He went back to work on the dresser. Nina moved into the closet.

Two minutes passed.

"Anything yet?" she called.

"No. How about you?"

"Nope. That outfit last night was nothing compared to the rest of this stuff. A good third of it is women's clothes. Come here look at this thing."

"Is it a gun?"

"No I'd call it a jumpsuit."

"If it's not a gun, I don't want to see it."

"Oh, my God, look at these shoes."

She came out with a pair of red sequined high heels.

"You don't think they're Carter's, do you?" She looked inside the left shoe. "Size six. Are Carter's feet that small?"

"Will you knock it off? Do you want him to find us here? Get to work."

Joe moved into the bathroom. Nina went to the desk by the window. She pulled the drawers out one at a time and poured the contents onto the floor. She kicked at the papers and pens. She bent down and spread them out with her hands. She'd thought she'd heard something solid hit the floor but wasn't able to find a thing. She started to throw Carter's papers off the top of the desk. Half expecting something to jump up and bite her.

Joe, pulled jars and bottles out of the medicine cabinet. He tossed the towels to the floor. Hoping to hear a familiar sound of metal as it bounced off tiles. He groped behind the toilet. Looked behind the curtains. Instinctively he glanced at his watch. Time meant nothing. Cardinal was probably in the air by now. Time didn't mean a goddamn thing.

"This is looking pretty hopeless," he yelled to Nina. "Did you look under the mattress?"

"Not yet."

Joe picked up a container of women's dusting powder from the makeup table. He emptied it into the toilet. Nothing but fucking powder. He turned. He looked at the sink. He glanced away. Then glanced back. Something was fucking off here. He rubbed his eyes. Then rubbed them harder and found his vision blurring slightly. He turned the tap on and threw water into his face. He pressed his palms to the stubble on his cheeks. He threw more water into his eyes and onto his hair. Joe shook his head and went down for more water. It rolled down the back of his neck and onto his suit. Again he rubbed his cheeks and jaw.

Bang. Like a fucking shotgun. A bright white light seemed to flash through his brain. He straightened. Something was missing. Something was fucking missing. Missing from the sink. No razor. No fucking razor. He opened the medicine cabinet a second time. No shaving cream. No aftershave. He turned and yanked the shower curtain completely off its rod. No razor. No shaving cream. He called to Nina.

"Did you find an electric shaver in there?"

"No, but I think I found something else. This looks good."

There was excitement in her voice. Joe prayed for the best and ran into the bedroom. Nina was holding what looked like a small metal box. It was an inch wide and almost three inches long.

"What is this?" she said.

"Where did you find it?"

"On the desk. Under some papers. What the hell is it?"

"You're beautiful."

"Yes, thank you, but what is it?"

"It's an ammunition clip for a small-caliber semiautomatic pistol—a Beretta, to be precise."

The answer to Nina's question came from behind Joe.

The English accent was unmistakable.

It was Carter Perkins.

Thirteen

Carter smiled.

"Something told me I should have taken that clip with me to Torcello yesterday."

In one fluid motion Joe slid his left hand under his right arm, found his 9mm, and turned to face Carter.

"Don't try anything foolish, Mr. Bradlee. The woman will be the first to die. I can guarantee that."

Carter was holding a Webley-Fosbery .38-caliber pistol at arm's length. The pistol was the love of Carter's life and, finally, a last line of defense. The muzzle was kept pointed directly at Nina's head.

"I've never missed a target in my life, and I'm too old to start now. I can only assume, Mr. Bradlee, that under that lovely jacket of yours, you are armed?"

"Listen, Carter—"

"Please don't upset me. I received virtually no sleep last night. I've had some very disturbing nightmares. I've had far too much coffee and a rather frustrating day in general. I would hate for this pistol to go off accidentally."

" 'Cawdor shall sleep no more, Macbeth shall sleep no more . . .' " Nina said.

"Quite, my dear. Please take your hand out from under your jacket, Mr. Bradlee."

"I'll tell you what—"

"No, no, no. I will tell you *what.* Take your hand from your jacket. You have less than two seconds."

Joe dropped his left hand to his side.

"Thank you. That wasn't so difficult, was it? Now . . . Please take the weapon slowly out of your jacket—with your right hand. Place it on the floor in front of you. And move over to the closet. And again, Mr. Bradlee, nothing foolish, if you please. The woman . . . ? I'm sure you understand."

Joe did as Carter asked. Carter continued to train the revolver on Nina's head.

"So, you're a southpaw? That's the American word, isn't it?"

Carter crossed around the bed towards Nina, stopping only once, to pick up Joe's 9mm from the floor.

"Listen, Carter, I'm going to be up front with you. This woman means a lot to me. Let the two of us walk out of here together, and we'll disappear from your life for good. You have my word on that."

"Mr. Bradlee, you must take me for an absolute idiot. You? Let me go? You? A glorified policeman and nothing more. You won't disappear. And you can't be trusted for a minute."

"If that's what you believe, then fine. Keep me. We'll work out our differences. Let the woman leave. From what I've seen, you're not much into ladies anyway. . . . Kind of a pussy, actually."

Nina looked at Joe in disbelief.

"More so than you would think, Mr. Bradlee."

"Oh, I know all about you, Carter. The cat's out of the bag, so to speak. . . . Stay away from the woman, Carter. I mean it."

Carter had almost reached Nina. She scrambled to the far corner of the room behind the bed. Carter followed. Slowly. Methodically.

"Let the woman go and I'm yours."

"No," Nina cried.

"Nina, stay out of this. It's between me and Carter."

"Nina . . . ? Quite right. I had forgotten your name. That's not at all like me. Please accept my apology."

"Leave her be. You want a man, you've got one."

"I like my men younger than you, Mr. Bradlee. And darker. I almost wish your agent Reynolds was here. He is quite something, don't you think?"

"Reynolds is long gone."

"What a shame."

"Why, Carter? Why the getup?"

"I found a man's world more to my liking. More doors could be opened. Less restrictions were placed on me. You see, Mr. Bradlee: 'All the world's a stage/ And all the men and women merely players/They have their exits and their entrances/and one man in his time plays many parts'—so why not women? I play both parts, but alas . . . I'm never taken this seriously when I play the part of a woman."

"But you still can't stay away from the boys, can you?"

"I've always liked my boys, Mr. Bradlee."

Carter placed Joe's pistol on the writing desk as she passed, then continued toward Nina.

Nina's mind was rocking. Racing to keep up. She squeezed herself into the corner in a feeble attempt to disappear.

"Joe . . . ?" Nina almost whispered. "What's going on?"

Carter had now reached Nina. She moved her left arm behind Nina's neck and let her hand rest on Nina's shoulder. Carter's touch was that of a woman's. Nina sensed it immediately. She shivered. As though a piece of dry ice had just been dropped down her back. Carter pressed the Webley-Fosbery into Nina's ribs—just below her right breast.

"You're a very lovely woman . . . Nina. I can almost see why this man is attracted to you. You have very small bones."

"Leave her be, Carter. If you hurt her in any way, you're dead."

"A threat? I don't think you're in a position to threaten anybody, Mr. Bradlee."

"Listen, Jesus Christ . . . Fuck . . . Call me Joe, for Christ's sake."

Joe was desperate to stall Carter. To distract this woman. To keep her from harming Nina.

"Joe . . . That's such a pedestrian name, Joe. It makes me think of those horrible plastic toys—G.I. Joe. Were you a G.I., Joe?"

"I was in the Marine Corps."

"There's a difference?"

"To some."

"You're not so young. You must have been in Vietnam. She was a lovely country before the American G.I. Joe's had their way with her. I loved the beaches in the early days. And of course . . . the boys."

"Whatever you say."

"Then you didn't go? What a shame."

"I went . . . Jesus . . . Listen, Carter, why don't we do a little switch, here? A swap? Put the gun on me. Let Nina go. You don't have to let her out of the room. Just take the gun away from her. You're terrifying her."

"Oh, God, I hope so. Do you think she's wet? I know I am."

"You're a pig," Nina spat at her.

Carter took her free hand and grabbed Nina's chin. She yanked Nina's face down to her left shoulder. Violently. Then pushed the revolver into the expanse of Nina's exposed neck. Carter stroked the barrel of the Webley-Fosbery up and then down on Nina's skin. A vein in Nina's neck bulged. Turned a light blue. Joe took a step forward.

"Don't do it, Joe. It would make such a mess of this lovely neck. So much like a young boy's, don't you think?"

When Carter was sure Joe had frozen, she moved around behind Nina and lowered the gun. She then kissed Nina on the neck. Nina tried to twist away, and Carter pushed the pistol deep into her ribs. Nina arched her back off to one side.

Joe looked at his pistol on the desk. Carter caught the glance.

"Now, that would be a terribly foolish thing to do, Joe."

"Carter, listen to me. This is no good." Joe was groping. "If you fire that gun, the entire hotel will be up here in a second. Why don't you let us walk away? Nothing will come of it. You have my word on that. You have to believe me."

Carter lowered her face, parted her lips, and bit into Nina's neck. Nina winced, but she made no sound. A small drop of blood formed just below her right earlobe.

"Sometimes they like a little pain. Boys and girls alike. Have you ever noticed that, Joe?"

Joe's eyes bore into Carter.

"I'll kill you if you fuck with her. I'll come over this bed and tear you limb from fucking limb and feed you to the goddamn fish. You hear me, you son of a bitch?"

Carter quickly moved her pistol back to Nina's head.

"Relax, Joe. I've never killed a woman. Funny, I was just thinking of that yesterday. . . . When I had my Beretta an inch from another lady's temple. And then once again today. She was more a child than a woman. . . . But both times I found it impossible to do the deed, as it were. I froze for some strange reason. Something stopped me. Well, here we are, and . . . well, I say, there's a first time for everything, isn't there?"

Carter's gun hand began to tremble.

"Carter. Listen. Stop, for Christ's sake. Slow down for a minute." Joe took a breath. He stepped back two steps.

"Look at me . . . I'm not coming near you, okay?"

He held his hands out in an effort to calm Carter.

"Look, Carter, tell me something? Why did you kill Louis?"

"That was his name? Louis?"

"Jesus Christ. You killed somebody, you took another person's life, and you didn't even know his name?"

"Did you know the names of the people you killed in Vietnam?"

"It was a fucking war, Carter."

Carter wrenched Nina's neck again.

"Life is a fucking war, Joe. If you only knew . . ."

"Okay. Okay. Just stop, okay? . . . Why did you kill Louis? Just tell me that."

"A tragic mistake, really. Not for your Louis so much, but for myself."

"A mistake? What do you mean, a mistake?"

"My life would have been such a success." Carter brought the Webley-Fosbery up to the side of her own head and scratched her right ear. " 'O mighty Caesar! dost thou lie so low?/Are all thy conquests, glories, triumphs, spoils/Shrunk to this little measure?"

"Carter, you're not making any sense. Talk to me. Look at me. What do you mean, a mistake?"

"They look so much alike."

"Who . . . ? Who . . . ? What are you talking about? Who looks alike?"

"Your Louis and the Vice President."

"You thought Louis was the Vice fucking President? There's twenty years' difference in age, for Christ's sake. What are you, fucking blind?"

"Don't push me, Joe. I'm as upset about this as you are."

"Okay, okay. I'm sorry. Don't get excited. We can work this out. Tell me who hired you and I'll let you walk. I swear I will."

"You won't *let me walk,* Joe."

"I swear it. Who was it? Who put you up to it?"

"Do you think that the world is full of such small-minded people that they are incapable of doing something on their own? Without the guiding hand of some—man? Some overextended penis? 'No dick, no brains,' my father used to say. He drove it into me almost every night. . . . There was a great deal of mixed pain and pleasure in watching him die."

"No one hired you . . . You did this on your own . . ."

Joe shook his head.

"Jesus, Carter, why? Why . . . ? It makes no sense.

The man is a goddamn nobody. Why would you want to kill him? Why would anyone want to kill him?"

"He's the vice president of the United States of America, Joe. He is not a nobody. It's all part of a much bigger plan. Something I wouldn't expect you to understand. History, Joe. You are the small-minded person. You are the little man. Your story will never be told. You are the man history leaves behind. History is about to be changed. Altered. The world is about to go off in a different direction. I was to play a part in that change. It will all be remembered as one of the great historical tragedies. In the future the finest actors would have been called upon to play my part. I would have become immortal. I would have been the Booth, the Oswald . . . King Richard."

"Okay, talk to me about this, Carter. But slowly. You're not making any sense. What's this big plan?"

"As a philosopher, I have to believe it's better to go down in history as one of the great evils than to not go down in history at all."

"Right. Sure. If that's how you feel. You and Adolf. But you missed it, Carter. Don't you see that? You didn't get the big fish. This is small potatoes here. There's no big plan at work here. If you pull that trigger, you're dead. If I don't get you, someone else will. You won't get out of this hotel alive. The only way you can come out a winner is to drop the gun. I'll let you walk. You have to believe that."

"I'm afraid I can't do that. I can't believe you. And the reality is, it's over. It's over for me. I'm very much aware of that . . . And I'm weary, Joe . . . I'm very weary."

Carter dug his fingers into Nina's jaw.

"Women are strange creatures, don't you think? Sometimes even I have trouble figuring them out."

Carter brought the Webley-Fosbery over and positioned the muzzle under Nina's chin. Her hand was trembling. She was almost completely out of control. A tear formed in Nina's right eye and rolled down her cheek. It crossed over Carter's index finger.

"Carter. Don't," Joe said. "Don't do this. I'm going

to beg. Okay? I'm begging you, Carter. Don't fucking do it."

Joe stepped toward Carter.

"Don't move."

It was an order. Joe froze in his tracks.

"I've never killed a woman. Why do you think that is? And it's strange now that I think more on it. Women have never been my favorites."

Carter put her tongue to the drop of blood on Nina's neck and smiled.

"I suppose my life would be somewhat incomplete if I were to die without having taken a woman for myself."

"Carter. Stop. Don't."

Joe was pleading with her now. Carter's gun hand shook. The ivory sight bead on the barrel of the pistol dug into the soft skin under Nina's jaw on her right side. A new drop of blood formed there. Carter began to speak methodically once again, as if in a trance. As though she were counting down her last seconds on earth.

"My father and Glendower being both away,
The powers of us may serve so great a day.
Come, let us take a muster speedily:
Doomsday is near; die all, die merrily."

The explosion of the gun, or the cartridge within the gun, the powder, the black powder within the cartridge, was colossal. It was the most turbulent gunshot Joe had ever heard. The noise filled every corner of Carter's room. Every seam in the wallpaper. It wrapped around the curtains. It rattled the windows. It found its way into the bathroom. Into the closet. It actually made the empty coat hangers sway. It echoed off the walls. And hammered and jabbed and poked and punched Joe's eardrums. It streamed out past him. It flew through the door. Shot down the hallway. The stairway. Until it had reached every living soul in the Malvasi. All conversation within the hotel came to an immediate halt. All eyes looked in the direction of the explosion.

The air in Carter's room filled with the odor of sulfer. The burning smell of discharged black powder. The burning smell of flesh. The bullet had vaporized nearly all blood, flesh, and bone it had come in contact with. It had created a thin red mist. Joe could feel the warm dampness of the blood as it latched onto his hair. His eyebrows. The gore stung his nostrils. His lips.

The weight of death had been too much. It had pulled both Carter and Nina to the floor. Together they had slumped down onto the carpet. And disappeared behind the bed.

Where they had been standing, the peach-colored flocked wallpaper had been saturated with even more gore. Small pieces of scalp and hair and skin and brains clung to textured material. A trail of crimson led down the wall, as if leading the way. Beckoning the onlooker. "Come see the death that lay below."

From behind the bed Joe could hear the crawling and scratching of the living. Trying desperately to get out from under the weight of the lifeless. He raced to retrieve his 9mm. But stopped dead in his tracks when he heard the voice.

"Et tu, Brutus, motherfucker."

Joe spun around. A thin whisp of white smoke was still working its way out from the muzzle of Reynolds' Smith & Wesson .357. Reynolds smiled at Joe.

"Actually, the line is, 'Et tu, Brute?' The 'motherfucker' part was my own. Kind of makes it more contemporary, don't you think . . . ? At any rate, Carter was no Caesar, not by a long shot, so I felt I could take a few liberties."

"Fuck me."

"Yeah, well, it seems Mock didn't want my skinny ass on his lap after all."

Joe turned back toward the corner of the room. Nina was pulling herself up onto the bed and out from under the weight of Carter's lifeless body. The move took every ounce of her remaining strength. Nearly her entire right side was covered with Carter's blood. It matted her hair. It dripped from her ear onto her exposed neck and shoulder. Her blouse gave the appearance of being tie-dyed red on the right side. She called out to Joe:

"Oh, God."

Joe ran around the bed and took Nina by the waist. He dragged her free from Carter's weight. Carter's body settled back on the carpet with a noise that sounded more like a sailor dropping his sea bag after a tour of the Mediterranean. Nina hung onto Joe. She pulled him close. She clung to him. Clawing the back of his jacket. Trying to consume him. Trying to become one with him.

"Oh, God, Joe. God."

She pulled her face back. Carter's blood was now matted to Joe's cheek. She pushed her hair out of her eyes. She shook her hand. The still warm blood rolled down her fingers and onto the floor. Joe pulled her back into him.

"It's over. It's all over."

Nina trembled in his arms. He held her like that for two or three minutes. No one spoke. After an eternity Joe said to her, "Come on. Let's get you cleaned up."

He walked her to the door and stopped when he reached Reynolds.

"I owe you a big one."

"N-B-D."

"You should probably call Solfanelli, if he hasn't been called by somebody already. He's not going to like this. . . . I'll be over in my room."

"Right. Say, this wouldn't happen to be Nina Lake Wallace, would it?"

"Yep."

"Well, guess what? She checks out with Big Bertha."

"Thanks . . . Oh, before Solfanelli shows up, you might want to see if you can find any souvenirs here. Things we should save for ourselves."

"Right."

The couple left and walked down the hall. Reynolds

eased his way into Carter's room. He stepped over the door and went to the desk, where he picked up Joe's pistol. He looked down at the person he had just killed. Reynolds tapped Carter's left knee with his shoe, half expecting this almost headless corpse to say something. It didn't.

Reynolds then took a balled-up piece of paper from his suit pocket and carefully spread it flat on the desk where Joe's pistol had been. On the paper, in the Malvasi switchboard operator's handwriting, had been written, "No news is bad news . . . DOC." He then shuffled through the papers on the floor until he came up with another piece of Malvasi stationery featuring the same handwriting. This one read, "Green light on your article. Will pay top dollar. Expect confirmation within forty-eight hours. Advise of any difficulties . . . DOC."

Reynolds then folded both papers in thirds and placed them in his inside coat pocket. A voice brought his attention back to the doorway. It was Joe.

"Do you think you could come down and pick the lock to my room? We seem to have left our keys in there."

Joe looked down at the broken door on the floor.

"Obviously I don't have your finesse with these things."

Fourteen

It had been a long process. Almost four hours. Joe had been right. Lamberto Solfanelli had not been happy. Not for a single minute. The inspector had made the three Americans stay in Carter's room for his entire investigation of the shooting.

"Joe, you promised me you wouldn't kill this ... this person."

"I didn't kill her ... He did," Joe'd said—and had pointed at Reynolds.

That was pretty much how the conversation had gone. And Solfanelli had not been amused.

"What made you think Louis' killer was a woman?" Joe'd eventually asked.

"The footprints seemed to point to that. In addition, a second set of female fingerprints were found at the Locanda."

"The maid?" Nina said. Solfanelli did his best to ignore her.

The inspector kept the Americans in Carter's room much longer than he needed to. They all knew that. But the man was upset—and for good reason. Three murders in twenty-four hours. It had to be some sort of a modern-day Venetian record. Solfanelli seemed to take it all very personally.

Nina had cast her blood-stained clothes to the wind long before the inspector had arrived. She had no desire ever to see them again. The Malvasi management had been kind enough to allow her the use of a chambermaid's uniform—only for one day. They wanted it back. Pronto. They hadn't been very pleased with the situation either.

After two hours in Carter's room, Nina tried to get Solfanelli to let them leave by saying, "I've left my son alone. He'll be worried about me."

Solfanelli's reply was a facetious "*Signora,* your son has every reason in the world to be worried about you."

The inspector did, however, finally agree to let her use the telephone. But it came too late. The old Scottish woman at La Primavera had already called California. She had spoken to Nina's former husband. The TV producer.

His response to his missing ex-wife and stranded son was, "Well, why don't you wait a few more hours? I'm sure she'll turn up. I have house guests—and early tennis tomorrow."

Solfanelli released them at five-thirty, after giving them a "Leave my city and don't return in the near future" lecture.

The last thing Joe said to the inspector was, "Jesus, Lamberto, I almost forgot. Oscar Sanchez is chained to his fucking lamp."

Joe then handed Solfanelli the handcuff keys, and the three went back to Joe's room. And Joe called La Primavera one more time. He arranged for two rooms. One for himself. One for Reynolds. Nina spoke with Eubie. Then Joe called the Taverna La Fenice and made a dinner reservation for three adults and a child. Nine-thirty would do just fine.

The three Americans now found themselves in the cabin of Vittorio's pristine launch. Malvasi launch number four. They were on their way back to the Dorsoduro section of the city. And La Primavera. And Eubie.

"Mock knew damn well you had no intention of being on Cardinal when it took off," Reynolds said. "He's not an idiot. Far from it. In fact, the last thing he told me to do, before the chopper took off, was to go find you. And when I did, he wanted the two of us to pick Louis up. Take him back to his mother."

"I would have done that anyway."

"Yeah, he probably knew that also. . . . You may have your differences with Mock, but he loved Louis as much as we all did. Louis was a good trooper. Mock wouldn't have let anyone but you take him back to Philly. He has no use for the State Department. You gotta know that."

"I suppose so. . . . It's not going to be easy. Louis was an only child. His mother adored him."

Joe looked out at the water for a moment. Then back at Reynolds.

"You don't have to go to Philadelphia if you'd rather pass," he said.

"I'll go . . . I should be there."

Nina shivered in the poorly fitting Malvasi maid's outfit. Joe put his arm around her.

"I don't know what it is, but I've always been attracted to women in uniform."

She smiled at him and moved closer. Reynolds pulled Joe's 9mm pistol from his overcoat pocket.

"I picked this up from Carter's desk . . . when you two were washing up. You're probably feeling a little naked."

Reynolds held the gun out in his left hand for Joe to take.

"Did you find anything else besides that?"

Joe made no move for the weapon.

"Two messages: from someone, or something, called DOC. Mean anything?"

"Not to me."

"I also got Carter's telephone book. There's a number. I'll get it all to C.O. See what they can come up with." Reynolds waved Joe's pistol. "You want this thing or not?"

Joe didn't seem to hear him.

Reynolds set the gun on a silver tray by the window. Alongside a bottle of Pellegrino water. It sat there like a time bomb for three or four minutes. All three stared at it—no one said a word. Finally Joe picked the gun up and handed it to Nina.

"What the hell am I supposed to do with this?" she said.

"Anything you want."

She stood. Then slid the launch window open. The blast of cold air caught all three off guard. Joe moved in front of her. He held the curtain back away from the opening.

And with the power of a discus thrower, Nina hurled the pistol. The weapon flew out of the window. It traveled twenty feet and skipped three times across the Giudecca canal. After the third skip, it sank like a fucking stone. She turned to Joe. He put his arms around her again. And again they held each other very tight.

"My only other option was to shoot you with it," she said.

"Thanks," he said.

"I think Eubie and I should to go to Philadelphia too."

"Thanks," he said.

LOUIS CANE ZEZZO

'E was all that I 'ad in the way of a friend,
An' I've 'ad to find one new;
But I'd give my pay an' stripe for to get the beg
gar back,
Which it's just too late to do!

—R. Kipling